Two action-packed novels
of the American West!

SIGNET BRAND
DOUBLE WESTERNS:

MAVERICK MARSHAL

&

Thirty Notches

Other SIGNET Westerns You'll Enjoy

MAVERICK ☆ MARSHAL

by *Nelson Nye*

and

Thirty ◎ *Notches*

by *Brad Ward*

A SIGNET BOOK

NEW AMERICAN LIBRARY

TIMES MIRROR

SIGNET, SIGNET CLASSICS, MENTOR, PLUME AND MERIDIAN BOOKS
are published by The New American Library, Inc.,
1301 Avenue of the Americas, New York, New York 10019

FIRST PRINTING (DOUBLE WESTERN EDITION), NOVEMBER, 1978

1 2 3 4 5 6 7 8 9

PRINTED IN THE UNITED STATES OF AMERICA

MAVERICK MARSHAL

by

Nelson Nye

CHAPTER ONE

IT BEGAN with a big temptation—too big for a man like Frank to resist no matter what trouble it might run him into. Turbulence and violence had given him a rep. He knew that it was the bold men in this world who got their names in the pot. He also knew with his first sight of the town that he was never going back to punching cows for old Sam Church.

In a place like South Fork, which was a jumping-off point for outfits heading up the trail to Dodge City, a person had to be born on the right side of Gurden's saloon or be a part of the scum for the rest of his natural. Such, at least, was the established tradition. Now Frank saw a way of changing all that.

He was going to wake this place up!

Marshal of South Fork, he breathed, and reared back his shoulders.

He grinned as he thought of Honey Kimberland. Smallest waist, biggest smile, yellowest hair of any girl in the country; and as far above Frank as the damn moon—but there wasn't no law against dreaming.

She had been in Frank's mind ever since the day he'd hauled her out of that south-shore boghole where she'd run just in time to miss the horns of Church's bull. Frank had cut down the bull with his pistol (and worked half the next winter getting its cost off the books) before he'd realized it wasn't about to go into that muck even for a tidbit as tempting as Honey.

Four years ago—Lord how time flew! Frank wondered if she remembered, being not much over fifteen when he'd saved her. He recollected the look of her knees with the mud on them, and the way she had clung to him shivering and shaking. She'd been well filled out even then and he remembered the clean woman smell

5

of her hair. . . . He remembered too damn well, he thought wryly.

It was nearly full dark and the nighthawks were swooping when he came into town and worked his dun horse through the Saturday night crush. He put the animal up to the pole fronting Gurden's Saloon and sat a spell having his look along the street. Frank was a big fellow and a rough one with his burly brawler's shoulders. And yet someway, strangely, he was a little reluctant about the marshal's job, thinking back to that talk he'd had with John Arnold. Arnold, one of the town councilmen, was a man grown old in the cow game, closest to being tolerant of any of the local big owners.

"But why me?" Frank had asked when Arnold let it be known the Town Council was dissatisfied with the man they'd fetched in from outside to pack their tin. "Ashenfeldt's a tophand at this pistol-packing business. All I know is cows."

Arnold, smiling, shifted his cud. "You've made your mark in this town as a real scraperoo. It's these local sports who've put the skids under Joe. They won't try that with you—they'll know better. Besides," Arnold said, warming up to his subject, "you're ambitious."

Frank scowled. But it was true enough, he supposed. If he was ever to make any impression on Honey it was time he got known for something besides brawling and shoving cows' tails around. Still it wasn't a job he would voluntarily have gone after. He knew the riptide of pressures by which things around here were made to suit the big owners and could not resist taking a sly poke at the rancher. "You hunting a dog that'll come to your whistle?"

The tightening of Arnold's hands showed the shaft had gone home, but he said easy enough, "We've got to have a man who understands local conditions, one who'll know when to reach and when to leave well enough alone. You fit that to a T."

"What's old Church think about it?"

"I haven't talked to Church about it; the deal is up to

the Town Council. Pay is one-twenty a month. I could put it into cows for you, Frank."

It would be obliging Arnold to take the marshal's job, which meant it probably would suit Honey Kimberland's old man too. Kimberland generally pulled most of the strings that got pulled. Without at least his tacit approval a man couldn't look to get anywhere at all here. W. T. Kimberland *was* South Fork—and his daughter wouldn't be marrying any thirty-a-month cowhand.

Frank took a deep breath. "How do you know I can have the damned job?"

Arnold said quietly, "Push it around for a while in your mind. Council won't meet before Saturday night. If you want to take a whirl at it, come in."

So here he was, and it was Saturday night with the dust and the racket boiling out of the street and the town crammed with men who would just as lief gut-shoot a tinbadge as look at him.

Among the mounds of stored goods in the back room of the Mercantile, Krantz, who owned the place, sat around with the other two Councilmen, sourly nursing their secret antagonisms, paying little attention to the voices out front where his weary clerks, wishing mightily to be done, tramped about the gabbing customers, reaching down and stacking purchases absent-mindedly ordered between bursts of gossip.

Krantz pushed an already soggy bandana across the moist shine of his completely bald head. He said, "I don't like it."

Chip Gurden, who owned the Opal and could generally be counted on to front for the riffraff and drifters, sighed. "Seems like I remember you sayin' that." His glance sawed at Krantz's nerves. The storekeeper jumped up, frustratedly fidgeting and popping his knuckles while his eyes slewed irascibly from one to the other of them. "That roughneck! How can ve trust our lives yet, und our goots, to such a one?"

Gurden's saloonkeeper's face in the light of the lamps showed no more expression than one of his table checks.

Arnold said, "He'll be all right."

Krantz, swinging back, sat down heavily. "Yah! All right for you cow people! What about the rest of us?"

"If he don't stay in line, two votes from this Council will take the tin away from him," said Arnold.

Gurden nodded. He fetched a black stogie from a case and bit the end off. He considered it a moment, scratched a match and fired up. "That's for sure," he said dryly. He broke the match and put his foot on it.

"I don't like it," Krantz repeated.

"Vote against him then," Arnold suggested smoothly.

Gurden growled through the smoke, "Maybe Frank's got other fish to fry. We been here twenty minutes already."

Arnold said to Krantz, "You're the Clerk of this outfit. Call the meeting adjourned if it'll make you feel any better."

Krantz glared, affronted. "You talk like you was Kimberland. You know this—this *wildman* will look out for your interests. Py Gott! Gurden has bouncers. Me, all I got iss a fortune in breakables und a pair of scairt clerks! Ve got to haf some law in this—"

Someone's fist banged heavily against the door.

Krantz, still fuming, got up and unbarred it. Frank Carrico came in and heard the door slammed behind him. "So you're here!" Krantz scowled. Frank looked at the other two. "Thought I was expected."

"Begun to think you weren't coming." Arnold shoved a keg out.

Frank, settling his back to the wall, searched Gurden's face. "This deal suit you?"

"I'll string along."

"Yah—you got bouncers!" Krantz, with his head up like a dog catching wolf smell, demanded of Frank bitterly: "You understandt this chob do you?"

"Expect I could make out to get a line on it." Frank, knowing Krantz didn't like him, considered the storekeeper, grinning a little. "Main thing, I reckon, is to keep you fellers in business, ain't it?"

"Iss something funny? Why you grin? Ve got troubles —wild-eyed crazy galoots wit pistols. Py Gott, ve need protection! Las' night these trail hands wreck Fantshon's blace like a pig vind!"

"Where was your badge toter?" asked Frank.

"He done the best he could," Gurden said.

Arnold, clearing his throat, suggested getting down to business. Frank stared at the rancher, trying to lay hold of something. Top dogs in South Fork acknowledged no one but W. T. Kimberland and it was gnawing at Frank's mind that Arnold would be acting for W. T. right now.

Krantz blew out his cheeks and glared about him dismally, his look lingering longest on the face of the saloonkeeper. Gurden gave him no encouragement. Krantz swabbed his baldness again with the wadded bandanna and testily said, "Comes now Frank Carrico, a candidate for marshal. All in favor signify by saying 'aye'."

"Aye." That was Arnold, looking smug and mighty virtuous. Gurden's slow nod held a hint of wry humor.

Krantz said bitterly, "Lift your right hand and put the other on this book."

After Frank was sworn in he pocketed the keys the storekeeper gave him and picked up the paper on which were set forth the duties of his office, local ordinances and so forth. His glance went to Arnold. "Where's the badge?"

"We'll step over to Ben's," Arnold murmured.

Ben Holliday ran the local furniture emporium. When there was call for it he also furnished caskets at three times the actual cost. There could only be one reason, Frank reflected, for going to Ben's. He took a tighter grip on himself going over there, but when he stood with the others staring down at Ashenfeldt's body, he couldn't restrain a shiver. Peering at Arnold he said: "Who did it?"

Gurden's grin was thin and crooked. "Make a guess."

"Some drunken trail hand?"

"One of Draicup's crowd," Arnold said. Frank's eyes slitted.

Krantz said, "Didn't you know they vas back?"

"Which one?" Frank asked, sounding like something had got stuck in his windpipe. Three months ago, in a drunken brawl, Frank had smashed a heap of glass in Gurden's Opal bar.

The saloonkeeper now, with the remembrance of this coming alive on his cheeks, said, "Tularosa," and showed a huge enjoyment. "Maybe that star don't look so good to you now."

Frank reached down and got the tin from the dead man's vest. With his face hard as rock he fastened it onto his shirt front. His eyes cut at Arnold. "Draicup's crew still around?"

"Tularosa's here. Fetched in a wagon with a busted hub and him and another's laying over to wait for it."

Krantz, ever fearful of violence, said, "You can have the exbense of vun deputy—up to, that is, fifty dollars a month. If you haf to bay more it comes out of your bocket."

"How free a hand have I got with this job?"

Arnold said, "In what way?"

Frank waved the paper the storekeeper had given him. "This part about guns. Man would need an army to disarm every ranny that comes into this town."

"You asked for it." That was Gurden.

Arnold fingered his thin mustache. "What do you have in mind, Frank?"

"It's the rotgut," Frank said, "that puts these boys on the prod."

The sardonic enjoyment fell off Gurden's face. "Now wait a minute! If you think for one—"

"I was going to suggest," Frank said mildly, "that whenever they come into a place where they can buy it we make it a rule their guns must be checked at the bar. I'll undertake to make that stick."

"It would help," Krantz said, brightening.

Arnold nodded.

Chip Gurden said grudgingly, "I'll go along on that," and got up. "What are you figurin' to do about Tularosa?"

"What do you want me to do?"

"He killed somebody, didn't he? Put the sonofabitch in jail!"

Draicup, held to be rougher than a cob, hailed from someplace down in the brasada. He'd been here before and always drove a mixed herd which was road-branded Spur. He packed a thick wallet crammed with powers of attorney and had taken twenty thousand cattle up to Dodge. His passing last year had cost the town four men —three of these killed by this same Tularosa.

Knowing all this, considering it, Frank stood on Ben's steps and scowlingly eyed the street. Up till now he'd thought only of Honey and the prestige of being the Law in this town. Now he was forced to look at other things, the town itself, the obligations of this job, and he had his moment of dark, grim wonder.

Ranch hands, trail hands, tramped the scarred walks and stopped in clotted knots of drab color wherever they came across friends or an argument. Staring over the heads of this noisy throng, over the collection of rigs and paintless wagons wedged cheek by jowl into that restive line of stamping, tail-switching rein-tied horses, Frank's glance prowled the street's far side with some care.

Most of the whiskey was consumed in three places, all of them on Frank's side of the street. Directly across loomed the Hays Hotel. East, to the left of the place as Frank faced it and separated only by a vacant lot, was the stage depot, horse barns and Halbertson's hay shed. West of the hotel was the jail and marshal's quarters, Fentriss' livery with its pole corrals—a growing establishment doing considerable business at this time of the year catering to drovers. Next west was the Chuckwagon where a stove-up Church cowhand eked out a living cooking for those who cared for that kind of grub; he had plenty of vacant space on both sides of him. Farther west—the last building—was the blacksmith shop. Beyond was just grass, a ragged chewed and trampled sea of it, bed grounds of the trail herds.

On this side where Frank stood, dividing the respectable and sinful sides of it, was Gurden's Opal Bar, hang-out of horsemen, mecca of those wild ones howling up out of the south. Beyond Gurden's, looking west, was Bernie's gun shop, a pool hall with a red-lettered, Billiards, chipped and peeling across its front and, west of this, the Blue Flag saloon, another vacant lot, then Minnie's place, the wrecked Fantshon store and Trench Brothers lumber.

East of Gurden's, separated from it by no more than the width of Krantz's wagon pass, was the Mercantile where Frank had just been to meet with the Council and latch onto this job John Arnold had got him. Next in line was Ben's Furniture (where Frank stood now), Pete's Tonsorial Parlor, the New York Cafe where drummers and comparable local fry did their nooning, the Bon Ton Millinery, a bake shop run by a Swede from Istanbul, and Wolverton's Saddlery.

A little beyond, dubbed 'Snob Holler' by the bunk-house fraternity, were the homes of the merchants and socially elite. Clerks and artisans lived on the south side in a heterogeneous muddle of shacks congregated beyond Halbertson's hay shed. Behind the town, north of it, were the barrens leading into the Claybank Hills; between barrens and hills swirled the opaque crimson waters of the river that gave South Fork its name.

Peering again southwest toward the holding grounds Frank considered the dark mass of close-bunched cattle, knowing these would have no connection with Draicup whose own stock would now be strung out on the trail. This was an outfit just lately arrived, peaceful-seeming in the night but sure to have dumped more strange riders on the town.

Frank hauled Tularosa out of the back of this survey where he'd been crouched, emptily grinning. Frank had only bumped into the fellow once and had privately hoped never to see him again. Six feet four, rawboned and gangling—so thin, as someone put it, he could have crawled through the eye of a needle and "never got one damn hair outa place." The odd thing was that, except for his eyes, he didn't look like a killer. He had a lantern-jawed dished-up sort of a face framing clackety store teeth and a spatter of freckles. He was a queer guy to look at—with that wistfully sober kind of bewildered expression frequently glimpsed on small boys called up for a lecture. Inside he was nothing but a bundle of nerves, unpredictable, explosive as capped dynamite.

Frank reckoned himself seven kinds of a fool to take the job but turned west up the street, alert to each shape that dragged its spurs through the dust. Without sighting his quarry he pushed through the batwings into Gurden's Opal Bar, braced against the racket that rolled against him like a wave.

All the games were in full swing. Men stood bellying the bar six deep. There were a lot of strange faces but not the one he was hunting. A couple of men suddenly flanked him, grinning. One of these was Kelly, a man Frank had used to punch cows with—narrow-chested, fiddle footed, always looking for something he didn't have, but a fair enough hand in a pinch or a bender.

"Man," Kelly said, "you're sure stickin' your neck out!"

Frank passed it off and shot a glance at the other one. This was Gurden's chief bouncer, a fellow called "Mousetrap" who would tip the scales at about 280 and fancied himself pretty slick with a gun. He was new around here, a recent investment on the part of Chip Gurden.

"Better sign me up, Frank," Kelly said, "while you're able."

Frank grinned and, using his elbows, moved up to the bar.

Scowls twisted faces colored by resentment. Frank picked up a bottle and thumped the bar top for attention. Turning his back against the wood he faced the packed room and called out, "As of twelve noon tomorrow there will be no pistols carried where whisky is served. All guns will be left with the barkeep. That's a new town ordinance and it's going to be enforced."

He went out through an ominous silence.

The night felt cold against his face. He felt a chill digging into the small of his back.

Bill Grace, Kimberland's range boss, came along with a couple of punchers, showing no surprise at the sight of Frank's star. He stared up at Frank's face with the briefest of glances, jerked a nod and went on. The punchers looked back. Frank saw one of them grinning.

Cutting around the Blue Flag he stepped in through the rear, still without catching sight of Tularosa. He stood a bit, thinking. The fellow might be over at Minnie's or following his bent in the dark of some alley. He might be at the blacksmith's or feeding his face in the New York Cafe, though this last was out of bounds. Frank found himself listening for gunshots.

The Flag didn't have as much flash as Gurden's which flaunted framed women without clothes above its bar and a bevy of live ones not clad a heap warmer. This place wasn't as noisy though money was changing hands pretty regular. Young Church, old Sam's son, was at the bar getting rapidly plastered. Arrogance lay in the flash of his stare and when he saw Frank a surge of roan color rushed into his cheeks. He pushed away from the bar, still carrying his bottle, and reeled toward Frank.

Frank said, "Hello, Will."

Eyes ugly, Will Church floundered to a stop three feet away and glared belligerently. He indulged the manners of a drunken hidalgo surveying a truant peon. "You were told to stay out there at Bospero Flats."

"That's right," Frank said.

"Then why ain't you out there? You think those cows'll stay hitched without watchin'?"

Some of the nearer noise began to dim away as men twisted around or looked up from their cards. Frank's eyes flattened a little. "If they're worryin' you, Will, perhaps you'd better go see to them." Frank's hand brushed the star that was pinned to his shirtfront.

The wink of the metal suddenly caught Church's attention. He showed a sultry surprise. His mouth twisted with fury as men back of him shifted, the sound of this seeming as a goad to his temper. As heir apparent to the second largest spread in the country young Church wasn't accustomed to being talked back at. His cheeks began to burn. He had never liked Frank anyway.

Frank, smiling meagerly, was turning away when Church lunged for him, lifting the bottle. Frank's head whipped around. Ducking under the bottle he came up, tight with outrage, hammering four knuckles to the point of Church's chin. It sounded like a bat knocking a ball over the fence.

Church's head snapped back with all his features screwed together. The off-balanced weight of chest and head abruptly toppled him. He hit the floor on his back and skidded into the bar, the bottle jaggedly breaking against the brass foot rail.

Will Church climbed to his feet groggily shaking his head. He discovered the splattered whisky and his stare, coming up, found Frank. He let out a shout and came at Frank with the bottle neck.

Church was big, even bigger than Frank, with a bulging swell of chest and arm and the hatred of balked arrogance baring his teeth. He shortened his grip on the neck of the bottle to give more reach to the jagged shard. He looked like an ape above the glitter of the glass.

Frank asked quietly, "Sure you want to go on with this, Will?"

Church showed the brawn of a gorilla and about as much reason as he stood there shifting his weight, breathing heavily. Men were crowding in through the batwings as word of the fight ran down the street. Frank got hold of the back of a chair.

"Mind the mirrors!" the barkeep yelled. Somebody's laugh was a sound of hysteria. The faces around Frank grew tense and avid as he brought the chair up in front of him.

Now Will leaped, throwing up a hand to ward off the chair, attempting to dive in under it. One spur hooked into the cloth of a pant's leg and he went down, cursing viciously. Frank, prodded by past injustices, brought the chair up over his head; but something stayed him and he reluctantly stepped back, allowing the man to regain his feet.

It was while Church was trying to get up that the racket of shots came—five of them, close-spaced, whipping Frank around, scowling.

He let go of the chair. The batwings were blocked by a solid crush of onlookers. He put his weight against the edge of the crowd. "Make way!" He shoved the nearest man roughly, driving broad shoulders into the wedge, hurling them back with the ram of his elbows.

Someone swung at him, knocking his hat off. He could feel them stiffening. A man swung at Frank, yelling wickedly. Frank hurled him back into the crowd with black fury. He tore the gun from a fist and beat his way clear with it, leaving behind the wild sound of their temper. He stumbled into the night, his shirt hanging in ribbons.

He ran around the back end of the pool hall and came into Gurden's with the gun still in hand. He backed out almost at once, finding no sign of trouble, sprinting down the passage between the Opal and Bernie's gun shop. Coming onto the walk he caught the sharp bark of two additional shots and swore in exasperation. It was nothing more alarming than a string of whooping ranch hands letting go at the moon as they roared out of town.

Frank threw the pistol away and remembered his hat. For ten years that hat had been a part of himself but he didn't go back after it. He tramped instead into the Mercantile and bought himself a new one, black this time, and a dark shield-fronted shirt, going—out of deference to female shoppers—into the back room to get into it.

Coming out he looked around, hoping to catch a glimpse of Honey, having noticed a Bar 40 wagon out front. While he was looking Krantz grabbed his elbow. "You get him?"

"Get who?"

"Tularosa." The lamps' shine winked off the thick

lenses of the stroekeeper's spectacles. "He vas in mine blace."

Frank, swearing, bundled the discarded shirt into Krantz's hands and hurried through the front door. He stopped under the overhang, avoiding the stippling of light from the windows. He found it hard to make out anyone, what with so much in shadow and all the dust stirred up by the traffic. He looked for five minutes and decided to try Minnie's.

He got his horse from the rack, the big dun he'd come in on, a *bayo coyote* with black mane and tail and a stripe down its spine in addition to smudges about the knees. A black horse in this job would have probably been smarter but Frank, like most of those who rode after cattle, was sold on duns, particularly duns with zebra marks descended from the toughest Spanish stock in the land.

Still riled with himself Frank got into the saddle and pointed the horse toward the west end of town.

Minnie was a character, practically an institution. A lot of folks would have liked to see her moved but she had, in Frank's mind, as much right to her business as anybody else. She kept an orderly house, which was more than could be said for the likes of Chip Gurden. More he thought about the place the more convinced Frank became that he would find his man holed up there. Tularosa made no secret of his affinity for the ladies.

All the shades were drawn but there were horses at the tie rail—two roans, a paint and three sorrels. Frank tied the dun and took a last look behind him. He ducked under the rail and felt to see if he had his pistol, resettling its barrel lightly, not hankering for anything to balk his need if he were forced to put hand to it.

He threw off his dark thoughts and pulled open the door.

CHAPTER TWO

THIS LAYOUT had once been a food stop on the overland stage line between Elk City and Dalhart, and the face-lifting Minnie had given the joint had not greatly changed its flavor. The big room Frank stepped into had all the look of a stage stop bar. She had got the place cheap when town expansion had decided the company to remove to a site directly across from the New York Cafe.

The old potbellied stove still held its key spot in the middle of things. The scarred pine bar took up most of the left wall, the wall across from it being cut by three doors. No mirrors, no pictures; Five kitchen chairs were racked before the north wall, the south wall was set up similarly except that here only two of the five were empty. Strangers held down the other three, men Frank had never run into before. None of them much resembled Tularosa beyond their big hats, brush-scarred boots and the gun-weighted cartridge belts strapped about their middles.

Frank, after that one sweeping glance, darkly stared at the three closed doors to his right. The nearest, he remembered, let into the woodshed. The farther, opening onto closed stairs, gave access to the rooms above. It was the middle door that held his attention. It led directly outside behind the screen of the woodshed and was a means of escape for men embarrassed to be found here.

Frank, ducking out, left the door standing open and ran around the shed's bulk, eyes expectant, gun in hand. But if there was anyone lurking in these shadows he didn't see them. Holstering his gun, he went back inside, ignoring the truculent looks the men gave him.

Minnie's raw Irish voice came from back of the bar.

"Whativer are ye doin' a-runnin' around me place like a banshee?"

She was a big coarse-boned woman with an orange-colored pompadour untidily bushed above crimson cheeks. Thirty years ago she might have been handsome but time had taken away this advantage; she had given up bemoaning or bothering about it. She was interested in one thing—cash, like the rest of them. "What's that ye've got on yer shirtfront, Frank? Don't be tellin' me ye've turned plumb fool at last."

Frank grinned a little sheepishly, rubbed the palms of his hands against the thighs of his pants. "Any redheads around?"

"Redheads, is it?" She was watching him shrewdly. "I got the one from Saint Looey, if that's who ye're meanin'. I figured after the—"

"I'm not talking about fillies."

"Then ye're in the wrong stall. Do yer huntin' some other place."

Frank swung around. "What outfit you fellers with?"

Resentment was plain in the cut of their eyes. Minnie said, giving him the flat of her tongue. "Don't be rowellin' me guests, ye dom star-packin' blatherskite!" But after a moment the smallest one said, "Gourd an' Vine. Out of Corpus."

"Get shucked of that hardware if you come into town tomorrow. You can't go heeled in any place that sells whisky. Including this dive." Frank went out.

He could, of course, have searched the place, but not without laying up trouble. If Tularosa was here he'd have to come out.

Frank got on his horse. He scowled, knowing he couldn't afford to hang fire here. He had the whole town to patrol and the riskiest hours were still ahead.

He breathed a sigh into the darkness and swore irascibly. It was in his mind the Council had jobbed him, keeping Tularosa back until he'd taken the oath. Yet in fairness he had to admit he couldn't blame them. Nobody would have touched this job with a prod pole if it had been aired Tularosa was the first thing on the docket. The man was like a wild animal.

Frank shook his head and cursed again, and observed Danny Settles shuffling along with his sack, threadbare coat flapping around bony legs as he picked a muttering way toward the Mercantile. Probably going after groceries, trying to reach the doors before Krantz locked up.

Perhaps because he was a loner himself, Frank had always had a soft place in his heart for Danny Settles who was the nearest thing South Fork had to a halfwit. He had a cave or a burrow somewhere out in the Barrens. It was the measure of his queerness that he made pets of crawling varmints. He'd been around as long as Frank could remember, the butt of coarse jokes and a lot of fool horseplay, a wizard at repairing firearms and the credulity of a child. He pieced out a precarious existence doing exacting odd jobs for Bernie, the gunsmith, while waiting for the monthly pittance mailed West by his father, a Boston industrialist who had gone to great lengths to be shed of him. He was the result, it was said, of too much education.

Frank's thoughts went resentfully back to John Arnold. Arnold and Gurden had played him for a sucker. There was no doubt about it. They'd known Ashenfeldt was dead, and by whose hand, when they'd set this up for him.

He was mad enough to shove the damned badge down their throats. Yet even as this occurred to him Frank saw in his mind the face and shape of Honey Kimberland and licked parched lips. The one good thing, Frank guessed, in his life. Actually, he supposed, he'd ought to thank the damned Council for giving him this chance. But, hating abysmally to be maneuvered, he scowled at the dust-fogged shine of the Opal, knowing it was Gurden who'd kept Tularosa hidden till they'd got Frank clinched into the job. Chip Gurden had known Frank couldn't back down after that.

Frank yanked his six-shooter savagely out of its

leather and let the dun carry him across the hundred-foot width of the hoof-tracked road.

The blacksmith was still working by the light of a lantern. Frank, cutting around to come up from the holding grounds, caught the iron-dulled strokes of his hammer. Frank heard the mumble of voices as he moved up on the door. He walked the dun into the light of the lanterns, seeing the smith bent over his bellows and the squatted-down shape of a cow wrangler watching him. He was an old coot, this trail hand, weathered and wrinkled as a chucked-away boot. Frank, eyeing the both of them, spoke to the smith. "You got that hub ready yet for Draicup's wagon?"

The smith's head came around. "Why, hello, Frank. Just about, I guess."

"Don't turn loose of it till I give you the word."

The smith and that other one traded quick glances.

"I'm a-waitin' on thet wheel, son," the squatted gent said mildly.

This meekness didn't deceive Frank. There wasn't one trail hand in twenty who was not plumb willing, night or day, to tackle his weight in wildcats. Frank said to the trail hand:

"Slide out of that shell belt."

The mild eyes measured him.

The smith said nervously, "Man, that's Frank Carrico!"

The old man, grunting, finally let the belt drop.

"Want I should git it fer you, Frank?" the smith asked.

"Just hang onto that wheel till I tell you different." Frank backed his dun out of the light from the door. He'd been lucky! There was sweat all over him. His hands got to shaking till he had to grab hold of the horn to keep them quiet when he thought of what a fool he'd been to go and brace that jigger with his back wide open. If Tularosa had come up or been around someplace watching— Frank bitterly swore.

He picked up his reins and sent the dun toward the street. A glance swiveled over his shoulder at Minnie's revealed nothing suspicious. He drew a ragged breath. Worry could do a man in sure as anything! He fetched his face around for a look at the Chuckwagon. It was off there ahead of him, its canvas top a dirty blur against the lantern beneath its fly.

He fetched Honey back into mind, recalling the soft exciting feel of her with her heart pounding wildly and the smell of her tumbled hair whipping round him. The job was worth this risk if it would do what he wanted.

He wasn't sure it would. But let him once get this town to eating out of his hand and a proper respect slapped into these trail crews and he guessed not many doors would stay shut against him.

This was still a young land where what you did was more important than who you were or where you'd come from. Old W. T. wasn't a man to forget that. If half the stories were true *his* start wouldn't bear much looking into either.

Frank was forty yards from the subdued shine of the flapping canvas when he became aware of the stopped wagon. There was a girl holding the reins, and a horse-backer talking to her. This was about all Frank could make out, the moon being under a cloud at the moment. A little wind had sprung up, whipping their words away. He likely wouldn't have noticed them at all if he had been less edgy and they hadn't been caught against the light from the Blue Flag.

With Honey on his mind they took immediate hold of his interest. He kneed the dun toward them, remembering the wagon from Bar 40 at the Mercantile. He got nearer. He saw the girl shake her head and sway away from the fellow, saw the man's arm come up as he bent after her from the saddle. The girl reached for the whip. Snorting contemptuously, the fellow grabbed her.

Frank didn't wait to see any more. He slammed the dun into the other man's mount, catching him by the coat at the shoulder, yanking him back with an uncaring roughness that mighty near dumped him onto the ground. "Ma'am, is this galoot bothering you?"

In Frank's grip the man, who seemed to be on the

bony side, was in no position to do much of anything, suspended as he was halfway out of the saddle. His horse snorted nervously, dancing a little.

"Why, no, not particularly." Her voice was pleasant. It wasn't Honey's. She was new here. She didn't seem much excited—appeared more like she was smiling. It kind of made Frank feel foolish.

Perhaps she sensed his resentment. "I wouldn't want you to drop him under those hoofs."

Frank very nearly did. For, just then, the moon came out. The fellow twisted his head, and Frank felt like Jonah in the belly of the whale.

The "galoot" he had hold of was Tularosa.

Frank had time only to realize this—when young Church, taut with fury, yelled:

"Frank!"

Frank saw the glint of metal in Church's lifting hand. Tularosa began to struggle, trying to get leverage, trying to pull his far leg across the drag of the saddle. Frank was in a bad spot. He slapped the gunfighter savagely. Then he growled at Church, "Will, keep out of this."

"Don't use that tone on me, you bastard!"

Frank half turned the frozen mask of his face. In that fleeting fragment of time his mind absorbed details without conscious understanding or realization of it even: the still look of the girl, the forward clump of Church's boots, the collecting crowd closing in about them. Yet never for an instant did Frank's glance quit the man he had hold of. While Church in his drunken fury might shoot, there was not the slightest question about Tularosa. The moment that sidewinder got any leverage he'd latch onto a gun and he would damn sure use it.

The strain of keeping his grip, of holding the fellow off balance, was beginning to play hell with the muscles of Frank's arm. He could hear Church coming up and, made hollow by the torture of this impasse, he rammed a knee into Tularosa's chest. It fetched a grunt from the redhead, but too much of Frank's strength was concentrated on holding him. The blow did nothing to ease the deadlock that was pushing Frank toward the brink of disaster.

He sensed the girl was in motion. He made a desperate attempt to reach Tularosa's holstered pistol, but the grip that kept Tularosa from trying also balked Frank. The saddle-horn prevented Frank from reaching his own.

The girl cried: "Keep out of this!" and snatched up her whip. Frank heard the snarl of Church's breath. The thump of his stride broke around the near end of the wagon.

"I'm goin' to cut you down to size!" Church wheezed.

Frank's left hand, fisting, hit Tularosa on the side of the face. He struck once more but he couldn't get steam enough into the punches.

The gunfighter grated, "I'll remember you, mister," and tried again to get a boot braced against his saddle.

With the flat of his hand Frank cracked Tularosa across the bridge of the nose. The man yelled. Church fired. Tularosa's horse squealed and, flinging its head down, went to pitching. The gun-fighter's legs lost contact and the dropped sprawl of his weight dragged Frank off the dun.

They fell into a dust-streaked haze of flying hoofs. Frank lost the man. The smothery stench of powdered earth enveloped them and through this fog Frank glimpsed the bobbling approach of a lantern. The dim grumble of Church's steady cursing was lost in the racket of hoofs and shouts. Frank's need to relocate the killer became more acute with each passing instant. It was then, as Frank came onto his kness, that he discovered the full meaning of the word 'desperation'. In the fall or the rolling he had lost his gun.

He swayed aside, barely avoiding the lashing hoof of a horse. The dust was so thick he couldn't see two yards in front of him. His face and clothing were gritty with the stuff, his burning eyes were filled with tears. He faintly heard the girl cry out, and he was groping blindly toward her when hardly beyond the stretch of his hand a man sharply screamed. Frank's legs crashed into something yielding, upending him. Back of him someplace a gun's report bludgeoned out of the uproar.

The dust started clearing in an updraft of air. Horses and men materialized out of it and patches of oil-yellow light from the store fronts. He caught the shape of the wagon with the girl standing in it. Someone yelled, "*There he is!*" and Frank flung himself around just as Church fired again.

Frank came out of that crouch with a wildly furious swing that took Church full in the wind. Frank gave the big ranchman no time to recover but tore into him with a ferocity that drove Church back into the crowd. Frank jerked the gun from Church's grip and whacked him across the neck with the butt of it. Church yelled and Frank hit him again. Still yelling, Church fell.

Coughing, wheezing from dust and exertion, Frank saw the lantern throw its shine on Church's face. The crowd stood silent. One cheek showed a welt like a brand burn where Frank had struck him and there was a red streak of blood against the side of his neck. Church wasn't out but he was considerably more cautious. He finally squirmed over and was helped to his feet by some of the crowd.

Nothing Will Church did would have surprised Frank much. Old Sam, Will's sire, was a tight-fisted miser, and Will's mother was a cowed little wisp of a woman who never opened her mouth unless spoken to. In the five years Frank had ridden for Circle C (doing the work of a foreman on the pay of a horse wrangler) he'd never seen Mrs. Church let go of two words without first peering at Sam or Will for permission.

Young Will shook his shoulders together, glance bright with venom as he twisted his head from one side to the other. "You ain't done with this," he said thickly. "Gimme that gun."

"You ain't got sense enough to pack a gun, damn you. If you ever fetch another one into this town I'll lock you up like any other nuisance. Now get going," Frank growled, swinging away from him.

Men stepped back. Frank found his new hat and

picked it up, cuffing the dust off. The outer fringes of
the crowd began to dissolve in search of other amusement. The girl's voice called, "Marshal—"

Frank walked over. "You all right, Miss?"

She eyed him curiously. "Of course. You won't need
that gun to speak with me."

Frank looked down at Church's pistol and put it away.
The remains of his anger was still reflected in his cheeks
and the weight of regret over losing Tularosa sawed
across his morose thoughts till he glanced up and found
her smiling. He looked more closely then, for the first
time really seeing her.

She was not the kind a man would easily forget. She
had shape and there was an attraction of some kind
emanating from her that compelled his sharpest interest.
It was like a current running between them. Her voice
took hold of him too. She said, "I haven't thanked you—"

"No thanks called for, Miss."

He saw the flash of her teeth and, annoyed with himself, decided her attraction was simply the lure of the
unplumbed. Because she was new and unknown to him—

The man with the lantern, coming up, touched Frank's
arm. "Sorry to cut in but some of the boys over there is
beginnin' to talk rope, Frank."

"Rope?" Frank looked at him blankly.

"If you don't want him hoisted you better git over
there."

Frank grabbed the lantern and strode into the crowd.
Kelly stepped in front of him, barring the way. "We're
takin' care of this."

Frank brushed him aside and came through the mob,
not daring to believe, and saw the shape on the ground.
He brought up the lantern, feeling the breath swell inside
him. Luck! He remembered the scream then and looked
for blood. He rolled Tularosa over with his foot without
finding any. Caught by a hoof maybe, simply knocked
out.

"Couple of you gents pick him up and come with me."

Frank heard growls. No one moved. Frank's narrowing

eyes saw what he was up against. He set down the lantern. "Pick him up, Kelly."

"Stay outa this, Frank. That bastard's killed five men in this town!"

"That gives you the right to string him up?" Frank looked at them bleakly. "Not while I'm packing tin."

"Kinda feelin' your oats, ain'tcha?" One of Kimberland's outfit pushed up with a hand sliding over the brass of his shell belt. "Go sit in your office if you don't like the play."

"Take him!" somebody yelled from the back, and when Frank twisted his head the whole crowd surged against him. A Church cowhand swung at him, numbing the nerves at the side of Frank's shoulder. Frank rammed the flat of an arm into the fellow, driving him backward. A growl welled out of the mob. Someone fetched Frank a staggering blow on the head. Another tried to climb on his back. Frank shook him off and brought up Church's gun.

"If you want to play rough you'll find out what rough is."

Those nearest Frank backed off a little. He dropped into a crouch, got Tularosa half upright. Frank let the man sag across his left shoulder. He lurched erect, darkly considering the crowd, knowing that when he moved they'd make their try.

"Don't be so damned proud," Kelly growled from the left of him.

Last year Kimberland had lost two riders to Tularosa. Kelly, teamstering for Kimberland, certainly understood the temper of this bunch. There were other Kimberland riders in sight and these were getting set, grimly shifting to box Frank.

It occurred to Frank that Tularosa fully deserved anything these people were able to do to him. But he was a prisoner of the law now, Frank's responsibility, and to turn loose of the man would be to admit he couldn't cope with this. Frank said with the wind away down in his belly, "I'm drilling the first guy that gets in my way," and was about to start into them when hoof sound

climbed above the growls coming at him. Wood screamed
harshly against the gouge of a wheel rim as the wagon
came around in a shrieking half circle driven by the girl
straight into the crush of angry men.

There were startled shouts and oaths as the men jumped
back to avoid being trampled. One, moving too late,
was struck by the wood and knocked over. The vibra-
tions of his frightened cry were lost in the wagon's racket
as the girl braced herself against the pull of the wild-
eyed horses.

"Hurry!" she called impatiently, shaking the hair back
out of her face.

Frank heaved his prisoner into the wagonbed, catching
hold of the tailgate as she let the team go. Several guns
barked behind them as Frank vaulted up. The girl
swung the excited horses past the Chuckwagon's shine
and cramped them into a careening run across the trash-
littered open between the cook's dutch ovens and
Fentriss' livery. Climbing over Tularosa's jouncing shape
—the man was trying to get up now—Frank cuffed him
down and, ducking the battered brass-cornered trunk,
jarred onto the seat beside her. Breathing hard he
reached for the lines. The girl wouldn't yield them.

"County seat's Vega, isn't it?" she yelled in his ear.

"We're not heading for Vega!" Frank scowled over a
shoulder. "Cut around back of the jail."

"Are you crazy?" She kept the team pointed south
and reached for the whip. "That crowd—"

Frank closed his hands on the lines ahead of her
hands, sawing the horses around into the east and bringing them back through the grass toward the street again.
Fentriss' railed pens came out of the dust and he drove
to the right of them, fetching the team up behind the dark
jail.

He got the animals stopped and jumped down.
"Obliged," he mumbled, hurrying toward the back door.
He got the keys from his pocket and pushed the door
open. With bent head he stood listening, then came back
for Tularosa.

"I suppose," the girl said, "you've got your mind set

on a halo. Just watch out you don't wind up with a harp. Some of those fellows—"

"They'll get over it." Frank grabbed Tularosa's feet and pulled. The man was conscious but he certainly wasn't himself by considerable. He was able to stand with Frank hanging onto him. Frank steered him toward the door.

Angry shouts interlarded with hoof sound came from the street where mounted men were milling in cursing confusion. "Wait—" the girl cried—"I'll help you."

"You can do that best by—"

"Maybe I can pull that bunch off your neck."

Frank twisted to look up at her. "Now who's reaching for a harp! You want to get yourself killed?"

She untangled the lines. There was the flash of her teeth. "I'm used to risk." She shook out the lines and clucked her tongue at the team. "Ever turned a herd with a lighted match?" With a laugh drifting back to put a catch in Frank's throat, she fingered the horses into a run. Before Frank could say "Damn!" she was whipping them around the back end of the hotel. Past the dark barn of the stage company she put the team at the street, bouncing east on two wheels as she went out of Frank's sight.

The crowd yelled. Riders tore after her, streaking across the mouth of the alley. Frank, swearing, shoved Tularosa ahead of him. He slammed the door and bolted it.

There was a light in the office and a man in the corridor with a gun in his hand.

CHAPTER THREE

FRANK, FROZENLY staring, stood unable to move for the better part of a second, hearing Tularosa stumbling somewhere off to the left of him. Sucking in a long breath he came out of it, following the prisoner, pushing him into one of the cells, yanking the grill shut. He wiped the sweat off his neck and tramped on up the corridor. "A fine thing, peon, rambling around this place with a gun in your hand. You trying to get yourself shot?"

The other fellow laughed. "The gun is yours. I got your horse too. How does it feel, packing the tin in this town?"

Frank took the gun and put it away between belly and trousers. "For eighty a month you got the chance to find out."

"Not me. I'm comfortable—"

"You only think you are." Frank, turning, rummaged in the desk, got his hand on what he wanted and tossed a nickel-plated star at the other. "Pin it on, bucko. You'll find it beats misbranding cattle."

The man rubbed his nose, staring at Frank like he was trying to figure out just how much of that was meant. He was short for this country, heavy-built and dark with a bristling mustache that hid his mouth. He thought and spoke in the manner of a gringo but his name was Chavez and, mostly, folks eyed him with their heads to one side. He said, "You fool! How long would this town stand for *me* on the payroll?"

"My worry," Frank grinned. "Pin it on. I got a chore for you. Danny Settles came in about a half hour ago. I want him found and fetched over here."

Chavez's black stare dug into Frank bitterly.

"Go on, you damn loafer. Pronto."

"That soft streak, gringo, will one day be the end of you."

Frank waved him away and dropped into the chair. He took Will Church's pistol out of his holster. He said, "You find Tularosa's?"

Chavez shook his head. "Old man Wolverton got it." He scowled and licked his lips and shifted his weight from one foot to the other. "Frank, damn it, you don't want—"

"Get going, you sorry peon. We've got to have a jailer and who can we get but Danny without putting up more than the cost of his keep?"

He shook the shells from Church's pistol and only one of them thumped when it hit the desk. He'd been lucky there, too, he thought. He squinted through the dirty barrel, got a rag from the desk and was cleaning it when he heard Chavez leave. He shook his head, unconsciously frowning.

He reckoned there would be a deal of talk about him taking for a deputy a Mexican who two-thirds of them figured to be a rustler. Luck had caught Tularosa for him. He'd put a star on Chavez because he had to have a man no one else could hire away from him, a gun that would stay loyal. It was simple as that. The soft streak the man had charged him with didn't enter into his selection at all. At least Frank hoped he wasn't quite that much of a fool.

They'd all be watching him, weighing his actions, quick to turn to their own advantage any weakness he was careless enough to show. By Frank's observation a marshal's life was a touch-and-go thing, safe only so long as he could keep the whip hand. Gurden's hard malice would be all the time looking for a new crack to stab at; the storekeeper put no trust in him and Arnold would stand behind Frank only so long as it might suit W. T. Kimberland.

Pushing Church's gun aside Frank put his elbows on the desk. Still thinking, he slid them back and rubbed his hands along its edge, feeling less and less satisfied with this shaky damn perch he had got himself onto. If Kimberland was dreaming up a further expansion of Bar 40 range—and there was talk enough to indicate there might be truth in the rumor—Frank could see how the man would want a galoot packing the star who'd be inclined to see his side of things. This had been a bad year with not half enough rain and the syndicate was caught in a falling market with a heap more cattle than they had any grass for. Roundup was less than a week away and if Kimberland couldn't manage to get himself out of the bind he'd have to drive to Dodge and take for good beef considerable less than it had cost to raise. A lot of herds had been ahead of him while he'd sat here fidgeting in the hope of additional rain. There was still grass on these flats but—

A faint scratch of sound pulled Frank's head up. This quick he was cocked to send a hand streaking beltward but he kept the hand still and held the rest of him likewise. Too close to the desk and too late for it anyway. Tularosa's saddlemate—that old jasper he'd disarmed at the blacksmith's—stood just inside the open door.

That old coot had the look of a hungry wolf. He held a gun at his hip and the slanch of his eyes said he'd just as lief use it. "Git him out."

"Keys are in my back pocket," Frank said, looking disgusted.

"Son, I ain't aimin' to tell you twice."

Frank, shrugging, got up. He found it harder than he'd reckoned to turn his back on this ranny but Frank wanted it understood he wasn't about to go off the foolish end of this. With two fingers he fished the ring of keys from his pocket. "Now shuck the gun," Draicup's rider said.

Frank got up and let it fall out of his pants. The sound of its drop held a world of finality.

The old man said, "Git him outa there now."

A pile of thoughts churned through Frank's head and were discarded. He tramped down the echoing corridor with the old trail hand keeping plenty of space between them. No chance to whirl and grab. Too much promise of stopping a bullet.

"That you, Dogie?" Tularosa growled.

The old vinegarroon grunted. "Git that cage open, boy."

It was in Frank's mind that he might still manage to block this. All he needed to do was pitch these keys into one of the cells, into one of those shut and empty ones. Before this sidewinder got things in hand again Chavez ought to be coming into the place with Settles.

But Frank hadn't enough faith in the plan to go through with it. Chavez would walk into this blind and probably get himself shot. And they might drill Frank for spite. Tularosa took hold of the bars. He was grinning.

Three feet short of Tularosa Frank turned. "You—"

"Git that door open quick!"

The old geezer was in one hell of a sweat. It was even money he had watched Chavez leave. *"Don't shoot,"* Frank yelled—*"bend that gun over his head!"*

It was the oldest trick in the deck, but it impelled the man to make a choice at a time he couldn't afford to get tangled up in thinking. Frank flung the keys, saw them whack Dogie full in the kisser. The old fool fired but he was still off balance and before he could trigger again Frank tied into him, smashing him wickedly against iron bars.

Frank grabbed the man's gun wrist, savagely twisting, forcing the muzzle of the weapon away from him. Dogie fought like a wildcat with a panting ferocity that carried Frank back and came within a twist of breaking Frank's hold. The fist that was free slammed into Frank like a jackhammer. A bony knee slashed at Frank's groin. The old man's head nearly tore off Frank's jaw.

He tried again for Frank's groin and this time found it. Frank's whole body felt that knee going through him. He was lost in red fog. But Dogie, swinging the gun at Frank's head, didn't have as much room as he thought he had. The pistol's long barrel clanged against a cell bar, the blow grazed Frank's neck and Frank, staggering into him, bore the old man off his feet. So much violence seemed to have used the man up. Frank, half smothering him, found Dogie's wrist again, cracking it against the floor until the gun fell out of his fingers.

Frank, rolling clear of him, heard the wild grumble of Tularosa's cursing. Frank pushed onto his feet but that damned old ranny wouldn't own to being whipped. With the breath rattling around in him like a wind-broken bronc he was after the gun again, talon-spread hand almost onto it when Frank, snarling with outrage, stamped a boot on it, twisting cruelly. Dogie screamed. Frank, with a fistful of shirt, hauled him upright, slamming him back against the iron bars.

The old man looked bushed. The eyes rolled around in his head like loose marbles. Frank could almost feel sorry for him. He propped him up against the cell, holding him there by that fistful of shirtfront and, wondering reluctantly if he ought to call Doc, reached down the limp arm for that boot-bloodied hand.

Frank never did find out what hit him. Through the blinding explosion of pain in his head he had one final instant of full comprehension. The old jasper had possomed, played him for a sucker. Then something exploded in the region of Frank's guts and he swung down a red spiral into the black of oblivion.

CHAPTER FOUR

HE CAME back to the rasp of men's voices. There was a light above him someplace. He had a feeling of motion which abruptly ceased and a bunk's ropes aroused to exquisite torture every misused bone and muscle in his body. Through the swimming red slits of his squeezed-shut gaze he saw Chavez bending over him, muttering and scowling. He saw Chavez twist his head. "Get that sawbones," the Mexican growled.

Frank, shoving up, pushed him out of the way. Pain splintered through him. The breath got stuck in his throat. The room rocked and wavered. He saw Settles' white face and got onto his feet, reeling, swearing. By the feel of his ribs someone had put the boots to him. Anger came into his throat like bile. "Say something, damn you!" he snarled at Chavez.

The Mexican, considering him, said at last, "They got away."

Frank shut his eyes. Already, in his mind, he could hear the avid whispers: *Whipped to a standstill. Licked by a stove-up trail hand.*

Settles shuffled his feet, flapped his hands. "It's my fault, Frank. I'd got through at the store—"

"I know whose fault it is." Frank said bitterly, "How long they been gone?"

Chavez shrugged. "Long enough. Took a while to get you out of there. They shut you into one of them cells, took the keys. We had to saw out the lock."

Well, swearing about it wasn't going to help now. Frank ran a hand gingerly over his ribs and wondered if he should try to locate John Arnold. Settles, watching Frank's hand, asked if Frank was sure he hadn't better have the doctor. Frank squeezed his fists shut. Chavez remarked without giving it any importance, "That

35

woman's waitin' to see you. The one with the wagon."

Frank scowled but fetched his head around. "Where is she? What's she want?"

"Never said. I guess she's outside settin' in it."

Frank got Church's pistol off the desk. He guessed the least he could do was be civil. It certainly wasn't her fault he had let them get the best of him. He told Settles:

"Look around. See if you can turn up those keys." He sloshed on his hat, telling Chavez to hold the place down.

He saw his horse where Chavez had tied it. He saw the girl. In the light from the windows, as he stepped up to the wagon, he could see she wasn't at all hard on the eyes. Couldn't hold a candle to Honey but she was worth a second look. He asked, "What happened?" and did not think to take off his hat.

"I expect they didn't much like it."

"Didn't bother you, did they?"

Her shoulders moved. She put her hands in her lap. "I hear that fellow got away from you. . . ."

Frank's cheeks got hot. "That's right," he said bitterly. "It'll probably blow over." He didn't really believe that; it just seemed the thing to say. Gurden, for one, would make all he could of an old man getting the best of their marshal. If Gurden could talk Krantz around he'd have the star off Frank's shirt. Frank might try to horse others but he was honest with himself. "They give you any trouble?"

She shook her head. "Of course not." She seemed amused. "I told you I could take care of myself."

Frank expected she really believed that. He took in the blue corduroy skirt, the dark corduroy jacket and small round hat pinned atop her red hair—a kind of chestnut sorrel, he thought—and resentfully found her too cool.

Women had their place in this country and Frank would have been the last to deny it, but this girl was too self-possessed for him. "Well, thanks," he said testily, and was turning away when young Church came around the end of her wagon. Frank's mouth turned thin. "I told you, Will, to get out of town."

"I got something to say to you—"

"Say it and get going."

Church showed the umbrage that was smoldering inside him, but he had hold of himself. He looked sober now. "When this town's had enough I'll take care of you, Frank."

"Don't let the badge stop you."

"Never mind. Just remember I gave you warning." Church, wheeling, twisted his head to stare up at the girl. He managed a parched smile, touched his hat and went on.

"Who was that?" the girl asked.

"Will Church." Frank spoke shortly. He was in a poor frame of mind and made no attempt to conceal his irritation. "Will's old man owns six thousand head of cattle."

She smiled. "How many do you own?"

Frank growled, "None!" and was turning back toward the office when she said:

"Frank, I wonder if you could . . . ." Her voice trailed off and then came back more determinedly: "I'm trying to find—"

But Frank had closed his mind to everything but Tularosa and the stove-up codger who had whipped him. He went inside.

Chavez with a hip on the edge of the desk looked up, started to speak, looked again and kept silent. Frank dropped into the chair. "You got any ideas?"

"About what?"

"That rustling."

Some of the outfits going up the trail last year had been bothered by stock thieves and the word coming back was that these fellows were getting bolder. Chavez's look showed he understood what was in Frank's mind. His mouth tightened a little but he shook his head. "All that talk was hot air. I had nothing to do with it."

Frank considered him, then said gruffly, "The hell with it. One thing I *don't* have to worry about in this job is cattle." He slipped Church's gun back into his holster. He looked around for his own but guessed

Tularosa had got away with it. "What you reckon old Kimberland's up to?"

Chavez shrugged elaborately. "I expect," he said finally, "he probably wants to feel he's got the law in his corner."

Frank got up and tramped around. He felt jumpy as a frog. "I think the old pirate's getting ready to grab more range. Plenty of grass up there on the Bench. Enough to see him through for sure. Like to know what he thinks he's bought with this tin."

Chavez nodded. "He aims to get value. But Sam Church is the tight one—he wouldn't give a prairie dog room for a burrow. Hear you slapped Will's horns down."

Frank waved that away. "Danny found those keys yet?"

Chavez shook his head. "Will's eying the Bench, too. If he could grab off that grass they'd be as big or bigger'n Kimberland."

"You think Settles understands we're counting on him for jailer?"

"I told him." Chavez searched Frank's face. "Krantz won't like it."

"Hell with Krantz," Frank growled and, with a wrench of bruised muscles, got a drawer out of the desk and started pawing through it. He shoved it back with a grimace. "Wonder where Joe kept his liniment?"

"What am I supposed to be doing for that fortune the town's paying me?"

Frank squeezed a hand against his forehead, twisting his face up. He felt six years older than Moses. "Damn but I got a head! Hell, you can take over at two. Right now, if you don't aim to pound your ear, you can go and help Danny chase down those keys."

Frank stepped into the street.

The girl was gone with her wagon. He was sorry now for the rudeness he had shown her; he was sorry about a lot of things. He slapped the dun with tired affection and wondered how much longer Chip Gurden would be content to let him wear this badge.

It was turning colder. The wind was getting up. There was the feel of winter in it. Frank got his brush jacket off the saddle, shook it out and shrugged into it, swearing a little at the hitch of mauled sinews. He really ought to rub something into them.

He got onto the horse and sat listening a while. There was plenty to hear but the street didn't seem near as noisy as it had. He caught the bawl of a steer and peered off toward the bedgrounds, seeing only solid black beyond the shine of Fentriss' lantern.

That girl, it crossed his mind, may have come from the herd; he didn't, however, put much stock in the notion. Women, as a rule, didn't travel with trail outfits. He didn't want to think of her, didn't want to think about that jail break, either. He hoped Dogie's crushed hand was giving him hell.

The moon was gone, lost in a welter of piled-up clouds. No light at the smithy. The Chuckwagon's owner had given up, too. Must be getting on for twelve. Up the line, in front of the Flag, he saw four-five hombres with their heads together. He didn't hear any singing. Fiddle squeal poured out of the Opal where business was really whooping it up. He heard a woman's high laugh. East, near the bridge, a jerkline freight crawled wearily toward him. These were the bad hours.

Time to move and get into his job. He threw one final look behind and saw two men come out of the pool hall, gab for a moment and head for Gurden's. As they pushed inside Frank saw Kelly behind the batwings. Frank and Kelly had done a lot of helling around together while working for the Churches. Even after Kelly had quit and gone to hauling for Bar 40 they'd continued to see quite a bit of each other whenever, like now, Kelly got to town. These last few months they'd seemed to be drifting away from each other; Kelly'd been spending a lot of his time with one of the floozies who worked for Minnie. Still it was odd, now he stopped to think back on it, he hadn't asked Kelly to be his deputy. Perhaps, without knowing it, the man's connection with Kimberland had decided Frank

to pass him up for Chavez. He thought Kelly showed
poor judgment loafing around at Gurden's.

Frank pushed it out of his mind and rode east, passing the hotel and gloomily wondering if Honey was
spending the night there. She sometimes did on a Saturday night. When her father had business in town
she came with him. But he hadn't seen Kimberland,
only Bill Grace and some punchers and that Bar 40
wagon that had been pulled up in front of Krantz's
store. It wasn't there now. The Mercantile was closed.

Frank saw the barbershop lamp wink out. It was quiet
here around the stage depot. Halbertson's hay shed was
lost in the shadows. Beyond this, south, there were no
lights showing. Continuing east Frank crossed the
street's blowing dust in front of the freighter and,
rounding Wolverton's Saddlery, cruised into Snob Hollow.

It was the first time Frank had ever ventured this far
beyond the limits proscribed by the town for his kind.
It gave him a queer turn to be riding here now with
the town's approbation. Krantz's house was dark. Frank
knew which was which from many travels across the
range beyond the river with its fringe of willows. Wolverton's residence, too, was dark, and most of the others.
But there were lights behind the lumber king's blinds.
Probably throwing a party of some kind.

Prowling the shadows Frank turned back. Putting
the dun into the street at a watchful walk he continued
to frown as he considered his troubles, reminded of
hunger by the yeasty smells coming out of the bake
shop where the Swede, with his shirt off, was punching
up dough. Nobody showed on the walks east of Gurden's. Frank, smelling coffee, eyed the New York Cafe
but he kept the horse moving. He pulled up his collar.
That wind was getting some real teeth in it.

Frank reached the Flag. Its crowd had thinned, no
longer hiding the bar. He saw Gurden off in a corner
talking from the side of his mouth at Old Judge (a
drunken sot) who was the only appeal a man had around
here without he was willing to drive a hand beltward.

At any other time Gurden's presence in the Flag would have caught up Frank's interest, but right then he hardly noticed. Tularosa was on his mind.

He passed Minnie's and, going on to the Trench Brothers' yard, wheeled the dun well away from those black piles of stacked lumber. With the wind blowing through him he passed Minnie's heading back, and was deep in the shadows growing out of that vacant lot when the saddle jarred under him, telegraphing shock the whole length of his body.

The horse flung its head down and had already humped by the time Frank caught the sound of the shot. He had his hands full keeping the animal under him. He spurred the dun around in a crow-hopping circle but there was nothing to see. The bushwhacker was too smart to try his luck again with Frank watching.

Prodded by anger Frank went over to the Flag, re-membering Gurden. Frank was about to vault down, go charging in, when a shout came racketing out of the adjoining pool hall. Frank's head whipped around. He forgot about Gurden; what he saw pulled him over to the pool hall.

CHAPTER FIVE

FRANK CAME through the door of the pool hall like the wrath of God. Every face jerked his way except the face of Jace Brackley. Most were startled, some appalled, by the violent passions unleashed in this room; some relief, some resentment at Frank's arrival showed too. Will Church's florid cheeks were still twisted with fury. One white-knuckled fist gripped a cue, butt end out, raised like a club. Blood made a bright splash of color on the knob of it. A second cue lay broken near Brackley on the floor.

"Church," Frank said, "start talking."

"The bastard tried to knock me down!"

No one disputed this. Frank, staring around, jerked his chin at the nearest strange rider. "You boys with that trail herd?" When this was admitted he said to the other one, "You got anything to add?"

The man shook his head and looked like he wished he was someplace else. Frank, sheathing his pistol, stabbed his look back at Church. "Why'd Brackley jump you?"

Young Church said, affronted, "How the hell should I know? Them damn Benchers is apt to do anything." He tossed the bloodied cue away from him and gave Garrison, the hall's proprietor, who was stirring uneasily, a hard look. Garrison quieted. Church wiped his hands against the seams of his trousers and, with a black look at Frank, started to step around him.

"Stand hitched," Frank said. "You're staying right here until Jace comes around."

They were all watching Will, and Church with the weight of that pressure upon him swelled up like a carbuncle. "Who do think you're talkin' to, Carrico?" He drew a half step nearer, dark with outrage. Before he could loose any more of his lip, Brackley rolled over

42

with a groan and sat up. He looked around blearily and put a hand to his head. He eyed the blood on his fingers and, again reaching up, gingerly felt of the ear that had been half torn away. He pushed himself off the floor.

Frank said, "What happened, Brackley?"

The rancher, keeping his eyes on Church, took the hat one of the drovers held out to him. "Nothing I can't take care of," he said, and staggered out of the place without further talk.

Church, cracking a grin, made as though to start after him. Frank put a hand out. "Just a minute."

Will jarred to a stop, the dart of his eyes turning narrowly watchful. "Takin' that tin pretty serious, ain't you?"

Frank kept digging into Will with his stare. Church didn't like it and something shifty in the man began to squirm under so long an inspection. Again he started around Frank and this time Frank let him go. But at the door Will's bile caught up with him and he said, bitterly wheeling, "Give a thirty-a-month cow-walloper a badge to pin on and—"

Frank asked quietly, "You want I should shut that big mouth of yours?"

"Mebbe," Church sneered, "you better look at your hole card. For a jasper that's let a pair of saddle tramps sucker him—"

Something he saw in Frank's stare muzzled the rest of it. With a strangled oath he reached for the door, recoiling when it came suddenly at him. Kimberland's foreman, Bill Grace, came in from the night with a gust of cold air, turning all the way around to stare after the man as Church plunged blindly out through the opening.

"Well!" Grace said, taking a sharp look at Frank, "somebody sure must've shoved a burr under his tail. Ain't seen Will move so fast since the time that centipede crawled up his pants leg."

A couple of cowpunchers laughed. Danny Settles came in with his long coat flapping around him. His

unlined face lighted up when he saw Frank. "We found
those keys!"

"All right," Frank said, catching the grins. "You get
on back," he said curtly. "I'll be over there directly."

He saw Settles' face fall, but the man turned and went
out. The two trail hands, racking their cues, also left.
One of the others said, dourly critical, "You ain't hired
that halfwit fer anythin', hev you?"

"He's acting as jailer," Frank admitted.

Bill Grace said, "The town fool for jailer and a cow-
thievin' Mex for deputy. I expect the taxpayers—"

"Any pay Danny rates will come out of my pocket."

"All we need now is some of them Benchers on the
Council! I don't wonder that killer got away from you."

"You feel so strong about it," Frank said, "why'n't you
go run him down? Maybe they'd make *you* marshal,
then your boss could have things just like he wants
them." Frank hadn't meant to let go of that last, but the
words were out now and he had to stand back of them.

The Bar 40 ramrod looked him up one side and down
the other. "It's sure as hell time this town hired a *man*
to do its work." With another hard look and a snort he
departed.

Chet Garrison dug an elbow into Frank's ribs. "Looks
like you been told, boy." There was a vein of friendliness in the man's tone Frank hadn't looked for. A sug-
gestion of that spirit was in some of these other faces.
It warmed him, washing away some of his bitterness, allowing him to recover in some measure his sense of
proportion. He grinned tiredly and left and outside
climbed into his saddle.

The blow was whipping itself into a gale. He had to
bend his head against it. Everything seemed to have got
itself in motion; dust, trash—even the damned shadows.
What few horses were still at the hitchrails had sidled
around to get their rumps to the wind. Blinds flapped
and banged, but nothing disturbed the wail of the fiddles
coming through the doors of the Opal.

It was getting colder than frogs. Frank thrust his
hands in his pockets, content to guide the dun with his

knees. Then, remembering, he snatched his hands out again. He'd need every advantage a man could get if he bumped into Tularosa.

The dun was breasting the Mercantile, shuttered for the night, when a hunched-forward shape floundered out of the shadows. Frank's instant reaction was to reach for his pistol. Fear of ridicule was greater than Frank's fear of trouble. The man wasn't Tularosa. Believing the fellow was drunk Frank swerved aside but the man cut after him, clutching his hat, and Frank was close enough to recognize Kelly.

"Was figurin'" Kelly shouted, "you might could use a little help."

Frank put the dun into the lee of Ben's Furniture. Kelly, lurching after him, still clutched at his hat. He caught hold of the gelding's cheekstrap.

"Thought you were hauling for Kimberland," Frank said.

Kelly snorted. "Old friends come first."

"I've got Chavez now."

"Wind's swingin' around." Kelly brought the gray blob of his face back to Frank. "Heard about that. Won't be no use to you. Ain't nobody goin' to take orders from no halfbreed."

Frank stared down at him uncomfortably. He was tugged one way by ties of past friendship, dragged another by allegiance to the man he had hired. There was some truth in Kelly's words; Chavez would put some people's backs up. Town Council had ought to be thought about too. Frank could use them both till he got shut of Tularosa. But he could hardly afford to hire Kelly out of pocket.

Seeming almost to read Frank's thoughts the man said, "Hell, I'll work for nothin'. Glad to string along till these damn cows quit comin' through here." He let go of the dun, stepping back like it was settled. Frank said, thinking of Settles, "I can't just kick Chavez out like a dog."

A note of resentment put an edge on Kelly's voice. "Never mind. I ain't quitting a good thing to play sec-

ond fiddle to no Mex. If I don't rate top spot with you
—" He seemed to catch himself then. He made an irri-
table gesture. "What I mean— Damn it, you got Will
Church down on you. Gurden's still riled about that
killer gettin' loose. Krantz hates your guts. Now, with
this pair of yaps you've latched onto—"

"What you mean," Frank said, "is that I've made a
fine hash of this."

"I never said that!"

"You might just as well have. It's the truth."

Kelly stared up at him, hugging his coat, edging back
more to get out of the wind. "Hell, you know what this
town is! All I was tryin' to say is you've mebbe bit off
more than one guy can handle—"

"Hickok's handling Abilene."

"Hickok!" yowled Kelly. "What you need's *help*—
a friend at your back, another gun you can count on."

"I ain't heard of Bat Masterson hiring any bodyguard."

"You think you can gun-whip this town into line?
Talk sense, damn it to hell!"

"Does it make sense for you to quit a soft job to go
with a man who's apt to get burnt down before he's
two hours older?" Frank picked up his reins. "I've got
to get moving."

Kelly followed him, the gale at their backs now.
"Swingin' into the southwest—we're like to hev weather."
He relapsed into silence, hanging onto Frank's stirrup.

At the Bon Ton Frank wheeled the dun around. Keeping to a pattern was just asking for trouble; Snob Hollow
could look after itself for a spell. Coming into the light
from the New York Cafe he got hold of Kelly's hand
and grimly pushed the man's fingers across the swell of
his saddle, across the ripped place where the bullet had
struck. Kelly jerked back like he'd touched a snake.

Frank looked down at him with inscrutable eyes.
"That leather won't bite. Be thankful, old friend, you
ain't called on to help."

The teamster twisted his head against the slap of the
wind. They were passing Ben's Furniture before he

got enough breath back to make himself heard. "Tularosa?"

Frank shrugged. He seemed to be catching the habit from Chavez. "Him, or another. Don't make much difference to a stiff whose slug tags it."

They were opposite the jail, hardly ten strides from Gurden's batwings when Kelly pulled up. "Mebbe I better be turnin' off here. I—"

The hammering explosions of two shots, one climbing hard over the heels of the other, barreled through Kelly's words. Both men flung startled looks at the Opal. Frank, sending the dun forward, was out of the saddle on skidding bootheels, catching at a porch post, smashing into the half-leaf doors. Two more shots, slamming the doors, drove him back. He had no further thought for Kelly. He dropped flat to the porch planks, palming his gun, firing beneath the doors at the gangling shape diving through a side window. One of the doors jerked over Frank's head but he was already coming off of the boards, throwing himself headlong at the mouth of the alley.

He was too mad for caution but there was no one in sight when he looked into the alley. The man he had fired at was Tularosa and now, still staring, Frank found himself shaking as caution belatedly sank its hooks into him. He backed away from that slot and swiveled a look round for Kelly. The teamster wasn't in sight. *Gone up the other side*, Frank thought, and ran along the dark front of the Mercantile, feverishly pushing fresh loads into the cylinder.

At the entrance to the passage between Krantz's and Ben's Furniture he fell back a moment, listening, but the racket of the wind made hearing other sounds unlikely. He ran east as far as the barber's pole. Dropping into a walk, he moved up that dark alley. This blackness had an almost tangible quality, folding around him like the wrap of a blanket, cutting off the wind, reducing its clamor to a kind of muffled groan.

He stopped three paces from the passage's end but still heard nothing he could imagine was Tularosa. Frank knew the chance he would take if he looked. A cold sweat filmed his flesh as he moved into the open but no bullet came at him. In this moonless murk the killer could have crouched ten feet away without discovery.

Frank wanted to turn back but the words of Kimberland's foreman still rankled. He raked the dark with angry eyes, weighing his chances and not at all liking them. Frank, jaws clenched, moved forward, driven by the knowledge of his responsibility. If Frank had kept hold of Tularosa the man wouldn't be here now.

Several times Frank stumbled in the trash underfoot and twice his boots sent tin cans rattling but he reached the back of the Opal without having discovered any trace of his quarry.

Swearing under his breath, he went around to the front, pausing on Gurden's porch for another look at those swing doors. Then he stepped in and talk broke. He tramped down an opening lane and found Brackley. The man was dead. Frank's eyes stabbed Gurden. "Let's have it."

"Brackley come in here maybe half an hour ago. Said he wanted to talk so we went in the back room." Gurden's eyes were bland. "Turned out he wanted a loan."

Frank had been wondering what had fetched Brackley in. The man hadn't liked towns, hadn't been to South Fork more than twice in three years. "So you gave it to him. Backed, of course, by a plaster on his spread."

Gurden's mouth thinned around its tightened grip on his cigar. "Naturally."

"Got it handy?"

"It's in the safe."

"So you gave him the money and put the lien in your safe. Then the pair of you came out—and Tularosa shot him."

Gurden's eyes were bland no longer. They gleamed like bits of metal and there was color creeping into his beefy jowls. "I didn't see the man killed; I was still in my office when I heard the shots."

Frank discovered Wolverton in the crowd and tipped his head at him. "You want to say anything?"

The saddle merchant said, without looking at Gurden, "Jace came out by himself."

"And where was Tularosa?"

Wolverton shrugged. "I didn't see him."

Anger came into Frank's face then. "Did *anybody* see him?"

A Boxed T man said, "He came in by that door over there," and pointed across the room toward the gun shop. "He slid in just as Brackley came out of Chip's office. He yelled 'Brackley!' and when Jace turned, shot him."

A Kimberland rider said, "No argument or nothin'." And Bernie, who was by the bar, said, "Tularosa let go soon as he spotted Brackley—just yelled and shot while Brackley was still turning."

"Then jumped for the window, eh?"

"Close enough," Wolverton said. "There was a racket of hoofs and someone come onto the porch. That's when he went for the window."

"All right." Frank looked at Gurden. Then his glance singled out two punchers, Squatting O hands from farther upriver. "Pack Brackley over to where they've got Joe Ashenfeldt and hang around till I get there." His eyes snapped back to Gurden. "Close up."

In this town Chip Gurden was one-third of the law and he was not in the habit of taking orders from anyone. His reaction was instant. "Now look—"

Frank cut him off. "Take it up with Krantz or Arnold. I want this crowd out of here in three minutes."

Gurden's look swelled with hate. "If you think—"

"Clear this place," Frank said, "or I'll do it." He felt the man's fury swirling round him like a fog, but in the end Chip threw a hand up and his housemen got the exodus started. One of his aprons climbed up on the bar and started putting out lamps. Frank nodded at the Squatting O punchers and they picked Brackley up and joined the departing customers.

When the most of them were out Frank said to the Opal's proprietor, "We'll go into your office and you can show me that lien."

"Go to hell!" Gurden snarled and went into the back room, slamming the door.

Frank was minded to follow but Chavez came in with a double-barreled shotgun. Frank sent him after the furniture man, who was all the coroner they had in these parts. Frank had cooled some by then and decided to shelve the matter of Brackley's plaster until he could secure reliable opinions on the signature.

Leaving the place, he went back to the street and got onto the dun and sat a while, frowning. Then he picked up his reins and rode over to Ben Holliday's furniture place. There was a light at the back, and he got down and went in. Brackley was stretched out alongside Joe's body but the pair who had fetched him were nowhere in sight.

Back at Chip Gurden's the new bouncer, Mousetrap, stepped into the office and carefully shut the bar door. Gurden, eyeing the man bleakly, hauled a bottle off his desk and helped himself to a snort. He was putting it down when somebody's knuckles rattled against the back door. Mousetrap raised the hairy black of his eyebrows and, at Gurden's nod, went across to open it.

Kelly slipped in, twistedly grinning at the sight of the derringer disappearing up Chip's sleeve. "I warned you he was tough."

Mousetrap said, "I kin handle that feller."

"Why didn't you do it when he was growlin' over Brackley?"

Gurden said, "Shut up—both of you." He nodded at the whisky. Mousetrap passed and Kelly, eying the man derisively, caught up the bottle and lowered its level by a third. He set it down, smacking his mouth. Gurden said, "You tried for him yet?"

"Thought you was payin' to get that took care of."

"Where *is* that damn Tularosa?"

"Ain't nobody payin' me to keep cases."

"You know what I told you—"

"Give Tularosa a chance," Kelly grumbled. "He sure as hell took care of Brackley."

Gurden brushed that aside. "I want Frank put out of the way, and I got no time to waste foolin' around, either. You get after him, Kelly. Right away. Tonight."

"I already made one try," Kelly said. "It didn't come off. I hit his damn saddle."

Gurden fished a fresh stogie from his flower-embroidered vest. "What's the matter? You get buck fever? You got the best chance of anyone. You could walk right up and ram a gun in his—"

"That's what you think. I was around when a guy tried that on him once—"

"But you're his *friend*. Damn it, Kelly!"

"If he thinks so much of me howcome I ain't his deppity? I done everything but git right down on my knees."

"You think he suspects you?"

The teamster said uncomfortably, "How the hell could he?" but there was sweat on his lip.

Gurden struck a match and tipped it under his cigar. Through the smoke coming out of his mouth, he said, "You ain't handled it right. I'll think up a way." He put more smoke around him, rolling the stogie back and forth across his mouth. "Anything'll come out right if a man will put his mind to it." A contemplative look came into his winkless stare and he said in a kind of half drawl, "Wonder what made young Church jump Brackley?"

"He's tryin'," Kelly said, "to steal a march on Kimberland. He's had it in for W. T. ever since the old man told him to keep away from that girl."

"Kimberland told Will to stay away from Honey?"

"I thought you'd heard that." Kelly grinned. "He said things to Will, the way I got it, no man could take off anyone." His grin broadened. "Will thinks the old man needs that grass."

Gurden didn't care what Will thought, or Kelly either. As a matter of fact, he had himself put Will up to bracing Brackley and Brackley, suspecting as much, had come here tonight to tax Gurden with it and to warn him off. Gurden wasn't about to reveal the real truth of it; what had happened to Brackley was pretty near as good as stumbling onto a gold mine. Gurden knew that Kimberland wasn't worrying about his cows. All these feints he was making was to cover up that railroad. Kimberland wanted that Bench for the right-of-way it would give him.

"Well," Gurden growled, changing the subject, "you keep away from Frank. Get hold of Tularosa and send him over here right away. Soon's you've done that, get a note to Frank. Don't talk to him. Get a note to him and tell him you've got to see him in front of the bake shop tomorrow at noon."

This last was spoken so low that Mousetrap, ten feet away, did not catch it. But Kelly heard. The bristles of hair along the edge of his collar stood straight up at the back of his neck. What Gurden, in effect, was asking him to do was to set Frank up where Tularosa could put a slug in him. The saloonman got up and took Kelly's arm and steered him over to the back door. "Remember—" Gurden's breath on Kelly's cheek was like the kiss of death— "no mistakes this time, eh?"

With the door closed behind him and silently re-bolted, Chip Gurden turned, gold teeth glinting, and winked at the curious look Mousetrap gave him. He took off his boots and, carrying them, cut over to the door they'd come through from the bar. With no warning at all Gurden yanked it open.

A man spilled in stumbling out of a crouch as the light broke across him. Turning loose of the boots, Gurden caught the thin shape of his piano player by the front of his shirt and slammed the man bodily into the wall. The fellow cringed from Gurden's look, cheeks ludicrous with fright. "I—I was just comin' in to—"

"You're in now!" Gurden grinned. He flung the whimpering wretch at Mousetrap. "Take care of this joker." He stamped into his boots and stalked through the dark bar. The big clock above it said ten after two.

CHAPTER SIX

KIMBERLAND, UNKNOWN to Frank or Arnold, was in town that night, having driven in late with Honey and gone directly to his suite at the Hays Hotel. The girl had gone to bed, worn out. In the dark of his second-floor-front room W. T., still dressed, was very much awake. He was doing what he'd come to do, keeping track of his latest investments.

He knew something of Frank—a lot more than Frank reckoned—but all he knew about Tularosa was that the man rode for Draicup and was a dyed-in-the-wool killer whose guns could be bought. It went against Kimberland's grain to have to deal with such trash but in this case, not caring to be involved, he had no choice. It was imperative that Brackley be got rid of at once. W. T. had learned from one of the man's riders that Brackley would be in South Fork tonight. At considerable inconvenience Kimberland had made his arrangements, knowing something had to be done before this thing got out of hand. He had had two weeks to plan and had the deal pinned down letter perfect, but he couldn't sit back and let events take their course. His entire fortune was at stake, and the way things had recently been going he had to be where he could step in and take a hand if that damned hired killer didn't get the job done.

He'd had a session right away with Bill Grace and bitterly discovered what had happened to Tularosa when he'd been after that girl. But Tularosa had got free, been turned loose on the town again, and Frank apparently hadn't yet caught up with him when Kimberland had heard the guns pound over at Gurden's and seen the two punchers lugging Brackley away. So that part of it was settled.

Stepping back from the curtained window Kimberland

53

yawned and stretched contentedly. It was too bad about Brackley but a man had to look out for himself in this world and he had given the fool an out by offering to buy the damned spread. Brackley had no one to blame but his own bullheadedness. That road represented progress and no one had the right to stand in the way of a country's development. He guessed the rest of those Benchers would understand that now. And before anyone got wise to what was brewing he, W. T. would have that right-of-way in his pocket.

This was why he wanted the Bench, not for the grass —though he could use that, too. But the road came first, that was where his money was. When the Company got their preliminary report, a survey crew would be sent into the region and the value of land would go up like Apache smoke. Which was why he'd held back his beef so long, not for the rain but for how it would look to the rest of this country when Bar 40 scrapped boundaries and moved onto the Bench.

That high shelf would be the obvious choice of any survey. There was no other practical place for a roadbed. It wasn't only that he had to protect his investment; that Bench ran for twenty miles through this country and control of it would net a handsome profit to the man who could deliver it. Tomorrow Bar 40 would start moving cattle.

He heard the creak of the stairs and, guessing this would be Bill Grace again, went over and quietly opened the hall door. His foreman slipped in, and said as soon as the door was shut: "Gurden's bought into this!"

Kimberland grinned. "Joke—ha ha."

"It's no joke," Grace said.

"How could he buy in when he don't even know—"

"He knows, all right. First thing your star-packer done when he went over there was ask what Brackley was doin' in Chip's place. Gurden wiped off his mouth an' said he'd come for a loan which he had made him— *secured by a lien against Brackley's stock and range.*"

"Son of a bitch!"

"The point," Grace said, "is what do we do about it?

I told you when we took over Chip's ranch that feller was goin' to lay for you. You better let me shoot him."

If it was just Gurden, Kimberland reflected, it might be better to let him get away with this. But it wasn't just Gurden. Bar 40, on the climb, had tramped rough-shod over everyone. The slightest evidence of weakness would bring the whole bunch swarming, and Gurden wouldn't quit with this. He had too long a memory.

"I've got to think," Kimberland said.

"You better think fast if we're pushin' those cattle over there in the morning."

"How did Frank take it? I mean about Brackley's killing and that plaster of Gurden's."

"Acted damn suspicious."

"Good," Kimberland nodded. "Now has Chip really got a lien?"

"He'll damn well produce one—"

"Keep your voice down," Kimberland grumbled. "We don't want my girl getting up to come in here."

"She wouldn't know a jughandle from a tomato can," Grace said. "All she's got any time for is—" He let go of that line when he caught Kimberland's look. Abruptly then they were both standing tense, faces whipped toward the window. There was a far sound of shots, a sullen rumble like thunder with a shout lifting through it, thinly soaring, suddenly gone. The racket, as Kimberland threw up the window, could mean but one thing to any listening cowman.

"By God," Grace cried, "it's that trail herd!"

Louder, nearer, laced with the terrified bawling of cattle, that trampling roar was like the sound of an avalanche. Cries flew out of the street. The hall door burst open. *"Father!"* A girl with a quilted wrapper clutched about her ran barefooted past the scowling red-cheeked foreman, the loose mass of her hair tumbling about slim shoulders like a cascade of gold in the light from the street. "Father—?" More guns went off and there were yells from below. Bill Grace, swearing, dashed for the stairs.

Kimberland, still at the window, dropped a comfort-

ing arm about the girl's shoulder. The tautness of strain
was in his muscles, too.

Honey said, "I'm afraid—"

His watch said 2:30. He allowed her to coax him as
far as the rocker. "We're as safe right here as we'd probably be anywhere." He took the girl's hand. "Tonight
we've got a new marshal, Sugar. I think you could turn
his head very easily."

There was no change in the lovely face but her voice
was compliant. "Would that help you, Father?"

"I suppose," he said with just the right inflection, "a
woman might find the young scamp attractive."

"Do I know him, Father?"

He smiled down at her quizzically. "He's the fellow
who saved you from Church's bull that time." He spoke
as to a child. "Perhaps you'd enjoy having lunch with
him tomorrow. Of course," he added doubtfully,
"Frank's pretty much of a roughneck."

"I could do that," Honey said.

"Town's growing up. Never does any harm to be well
thought of by a marshal. Sort of like to have him get
the idea us folks from Bar Forty. . . . Look, just act
natural, Sugar. Friendly. That's all I want you to do."

FRANK, AT THE marshal's office, had turned in at two.
Danny was tipped back in one of the chairs against the
wall, snoring with his mouth opening and shutting with
each breath. Frank had left Chavez in charge of the
town. Sleep wouldn't come to Frank what with all the
banging and clatter being stirred up by that gale. His
thoughts were like horses; every fourth or fifth jump
they'd take him back to those bodies in the rear of Ben's
store. Chavez had shown up with Ben, and the furni-
ture-selling coroner had officially pronounced Brackley
dead. Frank had then assembled the contents of his
pocket which had included a dog-eared wallet. This last,
upon inspection, had proved to contain a handful of
silver and thirty-four dollars in hard-used bills. Frank
had stared at these blankly.

"What's the matter?" Ben had asked, and Frank had explained about the loan Gurden claimed to have made Jace. Chavez had looked frankly skeptical. Ben had asked, "What about those fellers that carried him over here?"

Frank shook his head and, figuratively speaking, was still shaking it. The men who had brought Brackley here might have taken the money if Brackley'd had it on him but Frank couldn't dredge any confidence from the notion. If a man made up his mind to robbery, where was the sense in leaving part of the haul? It would all have been in Brackley's wallet if he'd had it. Yet Frank had no doubt if he was made to, Gurden would produce a signed lien on Brackley's ranch. There was only one question about this in Frank's mind: Had Gurden had such a paper *before* Brackley's killing?

But this question bred another. Had Gurden arranged Brackley's death or had somebody else? He could foresee the kind of rumors that were no doubt already flying—that would certainly fly if Bar 40 put cattle on Brackley's range. Kimberland or Gurden—which one of them had hired this?

Chavez had put up Frank's dun or he might have gone on the prowl again. He needed sleep. This had been a hard night, about the hardest one he had ever put in. He got up, pulled his boots on, and walked over to the door. Danny was still snoring. Frank stood there a moment, thinking, then went back, got his hat and shrugged into his brush jacket.

He pulled open the door. The suck of the wind put the lamp flame out. Frank heard the shots then, the distant yell, the rumble that followed it. Swearing in the testiness of temper, he ran over to the wall rack and jerked down a rifle. Pausing only to make sure it would take the shells in his belt, Frank hurried into the street.

The night was wild with wind and tumult. The pounding rush of crazed cattle was like the roar of a giant falls. They were nearer now, coming fast, straight for town. He remembered with a sense of bleak irony telling Chavez that cows were the one thing he didn't have to worry about. Looking around, Frank could see there were plenty of others coming out just as he was, armed to do battle for the town's preservation. He caught faintly the excited whickering of horses where a dozen were still uneasily huddling in the grip of tied reins at the rack before the Flag. Why the hell didn't some of those fools climb on them!

The wind flapped his clothes, staggering him with its violence. Digging chin into his collar, he tried to beat his way against it, needing to get into the lee of something, knowing the danger of being trapped in the open. Already those fellows across the way had got under cover. Grit stung his eyes. Dust boiled up by the running herd got so thick he couldn't see ten yards in front of him.

He locked his teeth against their chatter, trying to find Fentriss' barn. To move at all was like bucking a blizzard. Above the racket of hoofs, the shots and the bawling, Frank caught the screech of rending wood, the yells and crash as a building toppled. Those steers wouldn't leave enough of this town for kindling.

He found a wall and stumbled along it, drunkenly reeling, cursing floundering feet that wouldn't track. He could almost feel the snorting breath of those beasts as the leaders funneled into the far end of the street, bawling, horns clacking. The gunshots sounded like cork stoppers popping. Frank reached the end of the wall and the wind hit him solidly, driving the breath back into him. The dust-laden gusts tore at him, half blinding him. He staggered through the stable's door hole into a blackness impenetrable as lamp soot. Loose boards shook and rattled. The place was noisy with the clamor of frightened horses. Frank wiped his streaming eyes on the back of an abrasive wrist.

Across the street through the blowing dust there were patterns of foggy radiance where turned-up lamps shone through the windows, but these didn't make seeing any easier to speak of. The dust cleared a little as the gusts slid into a lull. The herd had been stopped, was beginning very slowly to revolve on itself; but Frank knew, without riders, how chancey was this respite, how swiftly those steers would run again should something upset them. He took his chance while he had it and darted into the open, thinking to get up on the roof of the Mercantile where he'd be able to see a little better.

In the dust and confusion he miscalculated someway and wound up before the half-leaf doors of the Opal. He shouted for Gurden but got no answer. The stopped cattle were still milling in front of Minnie's. He heard Chavez's voice:

"Douse them lamps before you burn up this town! Pronto!"

This seemed to make sense to quite a number of folks. One by one the nearer lights winked out. The horses tied in front of the Flag had gone away with their hitchrail. Gurden hadn't locked up; Frank saw the batwings flap as wind picked up the dust again with a howl. Something flapped, too, behind the herd. Frank felt the ground quiver under him as every steer in it suddenly churned into motion. Frank dived for the Opal.

He knew where the lamps were. He got one, letting go of the rifle, and dragged a match across the seat of his pants. A lantern would have been better, but he took what he could get. His fastest wasn't any too quick. There they came, boiling out of the dust with their eyes big as wash tubs. As Frank crossed the porch and ran into the street some woman cried shrilly, "*Is he crazy?*" And then the herd was engulfing the street like a monster, so near he could see their slobber-flecked chests and the sharp wicked glint of their tossing horns.

Frank flung the flaring lamp high above them.

The herd broke like splatter, the whole front melting away, panicked by the sight of that flame diving at them. Several steers crashed head-on into buildings, adding their terrified bellows to the uproar, but the great bulk of the mass veered off south after the lead steer who, by the kindness of God, took for the largest chunk of open space in sight, trailed by his followers in a curve that tipped east back of Fentriss' livery. One crazed brute, lone-wolfing it up the street through the dust, almost ran Frank down while he was standing there shaking. He fired twice pointblank with his pistol, yet blind panic or momentum carried the animal the length of the Mercantile's front before collapsing.

Frank's legs folded under him. Cramps ravaged his stomach.

CHAPTER SEVEN

DRAGGING A HAND across his mouth Frank shoved up off his knees and got out of the street. There was much random shouting, lights were commencing to flare up behind windows as anxious merchants and the incurably curious came forth out of hiding to assess the damage. The wind—after the manner of that rail and those horses —seemed to have gone somewhere else. Frank could hear occasional gunshots but these were scattered, sporadic, probably mercy slugs for cripples. He supposed he ought to get back to the office where he could be found, but that plaster of Gurden's was still on his mind and he went down Krantz's wagon pass and thumped on the Opal's back door with his fist. He kept at it a long while before convinced he would not get any answer.

He dragged himself around to the front, unutterably weary, almost out on his feet. He guessed he ought to be hunting Tularosa but he just wasn't up to it. He went back to the office and, finding Danny Settles in the bunk, collapsed on the floor.

He woke up in the bunk with the morning sun nearly three hours high. He was so crammed with aches when he tried to move he didn't much care if he never got up. He heard steps outside and Danny Settles came in with his breakfast, his old-young face looking cheerful as a man who has just been handed a king full on aces. "Good morning, Frank."

Frank said contentiously, "Is it?" and grimaced.

Danny, chuckling out of the wealth of his good humor, put the tray down on the desk. Frank sat up. The sight of food nauseated him. "Better eat that yourself." He lay back and stretched out his legs. "Well?" he growled when he discovered Danny watching him.

61

"It probably doesn't amount to anything," Danny said, "but that pianist at the Opal—Sleight-of-Hand Willie—was over here before daylight. He looked pretty banged up—"

"What'd he want?" Frank asked, showing interest.

"He seemed to think you ought to know Kelly's into some deal with Gurden. Seemed to have the idea that gun—" He broke off as someone pounded the door.

"Come in," Frank said impatiently.

It was Councilman Krantz, the Mercantile's owner. His eyes looked like they would jump through his glasses. "That pizness last night—" He shook his head. "I haff mizchudged you, my poy. But you vant to look out for that Chip, he iss after you. He vas ofer to mine house pefore breakfast yet. He vants to take that star avay from you—says you von't enforce that new gun law."

"He was never more wrong in his life," Frank growled. He flung off the blanket and stamped into his boots. He'd lost his hat last night in the wind and reached for Danny's. He said, glowering at Krantz, "Do I look like the kind that would sell a man out!" and caught up his shell belt, slapping it around him.

Danny Settles, alarmed, said, "Frank, where are you off to?"

Even Krantz looked worried. But Frank had had about enough of Chip Gurden. "I'm going to do something I should of done last night!" he said hotly.

He tramped across to the hotel, went up to the barber's room and talked Pete into shaving him at the point of a pistol.

"But gol darn it, man, this is *Sunday!*" Pete protested.

"If you want to see Monday," Frank said, "get busy."

He felt more himself as he went down the stairs. He'd cooled off a little, too, and decided he might as well stop for a cup of coffee, secretly hoping he might catch sight of Honey. He had the dining room to himself except for Joe Wolverton who owned the saddle shop and, not being married, was enjoying a leisurely breakfast. Sight of Joe eating suddenly whipped up Frank's appetite. "Ham and eggs," he told the hasher. "Wreck 'em and fetch the java right away."

He was midway through this food when the swish of a skirt and the tap of high heels swung his face around. A warm pleasure rushed through him when he saw Honey moving between tables. He looked—as the saddle man later told his cronies—"like a winter-starved dogie catchin' a whiff of fresh alfalfa."

It was the first time Frank had got near enough to speak since he had saved her from Church's bull. She completely took his breath away but at least he had sense enough to drag off his hat.

"How are you, Frank?" She came right up to him and put out her hand. She saw the star on his shirt. "So you're our new marshal. Frank, I'm proud of you."

He felt her hand squirm and finally let go of it. Fussed up and grinning, he stood twisting his hat. She'd filled out a lot, he thought—looked prettier than a basket of chips. Honey, squeezing his arm, laughed up at him softly.

Somebody scraped back a chair and Frank, recollecting Wolverton, became self-conscious and awkward, knowing the man would be taking this in.

Honey, still hanging onto him, said, "I think—I'm almost sure—I will be staying over tonight. Abbie's been making some new hats for me. Perhaps we could get together for dinner . . . ."

Frank stared and gulped, his grin showed embarrassment. Then remembering his job he said glumly, "I'll be on duty tonight." But he wasn't on duty this noon—he wouldn't go on before one. He said, brightening, "Could I take you this noon?"

Honey, hesitating, smiled. "That will be all right."

"Swell!" Frank said, forgetting Joe Wolverton, and the waitress who was also watching them with an interest not untinged by envy. "Twelve o'clock?"

Honey took a deep breath. "We'd better make it twelve-thirty. I might not be through by twelve."

Giving his arm a final squeeze, she moved off toward a table by the windows where the hasher, stiffly smiling, was holding a chair out. She had been nourishing a hope of catching Frank for herself.

The marshal saw Wolverton drop some change on his table and then he noticed Gurden by the cigar case lighting a stogie. Gurden, completely ignoring Frank, was taking Honey apart with his stare. Frank was starting to shove up with his face black as thunder when Kimberland turned into the room from the lobby.

The boss of Bar 40, pulling off his gloves, said: "Hello, Chip—Frank, how are you?" even nodding to Wolverton as he stopped by Frank's table. A cropped black beard concealed the most of his expression. His shrewd eyes probed Frank's and he said with approval, "I think, from what I hear, you must have established some kind of a record last night, stopping that herd with a lamp singlehanded. South Fork certainly owes you a large vote of thanks."

With another brisk nod he went over to Honey. Frank stared after him like a man in a dream. Wolverton, coming up, said, "Nice going, Marshal," and clapped Frank on the shoulder.

Frank finished his meal in a kind of a daze. He probably didn't taste one thing he put into him. He got up when he'd finished and left a silver dollar beside his plate. He was halfway back to the office before, with a scowl, he remembered Chip Gurden. He shrugged and crossed over, intending to wait at the Opal; then he saw Abbie Burks.

She owned the Bon Ton Millinery and, according to the way Frank had got it, was the orphaned niece of rancher John Arnold. She was in her middle twenties and was not a bad looker. The trouble with Abbie, Frank had always imagined, was that she couldn't get over her New England raising. She probably wanted a man bad as any woman, he reckoned, but those she could catch she held off with her stiffness and those she'd have taken wanted something more cozy to warm their beds of a night. Frank had watched her at dances —had even swung her himself, but it had been like hauling around a becorseted flapjack. She hadn't spoke ten words the whole time he had hold of her. When the fiddles had quit Frank had said, "Thanks—Prudence," and gone off and got plastered.

But she seemed glad to see him this morning, actually breaking out a smile, though he could see it was quite a strain. When she held out a hand Frank perversely grabbed and pumped it like she was leaving him her will. Her cheeks got pink and flustered. "My—" she said as if she'd just run a mile, "you certainly gave this town something to talk about! I—I do wish you well, Frank. Uncle John was saying—"

"He still around town?"

"I—why, yes—I think so."

Now what the hell would she blush about that for? She said, her lips pale, "Please let go of my hand, Frank."

"Hell, I washed this morning—took a bath in the hotel."

"Anger brightened her eyes and she twisted away from him. "You don't understand—you don't even try!" And then her voice broke. "You don't know what it's like to—"

"Abbie," he said, "don't work so damn hard at it."

An indescribable look came over her face and without another word she hurried off toward her shop.

Frank rubbed his jaw. "Women!" he said, and cut back toward the jail. Then he remembered the ride he'd got mapped out to take and went along to the livery. While he was saddling his dun the owner, Fentriss, came up. Frank twisted his head. "You seen Arnold this morning?"

"Nope," Fentriss said. "Ain't seen hide nor hair of him. Lost John, hev you? Chip can't find his piano pounder, either."

Frank led the dun out and climbed into the saddle. Then he remembered the rifle he had left in the Opal, and rode back to the hotel and got down and went in. The rifle, of course, was only Frank's excuse for another look at Honey, but she and her Dad had already left. He spotted Gurden paring his nails at a table with two others who had just started eating. One was Ben Holli-day (coffins and furniture); the other was McFell who owned the Blue Flag. Gurden said, grinning, "McFell thinks your gun law ain't got enough teeth in it."

"I'll put the teeth in it," Frank said, "never worry." He put his eyes on Chip grimly. "I left a rifle in your place."

"Yeah. It's back of the bar. You aim to pay for that lamp?"

Frank tossed two coins on the table, lips twisting. "Where was you when I came back a while later?"

"Pounding my ear, I guess."

"You must sleep like the dead."

Gurden smiled thinly. "I sleep all right." He rolled the cigar across his teeth. "Now why don't you ask me what my place was doing open?"

"Suppose you tell me."

"Well, it seems like I had some company. Somebody tried to get into my safe. When are you going to start earning your money?"

"I suppose," Frank said, "he went off with that pa-per."

"That's exactly what he did." Gurden's winkless eyes mocked him. "But, being's I had a witness to the deal, I don't look for any trouble when it comes to taking over."

"You didn't say anything about a witness last night."

"Last night I had Brackley's signature. Remember?"

Frank leaned across the table, glance truculent. "You don't give a damn for the truth, do you, Gurden?"

"Oh, it's true enough," Chip said. "Go and look at the safe. You prob'ly scared him away when you come after that lamp. About all I can figure he got off with is five hundred dollar bills and Jace's paper. When I went in there about an hour ago I found this on the floor." He pulled a wadded-up square of cloth out of his pocket.

Frank shook the thing out and felt his stomach turn over. It was a neckscarf, pale blue, with a design of yellow horseshoes. Frank had seen it last night around the throat of Tularosa.

Chavez, as Frank swung into the saddle, cut across from the gun shop still carrying his shotgun. "What's new with Boss Gurden?"

Frank's stare swept the storefronts. He told Chavez what he had just learned from Gurden and showed him the scarf. "It's his wipe," Frank said bitterly.

The Mexican shrugged. "Chip might of picked that up anyplace." He twisted together a brown-paper cigarette. "He was out of this town about half the night. He rode in about five an' left his bronc back of Minnie's. Make sense to you?"

"Horse over there now?"

Chavez shook his head. "That Mousetrap jigger come an' got it about seven. Rubbed it off well as he could an' told Fentriss he'd had it out for a gallop. I seen that caballo before this guy got to work an' I'm tellin' you it was rode hard."

The most of Frank's attention was still prowling the street, digging into alley mouths, probing black door holes. He couldn't find one hostile sign but the threat of Tularosa, like a wildness, was all about him.

He wiped a dampness away from his lip and picked up his reins and told Chavez, "You keep your eyes peeled. I'm figuring to take a pasear out to Brackley's."

Chavez, staring over Frank's shoulder, said, "Hasta luego. He goin' with you?"

Frank, twisting, saw Kimberland on a powerful looking bay jogging leisurely toward the west end of town. With a growl he spurred after him, discovering another rider angling in at a lope. Frank overtook Kimberland at the edge of the lumber yard. W. T. nodded, pulled off his right glove and, fishing a pair of cigars from his shirt, passed one over. Frank bit the end off and accepted a light from Kimberland's match.

The other rider came up, a grizzled looking man in dust-grimed range gear and, setting back his horse, inspected them like a cat with a knot in its tail. "Who's goin' to pay for all them shot cattle?"

"Take it easy," Frank said. "You ain't the only one hurt."

"I'll sue this damn town!" the man shouted. Frank remembered him then as one of the chair-warmers he'd encountered at Minnie's. Gourd and Vine had lost a lot of stock, crippled and scattered, and you couldn't much blame him for sounding a mite ringy.

Frank said, "You one of the owners?"

"Lassiter. Trail boss. I'll spread the name of this—"

"Friend," Kimberland said, teeth champing his cigar, "let's take a more charitable look at this deal."

Frank, backing him up, said, "Your herd tore down a couple of business establishments and might have leveled the whole town if we hadn't got them turned. We didn't order that wind nor—"

"Wind!" The man spat. "Them steers was spooked deliberate!" He shook a fist in Frank's face. "Somebody's goin' to pay fer it!"

"If you'd kept your crew—"

"Don't give me that! I seen what happened. A bunch of guys come out of the dark flappin' slickers. Draicup warned me what this country was like. You cigar-smokin' bastards think all you got to do is scatter these drives an' after they've gone you kin pick up the pieces!"

Frank said, "That's pretty strong talk."

"This geezer," Lassiter said, "looks like that sonofabitch Kimberland I been hearin' about. Draicup tol' me if I got in trouble to yell. Man, they're goin' to hear me clean back to Corpus!" He spun his horse, glaring furiously, raked its flanks with the steel and tore off toward his camp.

Kimberland said, "He'll cool. Draicup *could* be hitting these herds himself; he's never too far when the cows start to run. But I don't think it's him. I think Gurden's back of it. Chip and maybe—" He eyed Frank inscrutably. "Here's where I turn off. If you're heading for Brackley's—" He let that go, too. "Frank, you're doing all right. Don't let nobody spook you."

The sun was beginning really to bear down when

Frank sighted Brackley's buildings. He wasn't surprised to see the wrinkle of smoke coming out of a stovepipe. The man had employed two riders on a year-round basis. Frank *was* surprised though when, in answer to his hail, the girl of the wagon stepped out of the house.

There were glints of burnished firelight in her hair. Frank was discovering what a girl with curves and a too direct look could do to a man. She had a rifle in her hands but when she saw who it was she leaned it against the weather-grayed wall and a gleam of interest came into her look. Her mouth curved into a slow smile. "Well!" She smoothed the skirt about her thighs and poked a hand at her hair. "You didn't lose much time getting onto my trail."

"What you doing here?" Frank asked suspiciously.

She said after a moment, "I could ask you the same. This ranch isn't a part of your bailiwick."

She wore a thin cotton print that displayed her figure with an almost insolent boldness. Her feet were bare but Frank was trying hard not to notice them. As though perceiving his discomfiture and divining the cause of it she laughed in a way that made his cheeks burn. "I'd of freshed up a little if I'd guessed you were coming."

"Where's the hands?" Frank asked, peering around from his saddle.

With that mop of red hair tumbled about her head she was still coolly watching when Frank pulled his glance back. "Seems they woke up to important business elsewhere when they found I was aimin' to stay on here."

Frank's jaw dropped. The unbridled magnitude of this woman's audacity seemed to have no parallel. By the shine of her eyes it was plain she was laughing, aware of his amazement and thoroughly enjoying it. Frank's mouth tightened up. "You can't stay here. This place belongs—"

"I don't expect he'll be usin' it."

It was that easy indifference, her total disregard for established forms and conventions, that riled Frank the most. This was a man's business here and she had no right mixing into it. Her eyes defied him to say so.

He said, trying to keep the outrage out of his voice, "Squatting's one thing. Jumping preempted land—"

"You're wastin' your time."

Frank tried hard to hold onto his temper. "You don't understand—"

"Name's Larren—Sandrey," she said, her sage-colored eyes bold.

"The point—" he began.

Again she cut him off, "Seems like Brackley mentioned—"

"You know Jace?" Frank was astonished.

Her mouth widened again. Her hands strayed over her hips, bringing out more noticeably the wild grace and suppleness of that strong body. Then she was laughing up at him. "You might almost say I was Jace Brackley's widow."

Will Church left town in an ungovernable rage some half an hour ahead of Chip Gurden's return from that mysterious ride Chavez had told Frank about. Will was shaking with fury and ran his horse the entire way, even flogging the foam-flecked animal around the last hairpin twist of the trail. Coming down off the slope about twelve minutes short of dawn he saw the black oblongs of his father's headquarters buildings. The yellow squares of two lamplit windows proved Sam Church was already up. Will cursed viciously. Not one damned thing had come off as he had planned since he had tangled with Frank Carrico.

He'd got no satisfaction from Gurden. Frank had made a fool of him and those clabberheads he'd trusted with carrying out the stampede had run the goddam steers through town—or would have if Frank hadn't broken it up. True, Will's friends could still get away with some beef, but it had been Will's intention to get Kimberland blamed. If the raid had been pulled off as planned, those stampeded steers would have been spread

across Bar 40 and the shortages, when discovered, would
have involved W. T. in more than just suspicion.

Will rowelled the staggering horse around the house,
dropping off at the back porch, leaving the spent beast
standing. Sari Church was bent over the stove frying
mush; Sam was just sitting down. He started to work up
a growl but Will cut him off.

"Get yourself another flunky—I've took all of your
crap I'm takin'." He sloshed coffee into a mug and was
turning to put the pot back when his father said, glaring:

"If you've quit me again you'll walk out of here
strapped."

"Strapped!" Will wheeled with such violence he lost
half the cup's contents. "All I ever *been* is strapped."
Then he grinned, maliciously enjoying this. "Frank quit
our ranch. He's already gone—and so are them cattle
you had at Bospero Flats. They didn't stray. I found
horse tracks!"

Sam Church pushed away from the table. He was
reaching for his gun belt from the back of the chair
when Will said, "You might as well forget them. Frank's
packin' Ashenfeldt's star." He laughed at his father's expression. "Your good friend Kimberland has crossed us
up."

"What's that supposed to mean?"

"Just what it sounds like. He's makin' his push."

Sam Church's cheeks looked as gray as a bullet.
"Where—?"

"The best place to start," Will said, "is Terrapin.
Brackley was killed in town last night."

Sam Church sagged back in his chair, mouth twitching.
"The killer," Sam said, "who done it?"

Will shrugged. "Who wanted that place? If you ain't
feelin' up to it, I'll ride over. Sooner we know how
things stand, the better we'll know how to cope with
that pirate—wouldn't surprise me at all to find he got
those steers we had over at the Flats. It's his badge
Frank's wearin', an' him that tolled Frank away from
there."

The old man seemed lost. "We better be gettin' our-selfs some gun-hands—"

"I'll take care of that," Will said.

"Where'll you get 'em?"

"There's guns around that can be picked up—"

"Drifters! Saddle tramps!"

"What the hell you expect? A Wild Bill Hickok!"

"We could do with a few like him," Church said, and Will secretly smiled. He reached over to the stove and filled his mug up again.

His mother said, "This grub's gettin' cold." Neither of them paid her the slightest attention. Will and old Sam were staring hard at each other.

Will said, "I can get us a man that's mighty near good as Hickok."

Church snorted.

"Tularosa." Will grinned.

Sam Church got halfway out of his chair. He let the shout that was in him fall back unuttered. He didn't like any better than Will did Kimberland's recent insulting demand that Will keep away from his daughter. His eyes turned craftily. In that moment he almost admired Will. "How much'll it cost an' how soon can we get him?"

Tularosa, Will was thinking, could iron out a lot of things. Including Chip Gurden, if he were offered enough. "If you'll put up a thousand dollars—"

Sam really unwound. He wasn't half through when Will headed for the door. "Where you off to?" Sam shouted. Will took hold of the latch. Sam jumped to his feet. "Now you listen to me, boy—"

"Don't *boy* me!" Will whirled in midstride. His eyes glared like a crazy man's. "Keep your damn money!" He slammed out of the house.

He wanted a fresh mount but rather than tote the saddle he dragged the reluctant roan he had ruined half across the hard-packed yard. Suddenly turning toward the horse with an almost incoherent fury, Will snatched up a length of chain off the ground and struck the horse over the head. The roan, screaming, reared back with bared teeth, showing the whites of his eyes. The reins were torn from Will's hand.

But the horse was too hurt to get away from him. Doubling the chain Will leaped for him, cursing. The chain struck the horse back of the withers, dropping him. Making broken, piteous, whickering sounds, the horse staggered up with a heave and stood trembling. Will lashed out again. The horse screamed like a woman. He went down in the front, and then the whole of him was down.

Will watched for a moment the feeble scrabbling of hind legs, then flung the bloody chain at him. He was hunting around for something else to lay hand to when Sam came out of the house on the run. The old man stared at the horse then at Will. He saw the shocked faces watching Will from the cook shack. He said tiredly, "What kind of man are you?" and Will's darting eyes, so frequently filled with affronted resentment, glared back with the look of a coiling snake.

"If I give you your way," Sam Church said, hating the sound of it, "what guarantee—"

Will, chopping him off, threw his shout at the men staring out of the cook shack. "Get away from that door!"

The faces faded. Will, breathing hard, walked up to his father, fists clubbed at his sides. "Take a look at yourself if you don't like what you see, an' then get out of my way. I'm through takin' your orders. This ain't the only big spread in the Panhandle. I can find other backers."

Will's head was filled with the sound of his voice. It seemed to travel all through him like the fire of raw whisky. He felt seven feet tall, rough as rock and twice as impregnable. Nothing could touch him. Nothing ever would again; and he wondered with a sense of incredulous astonishment why he had taken so long to break his father's authority.

He caught the glassy look of Sam's stare and laughed, exulting when Church cringed away from him.

Will considered the man with amused contempt.

"You've tramped so long in Kimberland's shadow you act like the rest of these fetchers and carriers, but I tell you the man can be handled. Gurden's goin' after him and while they're peckin' away at each other we can take over this country!" Will make a sudden discovery. "A man gets what he's big enough to take." He liked the sound of that and said it again with a whinny of laughter.

Sam shook his head. "You're forgettin' Frank Carrico."

Anger darkened Will's skin. "He'll die just as quick of a bullet as Kimberland." Arrogance showed in the swirl of his temper. His hands, convulsing, became intolerant fists. "We'll start with these hills. We'll take the Bench right away. Go fetch me that money."

CHAPTER EIGHT

FRANK, AT Terrapin, caught hold of her roughly. "Brackley's widow! What kind of talk's that?"

"Straight." Sandrey shook the hair back out of her face. "Why do you suppose he was in town last night?" When Frank, still scowling, said he'd gone in to see Gurden, the girl said, faintly smiling, "He came to meet me."

Frank stepped back, puzzled.

"It's true!" she said sharply. Frank's eyes called her liar. In all the years he'd known Brackley there'd been no mention of a woman. Besides this girl was too young —where could she have met up with him? "I don't know what your game is—" Frank said.

"There isn't any game. I came here in good conscience. He sent me the money. We were going to be married."

Frank looked at her sourly. "Where'd you know him before?"

"I didn't. He got my name out of a Heart-and-Hand magazine." Color whipped into her lifted face. She looked at him defiantly. "People do such things—"

"Some might—if they was desperate enough."

"How do you know Jace wasn't desperate?" Her eyes were dark now and bitter, the whole look of her taut as stretched hide. "It makes no difference to me what you think. I've got his letters. I've got a deed to this place!"

Frank's eyes became unreadable.

"A quitclaim deed to it and everything on it, signed over to me in Brackley's own hand!"

"I reckon you have," Frank said finally.

She didn't seem to like the tone of his voice. "I saw Jace right after Will Church jumped him last night. He

75

took me over to the hotel—that's when he wrote it. He got me a room; got pen and paper from the clerk—that pockmarked one with the warts on his chin. He'll remember."

Frank nodded. He could understand how Brackley might have done it, especially if the man believed that talk about Bar 40. The thing that Frank couldn't figure was this girl. On the face of it—to someone ignorant of local conditions—Brackley's ranch might hold a certain appeal. But Sandrey Larren—Frank shook his head. He had seen a couple of these Lonely Heart females, and the only resemblance between them and her wasn't showing. Why, with her shape and looks . . . .

"I've got a right to this place."

"Ma'am," he said, "I ain't disputing it. The graves are filled with folks who had rights. You'll move, one way or another."

"It's up to you to protect me."

"Then come into town where I might have some luck at it."

"I'm stayin' right here."

Suddenly fed up with this jawing, Frank said, "Why don't you try being reasonable for a change?"

She grinned. "I can take care of myself."

Frank reached out and got hold of her, roughly yanking her toward him as though by force he'd disprove her contention, revealing it beyond argument for the empty brag it was. But he had reckoned without the vulnerability of emotion. Contact roused forgotten hungers. By the time he realized what lay ahead, the lesson he'd been going to teach had gotten out of hand.

She came against him solidly. He had a wild thought of Honey, then Sandrey's breath rushed across his cheeks. Her mouth found his with astonishing firmness. The yard dissolved. Sensation blurred. It was just like crashing through the roof of the sky.

When they broke apart Frank was breathing hard. Everything around him tipped and spun like the way things would look from a pitching bronc. It was like coming up from the bottom of a spill.

"Well!"

The word winged toward him through incalculable space. Frank found her then, found her flushed and trembling. The breath was sawing in and out of the both of them. Sudden guilt barreled through him. His face got hot. He felt sweat come out on him. "Sandrey," he said through the roaring in his ears, "I sure didn't aim to pull anything like that!"

Her eyes were like coal in the awful whiteness of her face. He had handled her like a whore, and remembrance of Honey was like a knife twisting in him.

That was when she hit him, open-handed across the face.

He staggered back with stinging cheeks, blinking, not finding it in him to much blame her though. His blurry eyes picked her out again and he stared unbelieving. But that girl wasn't fooling. She was heading for the rifle. Frank piled onto his horse and got out of there....

He didn't know how long he rode. He felt meaner than a twitch-eyed centipede with chilblains. He didn't want to think about her and wasn't hardly able to consider anything else. Except, now and then, Honey. He sure couldn't leave Sandrey Larren here in the middle of what looked to have all the makings of a knock-down and drag-out.

Frank swore. It wasn't Kimberland who Sandrey would have to fear, but the riffraff these hills were full of—the scum who might or might not be teamed up with Gurden. W. T. might grab the land but these renegades would grab Sandrey. It turned Frank sick to think what might happen if some of that crew chanced to come on her out there—rifle or no rifle!

He abruptly discovered he was no longer alone. There was a fellow up ahead on a black-and-white knothead, and the horse wasn't moving. The man wasn't, either. He was watching Frank sharply with a hand on his gun butt. He caught the flash of Frank's star and sat back, smiling sour-like, saying:

"Some pretty hard cases sifting around through these parts. Thought you might be one of them." He was garbed in an out-of-press store suit but hadn't the air or manners of a dude. He looked perfectly at home in flat-heeled boots that laced up the front, and had a turned-sideways nose below a pair of cagey eyes.

"Looking for something?" Frank asked conversationally.

"I been looking for snow but it keeps getting hotter." The fellow blew out his breath and wiped his face with a coat sleeve. "How far are we from Vega?"

"Pretty fair piece. Nearer South Fork. About a forty minute push if you happen to be in a hurry."

"It can wait," the other said. "I'm just ambling around. Expect you know most of the stockmen hereabouts?"

"Most of them." Frank could be cagey too. This guy was no tramp. Kind of hard man to place. Didn't look like a range dick. "What's your angle?"

"Just taking things easy." The fellow dug a couple of cigars from his coat, considering their tatters. Frank shook his head and the man put one back. He seemed to reach a decision. "Whereabouts does the Brackley spread lay from here?"

"Which one?" Frank said blandly.

The stranger scratched a match on the horn of his saddle. He lapped the tatters and presently, blowing smoke, broke the match stick and dropped it. "Didn't figure there was more than one."

"How long you been ramming around through these hills?"

The man faintly grinned. "I guess that's a fair question." He didn't seem in any great sweat to answer it.

Frank asked: "What's your business?"

The man observed brightly, "That's a marshal's badge, ain't it?"

Frank whipped his gun out. "You sooner talk here or in town?"

The man grinned. "Guess there ain't no reason you shouldn't be let in on it, everything considered. "I'm advance scout for a survey crew." Observing Frank's skepticism, he added reluctantly, "Like to keep this confidential if I can. There's some notion of putting a railroad through here."

"Keep talking."

The man shrugged. "Pretty definite now. One of your local men—fellow named Kimberland—has a wad of jack tied up in the deal. You can see why we'd want to keep it quiet for a while."

"You mean options?"

"Well—yes."

"Giving the big frogs a chance to get fixed, eh?"

The man said, "I'm not running the Company."

Frank asked, "Going to bring your road across the Bench, eh?"

"A road's got to be practicable if it aims to make money."

"Brackley's dead," Frank said. "Killed in town last night." Now Frank could understand why Brackley had been killed.

The man kept his face straight but there was a shifting back of his eyes like smoke. Frank picked up his reins.

The man rubbed his nose. "Somebody'll probably take it over."

"It won't be Gurden," Frank said pointedly.

CHAPTER NINE

DUST-SPLASHED and taciturn Frank pulled into South Fork at a little past eleven. After studying the street he wheeled into the gloom of Fentriss' stable. The bald-headed proprietor came up, mopping at his face. Frank, getting down, allowed that he was minded to look over the spare mounts. They went out to the corrals which showed evidence of repairs. Frank considered a blue roan, a squatter, that was fifteen hands without a patch of white on her.

Fentriss leaned on his hay fork. "You fixin' to buy or borrer?"

"Rent," Frank said, and stood silent a moment. "Get her ready," he said, and abruptly walked off.

Back in the street's sun glare Frank passed up the jail, went by the hotel and, ignoring the stares of a couple of townsmen, cut over to the New York Cáfe and stepped in. He took one of the twelve empty stools at the counter and distributed a part of his weight on his elbows. The pungent aroma of corned beef and cabbage made a strong bid for notice in the overheated room. At a corner table near the end of the counter Old Judge, hunched over his plate like a dilapidated vulture, sat gumming his food in preoccupied silence. "How's tricks?" Frank asked. The old man ignored him.

The biscuit-shooter, wiping hands on her apron, came from the back and hung out a tired smile. "Hi, Frank—what'll it be?"

"Slab of pie—make it apple, and a mug of black java."

The girl poured the coffee and slid the pie in front of him. He drank half the coffee at one gulp and then said, sniffing, "I'll take a bowl of that soup." The hasher dipped and passed it. "Crackers?"

Frank shook his head.

"How does it feel to be totin' the tin?"

"About like the pea in this bowl of hot water. Better give me them crackers." She pushed a plate down the counter and Frank broke up a big handful. The girl came back and leaned over, stacking some cups under the counter. She straightened up. "Thought you'd be eatin' with Honey Kimberland this noon."

Frank said, "It ain't noon yet." He finished the bowl and swung around to Old Judge. "What was you and Chip Gurden finding so profitable talking about last night?"

Old Judge, suddenly strangling, took on like a bronc with a clot of hay in its gullet. The hasher hurried over with a glass of water. "Watch out," Frank said, "you'll rust his pipes with that stuff." When the judge came up for air, Frank said, "Now that you've got that off your chest, how about answering my question?"

The old man wiped his mouth and eyes. "I don't know what you're talking about."

"It's about the size of a plaster on Terrapin. You don't have to play so innocent. That lien, if he's got one, ain't worth the paper it's written on. You can tell him I said so."

The judge, a bit shaky, got out of his chair. He appeared so disturbed by what Frank had said to him he went off without leaving the price of his meal. Frank tossed the girl some silver and dug into his pie. She dropped it into the till and said, half indignant, "He's like to be sick for the rest of the day!"

"Do him good." Frank finished the pie, paid and grinned up at her. "Don't worry about Judge. Next to Chip Gurden he's got the strongest gut in town." He took a look at the clock. It said ten of twelve. Frank went out and settled his shoulders against the front of the place in the shade of its overhang. He saw a kid pushing a hoop coming toward him from one of the alleys. Frank dragged a sleeve over his star and tried to think about Honey, but all he could see was the face of that sorreltop he'd left out at Brackley's. Chavez came into the street on his horse from the direction of Halbertson's. They considered each other and Chavez cut over.

The Mexican said, "Pretty quiet," and then leaned out from the saddle. "Them trail hands is raisin' a hell of a stink. Claim Kimberland's back of that run-off last night; say a lot of their stuff has got mixed in with his. If that's right there's somethin' fishy, they was headed the other way. And they're still throwin' fits about all that dropped beef."

"What become of it?"

"Well," Chavez grinned, "you can't prove it by me. But a lot of people around here is goin' to really fill up today."

He rode on. The kid wabbled his hoop up to the front of the cafe, regarding Frank with bright eyes. "Got a note fer you, mister." He dug a bit of paper from his jeans and passed it over. Frank tossed back a quarter. "Geez!" the kid yelled, and tore off like a twister.

Frank looked at the note. Signed "Kelly," it read: *Be in front of the bakeshop today at* 12 *noon.*

Frank peered through the window. Two minutes. He recalled the message Gurden's piano thumper had left for him with Danny, about some deal Kelly was in with Chip. Wants to explain that, he thought, and shook his head. Nothing, anymore, was solid white or solid black. Everybody it seemed was daubed with something. Everyone but Honey. In another half hour they'd be putting on the nosebag.

He struck off toward the bake shop. He wasn't going to have much time with Honey for at one o'clock he was due to take over patrolling the town; and he still hadn't figured what to do about Sandrey. He wistfully remembered the job he had quit and halfway wished himself back at Bospero Flats where life, though dull, had been simply a routine matter of eating, sleeping and watching cows' butts while they fed on the landscape. He had frequently bemoaned in those halcyon days being maneuvered into the position of being Will Church's keeper—now he was saddled with an entire town. Frank was out of his depth and he finally knew it.

He was abreast of Abbie Burks' millinery, with the bake shop's front in plain sight when, just like a hand had reached out to stop him, something pulled Frank up. He looked around perplexedly, and so discovered Kimberland riding in from the south. The Bar 40 boss waved, calling out some rigamarole which Frank, at this distance, couldn't make head nor tail of.

Frank got to within thirty feet of the rancher when Krantz, vastly excited, bulged around the near end of his store. "Gott in Himmel!" he gasped, floundering up to Frank and catching hold of him. His eyes were like peeled grapes behind the lenses of his spectacles. "Kvick—com kvick," he urged, wheezing. "In the back of mine blace you should see—"

W. T. Kimberland's shadow fell across the store-keeper. It seemed like Krantz's breath slid even farther out of reach. Sweat gleamed on his cheeks like lard.

"What's up?" Kimberland said, eyeing him curiously.

Krantz glared. "It shouldn't happen to a dog!" He tugged at Frank's arm and Frank let the man pull him back into the alley.

Kimberland swung down, moving after them. "Someone get hurt?"

The remark angered Frank. Krantz hauled him around the back end of the Mercantile toward a welter of boxes out of which barrel staves thrust like a scatter of rib bones.

The marshal's eyes widened. It was Gurden's piano man. With his neck folded over a crate top and his button-shoed legs flopped out of its bottom he lay like a drunk in the last stages of stupor. His brown derby, upended, lay a few feet beyond him with a break in its crown. Frank saw his head then. One look was enough.

"God above!" Kimberland muttered. "What'd they do—beat his brains out?" He backed off looking bilious, half lifting an arm as though to defend himself. "Who'd do a thing like that—and for what?"

Frank eyed the storekeeper. "You got any ideas?"

Krantz, making retching sounds, turned away and was sick. Frank ran back to the street, his eyes searching for Chavez while he thought of Sandrey alone out at Brackley's.

Kimberland caught up with him. "This is a terrible thing—"

Frank turned on him, snarling. "What are you fixing to do to this country?"

The Bar 40 man was taken aback. Now a dark core of watchfulness got into his stare. "Why, Frank, all I've ever done is try to improve this miserable country."

"You think that railroad's going to be any good to it?"

The man stared thoughtfully. "So you know about that." A little silence piled up, and then he said, speaking earnestly, "Of course it will. It's bound to! We'll be a shipping point instead of just another two-bit town upon the trail. Hell, I've put my money into it—every cent I could spare. I've even borrowed to bring that road here!" He swung his arms. "There'll be a great future—"

"You mean for them Benchers, or just for yourself?"

Kimberland let his arms drop. He stepped back, looking startled. But he covered it, chuckling. "Thought for a moment you meant that."

Frank caught sight of Chavez then and waved him toward the back of Krantz's place. Chavez nodded. Frank looked at Kimberland. "How are you figuring to benefit them Benchers?"

"Frank, talk sense," Kimberland said.

Frank sent his glance over the street, out into the hot glare, observing the sand-scoured fronts of the buildings, oddly surprised to find no change in their appearance. Birds were still chirping. Only in himself was the film of winter's ice apparent, crackling out its warning, skewering him with a million needles. His eyes, hard as jade, found Kimberland's face. "My Dad was one of those Benchers."

Kimberland was silent, a shade tighter of lip but obviously considering, casting up his impressions with that same cold assurance which had carried him through every bind in his life. He said, very softly, "Don't get in my way, Frank."

It was the man's attitude, as much as it was anything, which brought all of Frank's anger into sudden sharp focus.

Kimberland growled, "Don't be a damned fool!"

A mounting crest of excitement was in Frank now, the walls of his confusions crumbling away. The sheen of Kimberland's eyes, the pinched-in look about his mouth, was ample warning. But he said, thinly smiling, "I'm not fool enough to think I'll ever be able to pin anything on you," and saw the answering glint, the triumph and satisfaction which looked out of the cattleman's eyes. "But," said Frank, tapping a finger against W. T.'s chest, "if you molest those Benchers in any way I'm coming after you, mister."

CHAPTER TEN

It was good while he'd been at it but, watching the Bar 40 boss ride off toward the hotel, Frank understood the futility of using such talk on a man like Kimberland. A kind of baying at the moon. W. T. Kimberland was king in this country.

All the confidence and good feeling was washed out of Frank, leaving nothing behind but cold emptiness. The whole shadowy pack of old worries closed round him. He forgot his surroundings in this grim absortion. Kimberland's influence would rip the star off him—

He felt the breath of the bullet before the report of the shot slapped the fronts of the buildings. Frank dropped, yanking his sixshooter, rolling frantically for the alley mouth. A slug kicked splinters off the corner above his head. He was beginning to believe he was going to reach shelter when something with the shock of a forty-pound sledge slammed him into the wall.

He shot twice from that position at the disappearing back of a man fading around the far side of Fentriss' stable. Frank got his legs under him and lurched to his feet. The whole left side of his chest felt numb. There were calls and questions as men piled out of the nearest doorways, but Frank hardly noticed. He ran across the street, cutting east of the stable since the man obviously would not be crazy enough to try to escape through that open stretch west of it.

At the back of the place he looked in both directions and saw no sign of the man. It did not seem reasonable to assume he'd reached cover in so short a time without somebody seeing him. The fellow's very haste would have attracted attention. So he must be in the stable. Shutting his eyes for a moment Frank dived through the side door. His gun was ready but there was nothing to fire at; he could see well enough to have spotted movement. He yelled for Fentriss.

The man came in from the pens. "I've got her ready— What happened to your badge?"

Frank looked down at it blankly. "Where is he? Where'd he go to?"

"If I knowed what you was talkin' about—"

"Tularosa! Didn't you see him?"

"No—and I don't want to!" Fentriss growled.

"He must be hiding around here someplace."

"Then I'll be back when he's left."

Frank said, swearing, "You can help me look, can't you?"

"No, sir! I ain't about to look for no killer!" He grabbed both hands to his hat and backed out of the place.

Frank got to work. He went over that stable with a fine-toothed comb, he checked the pens outside, but he did not find Tularosa. He was minded to swear in a posse but knew as well as he knew his own name how much good he could expect from that. They would all be like Fentriss. It was Frank they'd pinned the star on. It was up to Frank to catch Tularosa.

Still fisting the gun he moved out back of the jail, alert and still edgy, but taking enough time to examine the ground. There were plenty of tracks, most of them too recent to pick out the ones he was hunting. Tularosa must have been past here. Next door was the hotel and beyond that Halbertson's hay shed. Then the shacks where the bulk of this town had their homes. He wouldn't have a Chinaman's chance singlehanded. Someone was almost bound to have seen the man but Frank could understand no one was going to admit it.

Chavez caught sight of Frank and cut over. "I heard the shots," he said, "but I was prowling the lumber yard. What happened to your badge?"

Frank eyed the bent metal. "Another half inch and that slug would of got me." He looked frowningly back in the direction of those shacks. Chavez, reading his mind, said, "I'm game if you want to try it, but the chances are he's pulled his freight."

"I suppose," Frank scowled, and then caught sight of his shadow. "Hell!" He suddenly remembered Honey Kimberland. "I'll take over at one."

He hurried back to the stable and, twisting the stirrup, stepped into the saddle. "Takin' off?" Fentriss said, and Frank looked down at him. "I'll be around. Seen any more of that herd boss?"

"Man, is he hot!" Fentriss passed up the blue roan's reins. "They're out combin' the breaks. Sent one of his hands after Draicup. If that jasper comes back with them wild men of his we're like to—"

But Frank, just now, wasn't interested in Draicup. He stopped by the jail but didn't see the jailer. Already late, he was about to move on when Chavez swung into sight between buildings, shotgun cradled across his knees. Frank cut over, repeating the gist of his powwow with Kimberland. "If you want out, say so."

"Ha!" Chavez grinned. "Have you found a good hole to crawl into?"

Frank scowled. "Where's Danny?"

"Ain't seen him. If he ain't over to the jail he's probably feedin' his face."

Frank said, "If anything comes up you'll find me doing the same, at the hotel." He sent the roan toward its rack. He got down and walked into the lobby. Bernie, the gun-shop man, put down his wrinkled copy of the Dallas paper and tossed Frank a nod. "Anything new?" Frank grunted, not seeing Honey, and went along to the cigar case where he treated himself to the luxury of a ten-center. He bit the end from the weed and put his back against the show-case. "Soon as I get through here I'm going after Chip Gurden."

Bernie looked at him sharply. He was a heavy-set man with a well-fed look, one of the town's more substantial citizens with a home in Snob Hollow and a bank account that, by some people's tell of it, would have choked a grown herd sire. Bernie studied Frank's countenance. "Think Draicup will be back?"

In the way he put the question there was an undertow of worry that brought Tularosa back into Frank's thinking. "I don't know," Frank said, frowning. "I can't see why he would though. Gourd and Vine troubles ain't no skin off his nose."

"Maybe," Bernie said, "you better get W. T. to let you deputize some of his crew. Just in case," he added grimly.

Neither man noticed the tap of heels on the stairs, neither of them saw the arrested shape of the girl. She was off to one side above the level of Bernie's chair and Frank was too much worked up to take his glance away from the saddle merchant. He said uncomfortably but with an edge of defiance, "I don't think Kimberland's in any mood to oblige me."

Bernie's glance was puzzled. "Put you in, didn't he?"

Frank had always known this town kowtowed to Kimberland just as the smaller stockmen did. When there weren't any trail herds, Bar 40 and its satellites—Arnold and the Churches—were the standby of these shop keepers, all that kept them going. Frank wondered if they guessed what Kimberland was up to. Probably not. Like enough they wouldn't give a damn. But he had to try. He said, "There's been a—"

"Been a what?"

Frank wondered how he could make Bernie see this when it wasn't even clear in his own mind. "Those fellers on the Bench—"

"Trash!" the merchant said contemptuously. "They wouldn't know a fine gun if it hit 'em in the eye!"

The clerk, back of Frank, put his oar in. "Except for Brackley puttin' that woman up here last night we've never got a nickel's worth of business off the bunch of them—and don't look to, I can tell you."

"Well, a man has to make a living," Frank said. "But—"

"Look," Bernie scowled. "There's good grass on that Bench. This drop in the market's caught Bar 40 over-stocked. There ain't a man in this town would honestly blame W. T. if he took over that whole range. It's too bad about Brackley but you can't—"

"I did," Frank said, and squared his shoulders. "It's not a question of grass. Kimberland wants that whole Bench and I've warned him to stay away—"

"Why, you damned fool!" Bernie leaped from his chair, white and shaking with outrage. "Kimberland's practically *made* this town! If it wasn't for him—"

Frank suddenly discovered Honey on the stairs. The expression on his face and the direction he was staring pulled the saddle man's head around.

Red faced, still glowering, Bernie dragged off his hat. "Your servant, ma'am, and pardon. . . ." He let the rest trail off with another black glare at the marshal.

Never had the girl looked more desirable to Frank. Looking down at them she held her head a little back, some trick of light on that shadowed stair bringing out the delicate structure of her face, heightening its proud beauty beneath the gleam of spun-gold hair so that she seemed the very embodiment of all that was fine and farthest from Frank's reach.

He wasn't bucking her old man so much because of what Kimberland was cooking up as because of the way the man hoped to come at it, treating those Benchers like a pack of damn Indians. Not that Frank liked them or they liked him. They were a stiffnecked bunch of penniless polecats, too cross-grained to work and too shiftless to neighbor with, but Frank wasn't going to see them shoved off their places just because they were trash in the eyes of these moguls. He had been trash himself until this star pulled him out of it. In their books, anyway.

A brightness came into his look, peering up at her. There was no hesitation in the way she faced Bernie. A kind of smile had parted her lips, deepening their color against her pale cheeks. Not many could have carried off so well the unenviable position in which Frank's words had placed her. His thoughts embraced this with relief and in humility as he sensed the gathering fierceness with which she meant to defend him. He could now admit, within the privacy of his perceptions, that he had been a little worried. Yet he had known she would understand; she could not have been herself, the guiding light of all Frank's reaching—the very core of every dream—and acted differently. To have shown less compassion than himself was plain unthinkable.

Frank's heart swelled with pride. It gave him the courage to say, "They've got some rights, too. They're not animals, Bernie."

The merchant half lifted a shaking fist, so furious it seemed as though he must burst. He twisted his glowering red face up at Honey. "You going to listen to that kind of guff? Bring this fool to his senses or—"

Honey giggled. Her eyes encountered Frank's and she laughed right out, uncontrollably. "Oh dear—" she gasped, blinking, holding onto her side. "Of course he's a fool. A bumptious, ignorant, spur-clacking nobody! Why else do you suppose Father gave him that star!"

CHAPTER ELEVEN

FRANK STOOD like a man in the clutch of paralysis. Each contraction of his heart held the impact of a fist. He had a giddy sense of motion, of being alone on some high point with the wind rushing round him and nothing to catch hold of.

He drew a ragged breath and his stare found Bernie. The man's face hung in mottled folds against the bones which upheld it. His eyes bulged like the eyes of a frog. Now his lips writhed away from the rotten stumps of teeth locked together.

It was the clerk's hysterical grip on Frank's shoulder which finally got through to him, bringing him out of it. He let go of Bernie's throat, saw the clerk's scared face and shoved the man stumbling out of his path. He went through the door blindly and onto the porch. All he could see was Honey's face tight with scorn. Breath began to come into him. He saw this town as the place really was. The fault was his for imagining he could pull himself up by his bootstraps.

He jammed fists in pockets and felt the crackle of paper. *Kelly's note.* He glanced at his shadow, checked the guess by his watch. Too late. His eyes raked the dusty glare of the street, noting its emptiness while a resolve solidified behind the tough planes of his cheeks.

Chavez came along heading west toward the office. "I'll take over," Frank said.

Chavez nodded. "Somethin' I don't savvy back there." He flung a dissatisfied look over his shoulder. "Could of swore I heard a woman yell."

Chavez was a bundle of contradictions. His mother, dead in childbirth, had been with a road show which had gone to pieces in Dalhart. She had put herself beyond forgiveness by marrying his father, a Mexican horse breaker who'd been working for Sam Church at the time. Frank had heard several versions of the story but all agreed Church had hounded the man out of the country. Frank could imagine what Chavez's boyhood had been with a father tossed from pillar to post and the blood of two races forever clashing inside him.

"Where was this?" Frank asked, scowling.

"Passing the bake shop. Could of been wrong. Might of been that hasher at the New York Cafe. Could of been a horse."

"My worry," Frank said, and crossed over to Gurden's. The gambler, back of the bar, had both arms anchored to a spread-open newspaper. He looked up, face tightening, as Frank stepped in. At this slack time, in addition to Gurden and one of his dealers laying out a hand of sol, there were only three other men, local customers, in the place. Frank didn't miss the way these quit talking.

"Where's Mousetrap, Gurden?"

The saloon owner shrugged. "When he ain't on duty his time's his own." He plopped the butt of his stogie into a spittoon. "Shall I say you been lookin' for him?"

"I've got a cell looking for him if I happen to lay hands on him, and I wouldn't be surprised but what I can find room for you. Why are these gents toting guns in your place?"

"Now look—"

"You know the law. You helped make it."

Frank continued to stare until the saloonman's face showed his hate and fury. When the stillness threatened to become too oppressive Frank waved a hand at the three bellying the bar. "Uncinch that hardware."

There were black looks and grumbling but the men complied.

"Now pick up your belts and head for the jail."

"You ain't serious—"

"By the time you get out you'll be a better judge of that." Frank waited till the men reluctantly started for the batwings, then he said, "You're through in South Fork, Gurden. You cut your string too short with

Willie. The next stage leaves at seven o'clock. Be on it, and take your hired thugs with you."

After he'd locked the men up, Frank, recalling what Chavez had told him, got his mare from the hotel hitch-rack, got aboard and pointed her east. At the stage depot he crossed the road's sun-scorched dust and stepped down in front of the New York Cafe. The place had no business.

The hasher was fanning herself back of the counter. She gave him a withering look. "You've shot your bolt, takin' up for them Benchers. I guess this heat must've scrambled your brains."

Frank managed a grin. "You can't scramble something you don't have to start with. Let's have another cup of that varnish you call java."

"And then tellin' Gurden to get out of town! You got a hankerin' for a coffin?"

"How the hell did you hear about that?"

"I heard it," she said. "The whole town's buzzin'."

Frank sagged onto a stool and tiredly leaned on his elbows. "Chip was after me anyhow."

She poured the coffee and put it in front of him. "Bernie ain't about to make no sheep's eyes at you—what'd you want to rough him up for? And Kimberland, too." She put her hands on her hips. "What you need is darn good talkin' to."

Frank saucered some of his coffee and held it up to blow at. "Seen Kelly around?"

"Kelly! Man, you better get your sights set on steerin' clear of Gurden."

"You been here all morning, ain't you?"

She shook her head like she was giving Frank up. "You know darn well I have. You think that Greek would let me outa this joint?"

"You hear anything a while ago? Like maybe some woman was yelling or something?"

She wiped her cheeks with her apron and regarded him queerly.

"Reason I asked, Chavez thought he heard something

last time he was by here. You know if Abbie Burks is home?"

She started to sniff then shook her head, looking paler. She leaned forward abruptly. "Danny Settles was over behind her place a while ago. . . . I know because I saw him. Jake'll tell you the same. He seen him, too."

Frank got down off the stool and stepped into the kitchen.

"That's right," the Greek said. He pushed a pan of dough back and wiped floured hands on his shirt front. "Skulkin', he was. I said so then and I'll say so now. Squintin' back over his shoulder an' all scrounch down like he was scairt someone would see him. Hell of a guy you should pick for a jailer. Right back of that brush," he pointed, "that's where I seen him."

Frank stepped out the back door. He went over to the brush and started looking around. In an alkaline spot that wasn't haired over with grass he saw fresh sign, the print of a boot heel. He found where this party had worked through the brush on a line with Abbie's back door.

He went over there and knocked without getting any answer. He tried the latch but the door was barred. "Abbie?" He jiggled the thing but no one moved inside the house.

"An' I'll tell you somethin' else," the Greek said grimly when Frank returned. "It won't be the first time that feller's been over there."

Frank went out to the mare and then went back to ask, looking troubled, "How long ago was this?"

"Well—" the hasher said, "it's been a couple of hours, I guess. About the time of that shootin', give or take a few minutes."

Of course, Frank thought. Knowing Abbie, he knew she'd take Danny in when he was probably scared half out of what wits he had left by those shots Frank had swapped with that damned Tularosa. Danny had gone to Abbie with the trust of a frightened dog. But why had she yelled—or had she? "You reckon she's out?"

The hasher couldn't give him any help there. "I never *seen* her go, if that's what you mean."

Frank went back to the street. He didn't want to break in. He'd look a pretty fool if Abbie was home.

He walked over to the mare. Abbie might have plenty of reasons for not coming to the door. She might have been working. He hadn't tried the front. He was starting to walk over there when he saw John Arnold turning in at the path. Arnold, glumly preoccupied with things in his mind, went through the picket fence without noticing Frank.

It came over Frank rather oddly that Arnold's look was generally perturbed whenever he seemed to be heading for Abbie's. Perhaps the rancher only visited his niece when the cares of this world got to weighing too heavy. It was a weird thing to think and yet in no way more strange than well-off John Arnold with a prosperous ranch permitting his kin—his only kin, far as Frank knew—to spend her time making bonnets for other people's women.

He had never happened to catch this angle on it before, and now was baffled to realize that never had he heard of Abbie visiting the ranch. Frank recalled the hasher's sniff and the unexplained color with which Abbie had told him this morning that she supposed her uncle was still around. It then occurred to Frank the strain he'd always sensed in her might spring from something other than a New England parentage.

A little startled, Frank suddenly saw Abbie Burks as the women of this town had, those good housewives and mothers he'd thought resented her good looks and the fact that she was in business.

The discontinuance of Arnold's knocking fetched Frank out of this thinking and he heaved into the saddle as Arnold's steps approached around the side of the house, and suddenly stopped. Frank might have gone to see what Arnold was swearing about except that, just then, he caught sight of Kelly beckoning from the doorway of the stage barn.

Frank put the mare across the street. Kelly abruptly

faded away from the door. At that moment, Frank saw the surveyor's scout he had met in the hills coming in from the west. The scout was half falling out of his saddle. Sandrey Larren, riding alongside, was doing her best to hold him on.

Forgetting Kelly, Frank swung toward them, touching the mare with the points of his spurs. A moment before, the town had seemed asleep on its feet; now men appeared from a dozen doorways—even Old Judge with a beer in his hand running out of the Flag to find out what was happening.

Frank reached the surveyor's scout and eased him down. Blood and dust were all over the front of him and his face looked like a mask of waxed paper. Sandrey's cheeks were drawn. Both horses showed lather. Ignoring the excited jabber around him, Frank hoisted the scout and carried him into the Blue Flag where he eased him onto a faro table. It was to be seen at a glance he was no case for a sawbones; the man had lost too much blood and there was froth on his mouth.

"Back up!" Frank growled as men crowded around them. His glance flashed to Sandrey.

She said, "Will he make it?"

Frank, studying the man, shook his head. "What happened?"

Sandrey drew a long breath. "He stopped by my place—it was just before noon. He gave this pitch about a railroad, said he wanted an easement. He came right out and offered cash money for it. I put him off, told him I'd have to talk first with my neighbors. He upped his price five hundred dollars—"

"Get to the shooting." Frank ignored the rest of them. He could tell by their looks of startled excitement this was the first they'd heard about any railroad.

Sandrey's eyes were smoky sage and she was still breathing hard. Frank understood this was emotion. She was fiercely angry. It was in all her looks, in the hand she put up to push back her hair. Her cheeks were pale but fright had nothing to do with this.

"It was the cattle," she said, "we didn't see the men

right off, only the cows. They were everywhere, like a sea of horns, bawling and staring wherever we turned. They must have shoved that whole six thousand—"

"Kimberland's got more than that," Frank said.

She looked at him straightly. "You don't get it. I'm talking about—Church. Will Church."

"You must be mistaken. The cows you saw were Bar Forty—"

"Tell him!" Sandrey said; and Frank followed her glance to the pain-racked eyes staring up at him.

"That's right," the scout whispered. "Circle C the brand was."

An angry muttering broke out back of Frank. Heels fell loud across the planks of the porch, and Sandrey said, "Young Church himself—the one who threatened you last night and then lifted his hat to me—came loping up with a couple of hardcases. He was feeling pretty pleased with himself. 'Sorry,' he said, 'but you can't stay here.' Then Mr. Fles—" her hand moved toward the scout on the faro table—"told Will Church he was barking up the wrong tree, that I was owner of Terrapin. He—" she looked at Frank fiercely—"never had a chance to say anything more. Church grabbed up a pistol and shot him. It all happened so quick I couldn't keep up with it. Both of Church's men had their guns out by this time. Church said 'Git!' and we done it. I'm pretty sure if we hadn't he'd have shot me too."

Frank could hardly believe Church had been such a fool. Yet, it was exactly what Will would do, given nerve enough. Somewhere he had found the nerve. Frank saw but two possible answers to this. Either Will had got backing for this defiance of Kimberland or, stung frantic by the loss of face he had suffered at Frank's hands, the man had gone hog wild.

There was a commotion back up front by the doors and Chavez, thin-lipped, intolerant of delay, came through the crowd blackly shoving men off his elbows. "That Burks woman has been raped and they're hangin' Danny Settles!"

CHAPTER TWELVE

THEY'RE AT the stage company's barn!" Chavez piled in the saddle. "I tried to talk some sense into them. Arnold tried, too. You know what a mob is! They're fixin' to use that hay hoist. . . ."

Frank's thoughts, and the wind, isolated him from the rest of what the deputy was saying. Frank was raking the mare with the gut hooks. Every fiber of his being rebelled against this and he cursed the loose jaws which had incited it. Settles had been no more capable of attacking Abbie Burks than a cow was of singing, yet these fools in their need to fight back at their fears . . .

Snarling, Frank crouched lower with the wind in his ears as they flashed past the storefronts, making the run in twenty-seven seconds. He cursed the white faces that twisted around at him. He slammed the roan into them, scattering them. He had a blade in his hand. He knew before she had slid to a stop—by the grotesque way Danny spilled to the ground—he had got here too late.

Frank appeared about ready to start killing the handiest. The stock knife in his fist gleamed sharp as a saber and the mob fell away, shamefaced, some yelling, stumbling over each other in their fright and their guilt.

Frank dropped off the mare, bent over Danny, unashamed of the glistening blur in his lashes. It wasn't that the man had ever been close—no two could have been farther apart than the gentle dead and this roughneck marshal. Frank's emotions were aroused by the utter uselessness of this, the sheer stupidity that would allow men to act so.

Throwing off the rope he got up, bone weary, and saw Arnold's grim-set mask of a face. Behind him was Chavez with his sawed-off. The rest were gone.

"Crept away like whipped curs!" the Mexican said.

"Go tell Ben Holliday," Frank said, "we've got some more business for him." When the deputy left, Arnold said, "Man can't reason with fools." He glared at Danny and swore. "That girl was my life. Should have married her long ago. Was too damned smug," he said, hating himself, "too stinking proud of being Kimberland's right hand to chance offending. Kimberland would never have understood my marrying a kept woman."

Frank pulled off his neckscarf and covered Danny's face. "I blame myself."

"No need to. Danny never—"

"I know that. But I went over there and knocked. I should have broken in."

"Wouldn't have made any difference. She'd been dead for some time. Beaten, raped—strangled. Never locked her doors. Danny said the place was locked front and back when he slipped over there. He was frightened, went for comfort. They found him in that brush back of Wolverton's after that Greek and his hasher . . . . *God!*

A putty-faced hostler came out of the barn. "I'll watch him," he muttered.

Frank set off up the street, the mare's reins in his hand, Arnold silent beside him. There were plenty of men standing around on the walks, but no one intercepted them, no one met Frank's stare.

Arnold growled, "There's just one son of a bitch in this country—that could have done this."

"Tularosa," Frank said. "He's here, but how to find him."

"I'll find him!"

Frank told him then about the scout, and Sandrey's story.

"I've sometimes wondered," Arnold said, "if perhaps Will wasn't back of this cow-stealing. Whenever the herds come through he's got money. He damn sure never got any from his father."

"I'm afraid Sam's in this. Will would never buck W. T. without help."

"He could be getting it from Gurden. That kid plays more than's good for him. Chip's got a bundle of his paper."

"I've told Gurden to pull his freight when that stage leaves tonight."

"He won't do it."

"I'm not expecting him to."

Arnold grinned at Frank bleakly. "What about W. T.?"

Frank sighed. "I reckon he'll fight."

Arnold said, "Here's where I leave you."

Kelly, when he had waved at Frank, had been minded to throw himself on Frank's mercy. He had beckoned Frank over to spill what he knew; but when Frank, distracted, had whirled his mare up the street, the teamster was left like a drowning man who has grasped at a straw and finds himself sinking.

He stared after Frank in a sweat of self-pity. Saw the reeling scout and the girl hanging onto him, but all he could think of was the look of Chip Gurden.

Desperate, outraged, half out of his head with the bitter emotions of a man whose best has never been good enough, he looked again at Frank and ran back for his rifle. All the twisted hate of the man's warped nature was prodding him now with galling remembrance of how Frank had always been one step ahead of him. He picked up the rifle and returned to the entrance in time to see Frank, carrying the stranger, step through the Flag's batwings.

Kelly cursed in a frenzy, then cunning came into the wild blaze of his stare. Frank would have to come out. Be a pretty far shot. Making sure the hostler was still at his feeding, Kelly returned to the door and, cradling his Winchester, settled down where he'd be ready. There'd be no slip this time.

A growing clamor across the way gradually crept through the shell of Kelly's preoccupation. Finally, irritably, he twisted his face around. A crowd was forming between the Bon Ton and the bake shop. Even as he watched, it broke apart and ran off in segments; but almost at once it began to regroup itself as two men came shoving another cowed shape; the sound of their voices brought Kelly out of his crouch.

They seemed to be having quite a wrangle. He saw the hasher from the New York Cafe swinging her arms about and the Greek from the same place nodding emphatically. Growing yells went up as Danny Settles was shoved to the front again and out of this uproar came the shouted word—*rope*. Kelly saw Arnold's furious features and saw Chavez break away from the crowd. Arnold dropped out of sight amid a flurry of blows and then the whole push was crossing the street. Kelly's horrified stare saw them heading straight for him. His shaking hands dropped the rifle. He ducked through the side door and clambered into his saddle, cuffing the horse with the rein ends, beating its ribs with his heels.

After Arnold left to go off somewhere on his own hook, Frank strode on to the Flag, tied his mare and went in. A few men at the bar were arguing about Danny's lynching. Frank looked at them bleakly and two or three remembered forgotten chores which took them away. Talk petered out and then Wolverton asked Frank, "What are you going to do about Church?"

"I'll take care of him." Frank bought himself a beer and watched a dealer setting up a faro layout on the scrubbed-clean table where the dead scout had lain.

McFell, the Flag's owner, wearing a brown derby and impeccably dressed as usual except for the folded newspaper protruding from his coat's left pocket, drifted in from the back and gave Frank the eye from a corner of the bar. Frank finished his beer and went over. "The young woman," McFell said, "asked me to tell you she would be at the hotel."

Frank nodded his thanks. He was in a black mood and painfully preoccupied with thoughts of his own, yet something about the other made him scrutinize McFell more closely.

McFell's lips quirked a little. "Tularosa, wasn't it?"

Frank considered this, frowning, and glanced up at the clock, astonished to find that it was near five.

McFell said, "If you was Will Church and figured to go whole hog, what would you do to copper the bet?"

Frank said quietly, "Hire that damned killer."

"I've a pretty fair hunch that's the way he's figuring."

"And how would Will get hold of him?"

McFell tipped his head to stare down at his hands. Frank guessed he was making his mind up how far he wanted to go. Still without looking up, McFell said, "I guess you know Chip's been holding a bunch of Will's IOUs. Tularosa was in Chip's back room last night before you put him in the cooler. If you was Will, and made a deal with Tularosa, what are the first two jobs you would give him?"

Frank said, "Fixing Gurden. Taking care of me."

"So," McFell said, "if you watch Chip . . ." and thinly smiled.

Frank went back to the street. A pair of cowhands were jogging away from Minnie's; by her door another was just quitting the saddle. Another gent was mounting in front of Fentriss' barn. Small gatherings of talkers studded the walks farther down and, closer at hand, two men alongside the damaged corner of Bernie's gun shop were eyeing him with what looked to be a somewhat strained attention.

Frank untied the roan mare and, swinging up, turned her toward them. The pair lurched apart. One of them, disappearing into the alley, was Gurden's new muscle man, Mousetrap. Frank let him go.

The other was Sam Church. He thrust out his jaw as Frank came up to him, scowling in that dog-with-a-bone way the marshal remembered. Naked malice and a number of things less easily deciphered were in his stare. "Don't come whinin' around for your money," Sam Church growled, "after the way you took off from Bospero Flats—lost me ever' damn one of them beeves!"

Frank said, "Shut your old face. And you'd better snap the leash back on Will. Shooting that feller—"

Church said with a sneer, "If you had any proof—"

"I got all I need."

Malice got into the old man's choking voice, that raw edge of arrogance that was Will's stock in trade, more insufferable in Will's father, more infuriatingly caustic and contemptuous. "If you want to get laughed out of this town, go ahead. Fetch him in, if you're able. Five separate people saw that skunk reach first."

"Just who," Frank said, "are you talking about?"

"That sneak Kimberland brought in here, that feller we run into at Brackley's. Tried to gun Will down— even got off first shot." He grinned like a toothless old wolf, throwing his head back. "If you're countin' on that skirt sayin' otherwise you're a bigger damn fool than W. T. took you for. A saloon slut! Who'd believe her?" The chin jutted forward from his turkeycock neck, his red jowls jiggling like wattles. "Sake of ol' times I'm goin' to give you a tip—git out of this country while you're still able!"

Frank watched the old vinegarroon stamp into the Opal. All these years that Frank had known him the man's cupidity and miser's caution had kept him in Kimberland's string of supporters, dancing attendance on the big pot's bubbling, glad of the crumbs from the mogul's table. Something big, something thunderous, must have happened to make Sam Church think he could safely fly in the face of Kimberland's wrath to make a grab of his own at this strip W. T. coveted.

Frank followed Church as far as the Opal's porch. Now he found himself staring at one of the handbills he'd had Chavez put up to acquaint all and sundry with the new restrictions and penalties having to do with the carrying of firearms. It was crude. Butcher paper. Hand lettered with pencil.

Frank suddenly woke up. He cuffed his hat a bit lower to give more reach to his eyes. The whole look of him sharpened. A grin cracked his lips that was like summer lightning.

CHAPTER THIRTEEN

HE FELT the kind of weird bounce a man gets in poker when he fills to an inside straight. He'd got into this jackpot trying to impress people with abilities he didn't have. The one thing he *did* have was the rep he'd been trying to get shed of. Turbulence and violence had put the meat on his bones and it was, by damn, high time he quit selling himself short. This wasn't as rough as it looked—couldn't be! The trick was to pick away at the deal. Packing the star made a man feel naked but the forces against him were flesh and blood too, heir to the same drawbacks Frank fought. Bring it down to individuals, man to man, and the deal looked different.

He stepped onto the planks of the Opal's porch, graveled to think he hadn't seen this before.

A hail caught him back as he would have pushed into Gurden's. His glance, coming around, found Krantz and Joe Wolverton hurrying into the street from the far side of the Mercantile. Krantz, waggling an arm, broke into a run. Frank paused, undecided, then stepped through the batwings with a gun in his fist.

The place turned as quiet as the day after the Fourth. A chair scraped someplace and the stillness built around this, chunk on chunk till it was like a solid wall. Frank's stare picked up four men at the bar, a townsman at the end of it and three strangers part way down. He discovered Bill Grace at a card table with two Bar 40 punchers and the bronc stomper from X3. It was the horse-breaker's chair which had been shoved back.

Frank said, "Where's Church?"

Nobody answered but the townsman standing solo at the end of the mahogany shot a nervous glance toward the door of Chip's office. Frank's eyes raked the rest of them. "Clear out," he said, "this place has been closed."

105

He gave them ten seconds and when nobody moved drove a slug at the horse-breaker's chair. This collapsed with a shattered leg, spilling the X3 man to the floor. The Bar 40 punchers lurched to their feet. Bill Grace, Kimberland's foreman, got up too but he took more time to it, eyeing Frank narrowly. The horse-breaker got up looking mean-mouthed and violent. More ringy than Grace, or perhaps less observing, he permitted his resentment to prod him into speech:

"Who the hell do you think you're hoorawin'!" He started for Frank like the wrath of God. A horse-length away the fellow's feet slowed and stopped. He seemed a bit less ruddy about the gills and began to sweat.

One of the strangers at the bar curled his lip and said, "Chicken."

Frank placed these three then, guessing them to have some connection with Will Church. They were hard-bitten customers, belted and spurred, obviously looking for trouble. All three were armed.

Frank's mouth turned thin. He took a long step forward, swapping his six-shooter from right hand to left. His right closed in the front of the nearest man's shirt and fetched him around in a staggering circle, suddenly letting go of him. Momentum did the rest. The fellow crashed into his cronies, knocking one of them sideways. The other, ducking, slapped leather, but before he could bring the gun into line Frank cracked him hard across the face with his pistol.

The man fell back, yelling. He managed to jerk off one shot that brought dust off the ceiling then Frank banged his weapon across the man's wrist. The gun dropped. Frank booted it. The man reeled against the bar, sickly moaning.

The horse-breaker backed away with both hands up. The man Frank had used to break up the play lay where he had dropped, eyes bulging. There was blood across his chin. Frank said to Bill Grace, "Take all three of them over to the jail and lock 'em up. Rest of you get out of here."

He saw Gurden staring from the doorway of his office. When the last customer got off the porch, Frank stepped up to Gurden. "Got this place sold yet?"

The saloonman stood with his mouth so tight the stogie began to sag as though his teeth had gone clean through it.

"Don't wait too long. That stage leaves at seven." Frank's shoulder cut against Gurden and the flat of Frank's hand—the one that was empty—pushed Gurden's chest, and this way the saloonman was backed into his office. Frank's grin licked at Church. "You're in bad company, old man. Get Will's IOUs back yet?"

Sam Church looked about to throw a fit. Fury crept into Gurden's stare, tightening even further the thin trap of his mouth. But there was in the man some caution which tempered this fury. He scratched a match along the wall and held it up to his mangled smoke but the thing wouldn't draw and he pitched it away.

Someone outside put his horse into a run and quit town, heading east, in the direction of Arnold's. Dust swept into the alley, buffly coating the dust already fogging the window. The mutter of voices came into this quiet and Sam Church growled, "Your time's runnin' out." Then, because he was a man with an unbridled temper, Church permitted himself one additional remark. "You're dead on your feet and ain't got sense enough to know it."

Frank stepped out the door, putting a wall to his back. "Sam, unbuckle that gun belt. Jail's your next stop. For packin' a weapon in a place that sells rotgut. Drop the belt and start hiking."

Old Sam's eyes whipped to Gurden. But the saloonman said:

"Count me out of this, Frank."

Church's face was livid. The upper half of him tipped. The stiffened fingers of his right hand suddenly tensed.

"When you draw that iron you're dead," Frank said.

A trapped desperation brought the bones of Church's face into more vivid prominence. Passion clawed at his guards, the violent urge to defy Frank—but doubt crept in and shame twisted his cheeks and not all his fury could push the hand to his gun.

"Shuck the belt," Frank said, "and let's get started."

Visibly trembling, the old man obeyed. The still-sheathed pistol thumped the floor. Church stared bitterly. Gurden nursed his hate in silence. Church cried in a high half-strangled voice, "When my son learns of this—"

"I'm counting on it." Frank smiled, and scooped up the dropped belt. "Take the side door. I'll be right behind you."

The whole street appeared to be watching as Frank, following Church, stepped out of the alley, got hold of the mare's reins and prodded the second largest owner in the country over to the jail. The stillness was funereal. Out of the corner of an eye Frank saw Krantz's dropped jaw, the sour smile of Wolverton; and was almost across the width of the road before the storekeeper recovered enough to call out. Frank, paying no attention, tossed the mare's reins across the pole of the jail tie-rack, and with gun still in hand followed old Sam into the building.

Kimberland's foreman, Bill Grace, looked up from his perch on Frank's desk, stare inscrutable. Gradually it widened as he took in the meaning of Frank's leveled pistol. Frank tossed Church's belt into an out-of-reach corner. "Good place for yours, Bill," he said, waggling the six-shooter. "I'm sorry about this, Bill, but right now I can't afford to have you underfoot."

The man got red in the face and began to swell up like a poisoned pup.

"Save it for the Judge," Frank said. "You'll look an awful fool if I have to ventilate both ears."

Bill Grace shut his choppers and uncinched his belt. He slammed it down on the desk and considered the marshal with a look of pure venom. Frank only grinned and tiredly waved him and Church down the corridor.

After fastening them in across the aisle from the others, Frank went back and picked up the two belts, dumping all the cartridges out of their loops and emptying both pistols, same caliber as Will's. He stowed these loads in his pockets and took a look at his watch. Twenty minutes of six. So far he'd been lucky. He didn't look for it to hold.

Will's pistol was a Peacemaker, same as the pair he'd just dropped into the drawer. The model was in much favor. Like the .44/40 Winchester, it shot a .44 caliber bullet weighing 200 grains, propelled by 40 grains of black powder, allowing one belt to carry the loads for both weapons, the only hitch being you had to stick to black powder.

Frank punched the empties out of Will's gun. Someone would sure as hell bring Old Judge into this with a writ to get some of these prisoners sprung. The keys were with Danny Settles and this whole deal might be wound up before anyone happened to think about that. True, the jail might be wrecked. So might South Fork, but it was a heap less likely with these boys in cold storage.

Fed up with their racket Frank got up and slammed the corridor door. This cut it down somewhat and he was pushing fresh loads into Will Church's pistol when Krantz's shape cut off the outside light.

"What you got in your ears? I like to yelled mineself hoarse," he wheezed, mopping his baldness with a limp bandanna. "Vot a blace! Too hot mit der sun und too verdammt cold vit'out it!" He blew irascibly through pursed lips and passed the damp cloth over the rasp of his cheeks. Scowling, he said, "You von't like this."

Frank thrust Will's sixshooter into his pants. "You've come for the badge, I guess."

"Badge! Is about this Kelly. Your friend he vas, hein? Mr. Holliday vants to know vill you stand goot for his burying?"

Frank looked at him blankly. "You trying to tell me Kelly's dead?"

"Ass a herringk— Blease! My arm iss not rubber boots." He massaged the limb gingerly. "He vas found on the road to Wega. One off dem trailherders found him. He vas shot in der back."

Kelly dead! It didn't make sense until Frank remembered the message Danny'd given him from Sleight-of-Hand Willie, the Opal's piano man. *Tell him Kelly is into some kind of deal with Gurden.* And Kelly, by that kid, had sent a note asking Frank to meet him—and later had beckoned Frank urgently from the stage barn.

It all added up. Kelly had tried to warn him and, when he couldn't, had got scared and run for it. But what had there been to warn? And then Frank had it. *Tularosa!*

Something came over Frank then and he got up with an oath. Lifting the storekeeper out of his path, he rushed into the street. W. T.'s saddled black was in front of the hotel and Frank cut that way, breaking into a run. He took the steps three at a crack and crossed the porch at one stride. The clerk, frightened and paling, shrank back into his clothes. "What room's she got?" Frank growled, looking wicked.

"T-T-Twelve."

Frank dived for the stairs, making noise enough for a band of wild horses. At the top, breathing hard, he caught hold of the bannister, spotted the number and was lifting his fist to bring it down on the panel when the door was pulled open. Frank, swearing, commenced to back off.

Honey looked at him coldly. "What is it now? I thought another stampede must be loose on the town."

Frank dragged off his hat. "I guess I got the wrong room."

Honey's eyes looked him over like a horse up at auction. "If you came to patch it up you're wasting your time," she said, closing the door.

Frank clapped on his hat and dubiously eyed the line of shut doors. He was thinking of going down for another try at the clerk when a door was pulled open a couple of yards to the left.

"Were you hunting me?" Sandrey asked.

Frank looked powerfully relieved. He hadn't realized what a strain he'd been under until he saw her standing there, unharmed.

He said, "Whew!" and then grinned. But she didn't

grin back and Frank, turning sober, decided she hadn't much call to like him and no call at all to let him inside. "If we could talk for a couple of minutes," he said, and she surprised him by moving aside.

He went in and she closed the door, putting the backs of her shoulders against it, gravely regarding him.

Many washings had tightened the thin stuff of her dress. She seemed thinner than he'd remembered, like maybe she hadn't been eating too good. The waning light from the window put hollows in her cheeks. One hand went up to the red mop of her hair and she appeared of a sudden to be breathing more deeply. All he could think about now was her nearness, the feel of her pulled hard against him at Brackley's.

"Wouldn't you like to sit down?" She moved away from the door. "Take that chair. I can perch on the bed."

She didn't seem bothered or much put out by him being here. He remembered Sam Church's words but her eyes watched him straightly; she was more composed than he was. He suddenly reached out, catching hold of her shoulder.

He couldn't make anything out of her look.

The warm aliveness of her flesh soaked up into his fingers and he jerked the hand away. A saloon slut, Church had called her. Frank didn't know whether he hated her most or the man who had named her. She said:

"I thought you said you wanted to talk to me?"

He told her in a stone-cold voice what had been going on, about the railroad and Kimberland, Gurden, all the rest of it.

"And you've got Kimberland's foreman and Sam Church in jail. Of course you know you can't hold them.

"I'll hold them," Frank said, "or long enough anyway to get this deal straightened out."

"What will you do?"

"I jailed Sam Church to put young Will where I can grab him."

"Somebody'll carry him word but he won't come alone."

"That's all right." Frank took a turn. "Having his right bower in clink ought to slow Kimberland down some."

"I can't see Gurden riding tamely out of the picture. Especially if, as you seem to believe, he was hatching some kind of crooked deal with that road scout. And then he's got that forged quitclaim. Or, rather, *if* he's got—"

"He doesn't know about you, does he?" This was what had brought Frank over here, the fear that Gurden knew and might have turned Tularosa loose on her.

"I haven't seen Gurden," she said, "but if he's the same Chip Gurden who owned the Red Quail over at Brady it's not likely he'll have forgotten me. I used to sing there," she added, returning his stare with a look half defiant.

"Brackley know that?"

There was no humor in Sandrey's smile, but it was Frank who seemed uncomfortable.

"Anyway," he said, too hurriedly and with too much emphasis, "what I meant was does Gurden know about you and Brackley?"

Sandrey, watching him, shrugged. "Does it matter?"

Frank felt the need to square himself but couldn't find the words, tangled up like he was; and the girl presently said, "Gurden's not going to beat me out of that place—or Church, either. I'll find somebody—" She broke off and said, "What makes you think jailing Sam will fetch Will in?"

"He might leave his old man stew for a while, but those three hardcases I've latched onto is something else again. He's got to bust those fellers out or he'll find himself without any hands."

"He must have other—"

"He's got others, all right. It's a matter of salt," Frank said, "of principle. When a man hires out his guns he expects the backing of whoever he's working for. It's part of the code. Will has got to come through for these boys or lose the rest of them."

Frank looked around. He saw the road scout's pistol, at least he imagined it was his, beside the washbowl on the chest of drawers. "Keep that thing handy and stay in this room. Don't open for anyone. Understand?" He waited till she nodded, and then went into the hall, pulling the door shut after him. "Shove that chair under the knob."

"Frank—"

He started down the stairs, glad to be quit of any hold she had on him, relieved to get away from those too-steady eyes. Still scowling at tangled emotions, he found Wolverton and Krantz staring out of the lobby.

Frank said, "Anyone seen Arnold?" and came off the stairs while they were shaking hands. McFell, of the Flag, came in, looking curious, and a jabbering came with him out of the street. Frank said to McFell, "That trail boss around?"

"Can't prove it. Last I heard they'd moved onto Bar 40 . . . ." He threw a look over his shoulder and stepped away from the door.

W. T. Kimberland stepped in, saw Frank and strode toward him. "Frank! You've got to do something. This situation's intolerable!"

"You referring to Bill Grace?"

The rancher's mouth shaped the name as though it were some kind of edible; then his eyes began to stretch. He chewed at his lip. Frank watched coldly and Kimberland said, "You might remember how you come to be packing that—" and let it die. A silence enveloped them and grew and reached out to embrace the whole dimensions of the room. Something broke in Kimberland —you could see it run through him like undermined timbers falling after a trembler. The harsh lines of his face were like folds seen through water; and Frank wondered on what sort of facts the cowman's rep had been founded. It was like watching a landmark crack up, he thought bitterly.

W. T. Kimberland's eyes lowered. His clothes seemed too big for him. "I've been framed," he said thickly.

Frank said, "At least you know where I stand."

"You've got to believe me!" Sweat was on Kimberland's face like a dew. "I've done a few things—"

"Like getting rid of Brackley?"

Kimberland hung there. He couldn't get the words out.

There was contempt in Frank's stare. "You put that killer up to it."

"Frank, as God is my witness—I haven't spoken ten words to Tularosa in my life."

"What was Bill Grace supposed to do?"

The rancher's glance squirmed away. "I—he wasn't supposed to do anything."

"I've made sure he won't. If you're in a bind why don't you go to your friends—all those fine ranchers you've led around by the nose?"

The man stared at him numbly.

Frank said at last, "What do you want me to do?"

"Stay out of this. Don't push—"

"First you tell me I've got to do something. Now you want me to stay out of it. Don't you know your own mind?"

The man's look was gray with pleading. "You've let Tularosa go. Can't you do as much for Grace?" He hauled breath into him. "Give me a chance, man! I'll take my losses. I'll stay off the Bench. I'll—"

Frank's grim look stayed the flood of easy assurances. "Will you send your crew to protect those people?"

Kimberland groaned. "Do I have your strict promise—"

"You don't have any kind of promise. You're on probation. What happens to you will depend on the rest of it. On what I think *ought* to happen."

Kimberland looked his full age in that moment. "You don't leave me much choice." He scrubbed a hand over his face. "I was a big man this morning; I'll be lucky tomorrow if I've still got a horse. All right." He turned to the door. "I'll do what I can." He went out through dead quiet.

"Py Gott!" Krantz exclaimed, staring unbelievably at Wolverton. Frank quit their company. McFell, staring after him, cleared his throat, shook his head. It was Wolverton who said, "Now we've seen—*everything!*"

There was quite a passel of men on the street, Frank discovered. Quite a bunch right in front of him, motionless, watching him. Kimberland's black was gone from the hitchrail. The sun was gone, too. Down across from the New York Cafe the stage company flunkeys were leading out fresh horses. Frank prowled a glance at the men grouped in front of him. "Any of you care to volunteer for a little duty?"

A couple shuffled their feet. Two or three grinned derisively. But finally one of them, flushing a little, asked to be told what Frank had in mind. "Well," Frank said, "it's like this," and told them what Will Church was up to. "I've got three of his bunch locked up in the pokey —leastways I guess they're a part of his outfit. If they are, it stands to reason he's going to try to bust them out. He may bring some help. I want to lay hold of him on account of that road scout being killed."

Several men exchanged looks. These drew off to one side where they stood muttering a moment. Then one of them asked, "We git paid for this deal?"

"Sure you'll be paid. You'll be full-time deputies for as long as you're needed. How about you?" he said to the blacksmith.

The smith looked around and reluctantly nodded. "Expect I owe you that much, lettin' that feller get away with that wheel." He moved over with the others.

Frank said to a leather-cheeked man, "How about you?"

"Ain't got no rifle."

"Plenty in my office. Plenty of cartridges too."

"I dunno. My ol' woman—"

"Before I swear you in," Frank told the others, "I suppose you should know there's one other thing I may be needing your help with. Tularosa's still loose and—"

"No!" the smith growled, glaring up at him. "I don't want no truck with that damned killer!" He wheeled away, glowering. The other volunteers looked at Frank with stricken faces. "You were hellbent to hang him last night," he reminded them. But last night wasn't now and Tularosa lying unconscious was a totally different story from this killer at bay with guns in his fists. "Not me!" someone gasped, and they melted away.

Frank, squaring his shoulders, headed for Gurden's alone.

CHAPTER FOURTEEN

CHAVEZ, ON his horse and still toting his shotgun, angled into the street towing Frank's blue roan mare. Frank shook his head but the Mexican came on, grinding an elbow against his star.

"You stubborn damn peon," Frank growled at him, "stay out of this."

Chavez's teeth made a paler streak against his face. He cupped a hand beside his ear and Frank, glancing back, could see that the stage was about ready to roll. He pulled up to give Gurden a chance to get on it, if he was going to. "I'll keep 'em off your back," Chavez said, and rode off to put the horses behind the wall of the gun shop.

Frank's eyes prowled the face of the Opal. The drawstrings of time were tightening night's shadows, deepening their encroachment. No light showed back of Chip's windows. The Blue Flag was lit up and there were lights in other places, including the stage depot.

He saw Chavez striding toward him and sent him down to check the passengers. Gurden wasn't likely to be making the trip but Frank supposed he'd better wait until the stage had departed. Sending Chavez over there would probably keep the Mexican out of this.

As Frank waited he seemed to catch the mutter of hoofs. Quite a number of notions were keeping him company, few of a nature that would help him relax. The scattered lights of the town intensified the obscurity of blackness untouched by them. The face of Sandrey came into Frank's mind; he heard the driver climbing up to his seat, heard him kick off the brake and yell to his horses. There was the crack of the whip.

Chavez called, "No go," and Frank drew Church's gun. Gurden had had plenty of time to get set for this.

117

There was nothing Frank could do now but walk into it.

Queer how swiftly the street had been deserted. The whole town was watching him now back of windows, in the shelter of doorways. Frank didn't too bitterly blame them. He was paid to take chances.

He stepped out of the shadows. Alertly scanning the Opal's dark front, he saw a shape duck across the boards in front of the Blue Flag and snatch at the reins of a tied pinto horse. The paint sat back, but cursing and hauling finally overcame its stubbornness and its owner pulled it into the safety of the Blue Flag.

The breeze slapped at Frank's coat and was like cold fingers at his forehead and throat. Each step he took required a mental effort. He had always figured walking to be entirely automatic and so was doubly astonished to find each taken stride a victory, each yard of gained progress an unmistakable triumph. The doors of the Opal were just ahead of him now. Another six strides would put him onto the porch.

Arnold, leaving Frank after the lynching of Danny Settles, prowled the town by himself for a while, poking through alleys, peering in through the windows of locked-up buildings, touring Minnie's, the Flag, the stage barn and Fentriss'. He spent a good deal of time before reaching the conclusion which had been forced upon Frank—that in a place like South Fork no man, singlehanded, could hope to run down a free wheeling sidewinder who was making it his business to keep out of the way.

But the rancher had resources not available to Frank and, once he'd been convinced of the fruitlessness of this, he got his horse and left town. It was Arnold's departure the marshal heard when he went into Gurden's office after Sam Church.

Arnold came to the river and rode over the rattling planks of the bridge. Abbie Burks rode with him and he made good time. It was barely six when he swung down at headquarters and set up a yell which brought his crew on the run. Arnold stripped his horse, saddled a fresh one. Inside twenty minutes, armed and mounted, they were riding.

Sandrey, after Frank went down the stairs, stood for some minutes facing the door without seeing it. Not recalling Frank's instructions concerning the chair she went over to the chest and stared into the cracked glass above it. Turning, she moved over to the window, observing how near night had come while she'd been up here. She saw Frank's features against the mauve shadows, the striking force of his stare trying to hide its bleak hunger. While she did not particularly like what she had glimpsed, the fact remained that he'd been concerned enough to come up here in spite of what someone had obviously told him.

She was honest enough to admit the man attracted her, but she'd come to this place on a hunt for security which she'd learned to believe was more important to a woman than any other thing.

She took a turn about the room and tried to see this in a practical manner. She'd come through a hard school and knew how treacherous was emotion. She could have Frank, she was sure of it; but she wouldn't get security. He had no money and poor prospects of ever latching onto any. He had the worst kind of job imaginable, a constant nightmare of suspense which she had no intention of living with. What else did he know? Punching cattle? Thirty dollars a month! Maybe sixty for a man who finally got to be a range boss. It was impossible, she thought, and went and stood again by the window.

The shadows were deeper now. Lamplight gleamed from a dozen scattered openings and the street looked deserted. She heard the stage roll out of town and smelled its dust and saw a man dive out of the Flag and another step out of the gloom near the Opal as somebody cried, "No go."

Unaccountably her eyes stayed with the man approaching Gurden's. It was so dark she couldn't make out the batwings but as he stepped onto the Opal's porch Sandrey suddenly knew that this man was Frank Carrico.

By the chill in the air Frank knew he was sweating. He transferred Church's gun to his left hand and wiped his right against his leg and took the gun back into it again. He was positive Gurden was in there. Chip was not the kind to throw away an advantage.

Frank felt for the walk with the toe of his boot and stepped up and came onto the planks of the porch. The hair began to prickle at the back of his neck. He felt his stomach muscles knotting. Never in his life had he so badly wanted to run. His mouth was dry. He had to stop and consciously moisten it. "Chip—" He put more strength into his voice: "Chip, I'm coming in."

A loose blind flapped off yonder and somewhere a dog howled. Frank could hear the creak of timbers, the tiny groan of the breeze curling round the eaves. This would be a hard winter, it was coming too slow. The crackle of paper whirled away up some alley, every slap of its racket tearing into Frank like splinters.

He struck the doors and went through, crouching low. A gun roared dead ahead, sending up its bright muzzle flash. Frank stepped widely to the right even while it was fading, and again as the gun went still. It was all he could do to keep the squeeze off his trigger.

Quiet regathered its hold and outside there was a restive stamping of horses which bothered Frank vaguely without his quite knowing why. There was a mumble of voice sound too low to untangle. The strike of shod hoofs went away through the dust and the wind came again with a rattle of sashes. The stillness thickened about Frank and the steady working of the clock over the bar beat out the passing time with a measured rhythm which became intolerable. Someone's shout carried over the street but Frank stayed in his tracks and breathed through his mouth. It was inconceivable that Gurden would brace him without another gun hidden someplace. Frank had to know where it was.

Patience paid off. What sounded like a hat struck and

fell somewhere to the right of him. Strangely cool now Frank grinned. The failure of the ruse to draw his fire loosened other sounds. The man who had done the shooting let his breath out, moved a little. Frank placed him behind the bar and considered his guess confirmed when a glass shattered back of him. A second glass hit one of the batwings, fell to the floor without breaking and rolled.

"Hell," Mousetrap said, disgusted, "I got him."

The clock ticked on. Mousetrap, moving around behind the bar, began to poke the spent shells from his six-shooter. "Want I should light a lamp?"

Gurden, Frank thought, would have liked nothing better but wasn't about to invite Frank's fire by replying. He was the cagey one; not in the class with Draicup's gunfighter, but even a small rattlesnake can kill. Until Frank could locate Chip Gurden he was stymied. If he fired at the bouncer the saloon boss would get him. It was too sure to doubt. It was the reason why Gurden had fetched Mousetrap into this—a beautiful decoy. Expendable gun bait.

Frank could hear the small sounds of Mousetrap reloading. These quit, and wind scratched across the black paper of the roof. The sound of the clock continued to hammer Frank's skull. Impatience rowelled him. Strain made his eyes burn.

Mousetrap said, "Well—here goes," and dragged a match across the bar. Before his hand reached the end of its swipe Gurden was driving his lead at Frank, too frantic and too fast, gambling on percentage as he had done all his life.

The first slug cuffed Frank's hat. The next twitched the upturned collar of his jacket, pushing him out of his crouch. He squatted, spotting Gurden behind an overturned table. Frank took his time, caring nothing about Mousetrap, closing his mind to the lead slapping around him. When he finally squeezed trigger Gurden straightened and pitched headlong.

Frank spun then, covering the bar, emptying the gun in a definite pattern, exploding four cartridges before the wild clatter of the bouncer's spooked flight. He felt the air from a door and stood, locked in violence, hearing an outside gun beating into the echoes and a sudden high yell that went cracked in the middle and was drowned in other firing.

Chavez, of course. But Chavez had a sawed-off and this racket came from saddle guns. Frank, remembering the horse sounds, added it up as either Lassiter's trail crew or Will Church and his rustlers. It was like Will, shooting from the dark, not caring who or what he hit. Will, all right—he'd probably taken over the town. But where was Chavez?

More firing broke out, a scattered volley of shots, not as near as those last had been. Surprised yells and cursing. And now, staring out of the Opal's front windows, Frank could see by the flashes that Will Church had his hands full. Will's bunch had lost control of their trap and now they found themselves caught in its jaws. From both sides of the street, from broken windows and door holes and the black slots of alleys, guns were pinning them down in a murderous crossfire.

Frank refilled Church's empty pistol and now remembered the rifle Gurden had left behind the bar, the .44/40 Frank had dropped here last night. He got it and checked it and filled it from his pockets and ran back through the batwings. A dark blob of horses were being hustled from the livery. Levering a shell into position Frank dropped the man who had hold of them. From a squealing pitching tangle the horses broke in every direction. Will's men, running to mount them, were caught flat-footed in the street without cover.

"Throw down your guns!" Chavez, that was.

Frank couldn't see him but caught the lifting glint of a gun barrel of a Church man, and fired just above it and saw a bent shadow reel away from its surroundings. A shotgun went off *prr-u-mph!* with both barrels. Three shapes lurched out of that howling commotion, and the rest yelled for quarter.

Frank ran into the street and the wind whirling down

out of the north tore his hat away. Chavez came out of the gloom with his Greener, limping a little, paying no attention to Frank's allusions to his ancestry. "It's a wonder," Frank said, "they didn't cut you into gun patches!"

The Mexican grinned. "Nobody uses gun patches any more." He laughed, full-throated, pounding a fist at Frank's kidney. "We got 'em, boy—we done it!"

Frank followed him, tagging after the rest, fastening his jacket against the bite of the wind. Like Chavez he was excited, but sober too, his mind filled darkly with the remembrance of falling men; troubled, moreover, by a disquieting hunch the kingpin hand of this deal had not been played.

Krantz came up, catching and wringing Frank's hand, short of breath but vastly beaming in the satisfaction of achievement. "Ach," he wheezed, "vot a pizness! Who sayss shopkeepers von't fight!"

Frank nodded. "You done a bangup job." He disengaged his fist. His glance, still uneasy, kept a roving watch.

He was prowling the edge of things seen but not definable. He even had the weird notion someone was following him although nothing he tried disclosed any sign of this.

He pushed into the crowd surrounding Church's crew. "Chavez," he called, "where've you put Tularosa?"

The deputy frowned. "Didn't bag him." Worried stares replaced some of the grins in Frank's vicinity and the crowd's enthusiasm took a noticeable slump. "What's more," Chavez said, "we didn't lay hold of Will, either. All we got was the scrapin's."

Frank grabbed the first dozen men he could lay hands on and sent them off to round up the loose horses. "Get 'em all," he said grimly, "including those at the tie-racks. We don't stop this here we never will without more killing."

He was afraid in his own mind the time was already

past when shutting the stable was going to do much good. He detailed other men to close-herd the prisoners and sent Chavez over to keep an eye on the jail. Bernie, Krantz and Wolverton he put to gathering weapons. "Go through the Opal, too, while you're at it. Take everything over to your place, Krantz, and—"

"Say, Frank," one of the unconscripted townsmen called, "this bunch of sidewinders Church fetched down on us looks just about ready for a jig on a rope."

Frank turned on him, furious. "Next feller mentions rope is going to jail!"

The man slunk away. Frank got some hard looks. He considered the prisoners but turned away without speaking. They probably had no more idea where their boss was than Frank had. If Will had got a horse he might be halfway to Dallas.

Frank looked for the pair Chavez had left by Bernie's but the passage was empty. The blacksmith, coming up, tapped Frank on the shoulder. "If you're lookin' fer them broncs, I seen Ben leadin' them off with some others. Boys're holdin' 'em all in one of them pens back of the livery."

Frank eyed the Sharps the smith was toting and told him to go over and see that they stayed there. He looked around him, still worried, and was about to head for the hotel to check on Sandrey when he thought he saw movement in the slot separating Ben's place from the barber shop. When he looked more carefully he guessed he had been mistaken. No reason for Will to be back there—nor anyone else, he told himself sourly. Keyed up like he was a man could see just about anything. He went on a few steps then swung around and cut over.

He stopped a moment in the deeper gloom of Ben's overhang, thinking the rifle might be more of a nuisance than help in close quarters. While he was debating abandoning it he got the feeling again of eyes boring into him and looked edgily around, discovering nothing.

Keeping hold of the Winchester, Frank stepped into

the alley. In the murk he paused, listening, testing the place for whatever it might tell him. But with all that wind he finally gave up.

Lifting Will's pistol from his holster he again stepped ahead. Midway through it occurred to him young Church might have arranged to play decoy on the chance of pulling Frank into a bind. This didn't seem too likely. He would have had to got hold of Tularosa; seeking and finding that fellow weren't the same. The man was like a damn wolf!

Frank stopped in his tracks. He'd heard nothing ahead of him or anything behind but the safety mechanism of primitive instincts was sounding an alarm.

He gripped the pistol with tightening fingers, taking comfort in the feel of it. Bending, he put the rifle down, trying from this angle to catch a larger view. He didn't discover anything and, straightening, went on, doubly conscious of the risk of sending a stray tin clattering. He couldn't be sure he had reloaded. Ten steps from the end of the passage he decided it was better to be certain than sorry.

He crouched again, forced to bring both hands to the task. The gun had five rounds in it. He glanced once more front and back and had just flicked open the loading gate to put one under the hammer when sudden awareness of danger brought his eyes up, rounding, frantic.

All his reflexes locked, seeing that shape so startlingly in front of him. He presently realized the fellow had his back to him, had ducked into the slot to conceal himself from something else. Even as this came to Frank the man in front of him wheeled and froze, stiff with shock.

Now that Frank could see in this gloom, enough reflected light reached the man from the street to reveal Will Church in the startled blob of those gone-awry features.

Church, recovering, stumbled backward, striving to reach shelter even as he brought up his hand. With Frank desperately scrabbling to get his gun into action,

Church backed out of the alley, the walls briefly lighting to the flash of his fire.

The double concussion hammered Frank to the
ground. It was like a white-hot iron had touched him.
After that he lost track. He knew a gun was still pounding but he didn't feel the bullets. Too numbed, he supposed; and got his hands on the pistol.

He pushed his chest off the ground and there was
nothing to shoot at. Will was down, writhing, groaning.
Frank thought the fool had shot himself—until his widening stare found the girl.

He licked cracked lips. He had to shape them twice
before her name got past the dryness of his throat. Then
he thought she didn't hear it.

But this was shock, delayed reaction. Her head came
around as he was getting to his feet. She dropped Fles'
gun and rushed into Frank's arms.

He had told her to stay in the hotel, to keep her door
shut, but "Sandrey—Sandrey!" was all he could say. She
seemed content; and it came over Frank that achieving
social acceptance in the eyes of Kimberland and people
like the Churches lacked a long way of being as important to a man as hooking up with a competent woman.

Now the crowd drawn by the shots was all around
them, shoving and jostling for a look at Will Church.
Sandrey said, hanging onto Frank, "When I couldn't
stand worrying about this fellow any longer I left the
hotel. I saw Will Church slip into this alley. Then I saw
Frank starting over here. I knew he was after Church.
I had that road scout's gun; I went round the other
side." She paused to say thoughtfully, "Church didn't
know about Frank, I guess. Time Church got to the
back I wasn't far off, heading toward him. I expect he
heard me, got rattled, ducked back and saw Frank."

"I was loadin' his pistol," Frank said disgustedly.

Sandrey squeezed his arm. "I didn't know what to do.
I was practically on top of him when Church brought
his gun up. I guess I kind of went out of my head. Next
I knew, Church was down and—"

"Yah," said Councilman Krantz. "Frank couldn't done no different. Justifiable homicide. Ve got a goot marshal. Ve goin' to raise his pay—"

"Give the star to Chavez," Frank said. "I'm getting hitched."

The storekeeper's shrewd eyes jumped to Sandrey and back again. "Veddingk bells, iss it? Ve vill gif you a bonus!"

Frank went over and bent down beside Will, others crowding around. Will Church wasn't going to make it. Frank got up. "Expect we could use that bonus, me and Sandrey, but—" Frank broke off. "Where is she?"

The whole crowd looked around, everyone staring toward the mouth of the passage. The pit of Frank's belly knotted and the cold got into the marrow of his bones. Backing into the comparative brightness of the street were two locked shapes.

Tularosa!

"Keep back if you want this frail to stay healthy!"

The man's left arm was wrapped around Sandrey's waist, making a shield of her. Frank was still holding the loaded pistol but might just as well have tried to attack with his teeth. As the outlaw backed into the shadows, Frank, unable longer to contain himself, started after them. The girl redoubled her struggles, making the gunfighter lurch with her efforts. Flame, like a snake, darted out of his hand. Frank, flung half around, crashed into the wall. When he got himself off it his left arm hung useless. He was barely in time to see Tularosa disappear with the girl in the direction of the river.

Frank stumbled into the street. Someone yelled from the darkness: "Arnold—Arnold!" and a thunder of hoofs swept over the bridge. Cut off, Tularosa came dragging the girl back, trying to make it to the livery. Frank saw Arnold's crew riding hellity-larrup but it was plain Tularosa would get under cover before they'd be able to come into range. The blacksmith with his Sharps was somewhere back of the stable but this was Frank's job and that girl out there was Sandrey.

"Now, Frank—now!" she cried, and hauled her feet up, folding. The full weight of her, hanging from the killer's arm, pulled him off balance and he had to let go of her.

Frank fired two shots and saw Tularosa stagger. He fell onto a knee and Frank emptied his gun.

Krantz came up, fairly bursting with excitement. "A goot marshal! Py Gott! Ve gif you two bonus!"

Thirty Notches

by
Brad Ward

FOR
Hank
Martha
Sandra
Doreen
Judy
Debra
and
Bonnie Erlene
O'NEIL

ONE

For the slender young woman on the high seat of the Conestoga wagon the nameless river before her was just one more in the seemingly endless parade of obstacles that had marked the passage West of her family; and she felt the bitter sting of tears. She was a tall, fine-featured woman nearing thirty, her face still smooth and white of skin despite the merciless glare of the prairie sun and the savage fury of the winds. There was strength in the firm fullness of her shoulders, and her rolled-up sleeves exposed capable arms. She gripped the hard leather reins tightly, with hands that were rough and red from exposure and hard work. But it was a long time since she had given consideration to the niceties of complexion and hands. Now, looping the reins about the footbrake handle, she pushed back a stray wisp of silver-blond hair and stood up from the spring seat.

The river had cut a deep channel across the flatlands, and now lay, a tan ribbon of muddy water, some seventy feet wide, moving turgidly. A mile or so downstream a stand of cottonwoods puffed green against the endless blue of the sky, and across the water to the northwest the faint blue smudge of mountains lifted the horizon. Otherwise, the prairie lay flat and unmarked in every direction, unbroken by even the silhouette of a tree. The vastness, the heart-aching loneliness of this land smote the woman, not for the first time, and once more her hand made the futile little gesture of brushing away the strand of hair that had fallen over her sweaty forehead.

There was movement behind her, in the body of the wagon, and she turned absently, her mind intent on the problem of the river, to check on the baby that lay in the packing-case crib behind the seat. A girl of twelve or thirteen came forward to stand there, her cotton-white hair shining in the sunlight. Her round tanned face was thoughtful and unsmiling. The baby moved restlessly, its cry a soft sound lost in the empty silence of the prairie.

"Change him for me, Sissy," Lydia Vail said in her gentle, soft-toned voice.

"All right, Mom." The girl picked up the child, balanc-

5

ing him in her left arm, gathered up a clean white cloth from a line strung the length of the wagon, and then clambered over the seat with a display of white cotton "jennies." The woman smiled and touched the girl's soft yellow-white hair.

"I don't know what I'd do without you, Joanie," Lydia said. Then, frowning, she lifted her head and stared at the flat expanse of grasslands about them. There was despair in her tired eyes, but she kept it to herself. Far behind them a thin mushrooming cloud of dust was rising. Lydia studied it for a moment, thinking perhaps it might be another wagon; then she shook her head. There was not enough density to the dust cloud for that; it was her guess that it was a single rider, moving across the plains toward the river ford.

From where the Conestoga wagon stood on the high bank, the ground dropped sharply to the river some thirty feet below. Although the rutted tracks it had been following did not end here, Lydia mistrusted the steepness of the bank, the slow movement of the mud-thick stream. She placed one hand over her eyes to shade them, while she studied the bank on the far side. The wagon track came out there, and angled on toward the distant smudge of blue mountains.

For a moment, despair held her tightly; then Lydia Vail shook her head and the strength of her jaw asserted itself "I'll have to try it," she said, half to herself.

From the bed of the wagon came a raucous snore. Joanie Vail looked up from the baby quickly. Her small brown hands had completed the change, and the baby lay contentedly in his sister's arms.

"Why don't Pa wake up?" Joanie asked.

Lydia Vail closed her eyes for a moment, then shook her head again. " 'Doesn't'—not 'don't,' " she corrected, quickly. "Your father is sick, Joanie."

The girl's chin set in firm lines. "Drunk, you mean," she said. "Mom, it ain't fair—him lettin' you do all the work—"

The lines in the woman's face deepened, and she shook her head. "Joanie, you're too young to understand. I won't have you saying such things about your father. He tries—God knows he tries—"

"Maybe he don't—doesn't—try hard enough!" the girl returned. She shook her head rebelliously. "Pa's always drunk. That's why we fell behind. The others'll be 'way

6

ahead of us—maybe there won't be no more Government land for us, an'—"

The little girl's voice droned into silence as there came a stirring from the wagon bed, and a haggard-faced man got up from the pallet he had been sleeping on and stood on unsteady legs.

"Lydia—Lydia girl—" His voice was lost, almost frightened. Then he saw his wife in the waning afternoon sunlight. He passed a shaking hand before his eyes and moved uncertainly through the narrow aisle that ran down the middle of the Conestoga wagon.

"I—I thought you were gone, Lydia," he said, falteringly. Beneath a four-day stubble of beard the weak handsomeness of his face shone clearly. He ran a hand through the dark mass of his hair, which he wore long. There were harsh yellow-gray streaks in the smooth locks now, Lydia saw. "It's a nightmare I always awake from. It's what I deserve, you know."

"Hush, Paul," the woman said gently, and touched his face with one hand. "Joanie is listening."

The man blinked his eyes to clear them, then laid an unsteady hand on his daughter's silver hair. She looked up.

"It's all right, Pa," she said. "Mom's makin' it all right."

"Sure she is, sweetheart," Paul Vail said. He tried to climb over the wide seat, but instead he sat down suddenly in the bed of the wagon, bumping the crib.

The baby began to cry, and Joanie bent swiftly over him. "Now see what you went an' did!" she stormed.

"Joanie, I want you to stop talking to your father like that," Lydia said resignedly.

Paul Vail got up, steadied himself, and climbed awkwardly over into the seat. "Never mind, Lydia," he said, softly. He managed a smile and shook his head. "Joanie, I apologize for giving you a damned fool for a father. You'd be better off without me."

The little girl turned to meet his eyes. "All right, Pa. You don't have to say it no more."

Lydia turned wearily. Her usually soft voice hardened. "Joanie, you're not too big to spank. I've had enough."

"Now, Lydia," Paul remonstrated, then shook his head and suddenly broke into anguished sobbing, hiding his face in his hands.

For an instant the girl stared with a stricken look into

her mother's face, then picked up the baby and moved back into the wagon.

The man broke off and laughed, harshly. "Self-pity is a damnable thing, Lydia," he said brokenly. "I've found more than my share. The child is right, though. I don't have to say it any more. You've heard all my excuses, all my lies. I've broken my word not to drink— How many times have I broken it, Lydia?"

The woman sat down on the seat, stirred as always by the weakness inside him. Her hands went to either side of his face, turned it toward her, and then she kissed him. "I love you, Paul," she said. "Nothing else matters." For a long moment she held him there, tight against her.

He drew back slowly. "I am sorry, Lydia. I'll make you no more promises I can't keep—but I will try."

"That's all you have to do, Paul," she answered. "Just try. Not just for me, but for Joanie and the baby—and yourself."

"Myself!" He laughed bitterly. "Of course you're right —as always." He straightened uncertainly on the seat, stared around at the wilderness. "Where are the others?"

"They've gone ahead. I couldn't keep up with them, Paul. Rogers said they would camp beyond the river. He said there would be a fork in the trail, and they would make camp there. It can't be far ahead if we push on."

Paul nodded, then stared at the river. He climbed up the high side of the wagon to look both up and downstream, then shook his head. "No help for it but to cross here," he said finally, climbing back down. "This must be the ford. We'll be all right if we keep 'em headed straight across for the other side."

He unwound the reins from the brake handle, and clucked to the team. The off mare shied at the abrupt decline of the bank, then headed down, forelegs braced. Paul Vail kicked the brake free, wavering in the seat as the wagon lurched forward but catching himself before he fell. The leather-lined brakes squealed shrilly on the steel-tired wheels. The horses made the steep downgrade, and the wagon creaked and jolted after them, then leveled out as they entered the brown water.

At first all went well, and the team pointed for the far shore. Here, where a sand bar had been built by eddying currents, the stream was shallow, and the wagon rolled steadily forward. Then, without warning, the off mare went under, and the Conestoga lurched with her falling weight. Scrambling, she found her feet and surged up, throwing the other mare out of stride. The wagon jarred over slick water-hidden rocks, slid sickeningly to the left, and the front wheel sank into a deep hole. As the wagon pitched crazily, Paul Vail lost his balance and fell heavily forward, striking his head against the rough iron of the brake handle. Lydia saw his eyes glaze, and the ugly red mark across the tender skin of his forehead.

Vail's fall with the reins jerked the team to the right, and for a moment the Conestoga careened wildly. Then the woman's strong hands caught the reins away from his grasp. As he shook his head dizzily and came erect, holding to the high front of the wagon bed for support, the frightened team plunged and bucked, trying to free the left front wheel from the hole into which it had plunged.

Paul Vail made a desperate lunge to take the reins from Lydia's grasp, and the heavy part of his forearm struck her across the face. Behind them, the girl screamed.

"Pa—the water's comin' in!"

Vail cursed, fighting the rearing team. The wagon tipped farther as the wheel dug deeper into the soft muck of the river bed. Lydia sat very still, a livid red mark across her cheek where his arm had struck her. Her face was white.

"Paul—we'll turn over," she said quietly, fighting hysteria.

"Damn it—I'm doing my best!" he yelled back savagely. Fright had sobered him, and he screamed at the team, trying to force them into united action. The horses, caught in the steady pressure of the river, disregarded the man's frantic cries and jerking of the reins and fought to get free of the restraining harness. The wagon rocked sickeningly, and the left rear wheel dropped into the hole. Water rippled over the high side, drenching Lydia. Joanie screamed again.

The sluggish torrent of the mud-heavy river pushed them to one side; it was all that kept the wagon from turning over. For one long, terrifying instant they balanced there, and for Lydia Vail it was too much. She covered her face with her hands; sobs racked her.

The desperateness of the situation and the sound of her sobs drove Paul Vail to a frenzy. "Shut up, damn it!" he yelled. His hands jerked on the reins, and the terrified team swung to the left in a movement that could throw them into the river.

"Paul, look out!" the woman cried out.

She stood up, and tried to grab the reins from him. He fought against her, his face gone wild, his voice shrilling curses at her. Then a horseman standing in his stirrups plunged through the water beside the wagon. The woman had a glimpse of a dark-skinned face, set and hard, and of sand-hued eyes that burned brightly, and then the rider swung in, and his hard right fist clubbed at Paul Vail's head. The blow shook him, and his mouth opened. Then the stranger's hand shot straight in, and Paul Vail dropped to the floor of the wagon.

"Pull the team in—hard!" the man yelled harshly. His light-colored eyes burned at her. "I'll give you a hand."

Lydia caught the reins and pulled back with all her strength. The stranger rode up beside the team, caught at the bridle of the off mare, and surged back in his saddle. Under the touch of the man's hand, the mare pulled back. The second horse shied, then backed. For an instant they held there, and the woman heard the newcomer's calm, unexcited voice talking to the frightened animals. They quieted quickly, standing bellydeep, the force of the slow-moving river pushing against them.

"All right—do as I say!" the stranger yelled back. "Give them a little slack, pull to the right—not too hard. Easy now!"

Beside Lydia, Paul stirred, put a hand to his head. His face was ashen. Then he was caught in the grip of helpless nausea, and bent double over the side of the wagon. White-faced, the woman fought to hold the team, urged them slowly to the right. She heard the stranger's encouraging call, saw him bend to lead the team to the right.

For another instant the wagon teetered there; thtn the team caught hold and their weight turned the front wheels to the right. The body of the heavy Conestoga rose, the wheels turned, and the straining team pulled it back to the level sand of the ford.

The rest of the crossing was simple, although Lydia let the stranger lead the team. They reached the far side, and the man on horseback angled them up the steep bank. They caught purchase, strained—and with a loud creaking the Conestoga rolled up and over. Behind them the unruffled river rolled quietly on, a tan ribbon across the face of brown eternity. Lydia shuddered, then gave her attention to the vomiting man still bent over the side.

The stranger rode up. She got a better look at him then. He rode a bay gelding, whose glossy hide was coated with grime where the river mud had fouled it. The horse moved easily, and the rider sat the saddle without effort or strain. He was a tall man, clad in brown trousers tucked into the tops of black leather boots that reached to just below his knees. His black frocktailed coat hung open, and a frill-fronted white shirt glinted in the sunlight. A black shoestring tie and a white flat-crowned Stetson completed his garb except for the black-leather gun belt that sagged across the flatness of his lower stomach. A heavy-handled revolver thrust up on his left-hand side. It lay across his thigh within easy reach of his right hand. His shoulders were broad, but he gave the impression of slimness. It was partly due to the narrow length of his dark face, she decided. His nose was prominent, with a white scar over its high bridge. His light-hued eyes gazed at her evenly, and she thought it would take a great deal to excite or disturb them. His chin was broad and square and, despite the fashion of the year, clean-shaven. There was a touch of gray at either temple, and when he pulled off his Stetson after looking at her intently for a moment, she saw that his dark hair was turning white. It came as a shock to her, for his face was unlined; his age might have been anything between thirty and forty-five.

The man looked at Paul Vail's shaken figure, and his face changed, hardened perceptibly. Vail looked at him from bleared eyes and shook his head.

"I was doing my best," he said defensively.

"Your best to spill the two of you into the river," the stranger said. His voice was flat, almost without inflection. "Didn't you see the markers set out to mark the ford?"

"No, I didn't see them," Paul answered. He shook his head again to clear it.

The stranger was looking at Lydia; she sensed rather than saw the interest she aroused in him. How long had it been since a man had looked quietly, intently at her like that? There was no disrespect in his eyes. He saw the livid red mark where Paul's arm had struck her, and she saw his eyes narrow. Involuntarily, her hand went to cover the mark.

"An accident," she said. "I—I bumped myself."

11

The stranger moved his shoulders. "None of my business," he said. Then: "This is poor country to be traveling alone."

"There are others ahead of us," Lydia said.

Paul Vail looked from his wife to the stranger. His soft-edged smile moved his mouth. "I'm sorry I panicked like that," he said. "Thank you for what you did. I would have tipped the lot of us into the river. My name's Paul Vail—this is my wife, Lydia. We're aiming to take up some of that Government land west of here."

The stranger moved, stared about him. His eyes hesitated once on the distant blue mountains, then moved steadily back. "Nesters," he said. "I wish you luck. Wyoming's a big place. I hope there's room for the trouble it will hold."

Paul Vail straightened slowly. "I don't understand you."

"Perhaps not," the stranger said.

Behind Lydia, Joanie moved, pressed close to stare at the mounted man. "Who is he, Mom?" she whispered audibly.

The stranger saw the girl, and his broad mouth softened. His smile changed his expression, broke the harsh flat planes of his dark face. *That's why he doesn't smile often,* Lydia thought. *He has to hide the softness inside him.*

The man's sand-colored eyes moved from the girl to the woman, held there. Then he nodded, almost reluctantly. "You're safe enough now. But I'd press on and join the rest of your party as soon as you can."

He turned the horse. Paul Vail called, "Wait." The stranger turned in the saddle. Paul Vail said: "We haven't thanked you properly. You haven't told us your name."

The stranger's face went to stonelike stillness. His smile hardened into something almost menacing. Then he said: "No, I haven't. Goodbye."

He touched the gelding with his spurred heels, and the horse jumped forward, settling in the course of a half-dozen running strides to a steady trot. Swiftly then, the horse and rider receded, a thin miasma of dust veiling them.

Paul watched him go. Then he shook his head. "Good riddance," he said.

Lydia said quietly, "He might have saved our lives, Paul."

Vail turned to look at her. Hard lines ran down his

handsome face. There was a swollen place along his jaw where the stranger's fist had struck at him. He touched it gently. "You're right—just as you're always right," he said, half bitterly. "Did it ever occur to you, Lydia, that a man could get tired of being always in the wrong?"

Vail bent forward, took up the reins, kicked the brake free. The wagon began to roll on toward the distant mountains. The baby began to cry.

"He's wet," Joanie said. "I tried to hold him up, but when Pa drove into the mudhole I fell with him. He ain't hurt."

"It's all right, Joanie," Lydia said slowly. "I'll change him."

The woman climbed over the seat, into the rear of the wagon. Joanie followed her back to the built-in bunk that stood to one side. The baby lay there. Lydia picked him up, quieting him. Joanie looked past her, through the opening up front where a narrowed horizon bobbed ahead of them. Paul Vail was huddled forlornly on the seat, one hand to his face.

. . *He's feeling sorry for himself,* the woman thought, and then was instantly ashamed of it. Joanie was looking at the receding haze that marked the passage of the lone horseman.

"I don't care what Pa says," the girl said rebelliously. "I like *him*."

For a moment Lydia stared out across the rolling flatlands ahead of them. She thought, *And the man liked me.* Then the baby began crying again, and her swift, gentle hands began to remove his wet garments.

ball closed his eyes. Fifteen years ago . . . Then a gun was a workshop, even though it carried with a strength ... fascinating sense of power. And it made the difference between a reckless-faced cowhand and a hard-faced man ...

TWO

The man on the bay gelding rode a half-mile before reining in atop a rising hummock. Turning in the saddle, he looked back. Through the thin shimmering veil of dust that marked his passage he saw the heavy wagon lumbering on. For a moment he watched it, a thoughtful frown between his eyes. Then a wry smile bent his mouth and he turned and rode on.

His name was James Ridgely Harbin, and he came from Texas. He was sufficient unto himself as few men can be, and his name and face were known wherever he roamed. But that was a distinction entirely unsolicited and unwelcome, for recognition usually meant only one thing to him: trouble.

Being completely honest with himself, he knew that the fault lay primarily with himself. But it was a fault he could not correct. He considered this now, as he rode on, and his face, for once unguarded, assumed grave lines. Instinctively, his right hand moved down to rest on the handle of his revolver, but the hard warmth of it did not reassure him. His long fingers moved restlessly over the black thornwood grips, and he counted the carefully grooved notches he had cut there. Fifteen notches on the right plate, ten on the left. Twenty-five in all. And for each one of them a man had died in some frontier town.

As he touched the grooves, he spoke names aloud. Slowly, and only twice did he hesitate. He tried to conjure up faces to match each name, but it was getting harder to do. Half of them he had hardly known at all. One he had never seen before in his life until the violent five minutes that ended in swift gunplay and the man lying dead at Harbin's feet.

In fifteen years twenty-five dead men rode the trail with him. It was a thought to make any man pause and think. There was a point where the wild kid with a gun had become a gunman, just as there was a point where the gunman had become a legend. And James Ridgely Harbin had passed both points long ago.

What had happened to that boy of fifteen years ago? The thought pressed in hard upon him, and Ridge Harbin

14

half closed his eyes. Fifteen years ago . . . Then a gun was a work-tool, even though it carried with it a strangely fascinating sense of danger. And it made the difference between a freckle-faced cowhand and a hard-faced man who wore his gun as casually as he wore his hat. Ridge remembered men like that, remembered the odd chill that had struck through him when he read the hell in their eyes, and remembered, too, that for a week he had left his gun in his bedroll. But there were better memories, of the jokes of his fellow riders, the odd warmth of being a part of a working crew. He was Johnny Harbin then, a kid with dreams in his eyes, and a softness about his mouth that had been ground away.

Riding into the home ranch in the teeth of a blizzard, the warmth of the bunkhouse windows shining into the night. The man-smells of the bunkhouse, the acrid stink of blackened pipes, the sharper bite of brown-paper cigarettes. The feeling of belonging—that was the hardest thing to forget. The knowledge there were men to side with you, men who would pull you out of a hole, men who would share your fun and your moments of high loneliness. Men like you, thinking the same thoughts, doing the same things, and today a drudgery to ride through so tomorrow and payday and town would be that much closer.

A hard life, filled with harsh realities; but a boy could dream. The rough edges wore away. You fought and you laughed—and that was another important thing. You knew how to laugh. And anger was quick, harsh, and violent—and gone as quickly as it came. Hard fists and the salty taste of blood, and the pain of a mashed lip and sore knuckles, and the man who had given the one and taken the other would ride beside you the next day and you would both laugh and feel a little ashamed of what had happened between you, and it would be forgotten; but the deeper feeling of friendship, of sharing a deeper bond, would not be forgotten.

But that was fifteen years ago. That was so long ago it seemed like a dream. A dream that had turned into an ugly nightmare of reality when you remembered the quarrel that fists could not settle. The sudden realization that the smoking gun in your fist had dropped a man dead at your feet. You stared into his filming eyes, and you read the shock and fear there, the stark, terrible fear, and your stomach turned over. A gun wasn't a tool any more. A

15

gun wasn't a part of the romantic swagger that made you feel grown up. A gun was a terrible, frightening thing, but you couldn't throw it away, you couldn't hide it among the few belongings in your bedroll—because you would need it again, and again, and again. . . . And somehow, any way you can, you had to keep your self-respect, and that meant never take the easy way. Never kill for money, and always, always fight down the growing sense of power that grips you with each dangerous man you down. Fight the killer instinct, keep it from making you into a kill-crazy animal like others you've seen.

He dropped his hand away from the gun and eased his weight in the saddle. Think of something else. Think of the women you've known. Think of the places you've seen. Think of anything but the men you have killed. It was a habit that Ridge Harbin shared with other men of the gun. But he used it consciously, and only after deliberately reminding himself of the things behind him. He had taken a penance upon himself that he would never forget the men he killed, that he would remember them and their names as long as he lived. For it was the only bulwark that stood between him and the callousness of the born killer. And that he could not honestly consider himself such was all that kept him going.

He admitted this now, and his wry smile came again. Then he shook his head. A man's quickness with his hands, his practiced deftness with a gun, his constant vigilance against surprise, his unrelenting instinct to strike back when hurt—these made the one difference between him and other men, and he would admit of no others.

Think of something else. Think of the women you've known. . . .

Think of the woman in the Conestoga wagon, and the weak-faced man who had almost killed them both. Think of her face, the strength of her shining through, the level eyes, the odd little gesture of brushing away the strand of hair from her forehead. Think of her, and the wagon, and the young girl and the baby; think of all of them, and envy the man who was too stupid to appreciate what he had.

Envy him the ease of sleeping at night. Envy him the knowledge he could put something off until tomorrow with reasonable certainty he'd be around to tend to it. Envy him the love of the woman who rode on the seat

16

beside him. Envy him, and hate him, too. Hate him and all his stolid kind for being what you're not. . . .

Harbin broke the thought off there. Bitterness was a sea a man could drown in.

The bay gelding moved steadily along the rutted tracks, and the blue hills grew higher. The sun began to edge down behind them, and the purple shadows of evening began to spread out from their base. The first coolness of night swept over the flatlands with the breath of the desert, and the man and the horse became darker shadows moving into the gathering dusk.

An hour after sunset, Harbin saw the first twinkling light of a campfire ahead of him, and soon afterward a score or more scattered some distance apart. For a moment he reined in and sat the saddle. Fires meant men, and there would be someone there who might know him. He accepted this as a logical possibility, and balanced it in his mind. Then he shrugged and urged the horse on once more.

The fires grew larger, and he approached them directly, riding easily, his left hand holding the reins high, his right hand casually across his lap. He saw the flicker of the firelight on the side of a heavy wagon, caught movement ahead of him, and reined in.

"One man—alone," he called out. "Traveling through."

A deep man's voice replied, "All right, ride in."

Harbin stepped the gelding into the outlying circle of light and pulled up. A big thickset man awkwardly holding a rifle in his hands moved toward him. The man studied him for a moment, then nodded.

"All right," the man with the rifle said. "You can ride through."

A woman stood in front of the fire, stirring a kettle. Harbin caught the smell of stew cooking. He eased his weight in the saddle.

"Will a dollar buy me a meal?" he asked.

"Hard money?" the homesteader demanded quickly. "Not scrip?"

"One cartwheel," Harbin said, and fished into his vest pocket. He brought out a silver dollar, and held it up so that the firelight caught it.

The man with the rifle looked at the coin, then at Harbin again. His smile came then. "Ma—set out an extra plate. We got company." He hesitated, then: "Light down an' eat, stranger."

17

Harbin climbed from the gelding, and moved toward the fire. The homesteader moved ahead of him. The man's acceptance had been final, for he set the rifle against one big wheel of the wagon.

"You'll want to wash up," he said. He led the way forward to the front of the wagon. A tin basin was set out on the tongue of the wagon, and a dirty towel hung beside it. Harbin removed his coat, rolled up his sleeves, and washed his face and hands. But he stepped across the wagon tongue first so that he could face the other man while he washed. If the homesteader noticed his action, he did not show it.

"Ain't meanin' to be inhospitable, stranger," the man said. "But these is hard times. Strangers ain't always welcome—because sometimes trouble rides their tail."

"You don't have to apologize to me," Harbin said slowly. He dried himself with the towel and put his coat back on.

"Hell, I ain't never been like that until now," the homesteader said. "A man rides in back home, you don't go wavin' a gun at him; you just ask him to light down an' stay a spell. Out here things are different."

"Not things," Harbin said. "Just people."

The other man frowned. "Yeah," he returned slowly. "Yeah. Look, my name's Palen, Hal Palen. We're from Michigan. Tired of farmin' somebody else's land. We've come west to find our own land."

Harbin said: "You don't have to follow me around. I'm not going to steal anything."

Palen frowned harder. "Hell, I never thought you was." He laughed, but his laugh broke off uncertainly. "Look, I'm tryin' to be friendly—"

"Sometimes it doesn't pay," Harbin answered soberly. "You don't know me, Palen. Maybe you wouldn't want to know me. I'll eat and ride on."

Something about the inflectionless tone of his voice held Palen for an instant. Then he nodded, too quickly. "Sure," he said. "Sure."

Harbin noticed that when the homesteader moved back toward the fire, it was to stand beside the rifle. Harbin had that effect on men, and it didn't always amuse him as it did now. The woman spoke then, and he went to her and accepted a plate of stew and a chunk of cornbread. He moved back from the fire and squatted down to eat. The homesteader and his wife watched him, and seemed reluctant to eat their own food. Their uneasiness disturbed him. He ate rapidly, and stood up.

"It was very good," he said. He laid the silver dollar on the plate and returned to the horse. The gelding took his weight, shied from the fire, then moved steadily into the darkness. Harbin didn't pause or look back. They would be standing beside their wagon in silence, listening for his hoofbeats to die away. Fear lay on them, fear of him; and Harbin realized that once again it was his own fault.

Why hadn't he just accepted the man's eager friendliness? The thought came sharply and unbidden. The answer was too clear: He couldn't afford the weakness of even a casual friendship. No man with twenty-five notches on his gun could. The slightest regard he tolerated for another man weakened him by that much. If a man took time to stop and think before he used his gun, that man's chances were lessened by that much. A man without friends held the advantage; there could never be any doubt in his mind. He could kill, unhesitatingly, passionlessly. . . .

Ridge Harbin frowned the thought away and rode into the darkness. He avoided the other campfires, circled them, and chose the right fork of the trail. It angled sharply toward the mountains which were looming closer now. A few miles farther on, where several rutted trails converged, the trail became a road. Harbin followed it until an hour before midnight. He had reached the first swelling rise of ground at the base of the mountains, and he left the road to ride some distance away before dismounting. He unsaddled the gelding, spread his bedroll after hobbling the horse, and lay down. Slowly the stiffness left his legs and back, and he relaxed, his hands behind his head, his eyes considering the stars that shone overhead. Their cold, dispassionate light held him, and for once his own bitterness was allayed.

There was no reason for it, but he felt good—as if this day had brought something new and pleasant to him. That happened all too seldom. He closed his eyes and thought back.

The day had been the same as any other of recent weeks. Aside from the incident of the nester wagon, there had been nothing—the nester wagon. The woman with the silver-blond hair and the work-reddened hands. One more casual meeting, without purpose and without significance, but he would remember it as he did others. The time he had ridden into San Antonio in the rain. Warm, thick rain beating against him, and the shine of lights across a muddy street. As if the lights were for him alone, welcoming him out of the darkness. Nothing had happened that night; he didn't even remember the hotel room where he had spent it. But for a little while he had sensed something happening that pleased him. And seeing the woman this afternoon had somehow been akin to that feeling.

. .I wonder how she would have looked if I'd told her I was Ridge Harbin? He opened his eyes and frowned up at the stars. Then he closed his eyes, and with the facility of a man who has spent most of his life on the trails between towns, he fell instantly asleep.

Once during the night he awakened suddenly, his right hand drawing his heavy revolver before his eyes had opened. For an instant he lay still, having rolled onto his left side. Then he caught the faint sound that had awakened him: the distant drumming of hoofs on the trail. The sound grew louder, and he distinguished the beat of two sets of hoofs; then the horses went past on the road and the sound of their passage diminished. Harbin sheathed his gun, rolled back, and slipped easily again into sleep.

He was awake before dawn. He rolled his bedding, found that his horse had ambled a few yards away in search of better forage, slipped the hobbles off the animal, and led it back. He had been an hour on the road before faint pink streaks lightened the sky, and by sunup he was deep into the mountain passages.

The road led across rolling benchland and finally cut between two mountain shoulders and climbed sharply for a distant pass. The gelding maintained his steady gait, but it was midmorning before horse and rider reached the summit. There Harbin reined in to rest the horse.

From the far side of the rocky pass, the road shot in sharp cutbacks down the steeper side of the mountain before leveling out on the plains far below. At the bottom of the sharp slope lay a broken, tip-tilted land that stretched outward for more than a mile, and from the height of the pass Harbin could see where the road wound through the brakes. Far across the plainsland lay an almost indistinguishable smudge that Harbin recognized as the flat silhouette of a prairie town. He rolled a cigarette with easy movements of his long-fingered hands, and considered the distant cowtown.

It had been three years since he had left Red Rock country, Harbin thought. What had brought him back? He frowned at the glowing tip of his cigarette. There was no reason: one road was as good as another; one cattle-town was the same as the next. He would stay in Red Rock for a few days, try to build a bigger stake, and then ride on. Maybe Red Rock would prove luckier than the last town he had hit, but he wouldn't stay long. His mouth was a straight grim line. Keep moving; never stay long enough in any town to get acquainted, to make friends, to have any regrets at leaving. It was a necessary part of his life to be a drifter like the many others who called no range "home."

Red Rock wouldn't have changed much, he thought. Cow country was always the same, from the Rio Grande to the Canadian border; and the men who lived on it were much alike. In the two decades since the War Between the States, and especially since the completion of the Union Pacific fifteen years ago, the cattlemen had come into their own. At this very moment it was estimated there were more than eight million head of cattle in the Territory, and Statehood was assured within a year or two. Wyoming was prosperous, and filled with growing pains. The Pre-emption and Homtstead laws had, within the past six years, brought hundreds of nester families West. And the rumblings of coming trouble were audible to all who traveled the Territory.

Harbin shook his head; maybe it had been a mistake to ride this way. He had no stake, no part to play; he was a free agent, riding through. Nevertheless, he had doubts. He was a man with a single purpose: To stay alive until the time a man's life depended upon his speed with a gun was ended. Harbin had no doubts that day would come; he had seen the taming of too many wild frontier towns not to be aware of the slow change that was coming to the West. But it would not happen today or tomorrow, and Ridge Harbin, in his own deadly way, was prepared to wait it out.

He flipped the cigarette away. Putting the gelding to the downward slope of the road, he sat the saddle easily. By the time he had ridden the last of the downgrade and wended his way through the broken land beyond, it was past noon and he was hungry. Three or four miles from the badlands he came to a crossroads, and the road that led to the north was barred. Across the parallel poles that formed the

21

wide gate a board sign had been nailed, and the wording was burned in with a running iron:

Nesters and Rustlers
TAKE WARNING!
This Is Three Horn Land
STAY OFF!

Beneath the lettering, in smaller printing, was the name *Vane Dallard.*

A man who had been sitting his horse quietly in the middle of the road reined aside as Harbin rode up. The man was past middle age; his belly rested against the flat inner surface of his saddlehorn. He wore no gun at his waist, but a rifle was lying across his lap. His clothes were worn linsey-woolen, obviously home-cut, and he wore the heavy thick-soled, broad-toed boots of the dirt farmer. His face was stubbled with a white beard that was streaked with brown tobacco juice about his mouth. He watched Harbin from narrow eyes, then spat to the ground.

"Vane Dallard and Jesus Christ—both powers unto themselves," the man said. His voice was a booming bellow. "It is given to no man to covet the whole of the earth —a truth that Vane Dallard and his kind will learn."

Something about the fat man nettled Harbin, and he pulled up. "Perhaps," he said, slowly. "But Three Horn is getting civilized, it would seem. The last time I rode this way, three years ago, there were nine crosses burned into the sign. Each one stood for a man Vane Dallard had hanged on Three Horn land."

The fat man listened to Harbin's flat-toned voice. Then he spat again. "They are not the only sins Vane Dallard must atone for, stranger. God will punish him."

"Perhaps," Harbin said again. "I also hope He has pity on the man who tries to do His work for Him—because Vane Dallard will have none."

The gelding walked on at Harbin's signals and the fat man sat his saddle, staring after them. When Harbin looked back, the man was still looking after him. The man's steady stare, without malice, without emotion of any kind, had made him uneasy. The fat man had accepted his own judgment, and nothing could shake it. His own self-righteousness would support him as long as he lived— which, Harbin thought grimly, would not be too long if he openly bucked the iron-handed Dallard.

22

Harbin remembered Vane Dallard well. He had worked for him for a month three years ago, and he had left the Three Horn ranch because he knew he would kill Dallard if he stayed. In a way, Dallard mirrored the hard certainty of the nester he had just passed. Only, Dallard had an awareness of his own strength, and a confidence that had never been shaken.

Harbin smiled grimly. Trouble. It hung over this Wyoming land like a pall of dust. It was reflected in the face of every man he had met; common talk revolved around it; and there could be no doubt that it would come to a head. There was more than $150,000,000 worth of cattle in Wyoming Territory, and a handful of men owned them all. And eight million cows required more grass and water and range than was available. And for every nester who claimed or pre-empted his 160 acres, a hundred head of cattle would die for lack of feed and water.

"Nesters and rustlers," Harbin said to himself. Dallard could have coupled them with lobo wolves and coyotes—except that wild animals could not read. Nesters and rustlers could—but would it stop them? Harbin thought of the fat-faced, white-whiskered man, and thought not.

But the trouble was not his own, and would not concern him. He would pass through this hostile land—

The shot came without warning. One instant Harbin sat placidly in his saddle, his thoughts for once away from himself, the next instant the hard flat slam of a rifle jerked him erect. His hat leaped from his head, and he felt the lead cut a strand of his white hair. Then, before the second, make-sure shot could be fired, he flung himself to the right, out of the saddle. Even as he was falling, his right hand freed his heavy revolver and brought it level, ready to fire.

THREE

It was long after midnight when Vail wheeled the Conestoga wagon into the group of standing homesteader wagons and reined in. He pulled the team to the far side of a low-burning campfire, and a man, who had been asleep under the wagon next to the fire, rolled out, a rifle in his hands. He blinked in the firelight, bent to throw on more wood, then advanced to greet Vail.

"Howdy, Paul," the man said. "We missed you, an' wondered if you'd turned back."

Vail looped the reins over the brake, and climbed stiffly down from the high seat. "We've passed the point where we can afford to turn back," he said flatly.

"You ain't the only one," the other man cut in. "I was just figgerin' I'll be damned lucky to see it through to where we're goin', let alone the rest of the year."

Paul Vail held his hands out to the warmth of the fire. The other man, Ralph Condon by name, studied him in silence as he stretched to ease cramped muscles. "You look like the wrath of God, Paul," he said.

"I look no worse than I feel," Vail answered shortly. "What I need—" He broke off to peer anxiously up toward the wagon. There was no movement there, and he relaxed visibly.

Condon grinned. "You an' me both. I got some applejack I been savin' for a cold night. Reckon this's it." He returned to his wagon, and came back presently with a brown crockery jug. He carried two tin cups in his other hand. He held them carefully and bent the jug over his free arm, letting the amber liquid gurgle out into the cups. He set the jug down beside the fire, and both men hunkered down on their heels.

Vail, accepting the cup of liquor gratefully, sipped at it slowly. "I hope we're not making a mistake, Ralph, pushing on this far," Vail said.

"You an' me both. I was talkin' to Gary Daniels, an' Gary says we'll be losin' some folks here. Some of 'em will turn south for the Tallows. But we been expectin' to lose some. Me, I'm dead set on gittin' myself a piece of Red Rock land. I heard a feller back in Indiana who'd been West in Sixty-six tellin' about how the Injuns just stuck a piece of wood in the ground an' next day found a tree'd growed. Reckon that's goin' some, even for a Hoosier to believe, but just the same the land's good. An' we can make it better. I'm carryin' twelve sacks of winter wheat in the wagon. Even dry farmin' can be made to pay —an' if we can get water we'll find what we come for."

"We were headed for Oregon," Vail said slowly. He frowned. "We won't make it that far." *Because I got drunk in Fort Abe Lincoln and lost most of our stake in a crooked game,* he finished silently. Bitterness pulled his mouth down. He lifted the tin cup and drained it at two gulps. Ralph Condon stared at him for a moment, then shook his head.

"Land is land," Condon said "A man can get back about as much from one piece as another if he tries hard enough. And this is new land, never touched by a plow since time began. Makes a man feel like maybe he's doin' somethin' special." He broke off. "Hell, I'm talkin' like Hellfire Gordon. Remember him, back in Fort Abe? Pulled out a month ahead of the rest of us. Reckon he's found his spot."

"I reckon he has," Vail agreed.

Condon yawned and stood up. "Hell, it's late an' you're tired. Better turn in, because Daniels said there'll be a meetin' in the mornin' at his wagon. It's two, three days through the mountains to Red Rock, an' two more from there to Wild Horse Valley an' the Government land."

Vail said, "Good night," then unhitched his team, and hobbled the horses. For a moment he stood beside the fire. Condon had left his jug there. Vail studied it, then looked up at his own wagon. He shook his head, guilt making him angry, and climbed slowly back into the wagonbed. Lydia stirred once as he lay down beside her. He kissed her, and she whispered, "Paul." Then, softly, she began to cry in her sleep.

In moments like this, Paul Vail cursed the weakness that kept him from being the man she needed. He lay still, eyes closed, breathing hard. The liquor burned warmly inside him, easing the tensions that held him, and presently he fell asleep and began to snore.

Lydia Vail was awakened by the baby just after dawn. For a moment she lay there, fighting a feeling of panic, of being lost. Then slowly she became aware of her surroundings, of Paul's recumbent figure beside her. His breath

25

reeked of liquor and he was snoring. She sat up, lifted the baby from the crib and rocked him in her arms, quieting him. Then she laid him down to dress him, and by then Joanie was awake. The girl's slim figure moved up the aisle toward her mother.

"Hold Jimmie for me, Sissie," Lydia said. "I'll make a fire. Try not to wake up your father."

"Yes, Ma," Joanie said. In the harsh light of dawn, her face was smooth, her eyes bright. She held the baby carefully, and he stopped whimpering.

Lydia climbed wearily from the wagon. A woman who was bent over a campfire straightened to look at her and to smile. "Mornin', Lydia," she called. "You folks got in pretty late, Ralph tells me. Ralph's gone for what firewood he can scare up. We'll end up usin' buffalo chips like always." The woman waved a hand. "No sense in keepin' two fires goin'. You're welcome to ours, Lydia."

"Thank you, Helen," Lydia said. "I want to warm some milk for Jimmie."

"He's a real good baby—I wish I could give Ralph a boy. I've seen him playin' with your Jimmie. Course he loves his girls, but—" The woman broke off. Then she smiled and looked down at herself. "Maybe this time we'll be lucky."

"I hope so, Helen," Lydia answered. She thought: *Why do people keep right on hoping when it seems certain not to work out for them?* She shook her head at the growing bitterness inside her.

Ralph Condon came up then. He was a short, thick-set man with a heavy mustache that hid the shape of his mouth. His eyes were placid, almost without life. He talked too much, and changed his mind too often, but he tried in his own way.

"Good mornin', Lydia. Paul ain't up yet? He looked tuckered out last night. Reckon he can use the rest. Sorry you folks got here so late, but it's good you made it up with us. Gary Daniels has called a meetin' for eight o'clock. Figger we'll be pushin' on by nine o'clock. Kind of a late start, but there'll be some goodbyes to be said. Three wagons're headin' south from here. The Morrises an' the Wrights an' the Holders."

"Kind of hate to see 'em go," Helen Condon said.

Joanie Vail climbed down from the wagon, carrying her brother easily. She grinned at the Condons. "Mom, if you'll watch Jimmie, I'll milk the goat."

26

Lydia took the baby. Helen Condon said, too quickly, "Let me hold him for you, Lydia." She took the baby. Lydia saw the hurt in Ralph's heavy-featured face, hidden almost at once. Then the homesteader grinned.

"Maybe we'll have a boy this time," he said. "How's about that, Lydia? Maybe you can give Helen some tips. Maybe she ain't eatin' right or somethin'?"

Helen Condon smiled. "Mrs. Benton was tellin' me of a needle trick, an' how it could always tell. I want to try it tonight. You ever hear tell of that trick, Lydia?"

Lydia nodded. "I've heard of it—but you'll know for sure when the baby arrives. Maybe it's best not to know ahead of time."

Ralph Condon looked down at Jimmie Vail in his wife's arms. He touched the baby on one cheek, then shook his head. "Four girls—time for a change."

"I'm sure you'll be happy no matter which it is," Lydia said. Again the odd tight look passed over Condon's face, and then he nodded, too quickly.

"Sure I will," he said.

Joanie came up with half a pail of frothy milk. "Goat's doin' better," she said. "Can I feed him, Mom?"

Lydia nodded. She watched while Joanie fed and changed the baby. Then she shielded her eyes and stared about the rousing camp. Children began to scamper between the wagons. The smell of cooking food filled the warm morning air. Joanie spread a blanket on the ground for the baby to lie on, and then helped her mother fix their morning meal of parboiled then fried salt pork and fried potatoes. Paul appeared, bleary-eyed as he climbed down from the wagon. He ran a hand through his rumpled hair, and grimaced.

"Mornin', Lydia," he said. "You should've called me sooner."

"There's plenty of time. The meeting isn't for a half-hour. Eat your breakfast. You'll need what rest you got, because Ralph says we're going to push on today."

Paul Vail nodded. He pulled the tin washbasin from its place on the side of the wagon, ladled out water from the barrel strapped to the side, and washed his face and hands. He returned to the front of the wagon and accepted his plate and cup in silence. He ate slowly, without speaking, and Lydia, who had already eaten, busied herself with cleaning the dishes.

Ralph Condon came up as he finished his meal, and

27

squatted down. He grinned. "That applejack must've knocked you out quick." he said. "Good for you."

Vail nodded. "You heard anything more?"

Condon shook his head. "Not yet. But Daniels is all ready. Let's mosey over."

Lydia paused to look up and watch them go. Paul Vail closed one eye in a reassuring wink, and she smiled at him. But Joanie frowned at her father. He read the dislike in her face, and it disturbed him. *It's my own damned fault, actin' the way I have,* he thought. And for the hundredth time he made new resolves that he knew he could not keep.

Gary Daniels was a big man, a full head taller than anyone else with the group of wagons. His hair and beard were streaked with gray, and his red-skinned face was determined. He stood in front of his own wagon and he raised his hands to quiet the men.

"All right, men," he said. "Here we've reached the partin' of the ways. Some of us will drive south—the rest, includin' me, will be headin' for Red Rock. You all know as much about your plans an' this whole country as I do. I ain't meanin' to start another argument, but I'm sorry that some of us are leavin' the group. We'll do better an' make a stronger start if we stick it out together—but you're all free. I just wanted this last meetin' so none of you will feel we're burnin' our bridges behind us. For the last time, I'm askin' each of you what you've decided to do. If any of you have changed your minds, speak up."

For a moment no one spoke, then a small thin man Paul Vail knew to be Homer Wright stepped forward. "I've been thinkin' maybe Gary's right—about us all stickin' together. When we left Independence I was aimin' for the Tallows country—but what the hell, it's all land, an' maybe I'd be better off to stick with the rest of you. I don't know what Morris an' Holder have decided, but I'm stayin' on."

Gary Daniels's big face split in a wide grin. "You make sense moren' any time since I've knowed you, Homer. All right, what about you other two?"

Charles Morris was almost as huge a man as Daniels, and his red hair stood like a red brush atop his bold-featured face. "I say what I've always said: The Red Rock country has always been cattle land. Vane Dallard's land. I had my bellyful of fightin' twenty years ago. Now I want land of my own an' a chance to farm it. Wild Horse Valley sounds like nothin' but trouble to me. I'm headin' south—an' the rest of you'd do better to follow me."

Gary Daniels frowned ponderously. "That's your right an' privilege," he said. "But anything worth while's worth fightin' for. Hell, not even Vane Dallard's big enough to buck the Government. It's Government land, up for pre-emption. One hundred an' sixty acres of the finest unspoiled land in this country waitin' to be plow-broken an' seeded. I know the Tallows country. I tried my luck there three years ago, and I'm tellin' you the story is the same there as anywhere else. The ranchers drove herds north after the War Between the States—thousands of 'em. All of 'em are Texans who think they own the earth they walk on. They'll learn they've got to live an' let live. There's Territorial Law—an' damned soon there'll be a State Law. It isn't the single man ownin' a million acres of grassland that makes a State—it's people like you an' me, plowin' the land, settlin' it down, makin' it liveable. An' there ain't nothin' can stop us if we stick together."

Daniels's big voice spoke strongly. They were swayed, and Charles Morris knew it. He shrugged his heavy shoulders. "All right," he said. "You others do as you please. I'm loaded an' ready to roll south. I'm leavin' the group in ten minutes. I ain't got time to make the rounds, wagon by wagon, so I'll say so long, now. I wish you all the luck in the world. You'll need it when Vane Dallard makes his move."

He turned around and walked away. There was silence in his wake, and Vail saw heads turn to look at John Holder. He was a dark-faced man, somewhat younger than the others. He shook his head. "I've changed my mind," he said. "I'm stayin' on. Charley, you'll have to go alone."

Charles Morris turned to look back. His face was grim. "I expected it," he said, flatly. "Goodbye, John." Stubbornness lay in him like a vein of iron. Vail saw Gary Daniels's shrug.

"All right, men," he said. "I feel better, now. That's eleven wagons of us. We'll make a nucleus of an organization wherever we make our beginning. It's three days to Red Rock. There's a Land Office there. Wild Horse Valley lies two days beyond. There are others ahead of us there, but I've heard there's a river, and better land beyond, open for pre-emption. We'll drive for Red Rock, stay on there three days before pushing on. You can get supplies, stuff you need there. Is there anything else?"

The meeting broke up, and Paul Vail returned to his wagon. Lydia was sitting in the shade, and she looked up as he approached. "All but one are pushing on for Red Rock," he said. He frowned. "There may be trouble waiting for us there."

Lydia smiled. "I'm not afraid, Paul."

"Of course you're not," he answered, and thought; *You're never afraid, Lydia. You're strong where I'm weak. But because of that I'll see it through.*

Paul was hitching up the team when he saw the Morrises' wagon roll past, taking the south fork of the road. Charles Morris's red head stuck erect, and he didn't wave or look back. Lydia saw his wife's face, strained and anxious-looking. Paul put his arm through hers, and she knew he needed her strength to curb the doubts that held him as he saw Morris drive away.

"It will be all right, Paul," Lydia said quietly.

His too gentle eyes probed into hers. "Will it, Lydia?" he whispered. "I feel odd, like something is going to happen to us. I couldn't go on without you, Lydia. I'm not much, and I've failed you too many times—but without you, I'm nothing."

"Hush, Paul," the woman said, and smiled and kissed him.

Then there came the loud shouting as the first wagon—Gary Daniels's—rolled away toward the mountains which lay closer now. The second wagon wheeled into line, a dog running and barking beside the team. Paul Vail helped Lydia to the spring seat of their Conestoga wagon, and they waited their turn to move out.

FOUR

For Ridge Harbin the instant that followed the rifle shots seemed an eternity. No matter how many times a man might be fired upon, there was a nerve-numbing terror to the thing that could not be denied, and it was like that now. Jarred violently from the saddle before he had time to gather his thoughts, he fell heavily, but landed, rolling desperately even as the second shot was fired.

The shock of his landing and the puff of yellow dust that shot up thickly about Ridge kept him from locating his attacker for an instant. The second shot missed his moving body by inches, then he leveled his revolver and fired three times, carefully placed shots that went where he aimed. He had caught the glint of blued steel against the flat brownness of rock and plainsland, and it was at this brief glimpse that he fired. He saw the white scoring of the rock his shots made, not an inch apart, and heard their whine as they ricocheted into the sky. He had the satisfaction of seeing the rifle jerked frantically back.

And a wild voice yelled, *"Keep off Three Horn land, you stinkin' sodbustin' bastard!"*

Then hoofs pounded, and he caught the wild veering of a horse off from behind the flat-crowned rocks. For a moment Ridge Harbin remained there, sprawled in the dust. Then he got up carefully and dusted off his clothes. He shaded his eyes and stared after the receding figure of the man who had attacked him. Then he shook his head.

He found his hat a few feet down the road, a jagged hole torn through it a scant half-inch above the band. Harbin thrust his forefinger through the front hole, and his lips pursed in a silent whistle. He looked again at the rider, but horse and man were gone; just thinning of dust hung in the air.

Harbin's frightened gelding had run some two hundred yards, but stood for him to come up. He patted the sweating, dust-streaked neck gently, then climbed into the saddle. Harbin's colorless eyes were narrowed. His conviction of being able to stand aside from the trouble here was shaken. Then a perverse thought struck him. *Do I look like a homesteader?* Even as the humor of the thought struck him, his eyes narrowed again, and his smile was hardly realized.

He had learned the bitter truth of never accepting a fact until it was proved, and automatically his mind began to sort through the incident just past. On the surface it was an overanxious Three Horn rider making a try for a homesteader, either to warn him or to kill him, depending on the attacker's accuracy of aim. Remembering the assailant's high-pitched quavering voice made Harbin's frown deeper.

Look at it another way: The rifleman had tried for a head shot. That meant he was sure of himself with a rifle and had no intention of missing. Just the slight downward thrust of Harbin's head had kept the bullet from striking between his eyes. And, to guarantee the accuracy of the head shot he intended to make, the rifleman had made the mistake of coming in too close, close enough for Harbin's pistol shots to strike uncomfortably near. And at that range, a man with a rifle held a distinct disadvantage over a man known to be a deadly shot with a revolver. The warning shout and the sudden flight were intended to throw him off.

Two interpretations of the same thought. Two meanings for the same set of facts. It was Harbin's own bitter past that made him select the second as the most likely. As he rode along, though he dismissed his brooding thoughts, he rode stiffly erect, cautious and wary. He had but one life to lose, but there were twenty-five dead men behind him to indicate the price he would demand for it. The thought returned to his smile, but it was a hard, warped mockery of amusement.

One point: If his second guess was correct, it posed a big question: Why had the attack been made against him? Of course, there could be several answers to that. For one, it could have been a man who hated or feared Ridge Harbin and wanted him dead badly enough to try his hand at dry-gulching. But against that possibility was the simple fact that Harbin had not announced his coming, had no intention of staying in the Red Rock country, and had not even known himself a few days before in what direction his drifting would take him.

It had been three years since he had been in Wyoming, and he remembered no enemies who might have carried a grudge. Still, the possibility remained. And there was one other: That someone, determined to bring the range

32

trouble between nester and rancher to a shooting show-down, had picked that moment to start things rolling. In a queer way it made sense; the rifleman had been determined on a kill. If he hadn't known Harbin, then it meant he didn't give a damn whom he dropped. A dead man on either side would be hard to talk away; it could start a holocaust of hate and destruction, and Wyoming was ripe for it as Lincoln County, New Mexico, had been five years earlier.

Harbin eased his weight in the saddle, his eyes scanning the roll-off of the hummock-dotted rangeland. The sky was pale azure, striped with wisp-thin clouds riding high. A thin veil of dust curtained the west toward Red Rock. Somewhere, almost lost in the flat distant, Harbin heard the piercing whistle of a locomotive. Red Rock was a shipping point for the entire Red Rock range. End of track, a town with the bars let down, living for the pleasure of the rancher and his horde of half wild riders.

Frontier town, a gigantic rangeland empire held in the grip of a few men, and a new force making itself felt, the westward expansion of a nation in the throes of regrowth following the disruptive years of the Civil War. There was a pattern to the building trouble that lay over the land, and Harbin's reasoning concerning the attack on himself was the logical outgrowth of it. He rubbed at his square chin with one slender-fingered hand, his brows narrowed with a frown.

If he was right, then the attack held no personal significance. It would not recur. He could pass through the Red Rock country. There would be no reason to stay. He should have been relieved, but perversely he was not. Too long had he drifted, from range to range, without a focal point to aim for. There seemed to be no security for a man like him. He had one chance to survive his times, to keep moving, to stay alert. Walk softly, keep to yourself, don't argue, never choose sides—and kill mercilessly and without hesitation when you have to. Pattern for the survival of a gunman. Set yourself apart from every human emotion and feeling, face every man you meet with the full knowledge you may have to drop him dead at your feet before you leave—and then you have a chance to live. Drift from town to town, and keep drifting; work when you have to, gamble when you can. Stretch your money between both. Hard and mean, wearing the days down one by one until the time comes when men won't carry guns as normally as they wear a shirt.

Kill—one word to describe the ending of a man's whole existence, the end of his private hopes and dreams, one word to cover the slow inward dying of the man behind the gun. Justify yourself to yourself however you can—but each time it gets harder to do. Each time the urge to damn the few principles you have left grows stronger. But you fight it down, destroy the hardness, withdraw more and more into yourself, live as you can by the code you have made your own—it is all you have.

And never expect anyone to understand, to see beneath the rock-hard face you turn to the world. Never expect anyone to understand that each terrible time you are forced to use your gun a little more of something fine dies inside you. There is no law to protect you but the six lead commandments you carry in the holstered gun at your waist. There is fear and death in the gun; but there is justice, the hard, fair justice of the frontier there, too, provided you never break your rigid code. Ridge Harbin had not yet broken it, and because of that simple fact he lived the way he must. His swiftness with a gun was only a last resort. He could still sleep nights.

To the south a puff of white smoke, thinning as it rose into the pale blue sky, caught Harbin's eye. He watched it grow and thin as a train puffed along the prairie toward Red Rock. He passed a buckboard, and the driver, a weather-beaten ranch hand, lifted an arm in greeting as Harbin swung by him. Off to the north, the dust haze thickened, and he made out the darker spots of cattle, and horsemen herding them to new range. In the dusty wake a chuck wagon followed, the dingy canvas top flapping crazily like a broken-winged bird.

Harbin passed the first sod-walled house, which was set in a cluttered yard. Two small Mexican boys ran shouting around the corner of an outbuilding, a half grown pup frolicking along beside them. Harbin passed another wagon, then two more, all big, awkward Conestogas, heavily laden with the possessions of the families who rode them. Homesteaders, a part of the welling flood of humanity that was heading West to the Promised Lands. One hundred and sixty acres, yours for the taking. One hundred and sixty fertile acres where you can grow anything. One hundred and sixty acres where a man can stand on his own two feet and make his way. Land where

34

a man's family can grow up and spread out. Dreams, and harsh, barren reality—where it would be hard-scrabble at best.

A young girl lifted her eyes to Harbin's tall figure as he rode past the wagon in which she traveled. Loneliness and gaiety fought for expression in her round face, and she smiled shyly at him. Harbin half lifted his hand, then let it fall, and rode on. The girl followed him with her wistful eyes.

Then Red Rock, flat against the horizon, the raw un-painted lumber of its slab-sided buildings silvering in the sun and weather. The street churned to yellow dust in the wake of countless horsemen and wagons. Long hitch-rails before false-fronted saloons, a tethered horse here and there, head drooping against the midday heat. Men hunkered down on the shady side of the street, hats tipped forward to shield their eyes from glare. Mead's Livery Stables, Henderson's Dry Goods Emporium, Miller's Mercantile, Jacob's Harness Shop; the clang of steel on red-hot iron from the blacksmith's shop, the bitter smell of stale beer from open-faced saloons, the long row of empty chairs across the sun-drenched veranda of the Cattleman's Rest; the A.B.C. Café, its windows glinting brightly; the sudden howl of a locomotive whistle at the far end of the street which was veiled with dust from the herd being driven into the loading corrals for shipment. All the multitude of sounds and smells of a frontier town, familiar, and yet oddly disturbing to Harbin.

He rode the length of Trail Street, left his horse at Mead's Livery Stables with instructions for the gelding to be handrubbed and fed. Then he returned to the boardwalk, easing the stiffness from his legs as he walked. The sun burned against him, a steady, heavy pressure. He crossed the veranda of the Cattleman's Rest and entered the shade of the lobby. He signed his name, wrote Dallas, Texas, after it, and watched the familiar start of the clerk as he recognized the name. The man's eyes went swiftly to Harbin's gun, and then to his face, in that order. The name, the gun, and the man; it never varied.

Harbin said, "Where can I get a square meal?"

The hotel clerk blinked. He seemed vaguely uncertain, awed by the presence of the man before him. Then he smirked. His voice was silkily smooth as he answered: "Try Dugan's Lunch, across the street. Dining room here

35

ain't open until four o'clock, but we serve damned good meals for a buck. Stayin' long, Mr. Harbin?"

Harbin bobbed his head but did not answer. He crossed the lobby, then paused by the door for a moment. He saw the room clerk scuttle from behind the desk, and move toward two men lounging in chairs tipped back against the far wall of the lobby. Harbin's smile widened, and he went through the door to the street.

The first homesteader's wagon rolled down Trail Street, the dust-covered team plodding slowly. A milk cow tied to the rear of the wagon ambled along, its udder flopping rhythmically. The girl who had smiled at Harbin saw him again now as he stood in the bright sunlight on the board-walk. Her head tipped back and she looked deliberately away. Amusement made Harbin smile despite himself.

At the same moment a buckboard hitched before the Prairie Flower Saloon backed into the street, and the front wheel of the Conestoga wagon rammed ponderous-ly into the rear of it. The light buckboard jounced, and the driver was pitched to his feet. For a moment the flighty team hitched to the ranch wagon danced; then the driver got them under control. The Conestoga continued to roll on, the driver calling out:

"Sorry, cowpoke—you backed into me."

"The hell I did, you lousy plow-walker!" the cowman yelled.

It was a casual accident that harmed no one and hap-pened perhaps twenty times a week in every town in the West, but the tension of these times made it assume an importance it didn't have. The homesteader, a big heavy-set man with a ponderous paunch, shook his head.

"I want no trouble," he said. "It was an accident."

The man in the buckboard flung the reins about the brake, and leaped to the ground, his face red and angry. "Like hell, you bastard!" he shouted, and ran forward. He leaped to the spinning hub of the Conestoga wheel, stepped up. The homesteader shook his grizzled head again.

"You got to have it this way!" he said. His right hand moved dexterously, and he laid the loaded butt of the whip he carried against the ranchman's head. The angry cowhand went off the wagon backward and sprawled in-ertly in the street. The Conestoga rolled steadily on, and the heavy-set man resumed his seat and flicked the whip over his team.

Harbin caught sight of the girl's pale, frightened face as she peered out at the cowhand. He was sitting up in the yellow dust, both hands to his head. Another man, a rider by his garb, shook a fist angrily after the departing Conestoga.

"You God-damned sodbusters think you own the world!" he called.

The man in the street shook his head dazedly, then rolled and came up to his feet. He staggered for a moment, then cursed bitterly, and his right hand went down to the holstered gun at his hip.

"Easy, cowboy!" Harbin called sharply.

The dust-covered, red-faced man swung toward him, then held there, strung taut, his right hand already on his holstered Colt. "The hell you say!" he yelled.

Harbin's crooked smile twisted his mouth. His frock coat swung open, and the upthrust handle of his revolver portruded from his left side. For an instant trouble hung in the balance; a single gesture or movement on the part of either man could begin something that would end only with the death of one of them.

A man's deep voice cut through the silent tension: "Hold it, Wayne!"

The stiffness slacked from the cowhand's body, and his right hand fell away from his gun. Across the street a man moved, walking with an easy, arrogant grace. He was tall, as finely built as a running horse, with the same lean hardness, the same suppleness of movement. He wore moleskin cloth breeches tucked into fancy diamond-top boots that had probably cost forty dollars, and his calf-skin vest had twenty-dollar gold pieces for buttons. His high-crowned Stetson was banded with rattlesnake skin, and a blue cornflower was thrust into one side. His face was lean, with symmetrical features and bright blue eyes that smiled continuously. Around his narrow waist sagged a horsehide gunbelt with loops of snow-white elkhide. The brass cartridges were polished and shown in the sunlight. He was a Wild West Show figure until you took in the hard flat lines of his mouth and chin, and then the outfit was forgotten.

He stepped diffidently into the golden dust of the street, walked three steps forward, smiling, then paused. He caught his first good look at Harbin, and the smile faded slowly. Then he shook his head.

37

"You're a lucky man, Wayne," he said in a deep-toned, good-natured voice. "In about a tenth of a second you'd've been layin' dead in the street. You'll buy me a drink for that." Then the handsome face lifted. "Hello, Ridge," he said.

Harbin relaxed. "Hello, Johnny," he said. "It's been a long time."

The man named Wayne looked uncertainly from one to the other. Johnny Lee grinned. "Joe Wayne, meet Ridge Harbin of Texas."

Harbin saw the color recede from the cowhand's face. Johnny Lee laughed out loud, enjoying the other man's frozen face and suddenly frightened manner.

"You'll never walk any closer to it than just now Wayne," he said. Then he sobered. "But you ain't paid to fight Three Horn battles. You climb back into that rig and wheel out of town."

"Hell, Johnny," the other man protested, "that lousy clodhopper—"

"Leave it lay, Wayne," Lee replied. He lifted his head, still smiling. "What's your stake, Ridge?"

Harbin shook his head slowly. "Nothing, doubled," he replied. "There was a girl in the back of that homesteader's wagon. Wayne might've hit her."

Johnny Lee was one of perhaps a dozen men that Harbin would have felt obliged to explain his stand to, and Lee knew it. The tension ran out of his figure, leaving him smiling, friendly.

"Then it's forgotten, Ridge," Lee said, and walked toward him. He stepped from the dust, then stamped his booted feet to remove what grime he could. "I'll buy you a drink," he offered.

"I'll let you," Harbin answered.

Johnny Lee led the way through the swinging doors of the Prairie Flower Saloon and straight to the bar. It was too early for much business except the habitual drunks, two of whom sat sprawled out at one table at the rear of the big room. The barkeep in the greasy apron moved up reluctantly from the paper laid across the bar which he had been reading.

"Howdy, gents," he said, then suddenly he frowned and as suddenly wiped the frown away. "Oh, hello Johnny."

Johnny Lee had always enjoyed another man's fear of him, and he had not changed, Harbin thought.

38

"Set up Dallard's bottle, Reb," Lee said. "This is a special occasion."

The bartender hesitated. "I don't know, Johnny, Vane gave me hell last time you got his bottle—"

"Reb, I'm going to kill you," Johnny Lee said. His deep voice spoke lightly, jokingly, but his smile was cold and serious.

The bartender swallowed heavily, then turned away. He came back in a moment with a black bottle. He set it on the bar, then put out two shot glasses.

"All right, Johnny," he said. "You can have what you want. You know that."

Lee's smile remained unchanged. "I know it, Reb," he answered. "See that you remember it."

Harbin said: "Why do you do it, Johnny?" It was a liberty he took for granted, and for a moment Lee's smile changed. Then he shook his head.

"There are too few of us not to speak the truth when we meet, Ridge," he said. "I'll tell you why. If you let one dog yap at your heels, pretty soon there's a whole pack of them. You've got a way of walking through them, Ridge. They leave you alone. Someday it will be the same way with me—when I've killed enough of them."

He spoke with certainty, but he did not believe what he was saying, no more than Harbin believed it. There was a difference between the two of them that would never be erased. And because that difference could make trouble between them, they ignored it.

Harbin said, "If you want it that way, Johnny."

Johnny Lee frowned suddenly, his handsome face hardening. "I'm kidding myself again, Ridge. It's a bad habit I've got. I can't break it. But what the hell? Who cares but me?"

"Nobody," Harbin said, in his curious flat tones. Lee stared at him for a moment, then laughed.

"If another man spoke to me like that, I'd kill him, Ridge," he said. "Why do I let you get away with it?"

"Do you really want me to tell you, Johnny?" Harbin asked gently. Their eyes met, and the bright laughing blue eyes dropped away first.

"Hell, no!" Lee said shortly. "Let's have that drink. It's Dallard's pet bottle, an' it's paid for. He has it shipped

39

in from New Orleans. Bet it costs him eight, nine bucks a bottle. It's good. Like you never had before."

They drank and the uneasy moment between them passed. But both knew the answer that Harbin would have given. The answer lay in the simple truth that Lee must always assert himself because he feared other men like himself, men like Ridge Harbin. And that fear would always hold him at a disadvantage. Nevertheless there was resentment in Johnny Lee, and it would grow.

Harbin said: "Thanks for the drink, Johnny. I'll return the kindness later. Time to chow down."

Lee hesitated. "You comin' back to Three Horn, Ridge?" There was a certain tenseness in him as he waited for the reply. The tension slackened abruptly when Harbin said: "No. Just riding through."

Johnny covered his relief with a smile. "Dallard will expect you to pay him your respects."

"I doubt that, Johnny," Harbin said, smiling.

"Flint and steel," Johnny Lee said softly, "makes fine sparks. Maybe I'm a bastard for saying so, but I like to see them fly. You rubbed him hard before you left Three Horn. He's never forgotten. You didn't call him to his face, but it was laid out, waiting for him to pick it up. He couldn't do it. I still remember the way he raved after you rode away, Ridge. He was like a madman. He never spoke your name, but he was hell on wheels. Nobody could do anything right for a week. He chewed the tail of every man on the spread. Nope, he hasn't forgotten Ridge Harbin."

"Then maybe he needs more time," Harbin said. "I'll see he gets it. Thanks for the drink."

He moved away. Johnny Lee watched him go, unsmilingly, Harbin knew. *He hates my guts,* Harbin thought. *But he enjoys the game of peers too much to end it before he has to. Just the same it will come to that someday.*

Ridge Harbin crossed the street to Dugan's café. He ate slowly, and topped the meal with three cups of black coffee. He paid his check and bought three cigars. He paused on the boardwalk to light one of the cigars, and stood there for a minute to consider the town. He had only thirty-odd dollars in his stake, and it was time to enlarge it. He had a choice. Three Horn would be building for the trouble to come, and Vane Dallard would hire him. The thought pinched Harbin's brows together in a frown.

When a man hired Ridge Harbin, he wanted his gun, and he needed it. It was the hard, simple truth. Just the same . . . His frown vanished. Thirty dollars would buy him into a poker game. With luck there'd be no need to hire out for Vane Dallard's dirty work. With luck—

A horseman came down the street, reined in in front of the Prairie Flower Saloon and dismounted. Harbin knew him at once. It was the man Johnny Lee had called Joe Wayne. He stood beside his horse for a moment, staring up and down the street. Harbin put his cigar between his teeth, let his right hand fall to his side. When he removed the cigar it was with his left hand. He stood quietly waiting until Wayne saw him. Harbin saw the sudden stiffening of the cowhand's back; then the rider moved across the street. He paused some feet from Harbin, legs slightly apart. His face was pale and set, and his tongue licked at his dry lips.

"I don't want you to think I'm afraid of you, Harbin," he said.

Ridge Harbin smiled. "It never occurred to me to think so, Wayne," he answered. "Let's leave it like that between us. I'll buy you a drink."

Wayne's sun-red face reflected indecision. Then slowly he shook his head. "I don't think so. I just don't want you thinkin' I'm afraid of you."

Harbin smiled, blew smoke out carefully. "Now you've got it said. All right, you're not afraid of me."

"I just wanted you to know," Wayne said nervously.

"I know," Harbin said. A familiar hardness inside him was setting, dangerously, and he fought to control it. Then he placed the cigar between his teeth and stepped from the boardwalk to the dust of Trail Street. Wayne watched him, his eyes widening. Harbin kept smiling, his hawklike features unreadable. He walked straight for the smaller man, striding slowly, evenly. At the last moment Wayne stepped out of his path, and Harbin walked past him. He didn't look back, but he knew the angry shame that filled the other man. *It's a mean, dirty trick,* Harbin thought, *but maybe it will jar some sense into his thick skull. This is the way it is, and he might as well know it.*

Harbin reached the far side of the street and turned slowly around. When he removed the cigar from his mouth it was with his right hand. Wayne recognized the contempt in the gesture. For an instant he held there, his red face working shakily; then his shoulders slumped, and he moved to the boardwalk and entered the first saloon he came to.

There was no satisfaction in the thing for Harbin, only a grim sense of having done what he had to do. He raised the cigar to his lips, but it had lost its flavor for him, and he threw it into the street.

A light step sounded beside him, and a hand touched his arm, gently. He swung about to face the girl he had seen in the homesteader's wagon. She was older than he had thought, seventeen or eighteen, and pretty, with a round face, and a tipped-up nose and eyes that looked as if they could laugh at most things. She was smiling, hesitantly, and spoke hurriedly.

"I—I saw what happened when Pa hit that buckboard," she said. "I told Pa, and he said it was all right to thank you for what you did. Pa sent me in for some supplies. He said it would be all right if I asked you to come out to supper tonight so he can thank you hisself. Our name's Chase—I'm Molly Chase."

Her cheeks were flushed, and she rushed over her words as if she had memorized them in advance. How long had it been since a girl like this had spoken to him in public? Even as the thought came clearly in his mind, a hard warning rang through him, and he stiffened, his face impassive.

"Thank you, Molly Chase," he said, slowly. "I'm honored. But you do not know who I am—and when you do know, you will know it was a mistake to have asked me. Just the same, I thank you for it. It makes us even for the day."

The girl was staring up at him. He touched his hat, and moved away from her. Molly Chase watched him go. Then, her cheeks suddenly redder, she turned and ran back the way she had come. At the door of the Cattleman's Rest, Harbin looked back, but the girl was gone.

FIVE

Paul Vail reined in his team at the mouth of the pass, where the road dipped sharply down toward the broken land at the base of the mountains. He shielded his eyes against the afternoon sun and stared out across the flat brown land. Lydia sat up straighter. Paul Vail smiled down at her.

"That dark streak there will be Red Rock," he said. "We'll be drivin' into town tonight. Two more days and we'll be in Wild Horse Valley."

The woman studied the harsh, barren grasslands that stretched as far as she could see, the flatness unbroken by tree or house. Paul Vail sensed the discouragement that filled her, and said: "It will be all right, Lydia. There's a river farther west, and trees. It isn't like back home, but it is a free, new country."

Always the dream, she thought, never the reality, the harsh, hard truth. But that idealism was a part of what she loved in Paul Vail. And she knew he would try, really try, this time, to bring the dream to reality.

Below them she could see the bobbing canvas tops of the other wagons as they rolled down the steep grade. Because of the cutbacks, she could see them all, big Gary Daniels's wagon in the lead. Teams, holding back, straining against the weight of loaded wagons, men riding the brake handles hard with their feet, cursing as the awkward Conestogas swayed dangerously near the edge of the roadbed.

Helen Condon waved to them from the rear of the wagon just ahead, and Paul lifted his hat. He smiled at Lydia. "Here we go." He clucked to the team, took a firmer hold of the reins, and let them pick their own pace forward to the first sharp downward dip of the trail. Behind them Joanie squealed as the wagon lurched forward.

"Oh, this is fun!" the girl shouted. She was holding the baby in her arms.

"Be careful, Joanie," Lydia warned automatically, and put her own feet up on the broad splashboard to keep from pitching forward.

Endless weeks, months of traveling. Heat and sun and

merciless desert winds. And now there were only two more days ahead of them. It didn't seem real that it could be almost over. Of course, only the first step would be over, and all the hard work was yet to start. But Lydia Vail had faith in the land; it would see them through, pray God. Paul would settle down, perhaps stop drinking so heavily. And even here in this harsh new frontier there would be people they knew. Other children for Joanie and the baby to grow up with.

Her thoughts scattered as the wagon lurched dangerously and Paul struggled, cursing under his breath, to get the ungainly wagon around a sharp cutback turn.

"Not so hard, Paul," she said once. He flashed her an angry look, but said nothing. He eased the grip, and the team worked together to make the turn.

Why do I interfere? she thought, miserably. *It infuriates him to have me be right, and I don't mean it that way. It's just that he doesn't know—No, that isn't true. He's failed so many times I can no longer trust him or his judgment, and he knows it, hates it, and in his own way is fighting against it.*

The last of the steep descent was safely made, and they wound their way through the broken rubble of the brakes. It was midafternoon when the Vail wagon, the last of the group, came into the flat open country again, and the settlers' wagons were strung out for a mile. Paul had not spoken for more than an hour, and Lydia was aware of the hard core of anger inside him, anger against her. It hurt her, but she accepted it.

Joanie sat between them, the baby on her lap, and Lydia looked now at her. The girl was thirteen, and already filling out. She would be beautiful someday. She had her father's dreamers' eyes, but the strength of Lydia was in them too. Lydia patted the braids of Joanie's silvery hair, and the girl looked up quickly and smiled.

"I'll be glad to get home again," Joanie said. "Course, it won't really be like back home, but I'll like it."

"Sure you will, honey," Lydia said, and frowned. Uncertainties still held her. What would life hold for Joanie and the baby?

The girl was staring soberly at the flat grasslands. She looked now at her mother. "I didn't want to come," she said slowly. "I hated leaving home. But now I'm glad. I like it here. I like the bigness. I'm scared, but I like it all." She paused. "You scared too, Ma?"

Lydia laughed softly and caught the girl's hand. "Of course I am, Joanie. But excited and pleased, too. It will all be new and strange and difficult, but we'll manage, and it will be worth while, and someday we'll think back about this time and laugh."

Paul Vail was listening, and despite himself he smiled. Lydia saw his smile, and thought that he could never sustain any emotion, not even anger, for long. Always and always something new would come along to attract him. There had been other women—Lydia cut the thought off quickly.

Paul: "It's worth all this trouble—wait and see. Lydia, I know we'll make it. This will be something to be proud of, something we've done by ourselves, without help from anybody—"

The wagons rolled steadily on, without pause, the drivers anxious now to get to Red Rock. An hour later they heard the piercing shrillness of a locomotive whistle, the first sign of civilization in weeks. They rolled past herds of range cattle drifting aimlessly. The gaps between the wagons closed, and they moved along the road as a unit.

It was late afternoon when the cavalcade of wagons rolled into Red Rock, and shadows slanted out across Trail Street. In the lead wagon Gary Daniels drove steadily on until a tall raw-boned man stepped from the boardwalk into the path of the wagon. He held up his right hand. Black mustaches drooped at either side of his jaw, and on his vest a silver star glinted in the dying sunlight. Daniels pulled up, kicked on the brake. The Vail wagon behind them was within earshot of the tall man.

"I'm Lou Colby, marshal of Red Rock," the tall man said, striding to the side and lifting his head to stare up at Daniels. He shook his head and spread his mustaches with one hand in order to spit to the ground. "Ain't there never goin' to be any end to you folks?"

Daniels grinned. "As long as there is free land for the takin', not much chance, Marshal."

Colby nodded. "I reckon that's right. Anyway, it's none o' my concern. We got law in Red Rock, an' city ordinances. One o' them says no homesteaders can camp inside the city limits. They's a camp of you folks out of town three-quarters of a mile. You drive right on through town. You need supplies, you come back in one or two at a time. I don't need to tell you this is a cow town. You ain't welcome here by most folks, but that ain't stoppin' you

45

from comin' anyway. But they's a right way an' a wrong way. I want no trouble—an' I'll damned well see there ain't none. South of the deadline is no place for home-steaders. End o' the month an' Saturday nights when they's a dance, you ain't welcome in town. Rest of the time get in early, buy what you need, and stay in your own camp after dark. No riders will molest you or your womenfolks there—I guarantee that. You pass the word to the others. Those rules got to be followed by all of you. The Land Office closes at three—but it's open at ten in the mornin', an' I suggest you appoint a committee of two, three of you to come in."

The marshal stepped back and nodded his head. Daniels waited a moment longer. "Marshal—we'll toe your mark. We want no trouble. But the folks with me will be askin' questions. We've heard of Wild Horse Valley—that's west of here, isn't it?"

"Northwest," Colby answered, and shook his head. "Good land—but not enough of it. Quite a settlement there now—with maybe a hundred families in Wagon-town with no place to go. But that's your lookout. Now roll them wagons out of town."

Daniels frowned, but obeyed, slapping the reins.

Lydia Vail turned to her husband. "What did he mean, a hundred families with no place to go?"

Vail shook his head. "How should I know?" he bit out, then more softly: "Sorry, Lydia. Reckon it was just his line of talk. We'll see in the mornin'. One thing, though —there ain't nothin' under God's blue sky that's goin' to keep us from the land we came for. That includes the marshal of Red Rock. It's hard to understand the way things are out here, Lydia. Apart from one-sided town lawmen like the marshal, there is no law, no justice ex-cept the kind a man can make for himself. It won't al-ways be like this—there's talk of Statehood for Wyoming —but in the meantime it's the reason for men like Ridge Harbin, the only justification they have for existing the way they do. They stand apart from the twisted local law —buck it in their own way. I won't say that way is right— God knows there's too much violence and bloodshed out here—but I can't say it isn't necessary either. These drifters who live by their guns are the element that bal-ances the scales; without them it could be worse than it is. They are a check and a warning to the men who would seize empire no matter the cost. And there is a lesson in that for people like us, Lydia. A hard lesson, but a true one." Paul Vail's jaw set stubbornly, and his eyes hardened. The woman beside him studied him for a moment, then shook her head and settled back on the seat.

For Joanie Vail, Red Rock was the first real excitement in days, and she sat on the outside of the seat, her right hand hanging on to the wooden top-bow. A cowboy riding down the street lifted his hat to her and deliberately winked. Joanie flushed, and Lydia had to smile at her daughter's obvious confusion. Nevertheless it made her think, and slowly a frown narrowed the space between her rounded brows. Joanie was growing up—too fast.

As they went through the town Paul Vail grew restless. "I've a mind to stop anyway," he said. Lydia caught the intent look he gave a passing saloon. She started to say something, then halted. Paul turned to look at her. He was expecting her to speak.

"Do what you think is best, Paul," she said slowly.

For a moment he looked at her, then frowned and looked away. "Better stay with the others," he said finally.

They left the town behind them, passed immense holding corrals for cattle shippers, then turned off the main road toward a stand of cottonwoods that puffed greenly against the darkening sky. The sun had set behind the mountains to the west, and the shadows of night were spreading over the flatlands. There was an encampment of thirty or more wagons clustered by the grove of trees, and two or three men walked out to meet them. Daniels's wagon stopped, and the others followed suit. Then Ralph Condon, who had walked up to the lead wagon, came back.

"We stop here," he said, cheerfully. "Land Office is open in the mornin'. Daniels has called a meetin' for nine o'clock tonight. He says to roll in anyplace. There's a creek down past that grove of trees with fair water. Them that's already here will meet with us an' fill us in on what's up. You'll never guess who's runnin' the show here —our old friend Hellfire Gordon, fat as a hog, an' mean as—" He broke off to grin up at Lydia. "We're in for some hellfire an' brimstone sermonizing."

He left, went back to his own wagon, and wheeled it out of line. Paul Vail hesitated, then followed suit. Condon drove his team forward, to the left of the grove of trees. He stopped just past the grove, where two other

47

wagons were parked. A large fire burned in an open place, and rocks had been piled to make a rude hearth for cooking. Two women were busy over the fire, but both looked up as the two new wagons rolled in.

"Wheel up ahead of me, Paul," Condon called, and Vail did as he was told. The place was good, sheltered from the afternoon sun by the trees, and close to a path that led down a sharp embankment into a gulley where the creek ran. Condon came up as Vail looped the reins over the brake handle.

"Best we're likely to do, Paul," Ralph Condon said. "Figger we might be here a day or two, so we'll make out here."

Paul Vail stood up and looked about. His eyes went back up the road toward Red Rock, and he licked at his mouth. "I'm out of tobacco, Lydia," he said. "I'll have to go into town. Come with me, Ralph?"

Condon grinned. "Helen wouldn't like it. Besides, Daniels said to stick close until we hold our meetin'. He's got somethin' on his mind."

"I'll be back before nine o'clock," Paul said. He avoided Lydia's eyes. "I've got to get some tobacco. I'll hobble the team and build a fire. You can fix dinner for you and the kids, Lydia. I'll be back as soon as I can."

Lydia hesitated. "Paul—" She broke off resignedly. "All right, Paul," she said slowly.

And later, when she was frying bacon over a low fire, Joanie came into the circle of firelight carrying a bucket of water from the creek. The girl set it down. "Where's Pa?" she asked.

Lydia shook her head.

The girl's mouth drew down stubbornly. "He's gone into town to get drunk again, hasn't he?"

"Joanie, please. I won't have you—"

"Have me what, Ma, tell the truth? Pa's a drunk—he'd be a drunken bum if it wasn't for you—an' he's doin' his best to get there anyway." The girl saw her mother's worn, tired look, then ran to her and held her tightly. "I'm sorry, Ma. I don't want to hurt you too. Pa does it bad enough, God knows."

For a moment Lydia held her daughter close. Then she managed a smile. "All right, Joanie. You're growing up. I've no right to keep anything from you. But it will be better when we stake our land, when your father sees his dreams turning into reality. It's hard for him, now; he's unsure, worried about us, Joanie, you and me and the baby. But it will be better."

"Sure, Ma," the girl said. "Sure it will."

But she doesn't really think so, Lydia thought. *My God, neither do I!* Though she tried to force the thought from her mind, it persisted despite her strongest efforts.

SIX

The morning of Ridge Harbin's fourth day in Red Rock came after a restless night of tossing and turning. He had fallen into an exhausted sleep an hour or so before dawn, and awoke before the sun was an hour high. The harsh morning light was softened by the dark green shade over the single window, and the holes and cracks in the material of the shade let in a myriad of light streaks. Dust motes danced along them, and the room was already getting too warm for comfort. He kicked away the single coverlet he had crawled under at dawn when the coldness of the night had become uncomfortable, then lay back and tried to relax.

Awakening was the hardest part of each day for him to face. It was always the same, except when he was on the trail, a restless urge to be moving on, as if it were desperately necessary to leave something behind him. He had long since realized the futility of ever running away from his memories. He lay still, gazing grimly at the ceiling.

Finally, he rose and began to dress.

The room in the Cattleman's Rest was identical with a thousand other Western hotel rooms, from the faded, peeling rose-figured wallpaper to the cracked white porcelain pitcher and bowl on the washstand. Over the bulge-bellied dresser a yellowing mirror hung crookedly, part of the silver backing peeled away, letting the ugly pattern of the wallpaper show through. On the whitewashed plaster wall that covered the tiny closet, some previous tenant had lettered with flourishing curlicues:

> *Maybe it's far, and maybe it's near,*
> *But anywhere else is better than here.*

Beneath the motto was a score or more of pencil-scribbled names and hearts and daggers, most of them worn away. Sunlight glistened through three closely spaced bullet holes in one wall, and beside it a name, *Nathan Wright, Abilene, Texas, 1878*. A spade-shaped outline covered the three bullet holes, and a larger outline formed the ace of spades.

Harbin turned to look up at his own revolver where it hung in its holster from one of the brass bedposts. He reached for it, pulled it free of the leather and lay back, holding the gun between his two hands. He touched the carefully cut notches with the tip of one finger, and his eyes closed as he remembered names and faces. His finger moved down one side, and he reversed the gun and touched the final notches. His finger rubbed gently at the inch of handle that was unnotched. What names, what faces would he remember because of the notches he might cut there?

He reached back and shoved the gun into the holster, then rolled over and sat up. He washed and shaved, then dressed slowly. The room was stuffy. He eased the blind up, unlocked and opened the window. It looked on the rubbish-strewn lot behind the Cattleman's Rest, and farther beyond, the hummocks of the grassland began, undulating in irregular waves toward distant mountains. For a moment he studied the land, a brown, flat road that angled across it, and heard the insistent call of the mountains and the promise of what might lie behind them, then shrugged it away as false, for he knew what lay beyond them.

He turned from the window, crossed back to the bed and took down his gun. He sat on the edge of the bed, broke the cylinder, and emptied the shells beside him. The blue of the barrel was worn away by constant handling. He went over the gun carefully with a rag, removing every trace of lint and dust. He checked the action, the tension, of the trigger carefully.

He laid the gun on the bed, stood up and buckled the gunbelt about his trim waist. He settled the holster into place over his left hip, and placed the gun in it. For a moment he frowned with concentration; then his left hand went down and around in one smooth flowing motion, and the gun came up level. The reverse draw was seldom seen, most men preferring the speed and certainty of the straight or the cross-draw; but for a careful few the reverse draw held an advantage. Naturally right-handed, Ridge Harbin had trained his left hand and arm until drawing and firing his revolver was almost a reflex action. Not that he neglected the cross-draw with his right hand; it was the most natural of the two and somewhat faster. But there were circumstances under which a man's right hand might be occupied during that split-second that was all that stood between him and death. The act of shaking hands, of scratching awkwardly, of raising a glass, cutting a piece of meat, lifting his hat—there were a thousand times when a man's right hand could be busy. But a man could always keep one hand free if he had to.

Harbin had seen men who wore two guns at their hips, but they were in the minority. And none of them bore a name for swift gunplay. He had tried a double belt with two holsters himself, as he had tried the cut-away, the bottomless, the swivel and shoulder rigs. All of them were discussed by men of the gun; but for Harbin the single long-barreled revolver, the cross-and-reverse draws, were the easiest to master.

True, he sacrificed something of speed in both. He had seen men who could empty their revolvers in a four-foot circle in less time than it required him to draw and place two shots. But his two shots would lie not an inch apart, and never beyond the radius of a circle a foot in diameter. And there was nothing that could break or disturb his intentness enough to keep him from placing those two shots. Not even a quickly placed shot in his chest, as one man had discovered in the instant before he had died.

Grimly, Harbin worked with his gun. His movements were deliberate, never hurried, and yet his gun would level out in one hand or the other with incredible speed. His feet could move, twist him to either side; he could fall forward, to either side, or backward, and still the draw could be made.

And each time, with the gun held out, he would check the alignment of the sights. Once he frowned; his shot would have miscarried by six inches at twenty feet. He shook his head. He picked a spot on the flowered wallpaper, held the gun rigidly out. He aimed deliberately, cocked the hammer, released it with the trigger. The target spot did not move from above the sights. His thumb and trigger finger worked faster; five shots clicked off as fast as a man could blink his eyes. The sights remained steadily on the target, without swerving.

His face wet with sweat, but satisfied at last, Harbin reloaded the gun and placed it back in the holster. He considered himself in the tarnished mirror over the dresser, a sardonic smile on his lips. His white hair was neatly combed back, his face surprisingly clear and youthful. He shook his head again, and picked up his coat but did not put it on. He carried it over his arm as he went out into the hall and locked his door behind him.

He left the key to his room at the desk in the lobby. Then he hesitated. He wasn't hungry, but he wanted coffee. He crossed the lobby to the dining room. It was cool and dark, and he started for a table at the far wall. He had crossed halfway when he heard hurried footsteps behind him.

"Ridge Harbin!" a man's voice called. But Harbin recognized the voice in that terrible instant before he turned with drawn gun. His instinct to strike had been strong upon him and almost—almost—he had made a mistake. He caught himself now and turning slowly.

The man coming up was grinning, holding out one hand. He was short, dressed in the Levis, open-necked shirt and vest of a rider, and carried a wide-brimmed Stetson in his left hand. His face was broad and freckled, and his hair was sandy red.

"Ridge," he said. "Jesus, but it's good to see your face!"

"Hello Herbie," Harbin answered. They shook hands.

Herbie Nichols kept grinning. "I heard you was in town. Johnny Lee said you was back. It's been a long time no see."

Harbin nodded and led the way to a table, and unobtrusively choosing the chair against the wall he sat down. Nichols sat opposite him. Harbin leaned forward, placed both hands on the table.

"Herbie—don't ever run up behind me again," Harbin said softly. His face still held strain. "I might have shot you."

Herbie Nichols blinked, and his broad mouth dropped open, then snapped shut. "Christ, I'm sorry," he said. "Just seein' you—even knowin' you was here, I was that tickled, I never stopped to think—"

"Forget it," Harbin said. The waitress came up, and he ordered ham and eggs and coffee.

Nichols said, "Double it," and the girl moved away.

A strained silence lasted for a minute until the waitress came back with their coffee, and then Herbie Nichols said, "Truth of the matter is, I rode into town to see you, Ridge."

Harbin spooned sugar into his coffee and stirred it. His eyes were expressionless, but his smile softened the hardness of his face.

Nichols frowned at his coffee. "I never thought I'd miss any man as much as I missed you when you pulled up stakes three years ago, Ridge. I used to think sometimes maybe I just liked to walk in your shadow, pretendin' I was big because you was. Maybe I ain't proud, but I try to be honest with myself. You taught me that. An' I learned after you'd gone it wasn't that. You were the best friend I ever had. I don't know what I meant to you—if anythin'."

Harbin's smile widened. "Friends are a luxury I can't afford, Herb," he said slowly. "But I made an exception in your case. Riding away from Three Horn by myself was a hard thing to do. But it has been done. It's better to leave it that way."

Herbie Nichols grinned up at Harbin. "Sure, Ridge, sure," he said. "I'm not tryin' to pick up where we left off. The pieces are scattered to hell an' gone. But I miss the old days here. Three Horn wasn't a hardnut outfit then; we had fun. Like the time we found Shell Buffano drunk here in Red Rock an' loaded him onto that cattle train. Hell, he was clear to Junction before he woke up—he never *did* find out what happened! That damned brakey threw him off at Selby, an' he had to hoof it eight miles back to town. I never seen a man as mad before or since."

Harbin thought: *I remember the good times, too, Herbie. I remember when I could walk and talk and act like a man instead of a lobo wolf. But that was a long time ago, when there were twelve notches on my gun instead of twenty-five.*

Harbin said, "A man can't live in the past, Herb." His voice was flat. "I won't forget those times, either. But they're gone."

"They sure'n hell are gone," Nichols agreed soberly. "Vane Dallard was always rock. Now he's flint, an' twice as ugly. Johnny Lee spends most of his time on the prod. Leastwise that part he ain't primpin'. He ain't rode fence in six months. He ain't a straw boss, but he walks like one. He's killed five men in the last three years. He's run off four, five more. He's ridin' high in the stirrups, an' to hell with anybody that gets in his way. An' Vane Dallard backin' his play to the limit. Like Johnny was a hired gun pointin' where Dallard says."

Their meal came then, and Herbie broke off. Harbin waited in silence, his thoughts going back three years. The old warmness he had felt for Nichols was stirring anew. The red-haired rider talked too freely and at the wrong times, he never seemed able to do anything right the first time he tried, and yet his shortcomings were a part of his likeableness. He wore his feeling like a coat, for anyone to see. And his friendship, once given, was inviolate; nothing could ever shake his faith.

Herbie chewed a chunk of ham, then washed it down with a swallow of coffee almost white with cream. "Nothin's the same any more," he said. "An' there's goin' to be trouble, sure's hell's hot. Dallard's fenced in the lower end of Wild Horse Valley, this side of the river, an' posted his notice it's Three Horn land. That ain't true. It ain't deeded. I seen the pre-emption lists of Indian land —an' that whole hundred-section piece, the best damned land in the whole Red Rock country, is on it. Some of these smart crackers are goin' to call Dallard's hand, an' there's goin' to be holy hell to pay."

Harbin lowered his fork slowly to his plate. He looked at Herbie carefully. "A man can stand his ground, or he can run, Herb," he said. "He can't do both."

The red-haired man nodded slowly. "That's the hell of it, Ridge. I ain't got the guts to do either one. I grew up on Three Horn; Dallard's pa was my first boss when I was fourteen. I never been anyplace else. I wouldn't know where to run if I was to start. I wouldn't even know how to begin bein' on my own. I'm drawin' eighty bucks a month, which is more'n double what any other rancher's payin' for hands. I still own that two-section piece my ma had. I still figger I'll run my own brand someday when I get enough saved." He stopped, looked closely at Harbin. "An' there's a girl here in town. We're goin' to get hitched someday."

Harbin said, seriously: "Dallard will pay more later. Scalp money runs high. You'll be able to afford your own spread, Herb—if you live long enough."

Nichols laid his knife and fork down. He frowned intently at his plate. "That ain't what I wanted you to say, Ridge, but I reckon it's the truth. You know, I'd feel better if you were back on Three Horn with me."

Harbin shook his head. "I'm riding through," he said. "Sooner or later."

Nichols raised his head, slowly. "Ridge—you've done it. What's it like—killin' a man you don't hate?"

"Too damned easy," Harbin said, quietly. "But I've never killed a man for money. I hope I never will."

"But"—Herbie Nichols lifted puzzled eyes—"I've heard—" He broke off uncertainly.

Ridge Harbin frowned. "Herb, you don't know me any more. I'm not the same. Nothing stays the same. You've changed too. Maybe not as much. But the change is there, just the same. A man has to have something to live by— a stand of some kind—even a man like me. If I lose that, there won't be anything left."

The other man looked away. His freckled face was drawn and pale. "The trouble is, most of us set our standards so high we can't live up to them. Once you break them it gets easier each time. I'm still trying to be honest."

Harbin was stirred despite himself. For a moment he hesitated; then he leaned forward. "Get out of this while you still can, Herb," he said, finally. "It's not too late now. But once things start, it will be. Ride south. It's still open range land in New Mexico and west Texas. You can buy out a two-bit outfit and build it the way you want it. It will take time, but it will work."

"I don't know, Ridge. I just don't know," Nichols said slowly. "Just the same, thanks for telling me what you think."

They left it like that between them, and later, when Harbin left the dining room, it was with a growing feeling of loss. There was a stubbornness in Herbie Nichols he hadn't remembered, and Harbin knew too well what it could lead him to. He shook his head, and went through the lobby to the boardwalk. He stood there for some moments, rolling a cigar between his fingers before lighting it. He smoked reflectively for a few seconds.

Ridge Harbin had been in Red Rock three full days. A longer time than he had anticipated, largely because luck had not smiled on him. He had something less than a hundred dollars in his pocket—and it was forty miles to the first town beyond the Red Rock country. There was a pressing urgency inside him to ride on, and a stubborn opposition to it that held him there. The main trouble, he decided wryly, was the simple fact he had no good reason for doing either.

He shook his head, and started across the street; then he stopped. Three horsemen came down Trail Street, their mounts lifting their feet daintily clear of the yellow dust. Harbin knew all three men. In the van, with the two others slightly behind him, rode Vane Dallard.

There was a natural arrogance about Dallard that made Johnny Lee's swagger seem artificial. His shoulders were broad and thick, and his hands were huge. He rode stiffly erect, looking neither right nor left, his left arm bent stiffly in front of him, holding the reins. The features of his face were heavy, almost gross, but the thinness of his mouth and the hardness of his chin attested to his strength of will. He rode past Harbin without turning his head, but Ridge caught the quick flare of recognition in his eyes—and with it something else he did not understand.

Johnny Lee rode to Dallard's left, and Joe Wayne beside Lee. Wayne saw Harbin, and his mouth drew down in an ugly grimace; his eyes never moved from Harbin's face. Johnny Lee lifted one hand, but did not speak.

The three riders passed, and Harbin stepped out into the yellow dust of Trail Street. Avoiding an oncoming freighter's wagon hauling supplies from the station at the end of the street, he made his way across. He walked the short block to Miller's Mercantile Emporium and went inside. He noticed that the three Three Horn horses were tethered in front of the Prairie Flower, although all three riders were out of sight.

Walter Miller was a short big-bellied man wearing a starched white apron that bulged grotesquely. He grinned. "By gosh and by damn, it's Ridge Harbin, back in Red Rock!" He placed a finger beside his red-veined nose and grinned. "Two bits says it's shells you want."

"You just won two bits," Ridge answered, smiling. "How are you, Walter?"

The fat man patted his belly admiringly. "Can't complain. Older, not a hell of lot wiser, but some bigger. A man's brain stops growin' when he's fourteen, but his belly don't. You're lookin' hard an' flat, Ridge. Older. How long's it been? Two, three years? Seems longer. It's good seein' you, Ridge."

Harbin drew his revolver, laid it on the counter. Walter Miller grinned. "You still carry that Schofield gun, Ridge? Thought you'd be packin' one of the fancy new Colts like the rest of 'em."

Ridge shook his head. "I'd like two boxes of forty-fives, Walter."

The fat man nodded, turned away. He placed two oblong cartridge boxes on the counter. "Since Colt converted to self-contained cartridges in Seventy-two, we've sold a million shells, I reckon. But not too many forty-fives. Most men are usin' thirty-eights. I still get call for forty-ones. Johnny Lee used 'em until a year ago when he bought one of Colt's new Lightning models. Funny thing, but it's a forty-five, too. Pack a hell of a wallop, those Army shells."

Harbin paid for the shells and left the store. He walked down Trail Street to the stables, got his horse, and rode out of town. A little less than a mile beyond Red Rock he passed a sizable wagon camp. A dog ran at the heels of the gelding for a little way, then ran off at a piercing whistle from a boy who watched Harbin from deep-set, unfriendly eyes. Homesteaders, the awkward, too heavily loaded wagons, Studebakers, Conestogas, and a dozen or more homemade prairie schooners. Over campfires, women were preparing meals; some were washing and hanging clothes on improvised lines strung between wagons, and others were shaking out bedclothes. There was a closeness that they shared that Harbin felt but could not participate in; he was an outsider, and their eyes followed him resentfully.

He rode on, and a mile or two beyond where the road turned from beside the creek he left it and followed the deepcut creek. He halted the gelding where the river had cut through a high swaleback ridge, leaving steep clay banks. He dismounted, left the gelding to graze among the thick grass along the riverbank, and made his way a hundred yards farther on foot. The creek angled sharply south here, and there was a shelf of land above reach of the water. He paced off seventy feet from the clay bank and made a mark. Using a stick, he traced the crude outlines of a human figure on the clay, then stepped back to consider it; it would do, he decided, and he returned to his seventy-foot marker.

Harbin drew the Schofield-Colt, and with slow deliberation put five shots into the smaller upper circle he had drawn. The pattern was good; only one shot had broken the exact four-inch grouping. But Harbin frowned. It took time and a deliberate aim to make a headshot; but every one would have to count. He reloaded the gun and fired five more shots. The center of the smaller upper circle was chewed away, and there were no scattered shots this time.

For twenty minutes, then, he drew and fired the Colt, varying position, moving with the shot, against it, to either side and by the end of that time the speed of draw and firing satisfied him. And not one shot had missed either the upper or lower part of the human-figure diagram. The clay was pitted and chewed away, and Harbin's upper body was wet with sweat. But there was no tremble in his hands. His smile was grim acknowledgment that he was satisfied.

He loaded the revolver for the last time, and had just closed the loading gate when he heard a sound behind him and spun about, gun extended. Johnny Lee was perched on the edge of the bank, squatted down, watching him. In the bright noonday sunlight his calfskin jacket glistened almost wetly, and his white Stetson was tipped jauntily back from his handsome, smiling face.

"You're good—too damned good," Johnny Lee said. "I give you that. I've never seen anyone as good. Unless it's me." His grinned widened, and he half jumped, half skidded down the steep embankment. He landed running, and came up even with Harbin. He wasn't breathing hard.

Lee's bright blue eyes sparkled with amusement. "You wouldn't want to see who's the fastest, would you, Ridge?"

The challenge struck at the perverseness inside Harbin, and his smile moved his thin lips. "I might," he said. "How do you propose doing it?"

Lee frowned, then brightened. "You hear that dog yapping? Some nester's kid's runnin' him back upcreek a ways. He barks, then stops. He's still now. We both draw and fire when he barks again. Your target's good enough."

Harbin holstered the Schofield slowly and shrugged. They stood, almost facing each other, arms at their sides. Their eyes met and held. In the silence came the hushed murmur of the creek running over stones, the soughing of the prairie wind. Tension grew between them.

Lee said suddenly, harshly, "Why in hell doesn't he bark?"

And almost with his words came the sharp yap-yap of the dog. Lee's hand was moving almost with the sound, a bewildering blur of coordinated bone and muscle. His gun came up level, spurted fire, and the explosion was followed so closely by Harbin's the shots were almost as one, and Harbin's second shot racketed right at the heels of the first two.

"High!" Lee said, bitterly. "But I got mine away first."

"So you did," Harbin agreed slowly. Lee's shot couldn't have knocked him off balance before his own two shots were away. There was a cold satisfaction in the thought.

A similar thought must have occurred to Lee, for he asked, "Where did you put them?" He looked uncertainly at the pocked face of the clay bank.

"I don't know," Harbin said, lying. He knew very well where they had gone; both shots had struck in the center of the larger lower circle. If they had struck a man, they would have been just above his belt, two inches apart, terrible killing shots that would have ended the fight.

Lee frowned uncertainly. Then he shrugged and grinned. "I was the fastest," he said finally.

Harbin matched his smile and nodded. "You were."

Lee asked, "Want to try again?"

Harbin shook his head. "I'm through for the day," he said. "Time for chow."

Lee looked up at the sun through narrowed eyes. "Yeah, guess it is," he said. "I followed you out here. Miller told me you'd bought shells. I figured you'd be along the creek bottom someplace."

Harbin kept his smile in place. "Didn't you have anything better to do, Johnny?"

The younger man grinned. "Yeah, but she's slingin' hash until six. Vane Dallard sent me. He wants to see you, Ridge. I don't know why, but it ain't hard to guess. Three Horn could use another gun."

"The one they've got is good enough," Harbin said.

Johnny Lee grinned back at him. "Sure, and I've told the old man that to his face. But Vane Dallard's a stubborn son." Lee shrugged. "It's no skin off my nose. Maybe I can pick up some pointers."

"You've picked up enough now, Johnny," Harbin said slowly. "All right. I'll see Dallard."

He led the way back upcreek to the gelding and swung into the saddle. Johnny Lee said: "Ride 'head. I'll catch up."

Harbin shook his head. "I'll wait for you, Johnny," he said.

The younger man climbed the embankment, and Harbin rode back the way he had come. He reined in when he reached the road to Red Rock. Johnny Lee's mount came driving hard; he slowed when Harbin urged the gelding on. Side by side, they returned to town. As they passed the wagon town, Harbin was again aware of the hostile stares of the people who watched them ride by.

"This is nothin'," Johnny Lee said. "You ought to ride

through Wild Horse Valley. You can feel the hate pushin' against you. Just the same, there are times like now when I wish things was different. Take a look at that nester heifer, Ridge."

A girl in a gingham dress was walking toward them, down the dusty road from town. In the bright sunlight her face was shadowed by the bonnet she wore, but the wind pushing against the light material of her dress outlined her slender figure in every detail. The girl raised her head as they neared, and Harbin saw the round, pretty face, the tipturned nose. It was Molly Chase.

The girl recognized him at once and smiled; then her eyes went swiftly to Johnny Lee's smiling features. Harbin saw the girl blush.

Molly Chase looked quickly back at Harbin and nodded. Then they were past and Lee was studying Harbin with renewed interest.

"I'll be damned," he said. "You do get around, don't you, Ridge?"

"I know her," Harbin said, almost reluctantly. He swung about to look at the man beside him. Lee had his head turned to stare after the girl. "Lay off, Johnny."

The gunfighter's expressive mouth curled in a mocking smile. "Staked your claim, Ridge?"

"No." Harbin met the other's smile evenly. "But I'd hate to have to kill you, Johnny." His voice was flat, and not for the first time Harbin could read fear of himself in Johnny Lee's eyes.

"I'm not sure you could, Ridge," Lee said, finally.

"Now you know a way to find out," Harbin returned. Their eyes met and locked, and Lee looked away first.

"All right, Ridge," he said slowly. "A nester's brat ain't worth fightin' for." He shrugged. "Forget it."

The subject was closed between them, Harbin knew; but just the same he had issued a flat challenge and Johnny Lee would not forget it. In front of witnesses Lee would never have backed water even that much. Harbin knew this, and thought of the split second by which Lee had beaten his draw. Ridge Harbin held few illusions, and none about himself. He knew he was good with a gun, as he knew the odds were for him bucking someone just a shade better sooner or later. The question that held him as they turned into Trail Street was a simple one: *Was Johnny Lee that someone?*

61

SEVEN

Vane Dallard stood at the far end of the long mahogany bar in the Prairie Flower, his broad back leaning against the counter, his bootheels hooked over the brass rail, his elbows on the top of the bar. He watched Lee and Harbin come in; though his granite-hard face didn't change, Harbin caught a slight narrowing of the rancher's eyes. To Dallard's left stood Joe Wayne, half swung around to face the doors, his face brooding and ugly. Beyond Wayne, Herbie Nichols stood silently, staring down into his glass of whisky.

Johnny Lee led the way toward Dallard, motioned Wayne back with one indolent gesture, and took his place at the bar. Harbin stopped in front of Dallard and said, "Hello, Vane."

The big rancher remained silent a little too long, then moved his head. It was a gesture of condescension that made Johnny Lee smile at Harbin.

Ridge said, "You talk too damned much, Vane," and started to swing around.

Dallard pushed erect from the bar. "Touchy bastard, ain't you, Ridge? All right, I'll say hello. It's been a long time. Nice weather we're havin'. How're things with you?" His voice was hard. "That satisfy you?"

Harbin turned back slowly. "My quitting Three Horn still rankles with you, doesn't it, Vane?" he asked curiously. He shrugged. "That's all right with me. You wanted to see me. You've seen me. What now?"

He stood with his hands at his sides, his face immovable. His eyes didn't leave Dallard's face, but he was aware of the men beyond Dallard, too, and they knew it.

Dallard's reaction was a humorless laugh. He leaned back against the bar, picked up a shot glass of whisky. "Reb, I'm buyin' Harbin a drink."

The bartender set a glass up beside Harbin. Dallard turned, picked up the tall black bottle, and filled the glass. Whisky ran over the edge of the glass and made a shining pool on the bar. Harbin realized then that Dallard was drunk. But his iron control was not weakened; there was a slight flush on his face, and his eyes shone brightly. Beyond that the liquor had no visible effect.

The Prairie Flower held other men, Harbin saw; one or two he guessed to be Three Horn riders, others who were not. But the bar was empty except for the four Three Horn men and himself. It was another mark of Dallard's character that men made way for him.

Dallard raised his glass. "I'm waitin', Ridge," he said.

Harbin shook his head. "I don't drink before I eat, Vane," he answered. "I'm hungry."

The rancher's face went redder, but he held his anger under control. He tossed off his whisky, threw the empty glass across the bar. "You won't bend an inch for God Almighty, will you, Ridge?" Dallard asked.

Harbin said: "You're not God, Vane. No matter what you think."

"All right," Dallard said thickly. "All right. I'm not God. I'm just Vane Dallard. But here in the Red Rock the difference isn't as great as you suppose." His lopsided grin broke the rock-hardness of his features. Beyond him Johnny Lee laughed his short nervous laugh. Joe Wayne glared openly at Harbin, and Herbie Nichols continued to stare morosely into his whisky glass.

Dallard straightened again. "You've made your little play, Ridge. That's all right with me. You've got to make a show. I understand that, I think. Like Johnny Lee an' his fancy duds. But it doesn't mean a damned thing to me. I'm buyin' you, Ridge. You and your toughness, and the gun you wear. Three Horn can use you. Two hundred a month and found."

As if the matter were closed, Dallard swung back to the bar. The bartender had replaced his glass and he filled it to the brim, spilling the red liquor on the polished wood once more.

Harbin felt the slow burn of heavy anger, but he fought it down. "Vane," he said, slowly and cleanly, "you can go to hell."

He saw Dallard stiffen, saw Johnny Lee lose his smile. Harbin waited a moment longer, wondering if Dallard had the guts to push it any farther. But the rancher lowered the glass to the bar and turned slowly to Harbin, face expressionless. Harbin stood there a moment longer, then backed two steps. Dallard's voice, oddly calm, stopped him.

"Ridge," Vane Dallard said, speaking carefully, no

thickness to his voice now, "Ridge, get out of the Red Rock."

Harbin smiled. "In my own time, Vane," he answered. Their eyes held for a long instant; then Dallard turned back to the bar. Harbin turned and walked out through the swinging doors to the street.

Back on the boardwalk, Harbin paused to light a cigar, feeling the tension draining from him. Why had it happened? He frowned. Though Dallard's arrogance was a natural part of the man, as natural as breathing, it did not fail to irritate Harbin every time he encountered it. That had been the reason he had left Three Horn years ago; it had been either leave or kill Vane Dallard, and Harbin could not escape the feeling he had only postponed something that was inevitable. And by refusing to bend to Dallard's arrogance, he had committed himself to something he wanted very much to avoid.

To Vane Dallard there were only two positions, with him or against him. And Harbin knew too well where he stood as of now. The perverseness of his nature made him smile again, and he walked along the boardwalk to the nearest restaurant. He went to the farthest table, and took the chair against the wall. He had just seated himself when Herbie Nichols came through the door into the café.

Nichols's freckled face was red, and he came directly to Harbin's table.

"Now you've torn it, Ridge," he said.

"No," Harbin replied, smiling. "I just didn't knit it back together again. All Vane Dallard has to do is leave it lay."

"You know he can't," Nichols said. "Dallard ain't built that way. To his way of thinking, you can't straddle a fence."

"Then he'll have to learn," Harbin said with finality.

"You plan on teachin' him?" Nichols insisted.

"No," Harbin said. "Look, Herb, things happen this way. You can run or you can stay put."

"Which are you plannin' to do, Ridge?"

Harbin frowned. "I won't run, Herb," he said, finally. "I can't. Johnny Lee said men like us can't afford to let dogs yap at our heels. If one does it, more will try. That's the way it is. I've known these things to wear themselves out. It could happen again."

"Not with Vane Dallard," Herb Nichols said grimly. "Just the same, I wish it could be squared. Sooner or later Dallard will make his try."

"And you'll go with Dallard, is that what you're trying to say, Herb?"

Nichols nodded. "That's the size of it, damn it to hell!" he bit out. "Ridge—you said you were riding through. Do it—now."

Harbin shook his head slowly. "Now I can't, Herb," he answered. "I need a stake to move on. But what's more important, Vane Dallard's made it impossible for me to leave now. I told you a man has to have a standard to live by—for a gunfighter it is a strange one. Have you ever wondered about the number of men I've killed, Herb? I've wondered too—wondered why there haven't been twice, three times as many dead men behind me. And I know the answer, too. Dogs hate and fear a lobo wolf, but they'll never tackle one if they are alone. Everyone out here listens to gun talk—men hold that same hate and fear of a gunman—and they follow everything he does; every move he makes carries its own significance. If I ride out of Red Rock today, I'll leave talk behind me —talk that will follow me no matter how far I ride. Talk that Vane Dallard faced me down, ran me out of Red Rock. And it will be believed by men who want to believe it and who are waiting for me to break. Such talk will kill me as certainly as Dallard could with his rifle. Can you see that, Herb?"

Nichols's bitter frown deepened. "Sure I see it, Ridge. Never run, never let a dog see or think you're afraid of him—hell, I know that, too." He shook his head. "I'm sorry, Ridge, but there's nothing more I can do. I'll say goodbye and good luck."

Harbin continued to frown. The old friendship he felt for Nichols made him speak. "Herb," he said softly, "let Dallard do what he has to—but stay out of it. You walk through enough mud, and some of it's bound to spatter on you."

Nichols stared into his eyes, then turned and left the restaurant. A poignant sense of loss assailed Harbin then, but he shrugged it away as the waitress appeared to take his order. Regret was a commodity that Ridge Harbin could not afford.

He ate the meal in silence, took his time over his coffee, and let the waitress refill his cup. He lighted a fresh cigar and smoked it thoughtfully, building thoughts carefully, emotionlessly in his mind, laying out the pattern of recent events in an orderly fashion, studying them carefully.

Johnny Lee was a known factor; to add Harbin's name to his growing list of kills he would chance almost anything but certain death. Joe Wayne and his uneasy denial of the fear of Harbin that gripped him was another certainty; Wayne would have to be cornered to be dangerous, and Harbin would know when that time came. Herbie Nichols—Harbin frowned. How far would Herbie carry his loyalty to Three Horn and the man that ran it? The thought bothered Harbin. And after Herbie there was Vane Dallard, the focal point of the whole matter. As Harbin had told Nichols, he would take no overt action; and it was most probably that Dallard would still avoid an open break. But Harbin had taken his stand, and he could not back away from it. Even if it meant trouble, even if it meant a showdown with Johnny Lee—even if it meant killing Herbie Nichols—

Harbin broke the thought off sharply. It would not come to that. Herbie would avoid being placed into a position from which there was no retreat, or forcing Harbin into one. It was poor solace, and Harbin placed little faith in it, but the fact remained that it was all he could count upon.

Returning to his room at the Cattleman's Rest, Harbin lay across the bed, his hands behind his head. Although the room was stifling hot, there was a slight breeze through the open window, enough to stir the dingy curtains. Without being aware of it, Harbin fell asleep. When he awakened suddenly, the room was dark and he was wet with sweat and trembling hard. He sat up slowly. Without lighting the single lamp on the table beside his bed, Harbin went to the washstand, dumped water into the washbowl and doused his face and head. He dried himself, feeling better, and removed his shirt to replace it with a clean one. He lighted the lamp after pulling the shades on his open window, and sat on the edge of the bed to smoke a cigar.

The same impatient desire to move on assailed him, but he dismissed it. He could not run from Dallard, or even give the appearance of running. He shook his head and frowned into the smoke.

It was after eight o'clock when Ridge Harbin left the hotel and walked up Trail Street. He walked slowly, and his eyes kept busy. Twice he slowed still more as he came abreast of lounging men in the shadows of buildings, but each time after a quick but careful scrutiny of the street he moved on. He paused again in front of the Prairie Flower Saloon, then threw away the last of his cigar and pushed through the swinging doors into the murky, smoke-filled interior. At the far end of the room a girl in a spangled dress sat on the top of a piano, singing in a sad, small voice. The bar was well lined, and at the scattered poker tables groups were playing earnestly beneath low, green-shaded lamps.

Harbin took his evening drink, then circulated around the room, pausing once or twice at tables, but each time moving on. No one spoke to him until he came to a corner table. Four men were around it, playing draw poker. Harbin recognized Joe Wayne first, then Herbie Nichols, whose back was toward the room. The man to Nichols's left was vaguely familiar, but it took a moment for Harbin to place him. It was the homesteader he had helped across the river four days ago. What had the man said his name was? Vail—Paul Vail. The man's eyes caught Harbin, and he smiled and nodded.

Across the table, facing the room, Joe Wayne looked up at Harbin and grinned. "Well, damn me if it isn't the big man himself," he said, too loudly. "Sit down and take a hand, Harbin."

Herbie Nichols turned in his chair, his face drawn and serious before he smiled. "Hi, Ridge," he said. "Sit in, if you want."

Harbin looked at Vail. Paul Vail nodded. "Shore," he said. "Harbin—Harbin—Ridge Harbin." He looked up again, too quickly.

"How are you, Vail?" Harbin asked. "Maybe my luck's in."

He took an empty chair, placed on the far side of Wayne, who moved around the table. Harbin sat down, glanced around. "Table stakes?"

"Sure." Wayne cut in. He riffled the cards in his hand. "This is a piker's game so far."

Harbin saw Vail flush, but the homesteader said nothing. There was a glass on the table in front of him, and he emptied it at a gulp. His face was red, and his eyes were hollowed. He had been drinking hard. At a guess, he had forty dollars in gold and silver piled in front of him.

Probably most of his stake, Harbin thought, half angrily. He remembered the handsome, pale-faced woman who had driven the Conestoga across the river. The damned fool didn't know when he was well off. Harbin looked at Joe Wayne. The Three Horn rider was frowning.

Herbie Nichols said: "Ridge, you know Joe Wayne, Paul Vail—this is Andy Trouper of the Rocking W."

Harbin nodded. Trouper was a small, weathered man past forty, with pale, unreadable eyes. Wayne riffled the cards again, and hailed a passing waiter. He ordered whisky all around, then set himself to the task of dealing five cards each. Harbin picked up his cards. High card was a queen, and he held a pair of treys. Vail lifted his cards, looked at them, and then smiled.

"I'll open," he said.

Harbin caught Wayne's almost open sneer. "Okay, sodbuster," the Three Horn rider said. "For what, two bits?"

Paul Vail flushed, but said nothing. He dropped three silver dollars on the table. The hand was played out, and Vail won with three sevens. Wayne threw his cards on the table and laughed rudely.

"Your pot," he said. "Your deal—make it as straight as the furrows you think you're goin' to run across Three Horn land."

Paul Vail frowned, then refilled his glass and drank it down. His hands were trembling as he picked up the cards. He riffled them clumsily, and Wayne laughed again. Wayne looked at Harbin.

"Pretty fast company for a farmer, ain't it, Harbin?"

Ridge let his eyes fix to Wayne's face. "His money's good with me, Wayne," he answered.

Joe Wayne's laughing face twisted half angrily. "Reckon you think more of nesters than I do, Harbin."

The Three Horn rider was on the prod, Harbin thought. He smiled thinly at Wayne. "To tell you the truth, Wayne," he said, slowly, "it doesn't matter much to me what you think."

Wayne grew red in the face, but said nothing. Herbie Nichols said: "For Christ sake, lay off, Joe. This is supposed to be a friendly game."

Wayne glanced angrily at Nichols, but held his peace. He frowned at Vail's awkward shuffle. "You heard the man, churn twister—it's a friendly game."

Vail continued to frown in silence, but dealt out the new hand. Twice during the play Wayne made contemptuous remarks, but each time Vail ignored them. Harbin knew that Wayne was reaching a dangerous stage of frustrated anger, and looked at Nichols. The freckle-faced cowboy shrugged but said nothing.

Paul Vail's luck was phenomenal. He won consistently, bigger and bigger pots. And Wayne lapsed into sullen silence. The pile of coins in front of him diminished, and the stack in front of Vail grew larger. The homesteader began to relax, to smile more often. He drank too much to be a good poker player, Harbin thought, but his luck was good.

The play reached the showdown stage, with a final hand being dealt by Vail, and Wayne's last dollar in the pot. Wayne's face was red, and his lips were peeled back over his yellowed teeth in an ugly grimace. Harbin eased his weight in his chair, aware of the tension in Wayne. Vail seemed unaware of it, and laughed as he laid down his hand.

"Sorry, gentlemen," he said in his mild voice, "but I've got a full house." He started to rake in the final pot when Wayne's chair scraped back, and the Three Horn rider lurched to his feet, grasping his edge of the circular table with both hands.

"Take it all you bastard!" he yelled, and threw the table into Vail's lap, dumping coins and cards onto the floor, and spilling Vail backward in his chair so that his feet shot up absurdly.

Harbin caught Wayne's movement before it started, and he swung sideways, the table missing him. Herbie Nichols, caught off guard, tried to come to his feet, got tangled with his chair, and fell heavily.

Joe Wayne moved forward, and his gun was clear of the holster.

"Look out, Vail!" Harbin called.

The homesteader was blinking as he sat up. His face was bewildered by the sudden turn of events. Wayne came at him, laid the barrel of his Colt across the man's head, smashing him to the floor. Blood spurted over Vail's face.

"I'll fix your clock, you card-cheatin' bastard!" Wayne yelled, and threw his gun down in line with the fallen man's body.

Wayne's intent to kill was clear, and Harbin found himself moving without conscious volition. His right arm chopped down sharply, breaking Wayne's aim, knocking his Colt across the floor. Other chairs were scraping around, and men were gathering fast. Wayne lurched around, his face twisted angrily.

"Stay out of this, God damn you!" he yelled.

"Try a man who packs a gun, Wayne!" Harbin bit out. He held there, face hawklike and intent, a tight smile on his lips.

Wayne swayed, breathing hard, his eyes rimmed with red, the veins standing out on his flushed forehead. He shook his head slowly, and glanced for his gun. He shook his head again.

"You'd like me to pick it up, wouldn't you, you murdering dog?" he whispered. "You talk big—but let's see you practice what you preach. I ain't got a gun now. "

Wayne took one step toward Harbin, bringing his hands up in knotted fists. Harbin could step back and draw his gun. It was what he should do, end it here and now, for it would never end until there was gunplay. He knew Joe Wayne's type, the fear inside him that drove him to prove it didn't exist. But Harbin's own code prevented that simple solution.

The Three Horn cowboy seemed to grasp Harbin's thought, for he lunged in suddenly, both hands swinging in vicious, jolting punches. Harbin blocked one, caught another high on his right cheek, and staggered, driven back by the force of the blow. Wayne yelled and bulled his head down and came on.

Harbin moved back under the force of Wayne's hard-thrown blows, avoiding most of them until a right caught him on the jaw, and he felt the numbing impact that sent him down to one knee. Wayne kicked up at his head, but Harbin avoided the blow, and caught Wayne's foot, twisted and spilled him to the floor. By the time Wayne regained his feet, Harbin's head was clear.

"You want it, cowboy," he said flatly. "You're goin' to get it."

"Try your luck, you nester-lovin' bastard!" Wayne shouted. He plunged forward, fist flying.

Harbin stepped back, shot out a straight left jab that rocked Wayne back on his heels, and moved in with a right cross that smashed Wayne's nose and sent blood spurting down his face and shirt. Wayne danced back, grinning crookedly, then lunged forward again. Harbin rolled with the blows, then straightened Wayne with a second left and struck with all his strength at the unprotected jaw. He felt the sledgehammer force of the blow jar him, and saw Wayne's eyes glaze. He teetered there and Harbin struck again and again, cold, efficient blows that landed exactly where he meant them to land. Wayne staggered backward, then his feet went out from under him, and he crashed into another table, overturning it, and fell to the floor with it, his head striking sharply. He lay still, sucking in tortured breaths, blood from his battered face dripping onto the yellow-gray wood-shaving curls that strewed the floor.

Herbie Nichols was pale but grinning. "Neat," he said. "No wasted effort. Short an' sweet, and Mr. Hothead Wayne's goin' to have plenty of time to think over his mistakes. I'll get him out of here, Ridge."

Harbin was breathing heavily, and a thin rime of sweat was on his brow. He nodded, then looked at the crowd of men gathered around him. They avoided his eyes, but their resentment showed clearly enough. They were range riders, to a man, and Vail was the outsider whose part Harbin had taken. Harbin had crossed the invisible line, and stood on the other side from them. Harbin might regret it, but he could not undo it.

He shook his head, half angrily, and bent to pull Paul Vail to a sitting position. Vail's eyes were closed, but when Harbin forced the lids open, the pupils contracted against the light. The head blow had lacerated his scalp, and the blow coupled with the whisky he had drunk had knocked him out; but there was no serious injury. He would sleep off most of the effects of both.

No one spoke, and none came forward to help as Harbin pulled the inert man erect, balanced him, then ducked low to catch him over his left shoulder. Harbin straightened beneath the weight, and eyed the onlookers.

"I'll thank one of you to put his winnings in his hat," he said slowly.

For an instant no one moved; then a man, caught by the coldness of Harbin's eyes, bent and scooped the coins from the floor into Paul Vail's battered hat. He handed it to Harbin, who took it with his free hand, crumbled it and stuffed it into the unconscious Vail's shirt.

The barroom was silent as Harbin made his way to the swinging doors, the men parting before him. Anger and hate and intolerance made the very room taut. Harbin's hard heels rang out on the wooden plank floor as he pushed through the doors. Outside, Herbie was holding

71

Joe Wayne erect in the saddle, and Nichols swung around to look once at Harbin.

"That sodbuster ain't worth it, Ridge," he said. There was regret in his voice. "Now all hell won't stop it."

Nichols mounted his own horse, still holding to Wayne, and spurred away up the street. Harbin stood on the boardwalk, his face grim. Then he shifted Vail's weight on his shoulder and turned in the opposite direction.

He was sweating by the time he reached the end of Trail Street, and breathing hard when the lights of the wagon camp twinkled out of the darkness. Harbin reached the first wagon, and a woman busy at a fire looked up sharply.

"You know which one is the Vail wagon?" Harbin asked.

The woman nodded, and pointed with a wooden spoon. "The far one over there."

Harbin said, "Thanks," and walked on.

Two wagons were parked together, with a fire burning in the clear space between them. A woman was sitting on a log in front of the fire, and she raised her head slowly as he came into the circle of firelight. It was Lydia Vail, and her face was tired, almost defeated. She stood up, the fire between them.

"Paul," she said. "Is he all right?"

Harbin nodded. "He got a wallop on the head, but no harm. It's mostly the quart of rawgut in his belly. He'll be all right in the morning."

The worry that had come suddenly eased, and she shook her head slowly. "Please put him on the mattress under the wagon. He can sleep there."

Harbin carried Vail there, dumped him on the ground beside the wagon, then rolled him onto the makeshift bed. Vail groaned, stretched out, then began to snore softly. Harbin straightened and turned back to the fire. The woman hadn't moved, but she looked up to watch him from clear gray eyes. Harbin touched the brim of his hat, and started to walk past the fire, but her voice caught and held him.

"Mr. Harbin," she said clearly. "Please wait."

Ridge stopped and turned back. He removed his white Stetson, and his white hair glistened in the firelight. The light made shadows on his sharp-featured face. The woman was not looking at him, but kept her eyes to the fire.

"There is coffee," she said. "I made it for Paul."

She stood up and looked at him then. Her eyes were level, oddly intent. He returned to the fire and waited while she poured coffee from a fire-blackened pot into a heavy crockery mug. She held the cup out to him and he took it. Their eyes met and held.

Despite the weariness in her eyes, she was beautiful, he thought. Her face and her ash-blond hair made a lasting impression on him. Still he said nothing, and she accepted his silent scrutiny without offense.

She sat again upon the log. "I'll thank you, Mr. Harbin, even though I know you don't want me to. You've helped us twice. I've talked to Molly Chase and she told me your name, what you did for them. This is the third time you've taken the part of—nesters—against your own kind."

He looked into the fiery red heart of the campfire. "My own kind," he said slowly. Then he shook his head, his eyes moving back to her face. "A lobo wolf, Mrs. Vail, has no kind. He can afford none. You place too much importance upon what I've done."

"Do I? I wonder." She was studying him. Paul Vail's soft snores were audible to them both. In the heavy Conestoga wagon the baby stirred and made little noises in his sleep. They heard Joanie's whispered reassurances, then silence.

The woman's eyes kept to his face. "If you won't accept thanks, perhaps you will accept friendship?" she asked quietly. "Not as a return on a debt, but with honest appreciation?"

"From you?" he asked slowly.

"From me—my family," she answered.

His smile flickered across his thin-lipped mouth. "Thank you," he said. He drank the hot coffee. "I should ask if you know what you're doing, offering friendship to Ridge Harbin—but I think you do know, and I thank you for it. But it's late and I must be going. Your husband will be all right in the morning." He drank the last of the coffee, then bent to set the cup on the ground. When the woman didn't speak, he turned away; then he came back.

His face was troubled. "Mrs. Vail, this is a hard country. There will be trouble. I think you know that and expect it—but I doubt if you can understand how serious it could be."

"I think I do understand, Mr. Harbin," she answered slowly. She turned to look back at the wagon. "But we have our lives to live, and Paul has chosen to come here. We will make our own way."

He hesitated there, the firelight playing across the ruthless set of his face. "I think you will," he said. "Women like you have a strength most men cannot understand. You will come through, but . . ." He frowned as he glanced into the darkness toward the sleeping Paul Vail. His eyes turned back to her. "I'll be here for some time. How long I don't know. It depends on several things. If you need me again—I will come."

He turned before she could reply, and walked from the firelight. For a few moments the sound of his footsteps came back to her, then only silence, broken by the sounds of the sleeping camp and the soft murmur of the creek below. For a moment she stared into the darkness after him; then, wearily, she climbed into the Conestoga to comfort the baby, who had started to cry.

EIGHT

Wild Horse Valley lay a little over forty miles southwest of Red Rock, a broad-bosomed gap between two horns of the Blue Line Mountains, a meandering stream called the Perdido River splitting its long length and emptying in turn beyond the wide mouth of the valley into the West Fork of the Trios. The road from Red Rock angled in from the northeast, through a pass in the East Fork of the Blue Lines, and it was along this road that the Vail wagon, in company with twenty others, had moved from Red Rock to the disappointment that awaited them there.

Just one of many disappointments they had found in the three weeks they had been in Wagontown, Lydia thought bitterly. The promised land—that was what they had all called it. But it was a broken promise for them—and for the hundred other families in Wagontown who seemed to be waiting for Providence to help them. At least, to Lydia's mind, they were doing little enough to help themselves besides endless complaining. Like that fat man Gordon, and his mousey wife, always shouting and raving and citing endless chapters and verse about the way things should be and never were. What was it Paul called him? "Hellfire" Gordon: that was it.

Lydia straightened slowly from the flat rock in the bed of the shallow Perdido where she was doing the laundry, and pushed back a stray wisp of her silvery blond hair. A grove of cottonwoods stood beside the river. Their Conestoga was one of a hundred wagons lined up along the stream. Beyond the camp, the brown length of the road edged the river toward the valley mouth, and beyond the ford that crossed the West Fork of the Trios, continued on across the grasslands that stretched to the far horizon. Grasslands that could fulfill the hope all of them held, with water from the West Fork for irrigation, and fertile land that had never known the bite of a plow. Land that Ralph Condon had crossed the river to examine and brought back in a bucket to show the others.

"Wheatland like I never seen before," Condon had said, staring back across the river, his face bitter. "Thirty head of cattle grazing on Johnson grass where wheat to feed a thousand people could grow."

75

The hopeless anger and bitterness of Condon's voice had been reflected in the faces of a hundred other men, but none except Hellfire Gordon had spoken. Lydia remembered Gordon swelling his huge chest, and shaking his fist in futile gesture at the small thing that forbade their crossing the river.

"Vane Dallard isn't God!" Gordon cried out. "He'll find that out."

And for once Condon had spoken back to him. "You fixin' to teach him, Gordon?"

In angry silence Gordon had stared at the post beside the road at the edge of the West Fork and at the board sign placed there. The legend was simple and to the point.

NOTICE
All The Land
South of the West
Fork of the Trios
Is Three Horn Range
STAY OFF!

Two hundred yards beyond the crossing of the river stood the mutely eloquent proof that Three Horn meant to keep its range, the fire-blackened mound that had once been a nester's hut, and beside it three mounds topped with rude wooden crosses.

Turning, Lydia looked up the length of Wild Horse Valley, dotted with the cabins and sod-walled huts of those who had been there first. The valley itself was checker-boarded with their fields, and they kept to themselves, unwilling to share with these Johnny-come-latelys.

Of course, the man in the Land Office at Red Rock had assured them that the lands beyond the West Fork were Government Land open for settlement, and that eventually the Federal Government would force Vane Dallard to give it up. But as Gary Daniels pointed out at the last camp meeting, that could be a long time coming, and few of the homesteaders were prepared for a long wait. Including us, Lydia thought, worriedly. Their hard money totaled less than a hundred dollars now, and they would soon need more supplies.

She bent, dipped the pair of long-handled drawers she was washing into the stream, laid them on the flat surface of the rock and began to pound them with steady, firm blows of a wooden paddle. Up the stream, Helen

Condon was busy at the same task, but taking more time. Helen was nearing her time, Lydia knew, and she looked once anxiously at the other woman. Helen Condon raised her head and smiled.

"One thing," Helen said bitterly. "It can't get any worse. Ralph's got it into his head to stick it out. I think he wants to cross the river and take a chance. Maybe Hellfire Gordon's right that the Federal Government wouldn't let Vane Dallard bother us."

"Then why doesn't Gordon move his family across?" Lydia answered quietly. She shook her head. Argument was useless. The men would do as they saw fit, and right now they saw fit to wait. And, despite her worries, it was a pleasant respite from the endless weeks of travel. Joanie was filling out, growing amazingly, and the baby was doing well. Even Paul had settled down, although he occasionally fell into morose moods that took him off alone. She knew where he went at such times, to stand on the north bank of the West Fork and to stare across at the open land beyond, hating it and the men who kept it from him.

The sun was westering by the time she finished her laundry and had hung it on the rope line they had rigged from the Conestoga to a nearby tree. There was a dull aching pain in the lower part of her back. She forced thought of it away and began to prepare their evening meal.

It was dusk, and Paul Vail had just lighted the lamp that hung from the end of the Conestoga over the rude table he had built, when hoofs pounded up the valley. Lydia saw Paul tense, a frown on his handsome face.

"Three Horn riders," he said, half angrily.

Across the table from him Joanie looked up at her mother. Lydia shook her head quickly before the girl could say anything to upset Paul. The hoofs veered toward them from the valley road, and a single horseman loomed up and reined in. He wore typical rider's garb, and was squat and heavy.

"I wondered if you was in this bunch, Vail," he said. His face was carefully expressionless. His eyes went insolently to Lydia, then shifted quickly to Joanie's face and stayed there. The man's rocklike expression broke and he grinned. "Damn maybe I ain't as mad at you as I thought. How about an invite to light down an' sit?"

Paul stood up quickly, his face paling, then flushing. "Get out of here, Wayne," he said, flatly.

The rider took his time looking at Paul, letting his eyes fix on Joanie as long as they could. His grin became lopsided. "You're sure unsociable," he said. "Maybe you've got me wrong. I could do you some good, Vail."

"There's nothing good about you, Wayne," Vail said angrily. "Get out of here."

Joe Wayne lifted one leg across his saddlehorn, and considered the tall man before him. "Now ain't that real tough?" he said. He looked again at Joanie, then lifted the reins, and his horse walked forward until Paul had to jump back from the table to keep from being stepped on. The horse's chest pushed at the table, and Joanie squealed. She jumped up and stood clear as the horse pushed the table over, the dishes falling with a crash.

Paul Vail started forward, but Lydia caught his arm and held him there. She felt the trembling of his body. Lydia said quietly, "Don't shoot him, Ralph."

Her words stiffened Wayne, and his eyes darted about. Then from the far side of the tree, Ralph Condon's voice said, "I'm tryin' not to, Lydia—but he's just beggin' for it."

Wayne kept his grin in place. He winked at Joanie, then touched the brim of his hat as he looked at Lydia. "A poor welcome's better than none," he said. "I'll be thinkin' about next time, ma'am." His eyes went to Vail and hardened. "I'll see you again, plow-walker."

He wheeled the horse, dug in his spurs, and galloped away. Beside her, Paul cursed savagely under his breath. "It's all right, Paul," she said. "We want no trouble."

Ralph Condon came into the clearing, his rifle under his arm. He grinned at them. "One ranny sent on his way," he said. "Maybe it'll teach him a lesson."

Paul Vail got control of himself and sighed. "I doubt it," he said. "But we can always hope. I've about had my fill of it, Ralph."

Condon frowned. "Movin' on? I'd hoped you wouldn't. Helen's about due, an'—"

"No, I'm not moving west," Paul Vail said. He stared up the valley in the direction Wayne had ridden. His face was set, more determined than Lydia could ever remember seeing it.

Condon stared at him, then whistled shrilly. "You mean you're jumpin' the gun—crossin' the West Fork?"

Paul looked down into Lydia's face, his own troubled, unsure. She said, "We'll do what you decide must be done, Paul."

Paul Vail smiled then, slowly, and nodded. "That's what I've got in mind." He held very still. "Somebody has to call Dallard's hand. It might as well be me. That's good land—you've said so yourself, Ralph. We'll find nothing better—probably nothing as good—farther west."

"I'm not sayin' you ain't right, Paul," Condon said. He scratched at his whiskered jaw. "Just the same, it's a hell of a big gamble. Three Horn is a big tough outfit. You tangled yourself with one of them in Red Rock. The same feller that rode in here tonight, I reckon, an' he'll jump at the chance to get even."

Paul Vail was very still, but Lydia still felt the trembling of his body. "I know that, too, Ralph. If we all moved at the same time, there wouldn't be any chance. But we won't. Gordon has most of them scared half out of their wits, and Daniels isn't much better. But if even two wagons made it across, got settled in, there wouldn't be any doubt the others would follow the lead pretty quick."

Condon pondered thoughtfully, then nodded. "Sure. You're right, only—would they make up their minds quick enough, before Three Horn decided to burn you out?"

"That's where the gamble lies," Paul Vail answered quietly. He looked once again into the gathering dusk to the north. "I've made up my mind."

He looked quickly at Lydia then, and doubt still filled his eyes. She caught his arm tightly. "I'm proud of you, Paul," she said softly. "Real proud." She saw what it did to him, the quick lift of his head, the old reckless smile he seemed lately to have lost.

Ralph Condon looked from one to the other of them. "You're probably both crazy," he said thoughtfully. "But then, maybe so am I. We ain't got money to see another winter through. With the new baby an' all, it's best we settle in, an' damned soon. You pull out of Wagontown, Paul, an' I'll be right behind you."

The two men grinned at each other, then somewhat selfconsciously shook hands. At that moment Ralph Condon's eldest daughter came running up. "Pa—better get back to the wagon. Ma wants you—she said to bring Miz Vail, too. She said the pains have started an' they're comin' awful fast."

Lydia took charge then. "Ralph, you and Paul put water on to boil—all the pots you can find. Joanie, you clean up that mess on the ground, then come to the Condon wagon. Maybe you can help."

Ralph Condon grinned, then shook his head. "A boy," he said slowly. "Please, God, let it be a boy this time."

Irritated, Lydia said sharply: "You'll know soon enough, Ralph. Now get busy. I'll go to Helen."

In the hours that followed, Lydia had no time for worries beyond the immediate concern for the woman in the Condon wagon. Twice Ralph Condon came to the rear of the wagon to ask if she thought he should ride into Red Rock for a doctor, and each time Lydia shook her head impatiently.

"The baby will be here long before the doctor could," she said.

Helen Condon's agonies quickened, and shortly after sunset the baby came. Lydia bathed the woman's pale, sweatstreaked face, then washed and oiled the baby. Joanie came at her call, climbing into the wagon with a fine display of white underskirts. Her face was sober but curious, and Lydia handed her the tiny baby. The girl took the child, her face suddenly softly smiling. Then her eyes widened. She looked up quickly at her mother.

"Mom, it's a—"

Lydia shook her head. "Be quiet, Joanie. Dress the child. The things are laid out there." Then she knelt beside the woman's bed.

Helen Condon opened her eyes. Tears rolled down her cheeks, and she was silently crying. "Ralph wanted a boy, so badly—"

Lydia made the woman comfortable, then took the child. "Stay with Helen, Joanie. I'll be back in a moment."

She went forward and climbed from the wagon, carrying the bundled child carefully in her arms. Ralph Condon was beside the fire, and he stood up now, his face gaunt with strain.

"Is it—" He spoke slowly, hesitantly.

Lydia said: "Helen is all right now. She's had a difficult time, Ralph. The baby is a girl."

"A—a girl—" He shook his head angrily, then turned around and strode away from the firelight, into the darkness beyond. Lydia stood there, watching him go. Paul came toward her and put his arm across her shoulder.

"He'll be back, Lydia."

"Yes, he'll come back, and he won't say anything, but he'll be blaming Helen silently always. Paul, why couldn't it have been a boy?"

80

Vail frowned. "Things don't always work out. Maybe there's a pattern to it we can't see. Maybe it's meant to be this way."

A twig snapped, and Ralph Condon came back into the firelight. He paused there, then came on. He stopped beside Lydia, looked down at the child in her arms. He smiled then, slowly.

"It's all right," he said. "I'll tell Helen it's all right."

He climbed into the wagon, and presently Joanie came out. She was crying softly, but her lips were smiling. "It's wonderful, isn't it, Mom?" she asked.

Lydia looked up at Paul, met his eyes, and smiled. "Yes, Joanie," she said, quietly. "It always is."

Paul Vail chose a morning three days later to roll out of of Wagontown, and the Condon wagon followed close behind. There had been a series of camp meetings, but no one else had offered to join them, and for once Paul had managed to remain resolute in his decision. It increased the sense of pride within him, and now as he drove the team down the brown road toward the West Fork ford, he was aware of the eyes that watched their progress. Let them make a start, and the others would follow soon. The thought lent him strength, and he turned in the seat to smile at Lydia, who sat beside him, the baby in her arms. Behind them Joanie stood erect, waving at her friends in the camp, proud that they were the first to cross. And this, too, affected Paul Vail, and strengthened his determination to succeed.

Only once, when they passed the Three Horn sign, did a frown furrow his brows, and he pushed it away. "Here goes everything," he said quietly, and put the horses to the clearly marked ford.

The river was broad but shallow, and the banks were not steep. Irrigation in the land beyond would not be a problem. He cracked the reins, and the team surged up out of the river, onto the level plains once more, and he pulled them up. He stood up in the seat. To the west a few hundred yards stood a small grove of trees, topping a low knoll that overlooked the bend of the river.

"Our house will be there, Lydia—our fields out here. I've staked it already. We'll make camp, break ground, and get settled before I file with the land office in Red Rock. One hundred and sixty acres will be ours. This is why we came."

The brown, hummock-rolling land stretched to the far horizon. In the great distance she saw the dark dots that were cattle.

"Fruit trees, a vegetable garden—and wheat. I'll plant forty acres this year if all goes well. It will take three years before all the land is broken. We'll have neighbors before then. This land will grow."

Always the dream, Lydia thought, but now without bitterness. She felt the touch of his new-found strength and determination, and welcomed it. She grasped his hand tightly. "Of course it will, Paul," she said softly. "Of course it will."

With all the problems that had confronted them, with all the talk and the harsh threats, the quiet crossing of the river into this brown, quiet land seemed strangely anticlimactic. Paul did not feel that, but stood erect to drive the team the remaining distance to the knoll he had chosen. Behind them the Condon wagon rolled steadily, Ralph Condon having chosen a piece of land farther up the river but adjoining theirs. Best to stay together as closely as possible, Paul had said, and Ralph had agreed.

The two men would work together to build their houses one at a time. The wagons would remain together until the first house was built. And it had been decided that the Vail soddy would be constructed first.

Paul Vail reined in atop the knoll. A slight wind rippled the green fronds of the cottonwood trees, and far below, the river rolled flatly on. Paul stepped to the ground, then reached up for Lydia, pride shining in his handsome face.

"Welcome home, Mrs. Vail," he said, and his arms caught her, lifted her to the ground. They stood close together and surveyed the new land. Warm contentment filled Lydia in that moment; then she stiffened abruptly. Far in the distance she saw a mounted man riding toward them. She saw him rein in, caught the flash of binoculars in the bright sunlight, and then saw that the man wheeled his horse and galloped off. A coldness ran down her spine, but Paul turned her away.

"Now we've come, there is nothing anyone can do about it," he said quietly. "This is our home. We will fight for it if we have to."

Warm, reassuring words, but somehow the dream failed him this time, for she felt the trembling of his body, and saw the frown that darkened his face.

NINE

Johnny Lee sent his roan mare kiting over the ground, and enjoyed the whipping of the wind in his face, the sense of freedom that running a horse always gave him. Johnny Lee was a product of the violent times in which he lived, an artificial product, for his surface personality and his concealed character were two different things. Johnny's swagger was not all bravado, for he had long since learned to recognize his true self, even if it did not always please him. There was the matter of his fear of Ridge Harbin; it was real, but he was not ashamed of it. His soft-walking in the presence of Vane Dallard was something else; it covered not his fear but his contempt for the man who hired others to do what he himself could not.

Johnny thought of this, and a crooked smile bent his handsome mouth. *Someday,* Johnny thought with grim satisfaction, *I'm going to gut-shoot the bastard just to watch him die.* And this, although Johnny would never have admitted it, was pure show, for in reality he was too much the man of fact ever to jeopardize the position he had gained. Vane Dallard was the tall man of this Red Rock country, and Johnny Lee enjoyed riding in his shadow. It made him big, too, and this was something more important to Johnny than the two hundred dollars a month Dallard paid him.

The roan had been running north toward the West Fork, and Johnny narrowed his eyes a little as he saw a horseman cutting over to intercept him. A frown narrowed the space between his dark eyebrows, and he made a show of loosening the Colt in its holster. He reined in as the horseman approached, and then relaxed.

Joe Wayne lifted one hand as he neared, and called out. "Hey, Johnny, wait up!" He spurred closer, then pulled up. His grin was crooked. "Two of them God-damn' nester wagons have crossed the river. They've staked quarter-sections up by the bend. You'd better tell Dallard."

Johnny Lee frowned. "Tell him yourself," he said. "I'm busy."

Wayne looked surprised, then shrugged. "Too busy to

earn your keep, Johnny?" he demanded. His smile was crooked.

Johnny smiled back. "They're goin' to be shovelin' dirt in your face, Joe, you keep talkin' like that."

Wayne's smile changed to something else, peeling away from his yellow teeth. He said, too quickly, "Just jokin', Johnny."

"Dyin's kind of funny, too," Johnny Lee said. "You're buckin' too hard for my job, Joe. Usually I don't care, for your kind come and go. Sooner or later you'll push a man like Ridge Harbin too far. But if you want it sooner, I'll oblige you, any time—remember that."

Wayne's smile was wiped away, and he frowned. "Sure, Johnny, sure," he said. "Hell, I ain't buckin' for your job. You're the Three Horn trouble man. But them two sodbuster wagons mean trouble."

It was Johnny's turn to frown, and he twisted in the saddle to look back the long way he had come, then turned to study the flat rolling land ahead of him. West Fork was not far away; he'd be there in another hour, and he didn't want to be late. He shook his head and smiled again.

"All right," he said. "You want my kind of work. Try your hand. You ride in an' tell the old man your story. Tell him you ain't seen me. Tell him you want the job. It's all right with me."

Wayne stared at Johnny for a moment, then asked, "You ain't kiddin' me?"

Lee shook his head. "Who the hell cares what happens to a couple of nesters? I got other things to do. Maybe there'll be some other things for you to handle."

"All right, Johnny," Joe Wayne said. His grin was back. "Leave it to me."

He spurred away then, and Lee sat his saddle to watch him go. "Sure I will, you two-bit tinhorn," Johnny said softly. There were a threat and a promise in his words, and he laughed to himself. Then he turned and dug in his spurs, and the roan settled to her work once more.

It was midafternoon before Johnny Lee reached the lower ford of the West Fork and crossed the shallow muddy stream. He rode carefully, at ease, but cautious. It would not pay to be seen by some clodhopper, he thought, then grinned. Just the same, the risk was worth it. He licked his lips and kept grinning as he let the mare pick her way through the thick brush that grew beside the river. A mile from the upper ford he dismounted, dropped the reins to the ground, and with a quick look around to make sure he hadn't been seen, pushed through the bracken to a well defined game trail that led toward a grove of cottonwoods some distance away.

He walked quietly, and came into the grove unnoticed by the girl who had seated herself on a fallen tree. She was staring toward the river with the abstract look of one lost in her own thoughts. For a moment Johnny Lee paused there to look at her. The afternoon sun, filtered by the cottonwoods that grew close here, shone on her yellow hair, outlined her slender figure. Johnny Lee licked his lips again and moved silently closer behind her.

"Lookin' for somebody?" he asked quietly.

The girl's startled gasp was followed by her quick turn. Her face was flushed, but she was smiling. "Oh, Johnny, Johnny!" she whispered. "You frightened me."

He came to her and she stood up to be taken into his arms. "You got nothin' to be scared of, Molly," he said. Hungrily, arrogantly passionate, he kissed her until she gasped and pulled away from him.

"Stop, Johnny," she whispered. "You don't know what you do to me when you're like this."

Johnny Lee grinned. "Sure I do," he said.

Molly Chase's blush deepened. "Reckon you do," she said finally, but without resentment. Her eyes moved over his handsome features, then they half closed. No matter how many times she saw him—and she had seen him often these past few weeks—Johnny could do this to her, make her breathe harder, make her legs seem weak. Johnny Lee was the promise of love and kindness, the promise of release from the drudgery of the settlers' life she hated, and she was blind to everything else he was. Johnny Lee loved her, and he would take her away soon —that was all that mattered. *God, how much I love him!* she thought.

Johnny watched her, possessively; then he would have taken her into his arms again, but she held him off with a hand on his chest. She took a deep breath, staring deeply into his eyes. "Johnny—when are we goin' to get married?"

Johnny Lee stepped back. His face was carefully bland. He half turned away, then sat down on the fallen tree. He pulled the makings from his shirt pocket, rolled a cigarette with practiced fingers, licked it and lighted it, keeping his eyes on the girl's face.

"I play games for keeps," he said flatly, aware of her fear of losing him, counting on it to make her bow down to his will. "I don't like people who don't trust me. That goes for women, too."

Molly shook her head slowly and began to cry. "You know I don't mean it like that, Johnny," she said. She came to him and knelt down in front of him. "But you don't know how hard it is, not knowing, seein' you ride away each time, thinkin' maybe you're tired of me an' won't come back. . . ."

Johnny Lee flicked the cigarette away and took hold of her shoulders. He slid off the tree to sit beside her on the soft loam. His hands took her shoulders, drawing her roughly to him.

"I'm back, ain't I?" he demanded, and kissed her possessively, almost rudely. He felt her tense, try to pull away, but he held her harder, and her own passion betrayed her. Suddenly she was all fire, burning at his will. Panting, they broke free at last, the girl's deep eyes meeting his.

"I love you, Johnny," she whispered. "No matter what, I love you."

There was an eager trembling in Johnny Lee's hands and body as he bent her to him. His normal caution was lost. His hands tore at the buttons on the upper part of her dress, and her protests grew feeble and died away.

Then iron hard hands caught Johnny Lee, tore him from the girl, smashed into his face, and drove him sprawling halfway across the clearing. He heard the girl's frightened cries:

"Pa—don't!"

Dazedly, Johnny sat up. He put a hand to his face, brought it away bloody. Senseless, insane rage drove at him. He saw the heavy-set man lumbering toward him, huge hands balled into knotty fists. He rolled quickly and surged to his feet like a cat.

"Get away from me, Chase!" Johnny yelled, but the angry homesteader kept coming. Behind him, Molly screamed.

"Don't kill him, Johnny!"

Johnny Lee stepped back before Chase's maddened lunge, and his right hand swung up his heavy Colt. With a vicious downward chop, he laid the length of the barrel against the bigger man's head, dropping him unconscious to the ground. Then Johnny stepped back, his mouth curling into a vicious snarl, and the Colt came down, his thumb cocking the hammer with smooth ease.

The girl heard the ominous click of the revolver, and threw herself forward. "Johnny, don't!" she cried.

For an instant Johnny Lee stood there, rage working in him; then slowly he lifted his head to stare at the girl. Her gingham dress was off one shoulder, and he caught the soft swelling of her breast, heaving now with fright. Johnny Lee shook his head slowly.

"I got to kill him," he said. "It's like I've got to kill him, now."

"No, Johnny," the girl said. "He's my pa—you can't!"

"He hit me," Johnny Lee said slowly. "You don't understand, Molly. Nobody can hit me and get away with it. Nobody." He extended the gun, centered the back of Chase's head in his sights.

"Johnny!" Molly screamed. "If you love me, you won't. Please, Johnny, please." She was crying, her face distraught. Johnny Lee stared at her and licked at his battered mouth. The salty taste of blood made him spit to the ground.

"What difference does it make now?" Johnny asked. His voice was without tension, without emotion of any kind. "You're goin' with me, anyhow. You can't go back to your own kind."

The girl stared at him as if she had never seen him before. Her eyes were wide, shock blanking them, dimming her tortured fright. *No, Johnny!* Her lips formed the words silently.

Johnny Lee smiled at her. The gun in his hand was rock steady, still aimed at Chase's head. "Never beg a man not to do something, Molly," he said in a curiously soft voice. "It just makes him want to do it all the more."

Still smiling at her, Johnny Lee pulled the trigger.

TEN

Vane Dallard stared up at the huge map of the Red Rock country that covered the west wall of his office, and his heavy features became ugly. One blunt finger touched Wild Horse Valley, then stabbed angrily at the dots that marked the Upper Ford of the West Fork River.

"Again," he said. "By God, they won't ever learn, will they?"

Joe Wayne looked quickly at Herbie Nichols. Nichols frowned, then shrugged. "Don't seem like it, boss," Nichols said.

Dallard whirled about to glare at Nichols. "Maybe it's because Three Horn is filled with damned fools," he flashed.

Nichols thought, *Including you, you bastard,* but only said, "I never laid any claims to bein' anything else."

Dallard crossed the room to his battered rolltop desk, threw himself into his high-backed leather chair which squeaked protest to his weight. "I won't have it," Dallard said. "By God, I'll see every damned nester in the Wyoming Territory dead before I'll let them have any more. They come in a handful at a time, grabbin' this section, then that one. Next thing, they've fenced you away from every damned drop of water, and your cattle die on the hoof."

Nichols said: "You've held 'em off a long time, Vane. But it's still Government land. You can't change that."

"I don't have to change it. But I can make it God-damn' costly to any man who thinks he can grab Three Horn range." He twisted about in the chair to glare at Joe Wayne. "You saw Johnny?"

Wayne nodded, his crooked smile fixed to his mouth. This was an opportunity he didn't intend to miss. "Yeah, I saw him, boss," Wayne said. "Said he was busy. Said to tell you I could handle it."

"Johnny Lee isn't running Three Horn, Wayne," Dallard said slowly.

"I know that," Wayne said. "Just the same, I can handle it as well as Johnny could. He said so himself. All I need is the chance."

Dallard studied Wayne with open curiosity tinged with contempt; then he shook his head. "I pay Lee for his gun. God damn it, he should be here when I want him."

"It's easy to draw down gun-pay when there's nothin' more to shoot at than coyotes," Wayne said. He knew he was going dangerously far, but he felt opportunity slipping from his grasp. He was aware of Nichols staring at him, gauging him.

Dallard laughed. "Ridge Harbin had twelve notches on his gun when he rode gun for Three Horn," he said. "Johnny Lee's doin' better. He's got fourteen notches on his colt. How many men have you laid low, Wayne?"

Joe Wayne flushed slowly, then shook his head. "A man has to begin sometime. I've got the nerve. That's what counts."

Dallard's eyes narrowed. "The hell you have," he said slowly. He lifted his head and stared up at the map again. "All right. We'll see. Move 'em out of there, Wayne. Do it fast and do it hard. Let the rest of them understand I mean it when I say that's Three Horn land. Take Nichols with you—and pick up Jesse Ord and his crew in the brakes. Tell Jesse you're runnin' the show. When it's over, you an' Nichols hole up in the line cabin at Broken Pine. There's grub there. I'll send for you when I want you."

Wayne kept his jubilation out of his face with effort. He grinned at Herbie Nichols. "Let's go, Herbie."

Nichols held there, frowning. "Look, boss," he said to Dallard. "Let me get Johnny, an'—"

Wayne's grin faded. "Cold feet, Nichols?" he asked. "I don't need him, boss. I'll go alone."

"You'll do what I tell you to do," Dallard said angrily. "Nichols, what's eatin' on you? Thinkin' maybe your pal Harbin's staked his quarter-section there?"

Herbie straightened slowly, and smiled. "If he has, it'll take more than Joe Wayne an' Jesse Ord to move him off. You'll be buryin' Three Horn men tomorrow."

Dallard's thick face reddened slowly. He stood up to lean forward, both hands on the flat top of the desk. "Nobody's going to stand in my way," he said, his voice pitched low. "That goes for Ridge Harbin and all the nester-lice God ever made. If you're yellow, Nichols, say so."

Herbie shook his head. "You know better than that, Vane," he replied. "You're mad, and you're talkin' wild. An' you ain't usin' good sense sendin' Joe Wayne. He's got the bit in his teeth, an' he's hell-bent he'll show you he can do a better job than Johnny Lee. That's all right with me, but you can go too far. You push any dog into a corner, an' he'll fight back."

Dallard stared at Nichols for a moment, then looked up at the map. "It's my land," he said slowly, clearly. "Three Horn land. We'll fight for it. We'll teach them a lesson that will be good for all time to come." His eyes came down to Herbie again. "You ride or you get off, Nichols. Make up your mind."

Herbie took a moment, then shook his head. "All right," he said. "You're dealin' 'em, Vane. Come on, Wayne, let's get to it."

Wayne let his anger show as he stared at Nichols. Amusement moved Dallard's mouth as he looked at the two Three Horn riders, then he said, "All right, Joe."

Joe turned around and left the office. Outside, on the wide veranda that sprawled across the front of the ranch-house, he stopped. "You son of a bitch," he said, "I ought to kill you."

Herbie laughed in his face. "You don't bother me, Joe," he said. "Dead men never do. And you're dead. If you don't push Ridge Harbin into doin' it, Johnny Lee will kill you sooner or later, just for the hell of it. Now shut up, and let's ride out of here."

Rage burned inside Wayne, but he kept it carefully under control. His crooked smile came, then went. "You won't dance on my grave, loudmouth," he said finally. "But that can wait."

It was still two hours before sunset when the two of them rode out of Three Horn and took the road north toward West Fork. They rode side by side, both silently intent on their own thoughts. For Herbie Nichols it was a grim, dirty job that had to be done; but for Joe Wayne it was an important step forward, and uneasiness rode Nichols. He dismissed it with an effort. What the hell, a man had to ride where the trail led him. Just the same . . . He thought of Ridge Harbin, and frowned. It still wasn't too late to ride free of Three Horn and never come back. It still wasn't too late to step aside. . . . Herbie stopped the thought, and his face grew grimmer.

The sun had set, and blue shadows outlined the heights of the jumbled, broken mass of rocks that formed the Blue Line Brakes, when they rode the tortuous trail that led to Jesse Ord's Broken O spread. Ostensibly Ord was a two-bit hard-scrabble rancher, but Herbie knew better. Vane Dallard was rough and willing to fight his own battles, but he was no man's fool, and Ord was a tool he could readily use without bringing any open reprisals against Three Horn. It was not the first time that Nichols had ridden into the brakes, not the first time he had been with Jesse Ord's crew.

Joe Wayne rode straight in, but Herbie pulled up. "Slow up, you damned fool," Nichols called out. "Jesse's touchy. The bastard'll have a guard out, most likely."

Wayne twisted in the saddle to grin crookedly. "Yellow, Nichols? He knows us." But just the same, Wayne slowed his horse to a walk until a loud hail came to them. A man scrambled down from a perch atop a high boulder to come up to them.

"Jesse's up at the cabin," the man said. "I'll follow you in. Jesse's been expectin' company."

Wayne laughed. "He's got it, now." He dug in his spurs and raced his horse on ahead into the narrow pass that opened into the tiny valley where the Broken O ran the few cattle it owned.

The lookout shook his head. "Joe's in a hell of a hurry, ain't he, Herbie?"

Nichols nodded. "Some fellers always are." he answered soberly. He shrugged. He didn't speak again as they rode through the pass.

Smoke curled listlessly up into the windless air from a crooked rusty stovepipe that angled from the shake roof of the ramshackle cabin. As they rode up, a tall thin man came out to stand on the porch, a brown-paper cigarette dangling from his slack mouth. The meanness in Jesse Ord was reflected in the hardness of his eyes, the sneering curl of his thin lips. He watched them ride up without speaking, and stood silent as they dismounted. Only when they stepped to the porch did he speak, a soft, almost whispering sound.

"Where's Johnny?" Jesse Ord asked.

"He ain't comin'," Joe Wayne said, self-importantly. "Dallard sent me instead. We got a job. You'll ride with us."

Jesse Ord's yellow-hued eyes narrowed, and he blew smoke from between his lips without touching the dangling cigarette with his hands. "Lots of men like to try walkin' like Johnny Lee," Ord said. "Most of 'em get killed for their trouble."

91

Again Wayne stiffened. "I'm gettin' tired of these cracks," he said. "If Dallard didn't think I was big enough, he wouldn't have sent me."

"Wouldn't he?" Jesse Ord laughed. "What the hell does Vane Dallard care what happens to you?" The outlaw shrugged his thin shoulders. "It makes nothing for me. You like it, you try to ride it. Where's the job?"

Wayne's anger kept him taut, but he controlled it. "Just out of Wild Horse Valley. Two nester families rolled onto Three Horn land across the West Fork. We move 'em back tonight—hard. Those are Dallard's orders. Afterwards we scatter. You do as you please. Me an' Herbie hide out for a few days."

Jesse Ord shrugged again. "Sure," he said. "Me an' the boys been gettin' fat layin' around." His yellow eyes grew intent. "Any killin' to be done?"

Nichols said quickly: "No. Dallard said move 'em out. That's all."

Joe Wayne twisted his head on his wide shoulders. He glared at Nichols, but said nothing. Jesse Ord watched the anger in Wayne's face, and amusement bent his thin mouth. One bony hand came up and flicked away the cigarette.

"All right. Sounds easy enough. We'll ride in ten minutes. You got time for a drink. You might need it, Wayne." The mocking amusement remained in Ord's voice, but Wayne, aside from a deepening of his frown, took no notice of it.

The last red streaks of day lined the dark sky when they rode out of the brakes. Joe Wayne rode just ahead of Herbie Nichols, and Jesse Ord and his two men rode behind them. None of the men spoke.

Now for Herbie Nichols the die was cast; there was nothing further to think about. Let Joe Wayne do what he wanted to do; in the long run it would not matter. There were the good years on the range, and there were the bad. Herbie Nichols had seen both. There was a strength in doing what you had to do, and he called upon it now, forcing away all other thoughts.

Nichols saw the campfire that burned on this side of the river first. He looked quickly at Joe Wayne's shadowy figure, saw the man stiffen, then rein in. Wayne waited for the others to ride up to him, then lifted his right hand.

"This is it," he said. "Two wagons, not far apart.

Jesse, you an' your men take the first one. Burn the bastards out, make 'em run for it. See they cross the river." There was a hard purpose in Wayne's voice, a surprising strength to it that Nichols had never heard before. "Herb—we'll take the far wagon. Ride in close, Jesse, an' wait until we make our move—then close in quick. Don't give the plow-walker a chance to fight back."

Jesse Ord's dry voice said, whisperingly: "Okay. Then what?"

"Scatter as you please," Wayne said. There was a sudden tightness in his throat. "Herb, you stick close to me."

Joe Wayne's lips were peeled back tightly against his teeth, and he was aware of a building excitement. He let it grow, seize him. He wheeled his horse with a vicious tug of the reins, sent it racing forward, upriver, swinging wide to come at the second wagon from upriver. He heard the pound of the hoofs of Nichols's mount behind him, and rode harder. The campfire grew brighter, divided into two fires, some distance apart.

Reining in, Wayne drew his heavy revolver, rested his hand across the horn of his saddle. "All right," he said. "Let's go."

Without waiting for Nichols's reply, Wayne dug in his spurs. His horse leaped forward, and at the same time Wayne's wild yell sounded. Downriver he caught the sharp report of guns as Jesse Ord and his two men rode in. Then the dark bulk of the wagon loomed up, the firelight playing on the dingy canvas sides. Straight to the fire Wayne rode, driving hard.

He caught the blurred movement as a man rolled out from under the wagon and stood erect. He was a tall lean man wearing an absurd white nightgown that blew about his thin shanks. He blinked about him in surprise. Then he stooped and came up with a rifle. Joe Wayne jerked forward and to one side. His long arm shot out and his revolver thudded heavily against the side of the man's head.

"Nobody to help you now, you God-damn' sodbuster!" Wayne yelled, in a frenzy of excitement. He swung free of the stirrups, and struck the ground at a run. The tall man, his face bloody, had sagged to his knees, and Wayne drove into him, slashing with the barrel of his revolver.

The man groaned and fell to the ground, and Wayne stood there, panting, his eyes wild.

Impressions flooded in upon Herb Nichols as he sat his saddle. Joe Wayne's vicious attack had been unexpected, and now the night lay silent again. Nichols caught the soft murmur of the river, the sigh of the fire as the night winds pushed at it. Red light splashed across the dark of night; he saw the bright crimson flowing down the fallen man's bloody face. Then from downriver he heard a woman's piercing scream, a man's wild yells, then the sharp, brittle crack of revolvers. Flames piled high downriver as the canvas tarp of the first wagon caught fire.

"Get busy, damn it!" Joe Wayne yelled. But Nichols sat stolidly, unable to adjust to the bitter reality of the moment.

Within the wagon a baby started to cry. A woman came out, hair disheveled, eyes wide with fright. "Paul!" she called, then: *"Paul!"* as she caught sight of his figure sprawled in the firelight. She climbed from the wagon, and ran toward him.

The baby's cries rose higher. The man on the ground sat up, shook his head. His eyes focused with an effort on Joe Wayne, and he half fell forward, hands groping blindly for his fallen rifle. Joe Wayne caught his movement and spun about, a grin splitting his face.

The woman saw the intent to kill on Wayne's face, and sprang at him. He met her with a quick slam of his gun, laying it against the side of her head. The blow knocked her off balance, and she fell heavily.

For Joe Wayne it was the culminating moment. His mouth fell slackly open, and there was a glaze over his eyes. His movements were beyond his control as he thrust his revolver out and thumbed back the hammer. It was the first time he had ever pointed his gun at a man with intent to kill, and his hand shook. He saw Paul Vail's pale, bloody face over the sights of his Colt, and his finger tightened with a jerk on the trigger. Vail slammed back as if struck with a sledgehammer, spinning around to the impetus of the slug. But he did not fall. Wildness twisted Wayne's face, and he thumbed the hammer again and again. His shots smashed into the night, struck Paul Vail, broke him, dumped him to the ground, dead.

Then Wayne became aware of the futile clicking noises of his gun, and his arm dropped to his side. He spun around and saw Herb Nichols staring at him with horror on his face.

Wayne laughed wildly and thumbed shells into his empty gun, thrust it back into the holster. "You yellow-bellied bastard!" he yelled. "Get busy!"

Wayne seized a burning brand from the fire, and moved toward the wagon.

"For Christ's sake—there's a baby in there!" Nichols yelled.

Wayne did not pause, but tossed the burning brand atop the sagging canvas top, which caught instantly and roared into bright yellow flames.

A slender figure came groping from the wagon, the baby clutched in slim arms. It was Joanie. Her long legs were revealed as she climbed down from the wagon. She was crying as she reached the ground.

Joe Wayne watched her and licked his lips. His mind was still in a turmoil, and excitement rose inside him beyond control. He saw the girl's slender figure, her softly rounded breasts under the thin cotton gown she wore.

"By God!" Wayne whispered. "By God!"

He moved toward the girl. Herbie Nichols saw him, and knew it lay with him to stop Joe Wayne. But the dead body of Vail lay sprawled in the firelight between them, and Nichols knew that he could not do it. Nausea gripped him, turned him weak. He saw Joe Wayne reach the girl and tear the baby from her grasp. The girl screamed, and cowered. With a single jerk of his arms, Joe Wayne ripped the gown from the girl's body.

Red firelight danced and played upon her figure, the high, firm young breasts, the whiteness of her skin. Then Wayne spun about to stare at Herbie, his face working. The caution of the beast made him turn to face the only danger present, but he read the fear in Nichols, and suddenly laughed.

"Dallard said to make them never forget. By God, they won't!" Joe Wayne said. He turned, caught the girl, and dragged her after him to his horse. His hands ripped thongs free, and he bound her hands, threw her bodily across his horse in front of the saddle. Then, laughing insanely, he swung up into the saddle.

Herb Nichols stood there. The woman Wayne had struck down came up. Her voice screamed at him: "Stop him! In the name of God—she's only a child!"

Joe Wayne watched Nichols fighting against the weakness inside him. Then, with a mocking laugh, he wheeled the horse and galloped into the night.

For a moment Nichols stood there, the woman's eyes burning hate into him. Then he turned and ran for his horse; but hard as he might run, he knew he could never leave behind the self-hatred that would ride forever with him.

ELEVEN

Ridge Harbin had remained in Red Rock for three weeks, making his evening rounds of the saloons, making a point of appearing wherever Three Horn riders clustered; but although he saw both Johnny Lee and Herbie Nichols, Vane Dallard made no appearance. While at first there was an obvious tension whenever he made a showing where Three Horn men were gathered, the tension lessened, and the fact became increasingly obvious that Vane Dallard would push his quarrel with Harbin no farther. To Ridge Harbin the fact was acceptable, although it made for an increasing restlessness within him. His ironic smile appeared more often, and on the evening of the twenty-fifth day he spent in Red Rock he saddled the bay gelding and rode out of the town.

Luck, this past week, had been favorable, and he rode now with more than two hundred dollars in his pockets and the assurance in his mind that he left nothing behind him. He let the bay gelding pick his own pace for a mile or more, then spurred him on faster. It was good to be free again, to breathe easily, to lounge as he pleased, to feel the open space about him. Mentally he promised himself it would be longer than three years before he rode again through this troubled Wyoming country. He rode west, without definite purpose, and stopped after midnight to bed down a few yards from the road. He made his fire, the sense of freedom easing the weight from his shoulders, and cooked his evening meal. He ate frugally from a bean can, and washed it down with cups of hot coffee. He smoked a cheroot over the last cup, listening to the night noises of the plainsland, enjoying the stillness. Finally he covered his fire with dirt and turned in.

Surprisingly, sleep did not come easily. He stirred restlessly more than once, and then sat up to smoke another cheroot before he managed at last to fall asleep. It was still dark when he awakened. The urgent call of the road made him roll out and ride on, although it lacked an hour of dawn. He was through the Blue Lines before sunup, and had worked his way down Wild Horse Valley by the time the sun was hot overhead.

He became aware of the turmoil in Wild Horse Valley long before he reached the grove of cottonwoods and Wagontown. He passed homesteads and saw men close by their huts and soddies. All of them carried guns in their hands and watched him from hard, suspicious eyes as he rode past. The men of Wagontown were clustered near the road, and Harbin saw for the first time the fire-blackened ribs of a Conestoga pulled off the road. He was aware of sullen stares as he rode in, and pulled up at the outskirts of the group to look at the burned wagon.

For a moment Harbin just sat there; then the old feeling of anger began to stir inside him. Trouble: he had smelled it from the day he had ridden into the Red Rock country, and now it lay about him, thick, smothering. The hate of these people was an almost tangible force, pushing out at him. Harbin swung one leg over the saddle-horn, and lighted a cheroot. A man nearby watched him with brooding eyes, and finally Harbin spoke to him.

"What's happened here?" he asked quietly. There was no emphasis in his words. The man studied him for a moment, then spat to the ground.

"Three Horn," the man said. "Vane Dallard's kept his stinkin' word. Johnny Lee killed Hiram Chase yesterday an' run off with his daughter Molly. Last night Dallard's Three Horn crew burned out Ralph Condon, puttin' a slug into his shoulder. That's his wagon over there. Then to make it a clean sweep, they killed Paul Vail an' clubbed his wife an' stole his kid."

Ridge Harbin stiffened, and his leg came down. The man beside him jumped back wildly as Harbin spun his horse. "Mrs. Vail—where is she?" he demanded. His eyes were slitted, and his face had become a hard mask.

The man held there, awed by the change in Harbin's manner. He stammered when he spoke. "She—she's over by the creek. The women are layin' her man out, an'—"

Harbin wheeled the horse, and his right hand threw the cheroot away. He rushed through the group of men beside the burned wagon and heard the angry yells that followed him as he headed for the riverbank.

He saw her silver-blond hair first, then her slim, upright figure where she sat on a rock beside the Perdido, staring dry-eyed at the turgid stream. Harbin swung down, and his hard heels rang against the loose shale as he walked toward her. She didn't look up until he spoke to her.

"Mrs. Vail," he said softly.

Lydia turned slowly. For a moment there was no recognition in her eyes, then she shook her head. "They won't go after them," she said listlessly. "I've begged, gotten down on my knees to them, but not one of them will go. Joanie—" She stopped, stared at him, then shook her head again.

Ridge Harbin moved closer. "Please tell me what happened, Mrs. Vail," he said. "I want to know."

She looked at him again, then slowly she nodded. "They killed Paul. It was a man Paul knew, called by name. Wayne, I think he said. There was another man with him. I tried to get the other man to stop him when he took Joanie—" She paused.

Harbin asked, his voice harsh, "Did you see them ride away?"

The woman nodded. "North," she said. "The second man followed Wayne and Joanie. They've had her all night. She's only thirteen—"

Harbin turned away stiffly. The gelding shied at the harsh touch of his hands, then steadied as he swung into the saddle. The group still stood about the burned Condon Conestoga, and made way for him as he rode through. Then he struck the road, and put the gelding to a run. He took the ford without pause, and swung right. He passed the charred remnants of the Vail wagon, and reined in long enough to study the burned-over ground. Then he lifted his head and stared north.

Not even Dallard would be crazy enough to take the Vail girl to Three Horn. And certainly Wayne would not. But Dallard would want to keep any proof of blame from the ranch, and had probably given orders to Wayne to hide out. Harbin tried to visualize this country as he had once known it. North. Broken Pine country. There had been an old line cabin up there near timberline. Harbin remembered it, had spent time there on hunting trips from Three Horn. He considered the possibility of it now, his face brooding. If he were wrong, it would be too late to do anything else. But there was no possibility of tracking Wayne through the fetlock-high sun-brown grass of the prairie. For a moment he stayed there, face blank and hard, his eyes dark with thought; then he turned the gelding north and dug in his spurs.

He pushed the horse hard, and rode erect in the saddle. But he kept his bitter, angry thoughts under rigid

99

control. As if sensing his master's grimness, the bay gelding ran without urging, maintaining a killing pace until Harbin reined him in where the flatlands broke and rose upward in swaleback ridges to the darkening ground of the foothills. The Broken Pine range, as Harbin remembered it, would not be used this late in the year, and twice he had to pause and consider, trying to recall elusive memories before riding on.

Even so, he missed the line cabin by more than a mile and had crossed into the timber country before turning back. Off to his left he caught the straight-stick look of white smoke, and instantly wheeled the gelding and sent him racing for it. The hut stood just below a ridge, sheltered from the northern winters, and was not visible until he topped the ridge and circled down toward the cabin. Two horses had been turned into the log-fenced corral beside the shack, but there was no sign of life other than the thinning stream of smoke from the rusted chimney. Harbin reined in and dismounted.

Even though there was a blind wall of the hut toward him, he walked with care. He touched the butt of his Schofield gun once before he reached the sod wall and turned a corner of it. The pine-slab door was closed, but beside it was a window, and Harbin moved up to it, halted to one side, then eased his head over to peer in.

The interior of the cabin was dark, but he caught the voices of two men, hard with anger. He recognized them both and drew back, frowning.

"—damned if I will!" Joe Wayne's harsh voice was saying.

In flatter tones, Herbie Nichols said: "Use your head, God damn it! Take the kid back. You keep her here, and you'll never live it down. Dallard'll kill you himself."

Joe Wayne's laughter rang out. "The hell he will! He said to make 'em remember our visit—an' by God this is one way they'll never forget. For the last time, I'm tellin' you to get the hell out of here if you ain't got the stomach for a little fun. Me, I'm goin' to enjoy myself—ain't I, honey?"

Through the grime-smeared window, Harbin saw the girl, huddled on a bunk, a dirty gray blanket draped over her slender shoulders, her white legs showing from beneath it. She was staring at her tormenter, but she wasn't crying. The strength of her mother was in her, Harbin thought, and a grim smile touched his lips.

Then Harbin's attention fixed on Herbie Nichols's pale face, and his smile faded. Herbie stood there, still fighting the fight with himself. Then, abruptly, he shrugged and turned toward the door. Harbin drew away from the window, ducked beneath it, and stood in front of the door. Rusty hinges grated, then the door came open and Nichols stepped through it and blinked in the bright sunlight. Behind him, Harbin heard the girl gasp, then the sounds of a bitter, though subdued, struggle.

Nichols started to close the door behind him, when he saw Harbin, and stopped. His face went gray, and his mouth slack.

"Go back inside, Herbie," Harbin ordered softly.

"Ridge—" The single word came from Nichols's lips like a groan, then he backed into the cabin slowly, moving his feet as if they weighed a hundred pounds apiece. Harbin stepped in behind him.

The girl had been forced back upon the low bunk, and the blanket had been torn from her. Her naked white-skinned body was visible in the vague light of the shack. Joe Wayne was sprawled across her, forcing her back, his lips seeking her mouth.

"Wayne!" Harbin's flat-toned voice slashed into the passion that gripped the Three Horn rider, and he jerked back as if stung by a monstrous bee. His short, thick figure wheeled crazily about. His face was panic-stricken, his eyes starting from his head.

Harbin said: "You've had your dance, Wayne—now you pay the fiddler."

Wayne's right hand streaked for his gun. Harbin bent to one side, and his gun came level, spat fire and a thunder of sound. His first shot broke Wayne's movement, smashed him stiffly erect. Harbin's second shot took Wayne in the center of his face. His nose and mouth dissolved in a bloody smear, and he fell straight down with his face to the floor. With a continuation of the same unbelievably fast movement, Harbin turned toward Herbie Nichols. For an instant Herbie stood there, face pale, his eyes staring; then he backed slowly through the open door of the cabin. Harbin followed him.

"You picked the trail you rode, Herbie," Ridge said, softly.

Nichols raised his face to stare up into the clear blue of the sky. His eyes were darkly shadowed, and a bitter smile twisted his lips. "I sure as hell did, Ridge, only—

only this wasn't my idea. I wouldn't have touched the kid. I want you to know that."

Harbin nodded. "I do know that, Herbie," he replied quietly. "It's all that kept me from killing you inside there."

Again Nichols stared up at the sky. "That means you'll let me go, doesn't it, Ridge? I can ride away—but can I ride far enough to get away from the stink of this? A man can get away with a lot of things out here, but some he can't. You can't steal another man's horse and you can't molest a child. We both know it was a rotten dirty business that won't ever be forgotten. You said a man who walked in mud would have to get some on him. I'm covered with it, Ridge. It's smothering me, and I feel sick to my stomach." He closed his eyes, then opened them to stare fiercely at Ridge Harbin. "I tried to stop Wayne. God knows, I wanted to stop him, Ridge, even if I had to kill him!"

"But you didn't stop him, Herbie," Ridge said gently. "That's the difference."

Herbie nodded. "I suppose it is," he said. He lifted his head. "I was afraid of Wayne, Ridge, but now it's over, I'm not afraid any more. I can understand myself better. I left the cabin, Ridge—I left the girl in there with him—but I couldn't have stayed out. I'd have had to go back in. Wouldn't I, Ridge?"

Harbin was silent. He felt the shame and disgrace of Nichols. "I don't know, Herbie. All I know is you didn't go back."

"Yeah, I didn't." Herbie Nichols looked past Harbin to the thickening stands of pine that swept up the sun-browned hills. He took a deep breath. "You'd let me go, Ridge—but what would I go to? A man can't outrun himself." Deep lines grooved his face. "God damn it, why can't a man walk his own path? Why does he have to face what he can't stand up to? There were things I always wanted to do, Ridge, like ridin' south, like gettin' married, like havin' a spread of my own. It's my own fault it's worked out like this. I didn't have the guts to stand alone. Just like I haven't got the guts to ride away now." Herbie broke off there, and suddenly shrugged. "To hell with it. I'll make it easy for you, Ridge."

"Don't be a fool, Herbie. Don't try it!" The words tore at Ridge Harbin's throat. He read the terrible determination in Nichols's eyes. Herbie's right hand made an awkward plunge for his gun at the same instant that he pitched himself to one side. He had his gun out, almost level, before Harbin's first shot tore him apart, slamming him back against the wall of the cabin. His shirt front turned soggy with blood and his eyes began to glaze.

"I—I still say you were the best friend I ever had, Ridge," Nichols whispered. Then he pitched face forward to the ground and lay still.

For a moment Harbin stood there. Then, with mechanical movements of his fingers, he ejected the three empty shells and replaced them with three fresh shells from the loops of his gunbelt. He holstered the gun, still looking down at Herbie Nichols.

Slowly he turned and reentered the cabin. The girl was sitting up, watching him with drawn, intent features. She had pulled the dingy gray blanket back in place about her.

"It's all right, Joanie," Harbin said, slowly. "It's all over now."

The girl stared at him for a moment, then stood up and came to him. Sobs wracked her slender frame. He took her gently in his arms. Then abruptly she stopped crying and pulled back. She stared down at the body of Joe Wayne, then looked quickly through the open door and shuddered.

"They're dead, aren't they?" she asked in her light, childish voice.

Harbin nodded slowly. "Yes, Joanie," he said. "Now go outside, and keep your eyes closed tight. There's something I have to do."

She looked at him from wide eyes, then turned and walked out of the cabin, and moved unsteadily some distance away. Ridge followed her, bent over Herbie Nichols's limp body, then caught him beneath his arms and dragged him back inside the cabin. He knelt beside him, closed his staring eyes, straightened his arms at his sides. Then Harbin stood up, frowning. He searched the cabin with his eyes. Then he found what he wanted, a five-gallon can of kerosene. He walked to it, lifted it to shake it; it was more than half full, and he removed the withered potato that covered the spout. He spilled the liquid over the dry board floors and across the cornshuck mattress of the bunk. Then he tossed the can to one side. He looked down once more at Nichols's inert figure, and whispered, "Goodbye, Herbie."

A match flared briefly in Harbin's hand, and he knelt to set a pool of kerosene ablaze, then backed hurriedly from the cabin, closing the door behind him. The girl stood outside, a touchingly small figure with the gray blanket pulled helter-skelter about her. Harbin smiled at her and whistled for the gelding.

The horse came up, lifting its head high. Harbin gentled the animal, then pulled the slicker from behind the cantle of the saddle and unrolled it. He gave it to the girl and she slipped into it. Then he boosted her up in front of the saddle and swung up behind her. The gelding stepped about, then settled to the climb up to the ridge.

Atop the swaleback Harbin reined in to glance behind him. The shack was burning freely, red flames licking up the slab door, and to the windowsills. The dry grass atop the sod roof was blazing, and a pillar of dense black smoke stood up into the pale blue sky. For a moment Harbin watched the fire; then he turned the horse and rode slowly back the way he had come.

TWELVE

Later that same afternoon Harbin eased his weight down atop the flat boulder that tipped into the turgid brown water of the Rio Perdido at the edge of Wagontown. The lines of strain still marked his face, and there was a hollowness inside him that would take days to ease. It was always like this after he had killed a man, he thought bitterly. Only, this time it was harder because one of the men had once been his friend. He frowned down at the featureless, almost oily surface of the narrow stream, then turned to glance back. The bay gelding was cropping long grass by the river's edge, and the saddle lay to one side.

Lydia and the Condon family were burying Paul Vail, he thought. He remembered the weakly handsome face of the man he had seen but twice. He remembered Vail's slender, almost womanish hands as he played cards. He remembered the far-away look of the man's pale eyes. The dream, for Paul Vail, had ended harshly, but for his wife and family, the silver-haired Lydia and Joanie and the baby—Harbin's frown deepened. A man's violent death was like a stone dropped in still water; the ripples spread. How many lives had he touched with his Schofield gun besides the twenty-seven men he had killed?

The thought pressed in upon him, and his right hand drew the Schofield Colt. His right index finger traced the ugly notches he had cut, one by one. For each cut a man's life. Grimly, Harbin drew a Case knife from his pocket and unfolded it. He studied the black thornwood grips. Slowly he began to cut another notch. His fingers worked methodically, and when the notch was cut deeply enough, he said the name, "Joe Wayne." And behind his narrowed eyes he visualized the Three Horn rider as he had known him. Then he began the next cut. He smoothed the edge of the last notch, and spoke Herbie Nichols's name slowly, and with regret.

Lost in the bitterness of his own thoughts, he didn't hear the woman until she spoke to him. He moved slowly, lifting his head to look up at her.

Her face was pale and intent, her eyes reddened from

tears. Her right hand made a little gesture, sweeping back a strand of the silvery hair from her forehead. She was looking at the gun, and now she raised her eyes to look into his face.

"There's room enough there for three more notches, Mr. Harbin," she said slowly. "I wonder what you will do then?"

He smiled ironically. "I'll buy another gun," he answered quietly.

She nodded. "Then you will go on killing, Mr. Harbin. Will there be no end to it?"

"There'll be an end to it—sometime," he said. He holstered the gun and climbed to his feet. "There's always an end, Mrs. Vail, for men like me. But I'm in no hurry to meet it."

She half turned away, and moved back to the bank with quick, lithe movements. He followed her slowly. Again their eyes met.

"I'm being unjust to you, Mr. Harbin," she said. "I should be thanking you, instead of condemning you."

"The truth is sometimes unkind, but it's never unjust," he said. "You're thinking it was a man like me that killed your husband."

She shook her head. "No, I wasn't thinking that. It isn't true. Joe Wayne wasn't like you. Neither was Paul. Perhaps if he had been more like you he'd be alive now." She stopped. "There were two men, Mr. Harbin. Joanie tells me you killed both of them."

Harbin's face settled into the hard mask she had seen before. He nodded. "There were two. Joe Wayne and Herbie Nichols. They're both dead."

The woman hesitated. "Joanie is a child, and perhaps she misunderstood, but she said the second man—Nichols —that you knew him, and that he seemed to be a—a—" She broke off.

He met her eyes levelly. "Herbie Nichols was a friend of mine," he answered quietly. "Once he was a close friend. Nichols meant Joanie no harm. But that was no excuse for him, Mrs. Vail. This is a time of black and whites; there is no room for grays. Herbie Nichols knew that, too. It's why he's dead."

The woman looked at him a moment, then one hand went out to touch his arm. "I'm sorry, Ridge Harbin," she said gently. "Very sorry. You'll be riding on now?"

His frown returned. He shook his head. "No."

He said: "I killed two Three Horn men. I will wait to see what Vane Dallard decides he must do about it."

She watched him, appalled by the hardness of him. "And if he does nothing?"

"Then I'll ride on."

She nodded. "But if he decides to fight?"

"Then I'll kill him," Ridge Harbin said flatly. His voice was level, almost toneless, but the light color of his eyes deepened.

Her face reflected nothing, but she half closed her eyes. "And it would mean no more to you than that?"

"I didn't make the rules I live by," Ridge Harbin answered. The lines down either side of his face were deeper. "But that doesn't mean I can ignore them, Mrs. Vail. Maybe I feel the same way you do about killing a man. Maybe I see blood on my hands every time I look at them. But staying alive means as much to me as to any other man, and I do it any way I can."

His answer surprised her, for she looked quickly up into his face.

For a moment she watched him, reading something behind the iron-hard mask of his face, sensing the bitterness that drove him, and then, slowly, she nodded. "I can see your side of it," she said. "But is there no other way?"

His laugh rang out, flat-toned and brittle. "Do you think I haven't tried? I've changed my name, I've run until I thought I'd left Ridge Harbin forever behind me. But each time he came back and killed a man. Those men wanted just one thing, to be pointed at as the man who killed Ridge Harbin. None of them knew me, or gave a damn for the fact that I tried to avoid them. They wanted just one thing: Ridge Harbin's death to wave like a banner of achievement. I'm tired of running from them, Mrs. Vail. I'll run no more. There will come a time when a man won't wear a gun as he wears a shirt. I want to see that time, and I will see it if I have to kill a hundred men to do so."

She nodded again, slowly, and turned away, but his voice stopped her. The afternoon sunlight glistened on the white streaks in his hair. "You'll be going back east now?" he asked.

She moved back to face him and shook her head. Again her hand made the swift gesture of pushing the strand of hair from her forehead. "No, Mr. Harbin, I won't be going back. There is nothing for me to go back to. We came west, Paul and I, to make a new beginning. Paul can't go on, but nothing else has changed."

His eyes widened. He saw again her strength. "Then you'll stay on here in Wagontown?"

She shook her head. "Paul filed on that land across the river. It is our land. Paul gave his life for it. I am going to try to see Paul's dreams come true." She looked quickly at him, as if expecting him to try to persuade her against it, but a smile eased across his face, softening it.

"One hundred and sixty acres is a lot of land," he said. "You'll need help to work it. A hired hand, Mrs. Vail. I'm taking the job."

For a moment she faced him, and their eyes met and held; then she said quietly: "It's getting late. The children will be hungry. Mrs. Condon and I are sharing a fire. I'll fix dinner. There'll be time tomorrow to cross the river and see what is left."

He watched her go then. He was puzzled by his own reaction, disturbed by something he could not name. Then he shrugged it away, and after a while made his way back through the grove of cottonwoods to the fire-blackened Condon wagon. Ralph Condon, his head in a thick bandage and his left arm in a sling across his chest, was surveying the damage. He raised his head to grin at Harbin.

"One hell of a mess—but it looks worse than what it is." He frowned. "Burned the tarp an' some beddin'. Didn't hurt any of the wheat or tools. I still got the makin's of a farm."

Lydia Vail was beside the fire, cooking. She lifted her head to look at him, then turned back to her work. The moment, for Harbin, held a surprising emotion he could not define. Ralph Condon caught his look and his grin broadened.

"She's a fine woman, Mr. Harbin," he said.

Ridge looked at him levelly. The beard-stubbled face was open and blunt. The homesteader said, "She's goin' to need all the help she can get."

Harbin nodded. "What are you going to do, Condon? Stay here in Wagontown—or move on?"

The blunt face grew surprisingly hard. The homesteader spat to the ground thoughtfully. "Well, I'll tell you. Things have a way of not workin' out for me. Like

108

all the bad luck we've had, like Vane Dallard runnin' me back across the river. But I been thinkin' a lot today. I was thinkin' when I helped shovel the dirt in on top of Paul Vail, an' I been thinkin' ever since. Maybe I'm just plain stupid—but I'm goin' back across the West Fork. I filed on that land. It's mine—or will be when I prove up on it. I'm thinkin' maybe Paul was right when he said the others will follow once somebody shows them the way. An' Vane Dallard can't buck us all."

Harbin felt admiration for this stubborn man, for the strength he could show when the chips were down. "All right," he said. "Maybe you'll carry Mrs. Vail and the children over in your wagon tomorrow. I'll ride on ahead tonight. I'll be there waiting for you."

Condon's eyes probed sharply at Harbin's face. "It ain't none of my business, Mr. Harbin—but you sure you want to mix in against your own kind?"

"Dallard isn't my kind," Harbin answered slowly. He turned and walked to the fire. Lydia smiled at him and handed him a plate.

"Salt pork and beans," she said. "It isn't much, but it's the best I can do."

"It's fine," he said. He squatted there on the ground and began to eat. Joanie joined them, smiling at Harbin. The resilience of youth had brought her back, and only the darkness of her eyes revealed the stress of what she had been through. She held the baby, and the wide-eyed child stared somberly at Harbin. The woman and the girl had accepted him, without question, without reservation, and it struck hard at him.

It was dark when Harbin rode out of Wagontown, letting the bay gelding pick his own pace. Once he reined in and looked back at the lights of Wagontown, the glow of lanterns through canvas, the gleam of campfires. Someone was playing a harmonica, and the tune carried clearly to Harbin. For a long minute he gazed at Wagontown, his thoughts in a strange and gentle pattern. Then he turned the gelding and rode on toward the river.

Harbin reined in a second time where Dallard had planted his warning post. *All the land south of the West Fork of the Trios is Three Horn land.* . . . Harbin urged the gelding closer and bent in the saddle to grasp the sign. With an effort he wrenched the plank from the pole and tossed it away from him. The act completed the change within him, and he was smiling as he put the bay to the ford and galloped across and headed upriver for the site Paul Vail had chosen.

He rode into the circle of burned-over grass and halted the horse beside the remains of the Conestoga. The night was still; the soft, lonely sighing of the wind, the deep-toned croak of a frog down by the river. Harbin dismounted slowly, and stared about him. In the silvery starlight the scene was stark and black. The charred remnants of the wagon, a mound of piled sod where Vail had started to cut sod for his cabin walls. The squared area was lighter in color where the sod had been cut away. For that moment Harbin relaxed the firm hold on his mind and allowed himself the luxury of planning ahead.

Here, where he stood, on the low bluff overlooking the river, he would build the soddy. Joanie and the baby would grow up here, the boy to fish along the banks of the West Fork, the girl someday soon to have a house of her own and a man to work their own fields. The completion of another man's dream, Harbin thought, and held no resentment for Paul Vail. In time, Lydia would feel the sharp sense of loss diminish. In time, Harbin's past would be forgotten. . . .

Wrapped in the warmth of his own thoughts, Harbin heard nothing until a soft step sounded almost directly behind him.

"Sucker!" Johnny Lee's mocking voice taunted. Then something slammed hard against his head, hurling him against the flanks of the gelding. The horse shied instantly, and Harbin fell forward to his knees.

He was aware of a dim, shadowy figure that loomed over him, and he tried to force his strangely numbed right arm to move toward his holstered gun. But the try was too late, far too late. He caught the gleam of bare metal raised high. Then the long barrel of Johnny Lee's Colt smashed a second time against his head, and for Ridge Harbin the world emptied instantly into a roaring black chaos.

THIRTEEN

Ralph Condon nailed home the last piece of siding on his Conestoga and straightened slowly to consider the fat-faced man who stood beside him.

"And I say he had the good sense to cut an' run for it," Hellfire Gordon intoned officiously. "God will see to it that Vane Dallard is punished for what he has done."

"I reckon," Condon agreed slowly. "But maybe He ain't in no hurry. Sometimes you make me wonder which side you're on, Gordon."

The fat man glowered, then turned and angrily strode away. Gary Daniels, who had been standing beside them, rubbed one thick hand over his chin stubble, his eyes narrowed thoughtfully.

"Gordon's a loud-mouthed blowhard," he said. "Just the same, it makes a man think twice about rushin' in. If Harbin didn't dust out, then Dallard took him out. Either way it leaves us by ourselves."

"Which is no better an' no worse than it was before," Condon cut in. He spat to one side. "Gary, we've talked this over until there ain't nothin' new to be said. Two days ago, when Ridge Harbin's gun was sidin' us, you made up your mind to roll with us. Now Harbin's gone. Maybe he'll come back, an' maybe he won't. Me, I ain't goin' to wait. If Vane Dallard or anybody else wants that land I staked out—they're goin' to have to kill me to get it. I seen Edwin Booth in a play once back home. He spouted a long spiel about a man facin' a sea of troubles, an' by facin' them down, endin' them. I go along with that. I'm packin' my rifle. I'm shootin' every bastard that comes within hailin' distance of my land. If I have to dig me a private cemetery, an' see that it's filled, I'm goin' to plow that land."

"Not if you fill the first grave yourself," Daniels returned.

"That's the chance I'm goin' to take. I've talked it over with Helen an' Lydia Vail. They see it the way I do."

Gary Daniels stared down the broad valley toward the river, and rubbed at his chin again, then slowly he nodded. "All right, Ralph," he said finally. "Maybe you ain't got the good sense to know when you're licked—but you got guts. It's time we made a stand—or moved on. Waitin' here ain't provin' nothin'. If Dallard's runnin' a bluff, it's time his hand was called. I'm movin' out with you. If I have anything to say about it, the rest of 'em will too. We'll see if Three Horn's got the guts to face down a hundred armed men."

He turned and walked away, and slowly Condon began to smile. Lydia Vail came around the wagon and looked after him. Her face was still pale and drawn, but the set of her firm jaw was hard.

"It isn't too late to change your mind, Ralph," she said.

"Reckon my mind's been changed too many times now," he said stubbornly. "But it's made up now. You ready to pull out of here?"

The woman nodded. "We've finished loading. There's nothing left to do."

"Except pray," Condon said quietly. "We could stand a lot of that. I'll hitch up the team. You an' Joanie pile in with Helen an' the kids."

With methodical calmness, Ralph Condon brought the harnessed team up and backed it into position. He finished and straightened from the task with a grin. "All right, reckon we're as ready as we'll ever be."

He climbed to the wheel hub, stepped over the high front of the Conestoga, unlooped the reins, and kicked the brake free. "Ha!" he yelled. The team lurched into the harness; the heavy wagon jolted, then rolled forward. Still standing, Condon wheeled the cumbersome Conestoga about and headed out of the grove. Grim-faced settlers stood beside other wagons, watching them.

When the team struck the road that led to the river, Condon reined in and looked back. "Reckon we're goin' it alone—again," he said soberly.

He lifted the reins, then tightened them as a man came up, running. It was Gary Daniels, red of face and puffing. "Hold it, damn it!" he yelled. "I'm rollin' with you. Give me ten minutes to finish loadin'. I'll be right behind you."

The big man turned back at a run. Lydia looked back at the grove of cottonwoods. She saw Daniels's big figure, and beyond him other men, loading possessions into their wagons, hitching up their teams. A tense activity stirred in Wagontown, a silent, intent activity that needed no eloquence to spur it on. The same stubborn will that had brought most of these men a thousand miles drove them now, grim-faced and determined.

Gary Daniels's wagon wheeled out of the grove, and almost directly behind it rolled another—and yet another. The sudden determination seized them all. Lydia saw the portly figure of Hellfire Gordon backing his team into the traces. Ralph Condon's triumphant laugh shouted out. He lifted the reins, kicked free the brake, and the partially burned Conestoga lumbered forward, the first of a lengthening train of wagons that rolled toward the river.

As they drove down the broad valley, Ralph Condon began to sing in a loud, clear voice, " 'Mine eyes have seen the glory of the coming of the Lord.' " Then Helen, sitting beside him, her new baby in her arms, sang with him. Joanie, beside Lydia, her round young face shining, sang too.

One by one the settlers behind them picked up the strong melody, and it rang out, in an odd harmony with the grating of wheels, the clatter of harness. The moment was a fine one, one they would remember with pride all their lives, and a fierce unity would hold them. Lydia closed her eyes and thought of Paul. *They're coming, Paul—as you said they would. I wish you could be here to see it, too. This is the dream you held, the dream the others could not see. It is real, now, Paul, as you always wanted it to be. . . .*

Lydia opened her eyes, and she was smiling. The river was close, and as Ralph Condon's team headed down the slight slope of the bank to the ford she saw a mounted man wheel his horse and gallop toward them. He rode stiffly erect, a part of his horse, and as he came toward them he bent and pulled his rifle from its scabbard. Ralph Condon saw the man but did not stop singing. He handed the reins to Helen, and picked up his own rifle.

Would the lone rider try to stop them? Lydia felt her pulse quicken as the Three Horn man rode in. Then abruptly he pulled up, swung wide to stare past them at the long line of wagons that rolled down the valley toward the river. For an instant he remained there, poised, menacing. The singing stopped, and in the sudden silence, over the grating noises of the wagon's passage, Lydia caught the rider's fierce yell. Then the Three Horn man wheeled his horse and galloped away.

Ralph Condon watched him for a moment. He stooped and laid his rifle down, and without speaking took the reins from Helen's hands. He urged the team through the turgid brown waters of the West Fork, standing up to drive them up the far bank. Lydia was aware of Joanie's hand pressed tightly against hers. The girl said suddenly:

"He'll come back, Mom. I know he will. This time he'll stay."

Lydia frowned, then looked down at her daughter. The girl was almost as tall as she, with beauty that shone from her face, and a haunting sadness about her eyes. What future would Joanie find here? But the girl had had enough hurt, and Lydia must shield her from more. She shook her head gently.

"Ridge Harbin has gone, Joanie. He had his reasons. You can believe that. But I don't believe he'll come back."

The girl's chin set stubbornly. "He will," she whispered. "I *know* he will. Nothing could make him quit. Nothing."

Lydia's frown deepened, but she made no reply. Ralph Condon pulled in the team, and Gary Daniels's wagon rolled up beside them. A new-found dignity and authority was evident in the erectness of Condon's figure.

"We'd better stick together. That was one of Dallard's men. Dallard will come a-runnin' now. We better make camp here close by the river. The men can ride out in groups to stake their land. But for now we'll do best by stayin' together."

Gary Daniels accepted Condon's authority without question, and nodded his head. Lydia saw him climb down and go back to the next wagon in line. Condon wheeled his battered Conestoga to the right, toward his staked land. The knoll ahead was where their own wagon had stood. She could see the black circle of fire-charred grass, the shapeless mound of cut sod. Her face stiffened, and she closed her eyes. *Oh, Paul, stand beside me now. Lend me strength to go on. . . .*

The firm pressure of Joanie's hand was warm in her own, and the girl's soft voice said: "It will be all right, Mother. Just wait and see."

Paul's words: *It will be all right. Just wait and see.* Lydia thought of his dreamer's smile, the gentleness of his eyes, the unusual certainty that had driven him those last few days, when he had seemed changed, with a strength he had never had before. Once he had told her, "Never let your dreams spoil reality for you—but even more important than that, never allow reality to spoil your dreams." The words came back to her now, strong and somehow reassuring.

One by one, the other wagons rolled up and halted. There was a stir of growing excitement in the new camp, but everyone spoke in low tones. Lydia worked with Helen Condon to set up their temporary quarters. Other families were unloading stoves, and the whang of axes on firewood resounded. Leaving Joanie with the baby, Lydia walked upriver to where their wagon had stood. Nothing had been touched, and there was much that could be salvaged. She looked down from the bluff toward the river, and then toward the clustered group of white-topped wagons below.

For a long moment she stood there; then she lifted her head. "Goodbye, Paul," she whispered. "I'll do the best I can. And I'll never forget you."

She set to work then, dragging things from the burned-out wagon. She found several bags of wheat, and a piece of charred tarpaulin to cover them. She found her trunk, which had withstood the fire fairly well. Only a few of the clothes in the top had been darkened by smoke. She worked quietly, without thinking, and it was almost dark when she stopped at last and brushed the hair away from her forehead. She felt better, stronger than she had in days, and she walked down to the river and along the weed-grown edge toward the camp.

The light of campfires was reflected in the slowly moving water. Near the center of the camp, the men were gathered. She heard Ralph Condon's voice, deeper, more sure than it ever had been before.

"Let Vane Dallard make his play," he said. "Keep together, work together. If he tries to burn one of us out, the rest will come a-runnin'. We'll stand together, by God—an' to hell with Vane Dallard and his Three Horn crew!"

The meeting went on for some time, and Lydia returned to the Condon wagon before it broke up. Later, in the makeshift bed she shared with Joanie and the baby beneath the wagon, she heard Ralph and Helen talking in low, muted tones, planning, dreaming of the tomorrows that would come. Loneliness came at Lydia then; but strangely, when she slept it was not of Paul she dreamed, but of another man who walked beside her, a tall, hard-faced man who wore a notched gun. . . .

Lydia awakened suddenly. For a moment she lay

there, confused, trying to gather her thoughts. She heard a man's wild yells, the urgent banging of a stick on a metal washpan, and she sat up. Beside her the baby stirred and began to cry. She picked him up and held him comfortingly against her breast.

Red streaks of dawn touched the sky. The campfire burned low. She heard the bustle of men, their harsh, serious voices. Then Joanie came running toward her out of the gloom.

"Mom!" the girl called out, excitedly. "They're comin'! Vane Dallard an' his Three Horn riders—a regular army of 'em!"

"Hush, Joanie!" Lydia said automatically, and got up. She had slept in her dress. She handed the baby to the girl and put on her shoes, buttoned them with numb fingers. Then she said, "Take the baby—and get in the wagon with Helen and the other children."

"But, Mom—I want to see!" the girl protested.

"Do as I say!" Lydia said shortly. She moved toward the wagon. She saw Ralph Condon, his trouser-braces pulled up over his woolen undershirt. He was grim-faced and carried his rifle in his hands.

"Now we'll see," he said. "Lydia, stay here with Helen an' the kids."

He moved away into the half-darkness as Lydia stood beside the wagon. In the growing light she could see the flat emptiness of the prairie stretching away into the darkness. Then the red streaks lightened to pearl, and the prairie stood out clearly, shadow-streaked and barren, and across that barrenness rode horsemen. She saw the high-blown dust of their passage suspended over them like a smear of black paint in the lighter-hued sky. Then Ralph Condon's half whispered words came clearly in the silence.

"My God! how many of them are there? Must be two hundred."

Then Gary Daniels's deeper voice, taut and hard. "Dallard's tried everything else. Now he'll stamp us out like ants under his boots, an' to hell with the consequences. I reckon this is it, Ralph."

The wire-taut silence held, and the horsemen drove in closer, in one tight group, the muted thunder of their hoofs growing louder, the black cloud of their angry coming standing erect into the sky above them like a poised, threatening fist. Then, against the sullen, des-

116

perate silence, Lydia caught the harsh metallic clicking of rifles as they were cocked.

"Some of us are goin' to die," Ralph Condon said softly. His voice was strangely matter-of-fact, without stress. "But a hell of a lot more of them are goin' with us." His voice lifted in a shout that rang down the length of the halted wagons. "All right, men—get ready—because here they come!"

FOURTEEN

Agonizing pain brought Ridge Harbin's head erect, and he opened his eyes. He saw the blurred hand holding a cheroot draw back from his face, but still felt the incredibly painful burn of the glowing tip on his cheek. The stink of his own burned flesh filled his nostrils, and he gagged.

Johnny Lee's soft laughter came to him, and when his eyes cleared again Harbin saw the gunman in front of him, still bent forward, the shallow eyes fixed to his own.

"Tall man," Johnny Lee said. "So tall. Tall enough to walk with the wind, tall enough to make the rest of us walk in his shadow. You ain't so damned tall now, Ridge Harbin, and you're goin' to be smaller."

Behind Lee, Jesse Ord straddled a reversed straight-backed chair, his face darkly thoughtful. He asked, "You havin' fun, Johnny?"

Johnny Lee's calfskin vest glistened wetly in the lamplight. He grinned. "More fun than tossin' a rattler in a sack."

"An' more dangerous if he ever gets loose," Ord said. His lean face tightened. "Why in hell don't you kill him an' get it over with?"

Rawhide thongs bound Harbin's hands behind him, held him to the chair he had sat in for most of the last two days in this small and dirty shack. Two days of hell, of Johnny Lee working off the hate that filled him. Harbin watched Lee's smiling, handsome face. The killer chuckled.

"I wanted to. You know why? I don't mind sayin'. Because I'm scared of him. But Dallard didn't see it that way. There's been enough killin' now to bring in Territorial Law. That he doesn't want. But them plow-walkers were countin' on Harbin, countin' on him big. Now they figger he's dusted out. They'll be wettin' their pants, an' they won't make a move. Some of 'em will pull out, headin' on west—an' it won't take the rest of 'em in Wagontown long to figger the odds against them and leave, too. An' besides, I needed this; I needed to see Harbin sittin' there takin' it, takin' any dirty thing I want to give him. It makes me feel good, Ord. Real good."

118

Johnny Lee balanced, rocking back on his high heels, still laughing. Then he turned to stare down at Harbin, and his mouth twisted. "Molly!" he called harshly. "Our friend needs some encouragement, Molly. Bring him some coffee."

In the shadows at the far end of the room a figure stirred, and Harbin watched the girl from impassive eyes. He remembered her, but not like this, her gingham dress soiled and torn, her feet bare and dirty, her face tear-streaked and marked with bruises.

"You remember Molly, don't you, Harbin?" Johnny asked. "You were the tall man then. You said: 'Lay off, Johnny.' That's what you said, 'Lay off, or I'll kill you.' You know somethin'? That didn't stop me, Tall Man. Nothin' will ever stop me. I get what I want—just like I got you."

The girl went to the black iron stove, poured coffee into an enameled cup, and brought it to Johnny Lee. The killer bent forward, holding the cup out. His smile was fixed and terrible, a mockery of amiability.

"You do remember Molly, don't you, Ridge?" he asked. "Remember this, you dirty son of a—" He threw the coffee into Harbin's face. The hot liquid burned, and the seared place on Harbin's cheek became living fire. He closed his eyes. Lee's crazy glee filled the shack.

Then Lee's laughter broke off, as hoofs pounded through the brakes and into the small valley toward the shack. Jesse Ord stood up quickly, and Johnny Lee spun about to face the door. Ord said, "It's just Randy gettin' back from Three Horn."

The rustler went outside, leaving the door open. Johnny Lee returned to stare down at Harbin. He puffed on his cheroot until the tip glowed angrily red. Lee's crooked grin moved his slack mouth, and he bent forward, holding the cheroot level with Harbin's eyes. His left hand went out, seized Harbin's hair to hold his head steady as he pushed the cheroot toward the seated man's face.

"I been savin' this, Tall Man," Johnny whispered. "I ain't goin' to kill you. Not me. Not now. I got better ideas. I'm goin' to blind you an' turn you loose. Ain't that a laugh? The great Ridge Harbin, feelin' his way, cadgin' drinks like any bum, an' talkin' about what he used to be. I like that. I like that fine."

Harbin watched the steady approach of the glowing tip of the cheroot, and he chose that moment to laugh.

"You're nothing, Johnny. An empty wind with nothing behind it." He spat suddenly. The blood and spittle struck Lee's fancy vest, staining it.

"You dirty bastard!" Lee yelled, and struck heavily with his left hand. Then he grasped Harbin's hair again, viciously, and jabbed the cheroot at his eyes. Harbin jerked his head painfully and the cheroot, missing its mark, burned into his forehead. Ruthlessly, Lee's iron hand lifted his head back.

Then feet pounded outside at a run, and Jesse Ord burst into the shack. His face was set and hard.

"Hell's busted loose, Johnny!" he said. "Dallard wants you—now! Them crazy homesteaders have crossed the West Fork—the whole damned layout of 'em. More'n a hundred—an' Dallard's ridin' in for a showdown fight. He wants you fast!"

Johnny Lee straightened slowly, reluctantly, and then threw the cheroot away. His grin was fixed. His breath came in hard, panting gasps. He froze, fighting the passion that held him, and visibly gained control over it. "Our little game comes to an end. Not the way I wanted it, Ridge, but maybe it's just as well this way."

Lee's right hand moved, and his Colt came out level. His twisted face kept smiling. "So long, Tall Man," he said. The revolver erupted smoke and flame, and something smacked into Harbin's left chest, spun him about, knocked him backward. It should have been a vicious, killing shot, but Johnny Lee had been too rushed. Harbin knew instantly the wound was not fatal, but went with the force of it and sprawled inert on the floor.

"You can bury him, Jesse," Lee said flatly.

The rustler's softer voice asked, "Yeah, sure—but what about the girl, Johnny?"

Harbin heard Lee's harsh laughter ring out again. "Keep her, Jesse—I owe you a favor. I'm through with her. But you'll have some fun with her." The girl gasped, and began to cry.

Feet thudded on the rude board floor as the two men left the shack. Then Harbin raised his head. Molly caught his movement, and stared at him with wide, startled eyes. Harbin shook his head, quickly, and lay still.

Long, silent minutes passed. Harbin felt his strength draining from the wound in his left side, but he forced himself to lie there motionless. Then hoofs pounded away, faded and were gone. In another minute or two, feet scraped outside, and Jesse Ord came into the shack. He grunted once from the doorway, then chuckled.

"Now that was mighty nice of Old Johnny, wasn't it, honey?" he asked, and laughed again. "I'll treat you nice. You be nice to me, an' I'll be nice to you. Fair enough, ain't it?"

Harbin caught a muffled struggle, the girl's gasp; then her feet moved lightly on the floor. "Wait, Jesse! What about him?"

Harbin knew she had pointed toward where he lay. He heard the rustler draw in his breath. "Yeah, him," he said. Then he laughed. "First things first. I'll cut him free an' drag him out to the corral. I'll bury him in the mornin'. Tonight—" He laughed again, harshly.

The man's boots thudded toward him, and Harbin took a slow, deep breath, drawing on the last of his reserve of strength. Hard hands jerked him around. Then he heard the hiss of a knife through the rawhide thongs that bound him, and he let his body roll slack on the floor. Jesse Ord bent to seize him, to drag him out, and it was then that Harbin made his move. He came up fast, his head butting into the other man's face, his hand clawing for Ord's holstered gun.

But he was too weak and too slow. With a sudden, frightened curse, Jesse Ord sprang back. His face was wild. Harbin came up to one knee, saw Ord's hand flashing for his gun. Then the girl's sharp cry sounded.

"Ridge!"

Harbin's head swiveled, and he caught the shine of metal thrown toward him. Instinctive reaction made him catch the revolver the girl had thrown. He felt the notched butt of it, and his face went hard and blank. Ord's gun was free and he was backing for the door wildly. "Johnny!" he yelled.

Ord fired once, but missed; then the gun in Harbin's hand bucked twice. The shots struck Jesse Ord's slight figure, tore him apart, almost broke him in half, and dumped him through the doorway as if he had been blown by a tremendous blast. In the yellow square of lamplight that lay outside, his dusty, booted feet stuck up starkly.

Molly Chase was crying in the sudden silence in the shack. A wisp of black smoke curled lazily upward through the light of the single shaded lamp. Harbin stood erect and rocked dizzily, shaking his head to clear it. He laid the Schofield gun on the hand-hewn table, placed

121

his hand over his wound, and probed at it gently. Lee's shot had taken him high, torn cleanly through flesh and muscle. His left arm ached, and he could not lift it.

"Get me some cloth, quick!" Harbin's flat voice rapped against the silence, and the girl pulled her hands from her face, then moved to obey. Harbin opened his shirt with bloody, trembling fingers, made a wad of the cloth the girl brought.

"You'll have to tie it for me," he said. There was a steadying calmness in his voice that kept her from breaking, and she nodded, her face white. Hesitantly, then more deftly, she placed a second pad against his shoulder where the bullet had torn through. He felt her shudder as she saw the gaping hole it had made.

"Hurry!" Harbin whispered. The girl tore the cloth into strips, bound the pads into place. "Tighter," Harbin said. He winced as she put pressure on the bandages. It was painful, but the bleeding would slow and finally stop.

Harbin rebuttoned his shirt clumsily and tucked it into his trousers. The girl watched him as he crossed the room, found his gunbelt on a peg beside the door, and buckled it on. He returned to the table, balanced against it until a moment of weakness had passed. Then he reloaded the Schofield gun. He returned it to his left-side holster, and straightened slowly.

The girl was watching him. "What am I going to do, Ridge?" she whispered. "I can't go back now."

Harbin's flat voice said: "Everybody makes mistakes, and everybody has to live them down. Ord's horse is outside. I've got two hundred dollars you can have. It's a start. You can go back, or you can run away."

She was staring at him. He said, harshly: "Only, you should know that once you start running, it's hard to stop. God knows there isn't much out here for a girl like you —but it's better than what you'll find on your own, no matter how hard it is."

He laid money on the table, and then moved toward the door. The girl stood silently in the cabin and watched him go. He stood by the door, staring down at Jesse Ord. "Twenty-eight," Harbin said tonelessly, and then stepped over the fallen man and into the darkness beyond.

Harbin found the bay gelding in the corral and saddled him. He moved slowly, carefully, conserving the strength remaining to him. For a moment, when he had finished, he rested, leaning an arm across the saddle; then slowly he lifted his weight up and settled into the leather. The horse danced a step, then settled down. In the lighted doorway the girl stood, watching him, the light outlining her worn, slender figure. He caught her voice as he rode away.

"I'm goin' back, Ridge!" she called out. Then the silence of the night closed him in, and he let the gelding pick his own way through the rock-strewn valley and through the maze of the brakes.

Harbin rode slowly, easing himself in the saddle, letting the gelding pick his pace, fighting the weakness that threatened him. In the long hours of that night ride, he fell into a half sleep more than once, to awaken suddenly, the pain in his shoulder a constant throbbing. But the bleeding had stopped, and Harbin knew he would have the strength to do what he must do.

He fell into a dazed sleep again, and when he awakened the sky was touched with red, and he was close by the West Fork River. He reined in there to orient himself. Keeping close beside the river, he urged the gelding on. The sky had lightened to gray, and the sun was just below the horizon when Harbin reached the point where the Perdido emptied into the West Fork. Here he halted again. The ford was close by, and he reined the horse to the left and up the clay bank of the river. He topped the rise, and pulled the horse in sharply, held by the tableau that lay there before him.

Here, on this side of the river, wagons were drawn up, and beyond them stood a line of men. In the wet-paint freshness of the new day their figures were stark and clear, and beyond them, like a series of statues, sat the mounted men of Three Horn. Taut and heavy lay the tension between the two forces facing each other. The sun tipped the horizon, and the hot light danced from naked steel in the grasp of many men.

For an instant Harbin watched the tableau. Then he lifted the reins and let the gelding walk forward. The movement of his coming was slow and deliberate and created no excitement in the tense men before him. As he closed the space between himself and the wagons, he heard Vane Dallard's bull voice.

"You'll go back—every damned one of you!" Dallard yelled. "You'll go back where you belong, or I'll drive you back!"

Thick silence fell in the wake of Dallard's roaring voice, and in that silence Harbin put his horse between the two forces. The gelding walked slowly forward, and Harbin sat stiffly erect, the sun now hot on his battered, bloody face. His hair was rumpled, and his shirt was black with dried blood. But his gray eyes were clear, and he sat erect in the saddle, the handle of the Schofield Colt across his lean lap.

Ahead of him, he saw Vane Dallard's massive, arrogant figure, balanced in his saddle, bold and proud and defiant. And beyond him the bright sunlight played on Johnny Lee's calfskin vest, shone from the bright red flower he wore through the braided horsehair band about his Stetson. Vane Dallard saw him, then, and Harbin smiled. Beside Dallard, Johnny Lee stiffened. Then his crooked grin slid into place, and he danced his horse out of the line to face Harbin. "Damned if you ain't a hard man to kill!" he yelled.

Ridge ignored him, and kept his eyes on Vane Dallard. The gelding plodded steadily forward, closing the gap between them. Only forty feet, then thirty, then twenty, and Harbin touched the reins, and the gelding stopped.

"Stay out of this, Harbin!" Dallard called out sharply. "It's none of your affair."

"You've made it my affair, Vane," Harbin answered.

"I know nothing of the kind!" Dallard flashed back.

Facing Harbin, Johnny Lee said: "He's mine, Vane. This is the way it should be. Me an' Ridge Harbin."

Harbin turned his head away from Lee, watching Dallard. "It is always like this with men like you, Vane," Harbin said. "There comes a time when you fight your own battles. Now is the time. There is no way out for you."

Dallard's pride and arrogance held him, but they were weakening. Harbin caught the swift glance he threw toward Johnny Lee. Lee laughed.

"You're wrong, Ridge. It's you an' me, like it was meant to be. *Look at me, damn you!*"

Without removing his eyes from Dallard's flushed features, Harbin said: "You're nothing, Johnny. An empty wind with nothing behind it. I'm facing the man I want. I'm waiting for you, Vane."

Tension gripped the lines of faces, opposed to each other, waiting for this grim curtain raiser. Minds and wills and bodies, prepared and ready for the struggle that had been building in these grim Wyoming mountains.

124

Rancher and settler, diametrically opposed in will and aim. And one bloody-faced man blocking that final showdown, pitting his iron will against them all, holding them motionless, baiting the arrogance, the strength of an empire builder.

Johnny Lee twisted in his saddle. "Look at me, Ridge!" he yelled again. "God damn you, I'll make you look!"

His right hand moved in that blinding gesture toward his holstered gun.

Harbin moved. His body bent to one side, and his right hand slipped down and partly up. His heavy gun thundered. The single glance he spared Johnny Lee was enough. His shot took Johnny in the head, smashed his handsome face, and tore out the back of his head. The sun glistened coldly along the polished steel of Johnny Lee's Colt, then that shine dimmed as blood splattered his hand and gun. He fell straight back from the saddle, his feet wedged into the stirrups. One booted foot came loose, and Johnny fell. His frightened horse jumped-kicked, then broke and ran, scattering the lined-up Three Horn riders, dragging the fallen Johnny, the gray dust dirtying his fancy clothes, and what was left of his bloody face pounding against the ground.

Vane Dallard sat still, his face gray. Harbin said. "I'm waiting, Vane!"

Dallard's dark eyes glanced down the line of his men. He read the answer there, and it enraged him. "Just one man," Harbin said. "Not an army to fight. They won't help you, Vane. It's up to you like I said it would be. I'm waiting."

The heavy Schofield sagged in Harbin's hand. Dallard studied it, then raised his head. His eyes sought the boundless horizons of this land he had built into a personal empire. His pride flowed back through him, and he stiffened. With incredible speed his hand moved, down and up. His holstered gun came free, spat fire and smoke, again and again, a ripping, shattering volume of sound. Wild, crazy shots—and Harbin broke them with a single bullet.

He lifted his gun deliberately. It bucked in his hand, and the shot knocked Vane Dallard from the saddle. He fell to the dirt on his hands and knees, and stared up at his conqueror.

"God damn you to hell!" he whispered through thick lips, and tried to raise the gun. The movement was slow, a

125

contest between death and his strength of will, and slowly that incredible power won it, bringing the gun up, higher and higher. Harbin waited an instant longer, then fired again. The shot smashed Dallard down into the dust and dirt. He lay still.

Harbin raised his head slowly to stare along the long line of Three Horn riders. His voice croaked out, a flat, inhuman sound.

"Thirty men," he said. "Who wants to be number thirty-one?" The gun raised, moved slowly. "You've seen two men die. Did you enjoy it? Do you want to die yourself? It doesn't matter a damn that there is nothing worth dying for left; it doesn't matter the price you pay. Kill and kill—and keep killing."

He started to laugh, a dead, dry sound. The man in front of him wheeled his horse without a word, and dug in his spurs, and like the fall of the first of a row of lined-up dominoes the riders of Three Horn broke and raced away, and the dust of their passage filled the sky, darkening it.

Harbin's laughter stopped. The sky was turning black. He stared up at it incredulously. He felt the burn of his wound, knew that he had torn it open, and that blood was flowing freely again. The Colt was heavy in his hand, too heavy to hold. He felt it slide from his grasp, saw it spin with crazy slowness to the ground. Then the blackness closed in tightly, and Harbin sensed that he was falling. Then the hard, brutal shock of striking the earth drove everything else into blackness.

FIFTEEN

Harbin raised the double-bitted ax high, and brought it down with all the force of his long back muscles, and felt the satisfying bite of the blade into the hard wood. Easing erect, he lifted his head to study the grayness of the sky, his face still gaunt and lean, but filling in rapidly now.

Three months since the showdown with Vane Dallard, three months of slow recovery, of pitting himself against this barren land. He turned to look back at the completed soddy, the smoke eddying from the chimney. The yard was cleared, and the gelding and the two Vail horses ran in the corral beyond the house. A full sense of satisfaction, of attainment, held Harbin in that moment, and he squinted again into the gray sky.

Winter was close at hand, the harsh, wind-howling winter of Wyoming. And after it, the spring plowing, the long rows of brown turned land. He stared across the broad acres, dotted now with other soddies, the green of gardens, the broken land where men had walked behind earth-turning plows.

Three months of contentment, a strange, growing contentment he dared not analyze. He frowned. He had changed in that time, changed too much, too desperately; yet, oddly, he welcomed that change.

He bent to load chopped wood onto his crooked left arm. He walked toward the soddy, and bent to drop the wood into the bin he had built and placed beside the door. Behind him he heard the pattering of running footsteps as Joanie Vail ran toward him, her face shining.

"Oh, Ridge—guess what's happened? Molly Chase an' Bill Ventnor ran away last night. They rode into Red Rock and were married. They've just come back."

Molly Chase with her pale, frightened eyes. Warmth filled Harbin, and he nodded. "I gotta tell Mom," Joanie said, and ran past him, around the soddy. Harbin frowned once more at the sky, then entered the house. He closed the door behind him, and saw his holstered gun hanging there from a peg. He studied it, and his face went grim. He lifted the belt from the peg, and carried it to the table. There were tiny red spots of rust along the blueblack barrel. He frowned, got a rag and a small bottle of oil, and sat down and began to work on the gun. He finished at length, and held it up to sight along the barrel. The notched grips felt strange in his work-hardened hand. The notches reminded him of something, and he drew his Case knife and opened it. He laid the gun on the table, and cut the twenty-eighth notch. He smoothed it and cut another. He was smoothing the third and last notch on the grip when Lydia opened the door. She stood at the doorway, and their eyes met. She closed the door behind her, and moved slowly to the table to stand beside him, staring down at the gun.

"Thirty notches, Ridge," she said slowly. "It's time to buy yourself another gun."

And, as suddenly as that, it was there before him, and no way to put it off, to delay it any longer. He stared at the Schofield, and the twin rows of notches. His right index finger moved along them.

A man can run only so far, and then he has to stop. He has to stop sometime, and make it stick. That was what drove Paul Vail, and he died to make it good. But he won, just the same. Maybe there will come a time when a man will ride up seeking the glory of killing Ridge Harbin. And maybe that time is past. Things are changing. But you must help to make them change. Ride away, Ridge Harbin; ride the trails you have always ridden before. They lead in an endless circle, and there is no end but death. But stop here and now, and you break that circle, destroy it forever.

Ridge Harbin stood up slowly, and holstered the gun. He walked across the room and hung the gunbelt on the peg. "A farmer doesn't need a new gun, Lydia," he said slowly. He watched her, seeing the sudden smile that broke the grave reserve of her face, sensing her beauty and her strength and her love.

For a moment they looked at each other, understanding between them. "The winter is going to be hard and cold," he said finally. "We'll need more wood. I'd better get at it." He turned to the door, opened it, and then stopped. He was smiling as he looked back at her.

"You might run down and ask Helen Condon to take Joanie and the baby tonight. Then get dressed. We'll be riding into Red Rock tonight."

The woman's smile was a softly wonderful thing. "All right, Ridge," she said softly. "All right."